MW01253663

This is a work of fiction. Names, characters, businesses, places, events and incidents are either the products of the author's imagination or are used in a fictitious manner.

Acknowledgements

Thanks to my wife, Lorraine for her constant encouragement and ruthless editing, and to my beta readers Neil Weir and Stew Jenkinson, and Abagail VanMerlin and Telann Erickson for a final proof read.

And my heartfelt appreciation to the members, instructors and critique group at the Alexandra Writers' Society in Calgary, Alberta, and the members of the Henderson Writers' Group, Henderson, Nevada for their support and critiques.

Table of Contents

Chapter 1 - The Old Plank Road

Algodones Dunes, California
July 31, 2002 - 6:20 pm

"Dad, can I go explore the dunes around the camp?"

Kurt stopped rummaging in a dusty backpack that was sitting on the back of a bright orange dune buggy.

"Robby, don't you want to build the fire tonight?"

"Sure, but after, can I go?"

Kurt nodded and watched Robby erect a small teepee of kindling; a technique they had perfected during their trip. Only a few more days and I'll have to take Robby back to Joleen. This father-son day, like the others, is going too fast. The visits that Joleen allows are never long enough. Smoke swirled into the sky.

"Can I go now, Dad?"

"Okay, but don't be too long. I found a neat ghost story we can read tonight. It's about the Old Plank Road. We'll explore that in the buggy tomorrow before we head off to Disneyland."

Kurt looked up at the sky. "And it's going to be a clear night so we can study the stars of the Navajo again."

Robby nodded, climbed the dune behind the camp and disappeared down the other side.

"Be back before it gets dark," Kurt shouted at the now vacant summit.

Kurt sat, his back against the wheel of the dune buggy, and pulled a book of short stories titled *Unsolved Mysteries of the Southwestern States* from his backpack. It was new, purchased only a day ago at a gas station. The story that had caught Kurt's eye was about three ghosts that haunt the Old Plank Road. He flipped through the book until he found "The Ghosts of the Old Plank Road" by H. Ivan Erickson.

Kurt skimmed the story.

It was late May in 1915. The smell of bacon and fresh biscuits drifted amongst the tents inviting the crew to Cookie's makeshift table. Four rough planks bridged the gap between the tailgates of two wagons forming a large table. A dented pan piled high with biscuits straddled the gap between two of the planks. Two blackened frying pans sat on one of the wagon tailgates, one with a mass of scrambled eggs, the other

2

heaped high with bacon. Cookie plopped a pail of cutlery and several tin plates on the table, grabbed a large triangle, and walked amongst the tents clanging out a call to breakfast.

It was a large meal for a work-crew of four, but Ezek, the boss, was planning to work the crew extra hard today. They had made excellent progress laying down the plank road across the desert sands. The old German, Hans, was a good worker, and to Ezek's surprise, even Mathew and his crippled cousin, Eleven-finger Jake, were doing more than expected. If they completed their portion of the road by week's end, they would all be in for a nice bonus. There were enough planks loaded on the row of wagons trailing off into the dunes to finish their part of the road; it was only a matter of pushing a little harder. With luck, they might even finish tonight, leaving a day to spare for the bonus.

Ezek finished washing up, turned and shouted at the cook, "Stop the ga'damn racket, you old Chinaman!" Cookie bowed, turned, and with a big smile gave the triangle one last loud jangle as he scurried off. Ezek shook his fist in mock anger. They worked many jobs together, and Ezek considered Cookie his closest friend, but he never let the work-crew know.

Hans, the German, walked over and surveyed the breakfast. He was almost seven feet tall with legs like small trees trunks and hands the size of spades. An always-smiling face, with sparkling blue eyes, framed by ragged blond hair, topped this monstrous frame. He could handle one of the large planks by himself, and was probably the main reason they would collect the bonus. Hans picked up a plate, filled it, sat down at the rough table, and began devouring the food. Ezek smiled. It would not be the last helping the giant would eat before they started the day's work.

Ezek grabbed a plate and looked at Hans. "Where're Mathew and ol' Eleven-finger Jake?"

Hans looked up, opened his mouth, and a large piece of bacon dropped out. "Auhgh, they went off that way." He pointed to a trail leading off over a dune. "I think maybe they go for da shit. D'know...they been gone for quite a while. Maybe they find da gold, huh?" Hans smiled.

"Ga'damn it!" Ezek said. "If they hold us up today with their stupid prospecting, I'll kick their asses all the way back to San Diego. Cookie. Hey, Cookie. Go up on that ga'damn dune and play that triangle of yours as loud as you can. Those two need to get here before I finish my breakfast, or they'll go without."

Cookie was about halfway up the dune when Mathew and Jake came running back along the track they'd made on their way out. They were waving wildly. Mathew stumbled in the loose sand, and Eleven-finger Jake landed on top of him. Jake pushed Mathew deep into the sand as they fought to regain their feet.

Jake was up first and ran across the plank road shouting. "We found a mine. We found a

4

mine."

Hans took another spoonful of eggs. "Again, yah? Hah, where's da gold, huh?"

Mathew ran up, spitting out sand. "No, we did. We did. We honestly found a gold mine. Jake found it. We were about our business, me on one side of a dune and Jake on the other. I finished, and all of a sudden, Jake, he starts shoutin' blue murder. So I climbs the dune, and there's Jake, head hanging over the mineshaft. Sand is right up to the edge, and it's starting to trickle in, so I tells Jake to get the hell away so he don't fall in. Then, we hi-tail it back here for a rope and a lantern."

"I'll get'em." Jake ran toward the supply wagon.

"Whoa," Ezek said. "You ain't takin' no ropes or lanterns nowhere. You sit down here and eat breakfast, and then get to road building. We ain't goin' to risk our bonus on any wild goose chase,"

"But the mine?" Mathew said.

"Probably not even a mine. More likely an old well, or just a hole."

"No, Ezek, it's not a hole. It's got a door," Jake said.

"A door?"

"Yah, a door. I was taking a crap. I put my hand down to steady myself and I just pushed the door open. It's got to be a mine."

"Wells have covers," Ezek said. "It's probably just a well. We don't have time. Eat

your breakfast.

"But, what if it's a mine?" Mathew said. "It could be a mine."

"Tell you what, if we finish the road today or tomorrow and get back to Yuma for our bonus, I'll let you take one of the wagons, and all the ropes and lanterns you need. You can come back here and search for your mine. Hans can come with you."

"Yah, I like da gold. I will help you with da ropes."

Ezek looked at Mathew and Jake. "Deal?"

They nodded and sat down to eat their breakfast.

The work went faster than expected. By the end of the day, the road was complete and they headed for Yuma.

Kurt stopped reading and checked his watch. Robby's been gone for quite a while. Should I go check on him? No, I'm starting to act overly protective, like Joleen.

Bellingham, Washington
Two weeks earlier - July 17, 2002 - 7:45 am

Robby dashed to the door. "It's Dad. Mom, Dad's here." He flung the door open.

Kurt grabbed Robby, hoisted him up. "How about a hug for your Dad?"

Robby gave him a quick hug.

"What, that's it? I come all the way from Saskatchewan and that's all I get? I didn't ask for a kiss."

Robby gave Kurt a big hug, and Kurt lowered him to the floor. "Hi, Joleen. Is he ready?"

"No, he needs to finish his breakfast. You hungry?"

"I'm fine. I ate at the motel. Robby, why don't you finish off your breakfast, then we'll load up your stuff."

"Kurt, why do you have to take him so far away? He's so young," Joleen said.

"He's almost ten."

"But he's never been so far from home."

"Joleen, he has. He's gone to the farm in Saskatchewan, that's just as far."

"Where are we going, Dad?"

"First, we'll go to the Oregon Dunes National Recreation Area. I've arranged for us to rent a dune buggy there."

"Dune buggy, great." Robby jumped off his chair and ran to Kurt.

"Yah, great," Joleen said. "Isn't that dangerous?"

"No more than driving to Wal-Mart, probably less, and we'll be careful."

"Yah, Mom, we'll be careful. Can I drive, Dad?"

"Drive? Kurt, you can't let him drive. No, he can't go. It's too dangerous."

Kurt looked at Robby and slightly shook his head from side to side.

"No, of course, he can't drive. He would need a valid driver's license. I will do all the driving, and

7

you know I'm a careful driver, right?"

Joleen looked down and took a spoonful of cereal. She chewed for a few moments and then looked up at Robby.

Robby stared back at his mother.

"You have to listen to your Dad. No driving and—"

"I will Mom. I promise."

"Kurt, you have him for three weeks. Will you be riding around on the dune buggy all that time? That's too much. Can't you do something else?"

"Joleen, we won't have that much time on the sand. We'll rent the buggy today, and check it out. Then, we'll drive for a couple of days down to the Pink Coral Sand Dunes State Park in Utah. The dunes there are small, and we can get used to the buggy. Then, we'll head to the Algodones Dunes in California. They probably cover fifty times the area. We can camp right out there."

"Is that safe? Camping on the dunes can't be safe."

"It's safe, we won't be alone; there'll be lots of other people out there. It'll be fun."

Kurt turned to Robby. "And there's a spaceship out on the dunes. We can search for it."

"A real spaceship?"

"Well, no, but they filmed Star Wars there. Maybe we can find the spaceship they built."

"So, you are going to spend almost two weeks at Algodones Dunes," Joleen said. "That's a long time. Can't you spend more time at Disneyland on the way home? You said you were going to go there."

8

"Disneyland, are we going to Disneyland?" Robby shouted.

"So much for the surprise," Kurt said.

"Sorry, but I still don't see why you are spending so long at the Algodones Dunes?"

"There's a lot to see, and Robby will learn a lot. On our last day, we'll explore the Old Plank Road. They built it in the early 1900's so cars could cross the desert. It will be a fantastic history lesson."

"So, for riding the dune buggy, that will be your last stop?"

Kurt nodded. "Last stop, the Old Plank Road."

Algodones Dunes, California
July 31, 2002 - 7:10 pm

Kurt found where he had left off reading the story and continued.

Ezek honored his promise. Hans, Mathew, and Jake went back to find their gold mine while Cookie and Ezek waited in Yuma.

Three days passed with no sign of the trio.

"Ezek, we go find them," Cookie said. "They been gone long time?"

"I think so. We need to get on to the next job."

Ezek and Cookie arrived at the gold-hunters' campsite at dusk.

"Look, there the wagon—but tent blow down," Cookie said. "Where are they?"

Ezek shrugged. "The horses don't have any water or food. We'll look after them first then we'll find those fools."

Cookie and Ezek tended to the horses and then followed a trail up, down, and around a number of dunes. They found a pile of ropes at the bottom of one of the dunes, but there was no sign of the trio.

"It's getting dark," Ezek said. "Let's go back to their camp. If they don't show up tonight, we'll look for them again tomorrow.

While Ezek repaired the tent, Cookie lit a fire, prepared a pot of beans, and warmed some sourdough biscuits.

Cookie took his triangle and clanged it loudly. "They come back when they hear this," he said.

Ezek's head popped out of the tent. "Ring that some more, Cookie, but louder."

Cookie smiled at Ezek, then dropped the triangle, and screamed, "I-eeeee."

Ezek turned to see Eleven-finger Jake, an axe lodged in his forehead, rising out of the sand. Hans and Mathew followed him. Without looking at Ezek or Cookie, they climbed the path leading up the dune. When they were about halfway up the dune, they faded and disappeared, only to rise out of the sand again and walk off in a different direction.

Cookie fell over Ezek as he rushed to hide behind the tent. "They ghosts," Cookie whispered. "Ezek, we not stay, go…we must go."

"Yep, let's get the horses hitched. You can drive our wagon; I'll drive the other one. Hurry, we'll leave the damn tent."

They left and the trio's bodies were never found. But dear readers, if you are out on the desert on a moonless night, you may see Ezek's crew wandering the Old Plank Road, just as they did that night of May 28, 1915—Eleven-finger Jake in the lead, an axe stuck in his forehead, and the others, following, with their ropes and shovels, looking for the lost mine.

Kurt closed the book and looked up at the evening sky. Stars were becoming visible in the blue-black of the desert's dusk; faint points of light that allowed him to look millions of years into the past. He pulled a copy of *Stars of the First People* from the backpack. It was a paperback, and the cover had fared poorly on the trip. But Robby enjoyed hunting for the First Peoples' constellations, and the cover could be repaired. Tonight, after the ghost story, he'd have Robby hunt for *Dilyébé*, the Navajo equivalent of Pleiades.

The sun disappeared behind a dune and Kurt checked his watch. Seven twenty—he's been gone for forty minutes—maybe I should call him. No, I'll give him a few more minutes.

Kurt added a few logs to the fire, leaned back against the dune buggy and closed his eyes. A wind was coming up. He listened to the sounds of the desert, a shuffle of dry leaves, a faint whisper of blowing sand, and—Robby's faint voice. "Help.

11

Dad, help."

Kurt leapt to his feet. Robby was in trouble.

"Robby…Robby, where are you?" Kurt shouted as he thrashed along Robby's trail in the loose sand.

His mind raced. If Robby's hurt, Joleen…she'll never let me take Robby anywhere again.

The cry was louder. "Dad, help me…hurry."

Kurt tried to move faster through the sand. He lunged over the crest of a dune and fell down its steep leeward face. Fighting gravity and momentum, he slowed his slide just enough to avoid a gaping hole at the base of the dune. Robby's sobs echoed up out of the hole. Kurt peered down. It was a black abyss. Nothing was visible. No indication of depth, nothing.

Chapter 2 - Connections

Nuits Saint Georges, France
May 28, 1915 - Noon

Brother Demetrios stood in the doorway to the sanctuary. The six torches that lit the room flickered and dimmed. He would refuel them when his eight-hour shift started. But for now, he would stand and watch Brother Fulgencio doze.

The straight-backed, cushion-less chair Brother Fulgencio slept in was designed to keep the Watcher from sleeping. But at eighty-seven, after an eight-hour shift, nothing could keep Brother Fulgencio awake. So Brother Demetrios came early and watched while the old man slept.

If Brother Fulgencio stirred, Brother Demetrios would slip out of sight and enter as if he had not been there. If Brother Fulgencio did not wake by the appointed time, he would step back and cough loudly until Brother Fulgencio woke. In either case, he would not embarrass the old one. This was Brother Fulgencio's last day; tomorrow, he would return to his home monastery in Spain. The Frenchman, Brother Gauthier, would replace him. Brother Demetrio stepped back out of the doorway. He could hear the Frenchman coming down the steps, talking to the third Watcher, the Englishman, Brother Layton. He greeted them in a loud a voice. "Ah, Brother Gauthier, I am so pleased you have arrived. Let's go in and join Brother Fulgencio. He is on watch." Brother Demetrio held his hand up signaling the others to pause. "How was your trip?"

"Slow, the war, you know, it has made travel difficult, but God provides. And Brother Fulgencio, how is he?" Brother Gauthier said.

"Shall we find out?"

Brother Fulgencio struggled to his feet, bleary-eyed, but awake. He extended his hand to Brother Gauthier just as a bright light, emanating from the center of the room, overwhelmed the dim light from the torches. They all turned to look. Atop a tiny pyramid, set in a pile of sand, a small orb glowed brighter than anything the brothers had ever seen. The room warmed as if heated by a fire. Brothers Gauthier, Layton, and Fulgencio fell to their knees and began chanting softly. "May the light protect us. Let the Master return to guide us. May the light protect us. Let the Master return to guide us."

Brother Demetrio stood silently, mouth slack, and watched.

The light atop the tiny pyramid shone brightly for three days; the brothers watched and prayed. Then the light died, leaving them to wonder if the Master was coming.

University of California, Los Angeles
July 22, 2002 - 2:00 pm

Amy Philips-Moore tapped away at her computer, searching the archives of various museums. She had been working to integrate her findings with previous theories for weeks now and she was getting frustrated. Her doctoral dissertation, "The Cultural Anthropology of the Early Navajo People," lay in disarray on her desk. It presented a number exciting new theories, but she was having trouble accessing museums to confirm her hypotheses.

There was a soft knock at her door, and Lisa Donald, her thesis advisor, walked in with a strange looking package. There was a hand-scrawled note on a mildew stained cardboard box. It proclaimed *Old Navajo Stuff.*

"Someone found this in the attic of a house about to be demolished," Lisa said as she passed the box to Amy. "They dropped it off at the main information desk, and it found its way to me. I haven't opened it, but who knows, it might be of interest to you. You can look at it later. Let's go for lunch first."

When Amy got back to her office, she slit open the lid to the box. Black powder drifted up, covering her hands and arms. A musty campfire odor assailed her nostrils. She opened the flaps on the box trying not to disturb any more dust. It contained a number

15

of items covered in a layer of black soot. She picked up one of the items and wiped it with a tissue. It was a small pyramid, about four inches high, with a one-inch diameter ball at its apex. It was extremely smooth, pale grey, and translucent. This is far more advanced than any Navajo artifact I have ever seen, she thought.

She put the object back and was about to pick up another item, when she noticed a small dark brown notebook stuck down in the corner of the box. The cover of the notebook was leather. It had been scorched in a fire, and most of the finely tooled inscription was gone, but she could make out, "*To Vla...deff, on yo... ...pedition ...Ameri..., ...r ......dra III, 1882.*" She opened the notebook. The edges of its pages were burnt black, but the thick leather cover protected the majority of each page. The text was legible, but she could not read it. The writing was in Cyrillic text, perhaps Russian. She'd see if Professor Grandich could translate it for her.

Sea Ranch, California
June 28, 2002 - Sunset

A couple approached, hand in hand, along a winding trail. Amil Fawaz, absorbed in his work, jumped as he caught sight of them. He moved quickly to clear the small bench in front of him and set his materials on the deck behind a weathered Adirondack chair. The trail passed at least twenty feet in front of the deck, and they would see nothing as long as they ventured no closer. He avoided eye contact and looked past them down the gentle slope leading to the bluffs along the ocean.

A mist drifted in off the ocean and drifted through the few pine trees that clung to the cliff tops. Their branches, bent away from the ocean by the ever-present wind, reached out to the hills, pleading for help in maintaining their precarious perch. Between Amil and the pines, scattered shrubs and bushes pushed up from the meadow. The grass on the meadow was long, and without a hint of green. Perfect, Amil thought, when he first scouted the trails. No-smoking signs were everywhere. He couldn't have chosen a better site. He would show these arrogant Americans that their day was over.

The couple proceeded down the path, without glancing at Amil, and then they turned and made their way up to one of the houses in the Sea Ranch estate. A few were small like the one he rented for two weeks, but most were large uninhabited second homes.

Amil surveyed those surrounding him. In Gaza, his brother's family, his wife's brother and their family, and the grandparents all lived in a house one-quarter the size of most of these. The wanton arrogance and waste of the Americans made his stomach ache.

They come, take the land, and then, like the Jews, build their houses.

He retrieved the material from behind the chair and went back to work. Everything had been easily obtained; small propane cylinders and cans of gasoline from camping stores; an array of relays and resistors from an electronics store; disposable cell phones, backpacks and motorcycle batteries from big box stores. To ensure he wouldn't attract attention, he purchased each item for cash at a different location. The final items, the blasting caps, were more difficult to obtain, but the Greek, his friend in Montreal, worked for a mining company and pilfered them, one at a time for weeks. The Greek simply put them in a CD case and mailed them to a post office box in Seattle.

This was the last of twenty units. He was confident in his work since he successfully detonated three test units on a deserted beach in northern British Columbia. They worked better than expected. A huge circle of flaming gasoline erupted as the exploding propane cylinder blew the gas can apart. Anything flammable in that circle would instantly burst into flames. Amil smiled at the simplicity of his design. He inserted a blasting cap into the outlet of the last propane cylinder and taped the cylinder to a gas can. He connected the blasting cap to a relay controlled by the cell phone ringer circuit. Finally, he connected a motorcycle battery to the cell phone. It would provide extra long life once he turned the phone on. He wouldn't even be in the United States when he called the phones to set off the explosions.

The previous week, he scouted the many trails that wound through the area to check cell phone reception. He selected his sites carefully. Each site contained lots of combustible material and was upwind from one of the houses. He'd start the fires at night and catch some of the owners in their beds. Each time he looked up at the houses, he felt the same knot in his stomach. The houses festered like boils on the landscape. The boils needed to be lanced or perhaps cauterized.

Yes, cauterized, he thought, just as my mother's wounds were cauterized after the Israeli attack. That butcher of a doctor used a piece of reinforcing steel heated to a red-hot glow in an open fire. Her screams still echoed in his head as he arranged the last propane tank, gas can, cell phone, and battery in a backpack. Tomorrow he'd plant the last device.

He leaned back in his chair, pleased with his work, and listened to the waves crashing on the beach. The ocean always reminded him of his childhood in Gaza, the light blue Mediterranean beaches, the warm breezes, and the laughter, bullets, and death. Here, the ocean was dark. The wind was cool, and often carried a gray sea mist inland. This sea would have been more appropriate for the Gaza coast. Yes, this mist hid a dark dangerous ocean with swirling tides and currents. Its dangers hidden, just as the Americans and Israelis hid their Imperialism behind false gestures and the myths of the Holocaust.

A bird darted up out of a shrub. It flew straight up, plucked an insect out of the air, and disappeared back into the shrub. Amil felt a tinge of remorse flow through him. He would destroy this bird's home and make him a refugee just like the Israelis did to him. But the shrubs would grow back, and the bird would be able to return. Perhaps he would return home someday, like that bird—but not yet. First, the

Imperialists, who came and took great chunks of his land, would suffer.

He stood, picked up the knapsacks and turned to go into the house. Sunset was approaching, and it was time for prayers.

Chapter 3 - The Light

Algodones Dunes, California
  July 31, 2002 - 7:40 pm

Kurt looked down the hole. "Dad…Dad, help, please." A shaky voice echoed up out of the blackness.

"Robby! Are you hurt? Can you see me? Damn, I should have brought the flashlight."

Robby's voice strengthened. "I'm okay, Dad. I just banged my knee a little when I fell."

Kurt tried to imagine where Robby was, based solely on Robby's frightened responses.

"Dad, it's so dark, I'm afraid to move."

"Stay still so you don't fall any further. I'll go and get a flashlight."

"No, Dad, please don't leave me. I can see you. Don't go, please. If I stand and reach up, you could grab my hand. Don't go."

"Okay, but don't move."

Kurt paused for a few moments and pondered his options.

"Are you right under me?"

"No, I slid away a bit."

"Stay exactly where you are and feel around before you move. Make sure there's no drop off."

"It just flat, Dad."

Kurt tried to keep anxiety from creeping into his voice. "Okay, crawl along on your hands and knees. Don't stand up. Don't stand until you are right under me. I don't want you to fall any further. Understand?"

"I understand; I won't fall. Don't go for the flashlight."

"Okay. You start crawling now and stop when you are right below me. Remember, go slow and feel your way."

Kurt waited. "Okay, Dad, I'm right under you."

"Good, now feel around again. Is there enough room for you to stand?" Kurt lay in the cool sand, head hanging over the dark void of indiscernible danger. What was Joleen going to say? What if Robby had—?

"Dad, there's lots of room. I'm up against a wall."

"Good," Kurt said. Thoughts of Joleen slipped away.

"Take your time; make sure there is no drop off. Stand up carefully, and when you're balanced, reach up, and I'll grab your hand."

The shaft began to brighten. A soft, reddish light bathed a narrow room or passage that led off under the dune. Robby was standing, his left hand against the wall. "Robby, what did you do?"

"Nothing, Dad, I just stood up like you said and put my hand on the wall for balance. I put my hand right here. Here, on these funny squares. They got letters or something in them."

The roof of the cavern was about a foot thick and Kurt forced his head further into the opening so he could see the letters. What is all of this, Kurt thought. As Kurt looked on mystified, Robby turned away and pointed to an area out of Kurt's line of sight. "Look! They're a bunch more squares, Dad."

Robby moved away.

"No, Robby. Get back here!"

The ground began to shake; the dunes groaned, and sand slid down towards the opening, and Kurt's prone figure.

University of California, Los Angeles
July 31, 2002 - 7:50 pm

Amy scanned the last page of the singed notebook and attached the file to an email to Dr. Grandich requesting his help in translating the journal. She hit send, rubbed her eyes and looked at her watch.

It's getting dark. I'm lucky to have an outside office. It's always nicer to work with natural light. But I guess I should turn on the light. I could strain my eyes staring at the computer screen in a dark room. She leaned back in her chair and closed her eyes.

The room brightened.

Has someone come into the office?

She sat up and whirled her chair around.

No, the light was coming from the old mildew stained box.

La Chambre Biblique - Paris, France
August 1, 2002 - 3:50 am

Brother Andrew lay on his back on a small foldaway cot and watched as one by one the six torches flickered and went out. He was in the new sanctuary under the small bookstore, La Chambre Biblique, in the heart of Paris, and didn't need to sleep there or sit wide awake through a eight-hour shift as the Watchers did in the past. No, if the pyramid awakened, the new alarm system would page him, even if he was not in the sanctuary.

Twenty-five years ago on August 15, 1977, when he was on duty in the sanctuary at Nuits Saint Georges, he was the only one to see the light. By the time he raised the alarm and the others came, it was out. Only once before in modern times in 1915 did the light awakened. It remained lit for several days, and all the brothers saw it. But that was eighty-seven years ago, and those Watchers died without ever seeing it awaken again. He would not let that happen to him, so he spent as much time as possible in the sanctuary during his two-month turn as the Watcher.

Today though, he would venture out into the noisy streets. He had been on duty now for thirty-five days He needed a little human interaction, even if it was simply the cold uncaring interaction of people about their hectic lives. He longed for his days in Nuits Saint Georges when he would dress in the white robes of the Cistercian Monks and visit the Abbey of Citeaux. Even though the monks practiced a voluntary observance of silence, their company provided more interaction than the streets of Paris.

Brother Andrew opened his eyes and struggled in the darkness to see the luminous dials on his watch. Was it time to get up? The dial glowed too weakly. Before he went out into the streets, he would refuel the ritual torches and pray. There were six torches—one for each Watcher. They were the only light allowed in the sanctuary.

The blackness in the room pulled at his eyes. They hurt as he stared up into the darkness. A hint of blue relieved the pain. It seems as if the sun was rising, slowly turning the night sky from black to the blue of the day. Yes, the blue ceiling and sand colored walls of the sanctuary were now clearly discernible.

Brother Andrew threw his feet off the cot and stood barefoot on the sand-covered floor.

It was happening again. He started to shake, and his knees buckled. He sat back down on the cot and turned his attention to the small pyramid that sat on the floor in the middle of the room, half covered by a mound of sand. The orb at the apex of the pyramid was now a brilliant ball of light, and he felt warmer. Yes, the orb was radiating pleasant warmth into the room.

After several minutes, Brother Andrew regained

his composure and stood up. Why was the alarm not sounding? A computer in an adjacent room was programmed to sound an alarm and send a message to the five other Watchers who would hopefully arrive in time to see the miracle. Brother Andrew made his way to the computer room where darkness cloaked a lifeless computer. He returned to the sanctuary to see the Master's light dim.

In the darkness he prayed aloud. "May the sands protect us. May the sands hide the secrets of the Master until peace reigns across the world. With peace let the light of the Master return. Let the Master return to guide us."

He repeated the verses six times then left. He would spend the day contacting the five other Watchers.

Tower Museum - London, England
August 1, 2002 - 2:50 am

John Smithers checked his watch. Where the hell is Peter? He's been on break for more than half an hour. I've been on duty for three hours without a break, and now it's time for my rounds. I'll miss my goddamn break. It's against the rules to leave the control room unattended, but someone has to make the rounds or there'll be bloody hell to pay. If the Sergeant at Arms happens by, and no one is in the control room, it'll be a real muck up. But they can't blame it on me. It's Peter's rotation in the control room—better he gets the blame than me.

Ever since Peter joined the Tower Guard, he's taken advantage of the rest of us. Even old Alfred said, "We need to get that bugger fired." Perhaps this will be the opportunity.

John left the control room, took out his key-card and entered Display Hall One. All he needed to do was hold his key card near the sensor on a station box by the door, and it read a chip in the card and unlocked the door. Some of the guards simply carried the card in their wallet and stuck their ass up against the sensor. Damned if I'll do that, bloody undignified.

Each station box had a small black plaque with the station number. Under the plaque were two small buttons, one green button which keyed a hard-wired intercom system, and a red button which triggered an alarm. The hard-wired intercom was necessary since the Tower's security system suppressed all cell phones and hand-held radios.

Wonder why my key card works, and radios and cell phones don't. John waved his card past the station for Display Hall Two. Nothing happened.

"What the bloody hell?"

He held his card closer to the station box just as all the lights went out. He waited a second.

Where are the emergency lights? He searched in the dark for the buttons on the card station.

"Green's on the right; red's on the left," he recited out loud.

He felt for the green intercom button and pushed it.

No response.

"Damn!"

Peter's probably not back yet; he'll be toast when they see the log on this. He pushed the button again and waited. Still nothing. It was totally black in the hall. He strained to see in the darkness. He pushed the button again just as the room began to brighten.

"Ah! Thank you," he muttered.

He looked over his shoulder expecting to see the main lights, or at least the emergency lights back on. But they weren't. Instead, a bright light came from behind the glass of one of the displays in Display Hall One.

"Fire! There's a fire," he shouted.

No one heard him

He reached for the red alarm button and pushed it. Again nothing happened. He ran for the exit and pushed the crash bar. It didn't open.

What's wrong? Oh, I remember, he thought, the crash bars are programmed to work only with a key card, or if the fire alarm is activated. Yes, I'll pull the fire alarm. He looked around, found the fire alarm and pulled it.

Once more, nothing happened.

He tried the door again. It still wouldn't open.

"I'm going to die…I'm going to die," he sobbed.

He looked back at the reddish glow in Display Hall One and threw his full weight against the crash bar in an attempt to force the door open. The room went dark again. Then, the lights came back on, the fire alarm began ringing, and the door opened. John fell through the doorway into the long hallway leading back to the central monitoring station. He ran down the hall and entered the control room just as Peter arrived from the other direction.

"What the hell's going on?" Peter shouted.

All the alarms--the main emergency alarm, the fire alarm, and sensor failure alarm for Display Hall One were ringing.

"Where the hell were you, Peter? John said. "I couldn't communicate with anyone. I couldn't get out of Hall One. You weren't at your post. You really buggered up. I could have died."

The Sergeant at Arms entered the room, "Buggered up—could have died—what have you two been up to?"

John and Peter stood there glaring at each other.

"Kill those alarms," the Sergeant barked. "What's going on here? Where's the fire?"

Algodones Dunes, California
July 31, 2002 - 7:50 pm

The sand flowed down the dune and up against Kurt carrying him away from the opening. He grasped the edge and struggled to pull himself back to the hole.

Robby was totally out of sight.

"Robby, get back here, right now!" Kurt shouted.

"Dad, Dad, there's a whole wall full of funny letters and stuff."

Kurt thrust his head down into the opening so he could see where Robby was. Robby reached out to touch the wall.

29

"Don't. Robby, don't."

Robby's hand touched a symbol on the wall. Kurt felt lighter. Dust rose from the sand around him filling the air with a dry powdery haze. The dunes seemed to grow higher. He pulled himself further into the opening and extended his arm. "Robby, grab my hand. Hurry."

Robby pointed as he moved towards Kurt. "There's skeletons over there, Dad. There's two of them."A ladder suddenly emerged from the wall, and Robby climbed up into Kurt's extended arms. Kurt stood up, pulling Robby with him. He wrapped his arms around Robby. A tear ran down Kurt's cheek. He looked back at the hole and saw the ladder retract.

"What the hell is going on here?" he whispered to himself.

He clutched Robby closer.

"Why did you go so close to that hole? Didn't you see it? You should have been more careful."

"But Dad, there was no hole. I went down the dune to look at the shiny rock. I sat on it and started to clean the sand away. The rock just slid open, and I fell in." The opening suddenly closed. Robby turned and pointed. "See."

Kurt bent down and pushed on what appeared to be solid rock. It didn't open. "What did you do? Where did you touch it?"

"I'll show you." Robby leaned down and touched a small dark area on the rock with his right hand. "Here, right here," he said.

Nothing happened.

"You sure that's all you did?"

"Yah, Dad. That's all I did." Kurt felt the ground calm. It stopped shaking, and he felt heavier. The dust drifted toward the ground. "We'd better get out of here," he said as the dunes around them slumped back to their original height. Sand poured down the slope. It was up to Kurt's knees as he struggled to push Robby up the face of the dune. Kurt and Robby gained the top of the dune and turned to see the sand fully cover the area where the hole had been. As the dust settled, the stars became visible in a clear night sky.

Kurt grabbed Robby's hand, "Okay, let's get back to camp. That's enough excitement for you today."

And more than enough for me, he thought. How am I going to explain this to Joleen—to anyone? Who'll believe it? I sure wouldn't.

Chapter 4 - Kings and Knights

Abednego carried an armful of firewood into a cave in the mountains west of the city of Marib. The cave overlooked the Gold and Incense Road that ran from Dana on the Arabian Sea to Gaza on the Mediterranean. He saw Meshach and Shadrach huddled close together, away from the Master, in fretful discussions.

Why had they left the Master unattended? The fire was almost out.

Abednego sat down beside the Master and tended to the fire. Smoke swirled upward to the roof. Dark shapes appeared and disappeared in the dim flickering light.

Abednego built a fire each night since they left the Empty Quarter, the *Ruba Al Khali*. There the Master used a wondrous device, a tiny pyramid

32

topped with a small orb that gave off a bright light and heat but no smoke. But today, he just lay there with the pyramid at his side.

Abednego longed for the *Ruba Al Khali*. The days there were full of joy and learning.

****

There they lived in a tent far from any source of food or water. Yet, each day the Master went into the desert and returned with water and food for them. They stayed for many months, listening and learning.

Then the Master weakened. His skin turned gray, and his large dark eyes lost their amazing translucence. "This is the end of my time with you," the Master said. "We came here many, many years ago with the seed of knowledge and hope. But yet, we were not successful. We have overstayed, and now we cannot return home. We will all die here."

Meshach said, "But, I am strong and healthy."

"No, not you. I am but one of three sent to guide you."

"There are others? Where?" Shadrach said.

The Master lay quietly for a while. "In the great kingdom to the east, and across a great sea to the west. I am now the first to depart, but we three are soon not to be."

"No, Master," Abednego said.

"Fear not. The light of many days will pass, but we will return. When the time is right, when the world is enlightened, we will come again."

33

"Master," Abednego said. "When will you come again?"

"I cannot be certain of the future, but in the north, near the end of the Gold and Incense Road, we have selected a child. He is of the proper lineage to do many wondrous things, but he must be guided. You must stay with him, and teach him all I have taught you these many months we have been together. With your help, he may lead your people out of darkness. Leave me here, in the *Ruba Al Khali*."

"No, we will not leave you here to die," Meshach said. "We will take you to a healer."

They left the *Ruba Al Khali* and travelled by camel many miles to the southwest, to Marib, the city of the Queen of Sheba, and the great Sabean healer, Uday. To their dismay, Uday could do nothing.

****

Now they sat in the cave above the Gold and Incense Road waiting for the Master to die.

The Master raised his head and motioned for Abednego. Abednego bent close to hear.

"It is time," the Master said. He took the pyramid that lay beside him and put it in a large leather pouch that contained a small sceptre and an object that looked like a third of a circle. He handed the pouch to Abednego. "Take these gifts, find the child I have told you about, and give them to him. Take gold from my camel. Buy new camels for your trip. Close the cave about me and hide the entrance. Go now."

"No, I will not leave you," Abednego said.

The Master paused and then took a laboured breath. "You will leave me, find the child and teach him what I have taught you."

"How will we find him?"

The Master raised his left hand, paused and took another breath. "Look for a baby like me." His hand fell to his side.

He exhaled slowly and whispered, "And there is another, you must meet him in…"

The Master died.

"No, no, no," Abednego cried as he clutched the body."

Meshach and Shadrach rushed over. "What will we do now? What did he say?" Meshach said.

Abednego looked at them, tears in his eyes. "We must find the child he told us about and give him these." He held up the leather pouch the Master gave him. "We are to close the cave, take gold from the Master's camel and buy new camels. We must go north, find the child and give him the Master's gifts."

"No," Meshach said. "We will keep the treasures till the Master returns. We will take other gifts, some gold perhaps, and some frankincense and myrrh."

"Yes," Shadrach said. "We have decided to keep the treasures."

"But we are to teach the child," Abednego said.

"That would take many years, and we have other things to do until the Master returns," Meshach said.

Abednego nodded but said nothing. Now he knew why they had not been sitting with the Master.

The next day they filled the entrance to the cave with stones and went to the nearest market. They bought frankincense and myrrh, and the strongest camels they could find. By nightfall, they were on the way north.

Perhaps the wandering star in the northern sky would be a portent of good fortune, and he could change their minds, Abednego thought.

Dome of the Rock – Jerusalem
October 1187 - Nightfall

Sir Roderick's handless left arm swung away from his body as he spun. His sword, fully extended in his right hand, found its target. The head of one of Saladin's warriors separated from its body and dropped to the ground. The body lurched forward, and blood sprayed the three Knights Templar who were protecting the well. "We must retreat. Meet at the Temple," Sir Roderick said.

They reached the temple and sat in a tight circle. Their robes were stiff from a mixture of dried mud and blood. Each took a small sip from a goatskin, passed from one to the other. The loss of the well to Saladin's forces meant that the small goatskin held the last of their fresh water. It stung as it passed over their cracked lips, but no sign of pain showed on their faces. "We can no longer protect the treasures of the Three Kings. We must give up the Temple and leave at once," Sir Roderick muttered to the ground. "There are only three of us left and we cannot repulse another attack."

"How shall we proceed?" Simon de Beaujeu, the smallest of the three, said. "We must move soon, or we will all be captured." His face was scarred and blood oozed from an old wound that showed signs of infection.

"I am not afraid to die," the third knight bellowed and stood. He was seven feet tall and his head almost touched the roof of the small room where they hid. "We must stand and fight. The three treasures—they cannot fall into the hands of Saladin. We cannot leave, I am not afraid to die."

"Sit down, Brother Hugh," Sir Roderick said. "We are not questioning your bravery."

"Yes, sit down, you overgrown bull," Simon de Beaujeu said.

Brother Hugh sat. "But the treasures?" he said.

Sir Roderick nodded. "We can find no more. We have searched for three years, and now everyone has abandoned the Temple. Nothing is left to find, we must protect these."He placed three objects on the ground in front of them.

"Yes," Simon said. "We must save what we have. We can return to search for other treasure later."

They all looked at Simon and nodded, but nobody moved. They could hear fighting outside.

"Let us fight our way out." Brother Hugh stood and grabbed his sword.

"No," Sir Roderick said. "This is not a time for the sword but for the head. If we fight we may lose these treasures. We will each take one and slip out of Jerusalem separately. We can make our way back to the fortress at Tyre and then on to France. If we are separated we will meet at La Rochelle."

"Agreed," the others said in unison.

They said nothing else and each of them stuffed a treasure into a leather bag with several gold coins and some personal belongings. They removed their bloodied robes and tied the bags to their waists in a guise of a large belly. They donned, dirty, but not bloodied monks' robes, and for quick access they placed their swords up their large loose sleeves. They nodded, raised their hoods, and slipped silently out of the temple.

Temple Villeneuve - Paris, France
Wednesday, October 11, 1307 - Early evening

Brother Philip wound his way through the streets around the Temple Villeneuve, the Templar headquarters in France. He stopped to gaze at the large stone stables where he frequently brought feed and bedding for the Templar's animals. At the nearby Cistercian monastery, his role was animal husbandry, and he could not help but admire the quality of care that the Templar extended to their horses. Of course, he did not approve of the Templar's use of these animals in military campaigns.

The Grand Tower loomed ahead, and he quickened his pace. Jacques de Molay, the Grand Master, had summoned him. Only once before had he visited Jacques de Molay. Then the Grand Master laid an array of artifacts before him—a small scepter, a pyramid with a small orb at its apex, and a small case containing a stone shaped like a third of a pie."I have heard of a brotherhood of six who have an article similar to this. He pointed at a small pyramid with an orb at its apex. Have you seen objects like these before?" the Grand Master said.

Brother Philip, not breaking his vow of silence, simply shook his head, no.

"Do you know of the brotherhood of the six?"

Again Brother Philip shook his head, no.

Jacques de Molay thanked him and dismissed him.

That was over a year ago, and he did not hear from the Grand Master again. Then, today, a rider brought a message to the monastery requesting his immediate presence. He was in the fields and it took him most of the afternoon to reach Temple Villeneuve. He arrived at the entrance to the Grand Tower and hesitated. Would the Grand Master be angry that he took so long?

He stood in front of a heavy wooden door; it was eight feet tall. An iron gargoyle sat atop each of three large metal hinges. Another gargoyle clung to the iron handle. Enough to scare off most adversaries, he thought as he reached for the handle. The gargoyle moved forward to greet him, and he stepped back from the door. A hooded monk scurried out, clutching a large burlap sack. The monk pulled his hood forward and looked away as he passed.

When Brother Philip entered the Grand Tower, he saw a line of monks waiting to see the Grand Master.

Each with their hoods pulled up and their heads bowed toward the floor so no one could see their faces. Why was everyone hiding their face? Brother Philip bowed his head, pulled up his hood and waited.

He peered out from under his hood as each monk was taken to a thick wooden door reinforced with metal straps. It opened, and they were escorted down a flight of stairs only to reappear a short time later clutching a burlap bag.

At last it was his turn. A knight armed with a sword led him down the flight of stairs, through several more reinforced doors and into a small room. The Grand Master sat at a small table, grim faced. A pile of burlap bags lay in the corner of the room. Two knights stood on either side of an open iron door behind the Grand Master.

The Strong Room, Brother Philip thought as he reached up and removed his hood.

"Ah, Brother Philip," the Grand Master said. He turned to an aide. "The treasures of the Three Kings," he said. The aide nodded and disappeared into the Strong Room.

"Brother Philip, the Templars are in imminent danger. We are dispersing our treasure amongst those we can trust. If we survive, you will be asked to return them, and if we do not survive, I trust that you will guard them as we have.

The aide returned with the artifacts Philip had seen on his last visit. He placed them on the table, wrapped each in burlap, and then placed them in a burlap bag drawn from the pile on the floor.

"These are the treasures of the Three Kings. They have strange powers and cannot fall into the wrong hands. You must take them far from here to somewhere safe. Do you know of such a place?"

Philip nodded. The treasures of the Three Kings, could it actually be? Then for the first time in twenty years, he spoke. "Yes, I know a place. I will take them to—."

The Grand Master held up his hand. "No, do not speak of the place to me. If I am tortured, I will not be able to tell. Do not tell those at your monastery where you are going so that they do not fall into danger. Simply slip away.

"Take these three bags of gold. They should be enough to provide for you on your journey. Go now, and may God protect you."

Brother Philip left as the others had, his head bowed, hood pulled fully over his face, clutching the burlap bag and the gold. He hurried back to the monastery and packed his few worldly possessions.

He left quietly in the middle of the night, made his way into Paris and caught a coach for the port of Calais. He made his way through England to Scotland and the Cistercian Abby at Melrose. Shortly after his arrival, word began circulating that on Friday, October 13th, 1307, two days after he left Paris, Grand Master, Jacques de Molay, and the rest of the Templars were taken prisoner by the soldiers of the King of France.

Chapter 5 - Roy

Algodones Dunes, California
  July 31, 2002 - 8:20 pm

When Kurt and Robby got back to camp, their campfire was out. Kurt watched as Robby built a new one.

"How's that, Dad?"

"It's good."

Kurt decided not to press Robby for more information on the evening's adventure. That could wait until morning. For now, they would continue with the nightly astronomy lessons.

"Sit here beside me, and we'll look at the stars. Can you find the Summer Triangle?"

Robby searched the sky, pointed out the Summer Triangle, and went on to point out the constellations of Lyra, Cygnus, and Aquila, whose brightest stars made up the Summer Triangle. Then, they found Dilyéb, and finally, in what had become an evening ritual, Robby took Kurt's binoculars and looked for the fuzzy star, the Andromeda galaxy.

"There it is, Dad. I found it. It's really clear tonight. How long would it take to get there?"

"I'm not sure, Robby, but it would take a long, long time. Even the closest star in our own galaxy is four light-years away. It would take a spaceship four years to get there even at light-speed, and we can't come anywhere near that, except in science fiction."

They sat quietly, Kurt's arm around Robby, scanning the sky, as the fire died.

"Robby, let's skip reading a story tonight. It's time to hit the sack."

Robby nodded in agreement.

"I'll set up the tent. You get the sleeping bags ready," Kurt said.

Robby fell asleep quickly, as though nothing unusual had happened, but Kurt re-lived the events. What if he hadn't heard Robby call? What if the door to the mine closed before he found him? What if…? And, why would there be a mine, with some sort of sliding door, out here in the middle of the desert? How could there be lights in it? There were no power lines anywhere nearby.

He would need some help figuring it all out. In the morning, he would call Roy Matacowski, his long time friend, and the most intelligent person he knew. He would ask Roy to help. If anyone could help him figure out what was going on, it would be Roy.

Barry Goldwater Air Force Range, Arizona
Wednesday, September 16, 1992 - 10:00 am

Kurt and Michael Walker watched as Roy Matacowski, a PhD in electronics and statistical control, ran through a final check on the equipment in a small bunker. The equipment simulated the proposed cockpit controls for the Firefly, an air-to-air missile. Orva Aerospace Ltd. developed the Firefly in Montreal, with Canadian Government support. If testing was successful, the U.S. would probably buy the missile, and as a result, Michael Walker, the Project Manager, was on site to witness the tests. They planned to test the Firefly in a number of steps, each more difficult than the preceding. The first step was to launch test missiles from the ground at a remotely controlled drone. The drone was small, slow and expendable. A number of pressurized containers filled with high-octane fuel used to simulate the exhaust of a jet engine clung to the underside of its wings. The heat-seeking Firefly would lock onto the simulated exhaust, and bring the drone down. If these tests were successful, they would move on to the next step and begin firing the missiles from aircraft.

Roy gave the thumbs up. "Okay, I'm ready, come to me my little sacrificial virgin."

Kurt launched the drone from the dirt road leading to the bunker, and now that Roy was ready, he brought it overhead and ignited one of the drone's high-octane flares. The simulated cockpit instruments in the bunker showed lock-on, and Roy pushed the button to launch the Firefly. It looked good. The Firefly bolted out of its launch tube. The exhaust trail from the Firefly looked like an arrow pointing straight at the drone. But at the last second, the missile veered to the right and flew by the target. A safety feature in the missile immediately detonated the warhead to ensure the missile didn't turn, and mistakenly return to a launching aircraft.

"That doesn't look good," Roy said. "What happened? Did it miss altogether?"

"It looks like the drone survived," Kurt said. "I'll bring her in so we can see how she fared."

Kurt worked the controls for a few minutes.

"Oh-oh."

"What's up now?" Roy said. "It appears she has a mind of her own."

"What?" Michael said.

"It appears she has a mind of her own. I can't control her, but she seems to be maintaining altitude and is just circling."

"Okay," Michael said. "Can we take another shot at her?"

"If Kurt can light another one of those high octane candles that is tied to her butt, we can give it a go," Roy said with a sound of doubt in his voice. "Don't try to light one until the cockpit simulator is ready for another shot. Give me a second."

Those few seconds seemed to go on forever. Maybe this is how time flows in actual combat. A heightened awareness that stretches time, Kurt thought.

Then Roy spoke and realigned time for him.

"The CPS is ready," Roy said, using the acronym

for the Cockpit Simulator.

"Okay, fire the candle on our reluctant little lady," Michael ordered.

Kurt lifted the safety cover over the switch and pressed the button.

"Nothing," he muttered and pressed again. "No go, Michael. Should I try the other flares?"

"Yah, let's hope something works," Michael said.

Kurt proceeded to lift the safety cover on each of the remaining flares, stab at each button and shake his head. "Nope, they aren't going to fire. I think we just have to let her run out of fuel and crash out there on the test range."

Michael nodded in agreement.

Roy looked up towards the corner of the room, something he always did, when he was about to deliver unwelcome news.

"One problem with that boss—our little darling appears to be headed toward the Auxiliary Field. Not directly, but in nice ellipses leading her ever closer. I think she has about forty minutes of fuel left. That's more than enough time to get there. Normally, the field is just used for emergencies, but…"

"But what?" Michael said.

"Well, usually they don't have aircraft at the field, but this month they have a load of fighters there. Some kind of exercise, or something. If the drone crashes into one of the fighters along the runway, with those five remaining flares full of pressurized high octane fuel, she could do a lot of damage."

"Not good—this is not good at all," Michael said. "What are we going to do?"

They all stood motionless, thinking, then Kurt said, "Why not call in the air force to shoot it down?"

"Yah, good idea," Roy said.

Michael nodded and reached for the phone, "Give me the Base Commander, this is urgent!"

Once he was connected he quickly explained the situation. In seven minutes, two F-18 Hornets were overhead. They lined up for an attack run. They each fired two air-to-air missiles at the tiny drone. None hit.

The three of them looked on from the bunker.

"Doesn't engender a lot of confidence in missile technology," Roy whispered.

In a few minutes, the Base Commander's helicopter landed at the bunker. He looked up at the small slow moving drone and shook his head. He grabbed his radio and spoke softly. In a few minutes, a small propeller-driven aircraft arrived. It made one pass and fired a few fifty-caliber machine-gun rounds. The drone exploded and plummeted to the ground.

The Base Commander looked over at the three PhDs. "That's the kind of reliable performance we need. And get your toys further away from the base before you send up any more unguided missiles."

Michael looked upset. He was the project leader, and he would have to answer a lot of nasty questions if details of this little fiasco got back to head office. He had pushed hard for early field-testing of the Firefly, and finally had received permission. This clearly went against established company procedure, and a number of senior technical staff had come out strongly against it. But there was money to be made by getting into production quickly, and Michael convinced management that early field-testing could cut several months off the schedule.

In the few weeks since Kurt joined the company, he realized that Michael could have just as easily been a snake oil salesman as a PhD in Aeronautical Engineering. Roy told Kurt that Michael paid for his undergraduate studies working as a used car salesman. At any rate, Michael was smooth. So when he said, "You guys try and figure out what went wrong. I'm going to see if I can fix things up with the Base Commander," Kurt was sure they would be just fine.

Michael left, and Kurt and Roy began pulling up and checking the limited telemetry sent from the missile. Roy decoded the information and cursed those who overruled his plan to collect more data. Michael might have had second thoughts about his team if he heard Roy cursing him. Roy finished reviewing the telemetry but nothing unusual showed up. "Ah, fu…ah feathers, turkey feathers," he said. "I'll have to start again—at the beginning. I must have missed something."

Roy was almost kicked out of MIT because of his swearing and developed his turkey feather curse as a substitute. Kurt could tell from the staccato string of turkey references that Roy was having limited success.

While Roy analyzed the telemetry again, Kurt pulled up the high-speed video. Nothing appeared wrong there either. The missile left its launch tube, picked up the heat source, adjusted course, and headed straight at the drone. Even without an explosive warhead, it should have knocked the little drone into the next dimension. Like Roy, Kurt started again to see if he had missed anything. He paused the video frequently looking for some anomaly. Nothing.

Then he shouted, "Tailfins!"

Roy leapt to his feet and rushed to Kurt's side.

"Look, the fins, the fins," was all that Kurt could muster.

About a hundred and fifty feet from the drone, the control fins on the rocket slammed into a hard turn position. As Roy and Kurt stepped through the next few frames, they saw the nose of the missile point away from the flare on the drone then—wham. The missile exploded. The shaped charge blew out of the front of the missile away from the drone.

"A piece of shrapnel must have put the drone's receiver out of commission. That's why we couldn't control her. But look there." Kurt pointed at the next video frame. "Most of the charge blew right by her."

Roy jumped up again, raced back to the telemetry log, keyed in a couple of commands and shouted, "There it is!"

"What?" Kurt said.

"See that," Roy said as he pointed to a small line that jumped upward just before the telemetry ended.

"That confirms it, something in the electronics, right?"

Kurt looked at the data, not seeing what Roy was

talking about. Roy's PhD was in electronics. He did his undergraduate work at the University of British Columbia, then a Masters and PhD at the Massachusetts Institute of Technology. When Michael hired Kurt he said that Kurt would be working with the brightest guy in the company. If Roy said it was the electronics, it was certainly the electronics, but Kurt couldn't see it.

Roy seemed to recognize the blank look on Kurt's face and pointed to the screen.

"That's the output signal from the heat-seeking sub-system's electronics. It's the input signal to the sub-system for the hydraulic fin control. See here, it jumps to maximum. That's what caused your control fins to go into a hard turn. I'll get the electronics from one of the other missiles and see if we can find out why that happens. While I pull out the electronics, maybe you could look at the mathematics we were trying to implement?"

Kurt pulled the file on the heat-seeker systems. Since he just joined the company, he had not been party to the original design, and everything was new to him. That was probably a good thing since it forced him to question everything. He went to work on the formulae, checking not only normally expected operating conditions, but also the extreme or boundary conditions. Experience showed him that unexpected errors often occurred at operational boundaries. Time flew by as he checked each equation.

Roy burst back into the room with a small gray cylinder in his hand. The wires on the electrical harness were cut and looked like the end of a brush. Roy waved the cylinder in the air. "They don't design these turkeys for maintenance, but I managed to get the little turkey-feathered nipper out with a wire cutter."

"Nice work—remind me not to let you work on my car," Kurt said. "How about breaking for some food?"

Their failed test started at nine that morning, and they hadn't eaten since breakfast.

"Do we have anything?" Roy asked.

"There are a couple muffins but who knows when they showed up here. That's it."

Roy looked at his watch, let out a low whistle, and said, "Yah, I'll call the base commissary and see if they will ferry us some victuals." He returned a few minutes later with a big grin on his face.

"Uncle Sam's pizza delivery on the way. If it's not here in thirty-five minutes, the Master Chef owes us a free round at the local bar."

"And if it is?" Kurt said

"Well, then we have to treat him to a night on the town in Ajo."

"Where?"

Roy shrugged his shoulders. "I don't have a clue. Doesn't matter though, it's almost a twenty-five minute drive to get here, so we're safe. He'll never make it on time."

Roy opened the electronic package, splaying its guts across a small portable workbench. Kurt returned to his equations. In their concentration, neither took much notice of a helicopter nearby.

"This could be it," Kurt said, just as the Master Chef strode in.

Nick Parozi, the Master Chef, clicked his heals together and saluted.

"Two Uncle Sam's specials with pepperoni, green pepper, mushroom, and extra cheese. And that's thirty-two minutes. You owe me one night in Ajo."

Roy thanked Nick and arranged to treat him the following Saturday night. Nick left with a glint in his eye, and a wink at Kurt, who hadn't moved away from his equations.

Kurt and Roy huddled together, pizza unopened, as the noise of the helicopter faded in the distance. Kurt had found a potential problem in the heat-seeking control algorithms. If the input from the heat sensors got too high, the algorithm became unstable, and directed the missile to make a sharp left turn. The output from the heat sensors should have been limited, but…?

Roy finished dismantling the electronics and began looking for the suspect sub-assembly. He found it and began comparing it to the design schematic drawings. "Turkey-feathered donkey butts, one and all," he said as he flipped open a file and looked at a small notation made in red pen. "Yep, turkey-feathered donkey butts, one and all."

"Okay, what happened?" Kurt said.

"Because we moved the field testing ahead, two special purpose integrated circuits weren't received. So what did they do? In order to meet schedule, the Assembly Team substituted an almost identical chip. Close is only good in horseshoes, hand grenades and tactical nuclear weapons. The substitute circuit can't limit the output of the heat sensors as the missile approaches the target. It's as simple as that."

"Can we fix it?" Kurt asked.

"Let's see if the real chips have arrived yet. If they have, we can have the rest of these babies fixed up in a couple of days. You call Michael. He should be at the motel."

Kurt called and explained the situation to Michael.

"I'll get on this and have an answer for you first thing in the morning," Michael said. Then obviously realizing the time, he added, "I mean before noon. You guys get some sleep. Oh, and by the way, I managed to smooth things out with the Base Commander. There's a small unused landing strip about thirty miles to the southwest. It has power and everything we need. We can fly the drone from the strip. It has a Quonset we can use as a workshop and even an old bunker. See you tomorrow."

Kurt turned to see Roy chomp down a piece of cold pizza and wash it down with day-old coffee. They finished the pizza on the drive back to the motel. At nine the next morning, Kurt's phone rang.

"They found them," Roy shouted.

"What?" Kurt said as he rubbed his eyes.

"The proper chip set. They'll have them here tomorrow; I can install them on site, and we can get the test-program back up. Should only take us a couple of days to get one of the drones flying. Only trouble is, we need to get those electronics units out of the remaining missiles without using the wire clippers."

They worked almost continuously for a week and concluded with a successful test. It was ten-thirty on Saturday morning.

Roy looked at Kurt. "Time for a tilt at the Ajo nightlife. I'll call Chef Nick and set it up for tonight."

Ajo, Arizona
September 26, 1992 - 7:00 pm

Saturday evening before they picked up Nick, Kurt asked the waitress at the motel restaurant about Ajo. She lived in Gila Bend, just north of the air force base, and had a pretty low opinion of Ajo."It's just a slut-filled slag heap," she said.

With more probing, Kurt discovered that Ajo was a mining town. Rockport Mining Company, in one incarnation or another, mined copper there since the early 1900s. As they approached Ajo in the fading dusk, in Master Chef Nick Parozi's beat-up Ford pickup, Kurt was not surprised to see the red sunset reflect off towering slag heaps. "Yahoo!" Nick shouted. "Free wine, women and song."

Roy and Kurt looked at each other and rolled their eyes. They could foresee a night at some dingy brothel paying for cheap booze and cheaper women for Nick. But to their surprise Nick blew by the town's few bars and headed up a side street. Soon he pulled up at a large community hall surrounded by randomly parked cars.

"This is it, boys." Nick smiled. "PPP."

"PPP?" Roy asked.

"Parozi's Pussy Palace," Nick said as he abandoned the car and dashed to join a crowd standing around at the hall's large front door. He arrived with a great leap, and then waited for Kurt and Roy to arrive and pay his entry fee.

As Kurt paid a dollar-fifty for Nick's entry fee, a voice called from somewhere in the line, "Hey, Nick, broke again?"

Another voice added, "Your food so bad the Air Force quit paying you?"

Then the line erupted in laughter.

Master Chief Nick Parozi is not unknown here, Kurt thought as Nick led them to a table. It was a bit too close to the band for Kurt's liking, but Nick pointed out, "It's close to the bar, and if you sit with your back to the wall, you can watch the chicks as they come in, and you can check out their moves on the dance floor."

Roy winked at Kurt. "Back to the wall, watch the door, Nick's a regular James Bond."

This turned out to be prophetic, as "back to the wall" prevented them from getting drawn into a brawl that started at a nearby table and spread when the brawlers fell onto an unlucky reveler, sitting at his table, facing the wall.

But the brawl was not indicative of the crowd which was made up of a mixture of people that included mine workers, Air Force personnel, and a large number of young women, many of Latin descent. As Nick explained it, they were all attractive and quite available since the town was short of men, or at least available young men who knew how to dance and came to the hall.

Nick also informed them that the hall, along with the adjacent Copper Creek Golf Course, had been donated to the community by Rockport Mining. Both sat on company property and were built and maintained by the company. Although not officially a donation, they were essentially community property since any resident of Ajo or employee of the company was automatically a member of the community association and could join the golf course for a yearly fee of twenty-five dollars.

Kurt thought the company was trying its best to make life enjoyable in the small out of the way town, and judging by the raucous good time everyone appeared to be having their strategy was successful. Kurt and Roy followed Nick's lead and danced with some of the ladies.

Nick seemed to know all of them. He escorted a couple of his prospects to the table, stating that Kurt was not fulfilling the obligations of his bet. "I think our bet required you to provide me and my friends appropriate libations."

Kurt agreed, but only if Nick turned over his truck keys. Kurt decided to hold off on the booze after he coughed up for Nick's fifth drink in an hour. The cost of the drinks was low, but the cost of letting Nick drive could be high. Kurt didn't want that responsibility. So, he resigned himself to be one of the few sober people around.

Roy also appeared quite happy to let Kurt be the

designated driver and put his arm around one of Nick's ladies.

"I'm Roy of the Great White North; let me buy," he said as he grabbed the money Kurt was passing to Nick.

Kurt listened as Roy explained that he had been born in an igloo, fought ferocious polar bears and made his living panning for gold. As Roy, Nick and the ladies wandered off, Roy was trying to stitch in an answer to Nick's question.

"How'd you get a PhD if you were panning for gold?"

Kurt chuckled as Roy's explanation faded into the din.

Chapter 6 - Handoff

Old Plank Road - Algodones Dunes
August 1, 2002 - 6:00 am

Kurt woke up early, built a fire and watched Robby sleep. Before he called Roy, he decided to call his boss, Michael Walker. Walker had moved to the Canadian Security and Intelligence Agency, and recruited Roy and Kurt into the computer countermeasures group that he headed. Michael answered, and Kurt quickly explained Robby's discovery and that he'd like to get Roy involved. Michael said nothing until Kurt was through.

"You said it had an active lighting system?" Michael asked.

"Right, and the light seemed to just come out of the walls. I never saw any real lights. Could have been indirect lighting I suppose, but the whole place had this strange rose- colored glow."

"So, it wasn't an old mine. An abandoned mine

wouldn't have lights. How about a current mine?" Michael said.

"Well, it's unlike any mine I've ever seen. The floor and walls of the place seemed to be highly polished."

"What about a ventilation shaft or something for some nearby mine?"

"I doubt it, Michael, there's nothing around here for miles, just huge sand dunes. There are no obvious mines anywhere nearby," Kurt said.

"Okay, then I guess you stumbled onto a secret U.S. military installation of some kind. I'll check with my contacts to see what we should do. I'll get back to you."

"One more thing," Kurt said, "there were all sorts of strange symbols on the wall, and when Robby touched one of them everything, sand included, seemed to float up. It could have been my imagination. I was quite worried about Robby, but I'm sure the dust just floated up."

"Static charge or something maybe, I'll find out. Can you get an exact location on the shaft for me?" Michael said.

"Sure, I have my portable GPS with me. I'll go out and check."

"Good, you do that and then sit tight; I'll get back to you. And leave Roy out of the loop for the time being."

Kurt woke Robby, and they walked back across the dunes to Robby's discovery with the handheld GPS.

"Why are you doing this, Dad?" Robby asked.

"Remember Mr. Walker; he's that old friend of mine?"

Robby shook his head, no.

"I told Mr. Walker about what we found, and he wants to know exactly where that door is located. So, we'll use the GPS to record the coordinates."

"Can I read them off the GPS, Dad?"

"Sure, let's go back to where you found the door, and you can do the readings."

Kurt handed the GPS to Robby, and they headed to the site of the previous night's adventure. "Turn it on like I showed you the other day and see if you can figure the coordinates out on your own."

When they arrived back at camp about twenty minutes later, GPS coordinates in hand, their campfire was almost out. "Robby, get the campfire going again while I get some bacon and eggs from the cooler. It's time we had some breakfast." Robby and Kurt finished breakfast and began packing up their camping gear. "We are running late, Robby, so how about we skip the Old Plank Road and head to Disneyland as soon as Michael calls back?"

"Yah," Robby said, "will we go to Disneyland, today?"

"No, I don't think we will be there in time, but we'll get into our hotel so we can get to Disneyland first thing tomorrow."

They went to work loading the dune buggy on the trailer and had just about finished packing up all their gear when Kurt's cell rang.

"I can't get much out of anyone on this, Kurt. But, the military guys down there want you to call a

Major Roger Wilkinson up at Edwards Air Force base at two this afternoon. Can you arrange that?" Michael said.

"Sure, Robby and I are headed to L.A. today. I'll stop along the way and call. What do they want?"

"Don't honestly know. I guess they just want to hear it firsthand. Keep me posted…and you and Robby have fun at Disneyland," Michael said.

****

Kurt and Robby pulled off at a rest stop at 2:00 pm, and Kurt called Major Roger Wilkinson. Kurt told him his story. Kurt could imagine what Wilkinson thought, and he was sure if it wasn't for Michael's high level CSIS security clearance Wilkinson wouldn't have been in the least bit interested. Major Wilkinson asked a couple of questions, and then after getting the GPS coordinates and Kurt's contact number, he thanked Kurt and said he'd look after it.

"Okay, Robby, we shouldn't hear any more about that. We can head to Disneyland now. Sorry about the delay."

"That's okay, Dad," was all Robby said. Then he sat quietly as they drove.

University of California, Los Angeles
August 1, 2002 - 9:00 am

Amy tapped on her advisor's door.

Lisa looked up. "Amy, come in. What's up?"

Amy was carrying a small pyramid.

"You won't believe what happened last night. This little ball on top of this pyramid lit up, just like a light bulb. But look at it, it looks like stone."

Lisa took the pyramid from Amy and examined it. "Where did you get this?"

"Out of that box marked "Old Navajo Stuff."

"Well, it's obviously not Navajo. Whoever labeled the box obviously didn't know what they were talking about."

"Maybe, but look at this." Amy put a singed notebook on Lisa's desk and sat down. "Look at the writing on the cover."

Lisa examined the leather cover. *Vla… …deff on yo… …pedition …Ameri…, T..r A…dra II, 1882.*

"I figured out whose notebook it was. The inscription reads 'Vladimir Villdeff on your Expedition to America, Tzar Alexandra III, 1882.' For some reason this fellow, Vladimir Villdeff, was on the Bureau of American Ethnology's 1882 Expedition to the Arizona Territories' Canyon de Chelly. He was involved in the early collection of Navajo artifacts. So, that could be some sort of Navajo artifact, except…well, why does it light up?"

Lisa held the pyramid to the light. "This thing is too polished to be Navajo. It appears to be stone; even the little bulb-like ball on top looks like stone. How can that light up? No, it's certainly not Navajo.

Someone must have put it in the box by mistake. What else was in there?"

"Well, there are a number of things that are undeniably Navajo, points and hide scrappers, but there are a couple of other things made of the same highly polished stone. There's a little thing that looks like a child's rattle with some thin hair-like material attached to the rattle part. The other thing looks like a small slice of pie. They don't look like Navajo artifacts either."

"Why don't you do some more research on the expedition and Vladimir…what's his last name again?" Lisa said.

"Villdeff."

"Right, find out as much as you can about him and the expedition. And why don't you post some pictures on the internet to see if anyone can shed some light on those strange objects."

Lisa picked up the notebook. "I thought the notes in the book might be Russian, so I sent a sample to Prof. Grandich. He agrees and is going to have his students translate the book in one of his language labs."

"Great, keep me posted," Lisa said.

Chapter 7 - A Queen

Tower Green – London, England
May 19, 1536 - Mid-morning

Thomas Cromwell, the first Earl of Essex, stood on the Tower Green. A bright clear day, he thought, not suitable for the execution of a witch. Where were the dark clouds and thunder?

He waited as she climbed the scaffold. It was higher than normal, and as she climbed, she stopped on each step to peer up at her fate. A French swordsman waited for her, a concession to a queen. No clumsy axe-man for her. Yes, that was good. Only last week he witnessed an execution that took three blows with the axe.

"Does she not look beautiful, more beautiful than I have ever seen her," a voice whispered from behind.

Cromwell turned, "Ah, Archbishop Cranmer, are you still smitten by the witch?"

Thomas Cranmer, the Archbishop of Canterbury, stood behind him gazing up as Anne Boleyn reached the top of the stairs and faced the executioner. Cranmer winced at the question. It was he who declared the marriage of Henry to Catherine of Aragon void and allowed Anne Boleyn to become Henry's lawful wife. He was the godfather of Princess Elizabeth, Anne and Henry's daughter.

"A witch, Lord Cromwell? Why, then, did you not charge her with witchcraft instead of adultery, incest, and high treason?"

Cromwell just looked at him and smiled.

The Archbishop knew full well why they did not pursue the charge of witchcraft. Had they not encouraged the king to marry Anne and break from the Catholic Church? Had Archbishop Cranmer not annulled Henry's marriage to Catherine? And had they not together killed the three witches born to Anne and Henry, and then declared them stillborn? Only Elizabeth, free of the mark of the witch, was allowed to live. If it became known that Henry fathered Elizabeth with a witch, Elizabeth's life would have not been worth a handful of grain.

Cromwell looked again at Anne. She was indeed beautiful. Her handmaiden removed her dull gray and black coat to reveal a brilliant scarlet gown. Good, he thought. She does look the harlot. She stood facing the swordsmen as he knelt in front of her seeking her forgiveness for what he was about to do.

Archbishop Crammer nudged Cromwell, and whispered, "Look, even now, she wears the gloves."

Anne always wore stark white gloves in public appearances. On her wedding day she raised many an eyebrow by not removing her glove, instead having the wedding ring placed over the gloved finger. She proclaimed, "As this white glove signifies purity so to the placing of the ring over the gloved finger signifies the binding of my chastity to King Henry. And as a symbol, I shall wear it ever so."

Archbishop Crammer continued in a low whisper. "And look! Even now, charged with adultery, she wears the ring over the glove. It is an abomination, it—"

"Shhhh!" Cromwell said. "She speaks."

Anne turned to face the small group of invited onlookers. "Good Christian people, I am come hither to die, for according to the law and by the law, I am judged to die, and therefore, I will speak nothing against it. I am come hither to accuse no man, nor to speak anything of that, whereof I am accused and condemned to die, but I pray, God save the king and send him long to reign over you, for a gentler nor a more merciful prince was there never. To me he was ever a good and gentle and sovereign lord. And if any person will meddle of my cause, I require them to judge the best. Thus, I take my leave of the world and of you all, and I heartily desire you all to pray for me. O Lord, have mercy on me. To God I commend my soul; Lord Jesus, receive my soul."

She turned and knelt, back straight and head upright as customary for execution by a swordsman. She whispered, "Clean and swift, dear sir, and may

God's mercy fall on both our heads."

The murmurs faded, eyes were averted. Death approached. The sword was quick and true. It was done!

"We must now finish the business." Archbishop Crammer turned and pressed Cromwell, "The witch's possessions must be destroyed!"

"What, not even a prayer for her soul, dear Archbishop?"

"Yes, yes," Archbishop Crammer said as he bowed his head and muttered a short prayer. "You know," he continued, "this whole affair started with her visit to the Abbey Melrose. Was it not there that the Cistercian monk gave her those cursed jewels? If not for him, she might be alive today. You should throw those trinkets in the Thames."

"No, I will not destroy them," Cromwell said, "but we must ensure that they do not fall into the wrong hands. " As Master of the Jewel House, I have just the place to keep them. They shall be safe." Cromwell turned his back on the bloody sight, "Let us go, I feel the cork on my stomach may fail me if we dally here."

Tower Museum – London, England
August 15, 1977 - 3:15 pm

Jane Seymour checked her watch and shook her head. Here I am a namesake, or perhaps, even a distant relative of one of Henry the VIII's wives; a Keeper of The Royal Jewel House and what am I doing? I'm acting as head mistress for this crew. She checked her watch again Three-fifteen, time to start packing things up for the day.

She was supportive of the Royal Families' initiative to provide employment for the physically and mentally challenged. But it was a challenge for her as well. Cleaning the Royal Jewels was not simple. Special techniques, chemicals, and above all, care was required. It was not possible to transfer twenty-five years of experience to such a diverse crew. However, in the year and a half that the program had been underway, nothing was broken, and the results of the cleanings were excellent. Yet, she did tire more on the days when this crew was under her direction; she shouldn't feel guilty about shutting down early. It took extra time to get the jewels stuffed back into that tiny safe that the security chief provided for them.

Only two more weeks, and we will be able to move into the new, spacious and secure Curator's Hall with the high-tech equipment and large storage lockers. That thought brought a smile to her face.

"Okay, girls, let's stop cleaning now and put your item back into the blue storage boxes they came in. Make sure you set them in place so they fit nice and snug. Once they are in place, I will come around and check. If the item is in properly, you can close and latch the lid. Then you will be through for the day." She watched her charges. "Remember; don't close the lid until I check."

Julia, sitting next to her, was already finished and looked at Jane. Jane looked at the little pyramid with the orb lodged on its apex; she checked its fit in the box. "Okay, Julia, close and latch your box."

The rest of the group lagged behind so Jane took the piece she had been examining and handed it to Julia. "Julia, could you put this piece away for me?"

It was an unusual item; it looked like a tiny ceremonial mace about eight inches long with strange hair-like material protruding from the small ball at the top. She hadn't figured out what the miniature mace was made of, but it did not tarnish, and didn't need any cleaning. The entire item appeared to be polished, almost transparent stone, even the hair-like protrusions, but that couldn't be; they were flexible and extremely strong.

Julia would easily handle that task; she was physically not mentally challenged. Julia stretched out her deformed hands. Jane handed the piece to Julia and turned her attention back to the others.

Rose was finished, and Jane walked over to check her work. The lights faded and went out. It was pitch dark. What happened to the battery-powered emergency lights? "Nobody move, don't set anything down, don't do anything." Jane worried the girls might panic and accidentally knock something off the worktable and break it.

"Everything is okay," she said, using the most reassuring voice she could muster. "I have a mini-torch in my purse. Stay nice and still while I get it."

She made her way to her chair guiding herself by touching the back of the girls' chairs. She had never experienced a place so utterly devoid of light. It actually hurt her eyes, as she strained to see. Finally, she found her chair and purse, fumbled with the clasp, rummaged inside and found the mini-torch. She tried to turn it on. Nothing. Batteries must be dead.

She reached in her purse again and rummaged for her lighter.

"Wait girls, I have a lighter. Just wait. She found it and, thankfully, it lit. She looked around the table at the girls. All, but Julia, had a look of panic frozen on their faces.

That's a lesson—I should always keep a lighter on my person.

"Okay, I want everyone to put whatever you are holding down on the table. Gently, gently; then get up and go to the door."

Jane planned to use the lighter to guide the group through the maze of corridors to the non-secure area where their parents or someone would be waiting to pick them up; but, as they set down their work and stood up, the lights came back on.

"Thank God," she said. "Okay, gather up all your belongings. I will guide you out just in case the power goes off again. With all the renovations, the rest of emergency lighting might also be out of order. I will come back to the secure area and finish packing things up and putting them away. Everyone ready? Let's go." She led her little procession out the door and down the hall.

Nuits Saint George, France
August 15, 1977 - 3:15 pm

Brother Andrew sat in the straight-backed cushionless chair, his eyes closed, deep in prayer. It was the praying that kept him awake. At fifty-two, he was the youngest watcher, but the eight-hour shift was still difficult. He finished his prayer and opened his eyes.

The small circular room where he sat was ringed with six torches. There was a small pile of sand in the center of the room. A small pyramid with an orb at its apex sat in the sand.

The torches were burning down so he would refuel them now before Brother Oswald replaced him. That would take the better part of the remaining forty-five minutes of his shift and keep him awake.

Andrew retrieved a large snuffer and canister of oil from a nearby storage room and proceeded to extinguish the flame on two of the six oil-fired torches. As he extinguished the second, the room brightened. He turned to see the orb atop the small pyramid begin to glow and produce a soft warm light.

Brother Andrew stood transfixed for several minutes, then remembering his duty reached for the bell rope and pulled it hard. Again and again he pulled the rope. The bell sounded throughout the Abby and nearby countryside—the first time in sixty-two years. Then he stood and watched as the light faded.

The room was once again dim, lit by only the four torches as Brother Oswald and Brother Joseph rushed in.

Radio Observatory - Ohio State University
August 15, 1977

Jerry Ehman wandered into a lab to check on the computers monitoring the Big Ear, a large radio receiver collecting signals from space as the earth turned. It was Ohio State's contribution to SETI, the Search for Extraterrestrial Intelligence.

Jerry casually flipped through pages of computer printout, and then stopped. He focused on an anomalous series of characters "6EQUJ5" that identified a radio signal—a 72 second narrow-band signal that appeared to come from a distant point in space.

Jerry circled the numbers on the printout and scribbled "WOW !" in the margin.

Chapter 8 - Joleen

Road to Disneyland - Southern California
August 1, 2002 - 2:10 pm

Kurt had seen Robby sitting quietly like this before, and knew what question was coming. It would be about Kurt and Joleen getting together again. How could he answer that? How do you tell him that you would gladly get back together but it was Joleen who wanted to stay apart? If only it could be like the early days.

****

Kurt sat at a table in the little Ajo dance hall, back to the wall, nursing his Coke on the rocks, watching the crowd. He turned to the door just as she floated in. She was stunning, a blonde in a short baby blue sundress; perhaps, stunning because she was the only blonde and only woman not wearing jeans or a dated flowered frock. She seemed to be held in some sort of awe by those who saw her. She stood in the doorway and looked over the crowd as a queen would her subjects. Then she glided over to a small group of people who were involved in an animated discussion. When they saw her they stopped what they were doing, and a space in their circle opened. She conversed easily within the group, and after several minutes moved on to another group. There, too, she seemed to hold court. Kurt couldn't take his eyes off her. Who was she?

As he sat watching this goddess, Nick returned. Apparently, Roy wandered off, and Nick needed someone to buy a drink.

"We're outa booze," Nick slurred.

"Tell you what," Kurt said. "You tell me who that blonde is, and I will give you a twenty. That should keep you and your friend in booze for a while, and by the way, you haven't introduced your friend."

"Oh, yah, this is Janice. We've been going together for over an hour now."

Nick better watch his tongue, or he may be in for a lonely night, Kurt thought as he stood and shook Janice's hand.

"Kurt, for two twenties I will go get little Miss House on the Hill, and introduce you personally," Nick said.

"Done," Kurt said as he handed Nick the twenties.

Nick stumbled off, in the general direction of the blonde as Janice and Kurt watched.

Kurt motioned for Janice to sit.

"Miss House on the Hill?" Kurt said.

"Yah, rich bitch," Janice said. "She lives in the house on the hill. She's the daughter of the mine manager. She thinks she's miss high and mighty."

Kurt looked from Janice across the room just in time to see Nick stumble into the group that the blonde was with. Nick seemed to know her and whispered in her ear. She excused herself from the group and to Kurt's amazement grabbed Nick's hand and walked toward his table.

As they arrived at the table, Nick turned to the blonde and with an enormous grin, he said, "Joleen, this is Kurt, Mr. Piled Higher and Deeper, as promised."

As Kurt rose to greet Joleen, Janice who had obviously heard Nick's little joke, blurted out, "Yah, you know, them there high soundin' degrees ain't that fancy at all, your BS is just what it sounds like, that MS stands for more shit and PhD just means piled higher and deeper."

Nick and Janice roared with laughter. Nick almost toppled over, and in his inebriated state probably would have, but Joleen reached out and steadied him.

Joleen looked Kurt in the eye. "You really a PhD?"

"Yes," Kurt said, "in control-systems engineering"

"So, what brings you here, and I don't mean ole Nick here?" she said as she guided Nick to a chair next to Janice.

"Can't really tell you."

"Makes you a bit mysterious," Joleen said as she dipped her head and looked up at him. "So what's your last name? Mine's Wallace," she said as she sat down and pulled him into the chair next to her.

Nick and Janice grinned and wandered off.

"Sigurdson."

"That's Scandinavian, isn't it?"

"Right," he said.

They were still at the table, hand in hand, eyes locked, talking and laughing, when the lights flashed on and off.

They looked up, surprised at the almost empty hall.

"Time to go. Drive me home?" Joleen asked.

"Okay," Kurt said reaching into his pockets for the keys. He looked around the hall for Nick and Roy but couldn't see them. "The boys must have gone home with their friends. Let's go."

Kurt and Joleen walked to Nick's old truck. It was chilly, and Joleen moved close to Kurt. This looks promising, Kurt thought as he opened the passenger door. Joleen looked up at him and smiled.

"Perhaps you should walk me home."

He was about to ask why, when he caught sight of the naked bodies of Roy and a woman, entwined on the seat.

Roy grinned in the faint light.

"Yah, why don't you walk her home, we'll be done here, shortly?"

It was only a short walk to Joleen's house. It actually wasn't on much of a hill. Must have just been the jealousy talking. Sometimes workers just need to take a shot at management.

To his disappointment, Kurt received only a light peck on the cheek. This gal wasn't giving things away as freely as Roy's friend. But she did invite him back the next day, Sunday, for a tour of the town and the mine.

"That will be great," Kurt said.

"One problem though, I don't have a car. We're driving Nick's truck tonight. I told him I would come back and pick him up tomorrow. If he doesn't want to stay in town, I'll—"

"Don't worry; I'll drive you back to the base tomorrow. See you at one o'clock," she said as she turned and disappeared into the house on the hill.

Kurt made his way back to the truck. Roy, now fully clothed, was sitting on the fender, a small cigar in his mouth. Kurt looked around. "Where's…"

"Margareet," Roy said. "She's gone home. Couldn't go with her. She lives with her brother and apparently, he doesn't take kindly to strangers fooling around with his little sister."

"Ah, that explains your little nudie episode in the truck. And by the way, I didn't know you smoked."

"I don't," Roy grinned. "It's a little something Margareet gave me."

"I hope that's the only little something she gave you. You may want to go see the base doctor for a little preventative shot."

Roy's grin faded.

"Let's go," Kurt said.

"What about Nick?" Roy asked as he climbed

into the truck. The stubby cigar still clenched in his teeth.

"In the arms of Janice, I expect. I will pick him up tomorrow. I am coming back to see Joleen."

"Back to see Joleen. Interesting…very interesting," Roy said as he flicked the cigar away, spit, and slammed the door shut.

Roy didn't say another word all the way back to the Gila Bend Motel. Out of the corner of his eye Kurt could see Roy studying him. It puzzled him, but he was pleased at the silence. He was happy to think of Joleen. He thought of her all the way back to the motel, thought of her as he lay sleepless in his bed, and dreamt of her when he finally fell asleep.

****

Robby turned to Kurt.

"Dad, mom says you met in a place called A-joe. She showed it to me on a map. It's right near Mexico, isn't it?"

"That's right. But it's pronounced A-hoe; it's Spanish. In Spanish, a word with a 'J' often sounds like an 'H'."

"A-hoe," Robby said.

"Right, that's it. Ajo. You were there. Do you remember?"

"No."

"I guess you were too young. Your mom took you there to visit your grandparents when they were still

78

alive."

"I don't remember them very much," Robby said and fell silent again.

Guess I shouldn't have mentioned them, Kurt thought. That seems to bother him as well. Thank goodness he still has his paternal grandparents, even if he doesn't see them very often. If only Robby could have known his maternal grandparents, things might have turned out better.

****

Roy bounced into the diner just as Kurt was finishing his breakfast. It seemed that his liaison with Margareet had raised his spirits. He sat down.

"I see you're finished. Can you stick around while I eat?"

"Sure on one condition, you buy me another cup of coffee," Kurt said.

"It's a deal."

Roy flashed the waitress a smile.

"Suzy, bring Kurt another coffee, please."

He then turned and looked Kurt in the eye.

"Now, what about this gal who looked in on my little show last night? Are you actually going down to see her?"

"I sure am. She is fantastic looking, and besides that, she's genuinely nice. She has offered to show me around the mine. Anyway, I have to go down and pick up Nick. That's if he hasn't been shot by a jealous boyfriend."

"You and your gal…what's her name?"

"Joleen Wallace."

"You going to take Nick on the tour with you," Roy asked, with a look of disbelief on his face.

"No, no, Joleen said she would drive me back."

"Good," Roy said, with an audible sigh.

"That would have been a disaster. How about I go down with you? If we can't find Nick, I can drive his truck back, and you can take off with Joleen. Besides, if we do find him, he may still not be in any shape to drive."

"Deal," Kurt said. "I'll go get cleaned up. You finish your breakfast and meet me at Nick's truck in twenty minutes."

The drive down was uneventful. Kurt daydreamed about Joleen, and Roy fretted about how they were going to find Nick. That turned out to be relatively easy. After checking the only restaurant open on a Sunday and not finding Nick, Roy suggested the morgue. Kurt wasn't quite as pessimistic and thought Joleen might be able to help. To Roy's delight, Joleen made one phone call and located Nick, still sound asleep at Janice's. Joleen gave him directions, and he left to chauffeur Nick back to the base, but not before he gave Kurt a wink and a lecherous grin.

Joleen spent the afternoon showing Kurt around the mine-site processing facilities. The mine was a much bigger operation than he had envisioned. It required a large staff which explained the crowd at the hall the previous night. The mine operation supported a lot of families in Ajo. After the mine, Joleen gave him a tour of the town. It didn't take long. Other than the hall, the golf course and more than a few churches, there wasn't much to see. Kurt assumed a Spanish Catholic influence led to the large number of churches. In general, the houses were small, but well kept. The exception was the row of houses which led up the street to the house on the hill. They had a Victorian look to them and got progressively larger. Joleen's was the largest. It was by no means ostentatious, but compared to the rest of the town, it was quite a step up. Now he understood how Janice could be a little jealous.

Joleen insisted that Kurt stay for dinner and meet the family. Joleen's father was a short broad-shouldered man. His hands were large, rough, and strong, Kurt noted, as he was greeted with a firm handshake and a pat on the back. His face was angular, weather beaten, and appeared as rough as his hands. You could have easily assumed he was one of the laborers from the mine. The eyes gave him away though. They were a light gray and seemed to look right into your soul. Arnold or Arn, as Joleen called him, graduated with a mining engineering degree from Arizona State. He had gone to work for the Rockport Mining Co. immediately upon graduation and rose rapidly to his first management position; a position which permitted him a secretary. When he was transferred to Ajo, he took her with him, not as a secretary, but as his wife.

Alice, Joleen's mother, was as soft as Arn was rough. She was blonde, a good six inches taller than Arn, and very well proportioned. Kurt could see where Joleen got her good looks, but the only identifiable characteristic connecting her to her father was Joleen's steel-gray eyes. Her mother had light blue eyes and a fair complexion. Scandinavian heritage, Kurt thought. He was right. She was from Minnesota and of Swedish ancestry.

Arn was particularly interested in Kurt's control-systems degree. He wanted to automate a number of processes at the mine and discussed them in detail with Kurt. Arn waited patiently at Alice's frequent interruptions with questions about Kurt's Scandinavian heritage.

Joleen just sat back and smiled as Kurt answered one question after another during supper. She whisked him off to the back porch while coffee and dessert were being prepared. She looked him in the eye, and said, "Good job." Kissed him on the lips and dashed back in to check on the coffee.

Kurt stood there on the porch, a full moon rising in the east over a small range of mountains, with his heart melting.

That kiss would have to do. Arn wouldn't hear of his daughter driving Kurt back and driving home alone.

"Too damn many drunken airmen and Mexicans on the road at night," he explained.

So Kurt spent another forty-five minutes answering automation questions while Joleen looked on from the back seat. When they arrived at Kurt's motel, Joleen jumped out and walked Kurt to his door.

She gave him a quick kiss on the cheek, and said, "Come on down next Saturday, and I will show you the Organ Pipes."

"Okay," was all he could get out. Joleen smiled and dashed for the car. His questions, about the Organ Pipes, would have to wait.

****

"Dad, how much longer?" Robby said as they navigated the LA freeways.

"Maybe ten minutes. We are going to stay at the Disneyland Hotel, so we will be fairly close. Maybe we can go over tonight if it stays open late. Look over there. You can just see the fairytale castle."

"Where?"

Kurt pointed.

"Oh yah, I see it. It's big. Let's go tonight, Dad."

"If it's open, we'll go."

Chapter 9 - A Russian and a Priest

University of California, Los Angeles
August 2, 2002 - 12:30 pm

Lisa was sitting in the cafeteria when Amy approached.

"Can I join you?" Amy said.

Lisa nodded and motioned to the empty chair across from her.

"You should try today's version of cream of lump soup. It's actually pretty good."

Amy forced a weak smile. "Lisa, I am having a lot of trouble tracing the artifacts they found on that 1882 expedition to Canyon de Chelly. The records at the Smithsonian show that a large shipment was received and put in storage, but no research was ever done on the material. There is absolutely nothing more in the online record that is of use to me."

"What about the Russian?" Lisa said.

"The only thing that I found so far is that he left the expedition and went to San Francisco. He continued to be supported by the tsar and made a couple of more trips to the area, but I guess the tsar lost interest and cut off his funding. Apparently, Vladimir teamed up with a Norwegian artist and collector, Fredrick Monsen.

"They set up a museum in San Francisco and used the proceeds from the operation to fund additional collecting and photography trips. By 1906, Vladimir had put together all of his research and was about to present a paper at a meeting of prominent archeologists, but the 1906 San Francisco earthquake and fire destroyed the museum. I couldn't find out for sure, but I think Vladimir was so severely burned trying to save his papers and artifacts that he never published anything. That little box probably contains all that remains of his work."

"Did you get any response on the internet post?" Lisa said.

"No, nothing yet, but it's only been up a little while."

"So that little box of artifacts is it. That's all we have?"

"Except for what's at the Smithsonian; I'm sure there is a goldmine of information there, but it's never been studied. I've drafted a letter asking if we could gain access. I was hoping you would sign it."

"Sure, bring it up after lunch," Lisa said.

Cairo, Egypt
August 2, 2002 - 7:00 pm

The room was cool and dry. A fine dust floated around a single light bulb that hung from a large beam, split and sagging from age. Steel doors occupied the center of three of the room's walls. Along the fourth wall, a bottle of water and a clock sat on a round table that was crammed against a small cot and coat rack. A sheet, blanket, and pillow lay in a heap on the bed.

A faint click broke the silence, and a small motor began to hum. Steel bolts pulled back out of one of the steel door. The bolts snapped to a halt, and the solid steel door opened on silent hinges. Rough-hewn wood covered the other side of the door. Large rusted, non-functional hinges and an ancient brass door handle completed the fake exterior. A man in a dusty burlap robe, with a hood pulled forward totally obscuring his identity, stood in the doorway. The passage or room behind the hooded figure was dark and gave no hint of its contents. The man stepped forward, closed the door, and watched the bolts slide back into place. He walked across the room to the door opposite the cot.

Grains of sand that somehow found their way into the room made the floor rough underfoot. How long had they lain here under the church? Perhaps they dated back to the days of the First Apostle.

He entered a few numbers on his cell phone. A motor behind the door hummed, and bolts clicked open. He stepped into a small room with white terrazzo tile floor and walls paneled in mahogany.

He glanced around the room. Phrases from the Koran in black lettering formed a border around the ceiling of the room. Small white clouds floated in a sky-blue ceiling illuminated with soft indirect lighting. An upholstered recliner sat next to a bookshelf that contained an ancient copy of the Koran sitting open on a golden stand. Next to it lay a dust-covered bible. Across the room, a black suit with a priest's collar hung on a rack over a pair of shiny patent leather shoes. A computer sat on a mahogany desk. A map of Europe and Asia hung on the wall behind the computer. Lines on the map led from a circle around the Gobi Desert to Bethlehem, Jerusalem, the Dead Sea, Yemen and Cairo. To the right of the computer a small glass box housed a small scepter lying on a blue velvet cloth. A left-handed black glove and sling lay next to the glass box. Everything was as he left it.

He sat down at the desk, typed in a few commands and waited. A picture flashed onto the screen. His mouth hung open as he leaned closer to the screen.

"How?" he said. "It can't be."

He sat for several minutes staring at the screen and then at the small glass box to his right. There on his screen was the picture of a scepter that appeared to be identical to the scepter in the glass box. But the picture also showed a small pyramid with an orb at its top, and a small object the shape of a small piece of pie. He enlarged sections of the picture and examined each object. The pyramid appeared identical to that which the Brothers possessed, and the scepter was identical to his, but the third piece, could that be the missing artifact? Yes, but could there be another pyramid and another scepter? Were there two sets of artifacts?

The alarm on his cell sounded. It was time to attend the meeting about Father Richard's access to the archeological site. He would have to research this discovery later, after his trip to Sana'a to investigate rumors about the Gold Scroll.

Before he left, he emailed the web address, of the site containing the pictures of the artifacts, to himself. Then he removed his burlap robe, hung it on a nail and slipped into the priest's garments. He slipped his left arm into a sling and proceeded to the third steel door in the adjacent room. Motorized bolts responded to his keyed command. He opened the door and climbed a set of steps leading to Saint Virgin Mary's Coptic Church.

University of California, Los Angeles
August 2, 2002 - 1:30 pm

Amy arrived back at her office just in time to see Professor Paul Grandich leaving.

"Ah, Amy, I left the old diary and the translation on your desk. It was a good exercise for my students. If you don't mind, I have kept a copy and will use it again."

"No, no, that's fine. I'm surprised at how fast you were. I thought it might be weeks," Amy said.

"Well, you looked anxious, so I copied it all and

divided it up amongst the students in one of my classes. The quality is a bit suspect, but if I do it with another class, you will probably get a darned good translation."

"That's great. Thanks, Paul."

Amy picked up the translation, and as she usually did, flipped to the back to see if there were any conclusions. She started reading the last dated entry.

Territory of Arizona - Canyon de Chelly - September 15, 1882 - eight in the morning

The expedition has been in the canyon for several months now, and we have made a number of significant discoveries. We investigated about fifty sites in the main canyon and several others in smaller canyons. The cliffs in the canyons are hundreds of feet high and provide protected building sites. Most of the ruins consist of mud brick structures built back under overhanging cliffs. One need only to construct walls as the overhanging cliffs provide natural roofs.

Today is our last at this site. I am almost thankful; for as a scientist trained in the archeological sciences at the University of Moscow, I cannot countenance the cavalier way antiquities are removed. Items are gathered at random without documenting which site they came from or to what depth they had been buried. The few pictures that were taken are without accompanying notes. Any form of academic study of the artifacts will be virtually useless. The tsar will be disappointed.

How do I tell this to Tsar Alexander, who personally sponsored my journey to the United States, and intervened to get me a position on the Bureau of American Ethnology's Expedition to the Arizona Territories' Canyon de Chelly? How?

Colonel James Stevenson leads the expedition. He is an excellent organizer and leader but not a scientist. He treats the mission as if he were a collector rather than an archeologist. I will go riding and think about how to tell the tsar.

Territory of Arizona - Canyon de Chelly - September 15, 1882 - three in the afternoon

I am ashamed. Am I also acting like a collector? No, I am not a collector; I am a true archeologist. I will keep this extraordinary find to myself; I will not disclose it to the colonel. The colonel would not understand its significance. It needs more study and documentation. I will return later and do a truly scientific job. My handling of the discovery will not be that of an amateur collector but that of an archeologist.

Earlier today I went riding. I left the campsite and its array of tents—artifacts and wagons were strewn across the canyon floor. The collection of antiquities, which to this point had been stored in a somewhat organized arrangement in a protected alcove under a cliff, was now being randomly packed in boxes and loaded on wagons. There were plenty of individuals to accomplish that, and I could not bear to watch.

I decided to make one more trip to the Mummy Cave. It was a ruin where we discovered and removed two mummified bodies. Stevenson decided to name the small ruin, "The Mummy Cave," and the canyon itself, "Canyon of Death."

I was on my way from the camp when one of the Navajo men who did not get work with the Expedition began following me. I had seen him at the camp several times trying to interest the colonel in hiring him. At first, the Navajo seemed to drift off in a slightly different direction, but once I was out of sight of the camp he quickly changed his direction and caught up with me.

"I have gift...ancient...the ancient one," he said, looking directly into my eyes.

I wondered; why is this man offering me a gift. I never talked to him before. Perhaps he thought there was still the possibility of a job.

"No, I cannot accept a gift," I said. I certainly was not going to accept a gift from someone obviously so poor.

"No! No! Gift from the ancient one. The Light Stone. I have it."

"What? What do you have?" I asked him.

The Navajo motioned for me to follow and

rode off in the direction of the Canyon of Death. That was the direction I intended to go anyway, so I followed. As we arrived at the Mummy Cave, I stopped, but my volunteer guide motioned for me to follow.

I had nothing else to do, so I thought that I might as well follow.

Soon the Navajo dismounted and walked directly toward a cliff face. Once again, he turned and motioned for me to follow, and then he suddenly disappeared.

If I was one to swear, that would have been the time. But, I simply blinked and stared at the cliff. Then just as suddenly, there he was again, like some sort of apparition, motioning for me to follow. The Navajo waited while I dismounted, then he disappeared again. Carefully, ever so carefully, I walked toward the cliff. When I was less than a foot from the cliff face, I could just make out a recess hidden in the folds of the cliff wall.

There was my apparition, crouched and motioning for me to follow. The opening was no more than three feet high and a foot wide. "Yes," I said, "I will come." We went in, the Navajo leading the way.

The small passage wound steeply upward for about twenty-five feet becoming wider as we proceeded. Then suddenly, I was standing in a large brightly lit room. I stumbled backwards at the shock. Then, as my eyes adjusted to the light, I realized that I was not in a cave but a canyon.

It was almost round at the base, maybe a hundred feet in diameter. The wall on one side was a sheer cliff while the other sloped upward to form a roof. There was an elliptical opening above, and a beam of sunlight shone through and reflected off the sloping wall, illuminating the canyon.

There were probably ten small well-preserved dwellings tucked under the sloping side of the canyon. In front of each dwelling was a stone fire ring. The ceiling was blackened from years of smoke from the fires, but the dwellings themselves were stark white. I could not believe my eyes. What a discovery! The sheer cliff wall had hundreds of indentations and channels carved into it. What were they for? I moved closer. The cave wall glistened in spots. Water! Yes! The cliff was weeping. The channels and indentations were for water collection and storage. These people were much more advanced than I thought.

"I am a Hatalii. In the white man's language, I am called a medicine man or shaman. My name is White Eagle. Come, I will show you."

He walked across the canyon to a space between the dwellings. I followed. The space appeared to be a form of town square with a small amphitheater facing the cliff wall. The wall was covered with exquisitely detailed pictographs.

White Eagle walked to the wall and pointed to a series of pictographs. "The ancient one lived with us for many years."

White Eagle's bony fingers pointed to a drawing. It showed two figures, one with a large head and large eyes, the other figure shorter with small eyes. They were standing in an amphitheater in front of a group of much smaller people, perhaps children. "He taught us many things," White Eagle pointed to the taller figure and then to the wall with the water management system, "and we lived in peace for many years."

Tears welled up in his eyes as he moved to the next drawing. It was a scene of battle with arrows flying and men fighting with axes. "Then the invaders came, and we had much fighting. The ancient one was displeased, and he said he would leave us and return only when we were again at peace. He gave us gifts."

He motioned for me to come closer and pointed to the next pictograph.

The drawings were small but with difficulty I could make out three things. One appeared to be like a piece of pie. The second item was what appeared to be a child's rattle. The third was a triangle with a circle on top.

White Eagle moved on. In the next pictograph, the smaller of the two men was holding the rattle. His hands were drawn much larger than the rest of his body to show his thumb on the large top part of the rattle and his fingers wrapped around the handle. Small perpendicular lines extended from the top part of the rattle. Lower in the drawing was the triangle with the ball on top. Many broad lines extended from the ball. White Eagle pointed at the smaller of the two men. "He was our first Hatalii. He was called Maker of Light. He could make the ancient one's light." He pointed at the triangle with the circle on its apex.

"The shaman could make a fire," I said. "He must have been very important to your people."

"No, not fire. Light. Bright light from here." He pointed at the picture of the ball on the triangle. "The ancient one's light." White Eagle walked back to the center of the amphitheater and bent over what looked like a circular stone altar about two feet high and a foot and a half in diameter. He looked back. I could see reluctance in his eyes. "I have watched you for many days. You are careful and treat our sacred things with respect. You are not like the others."

He stood motionless for several seconds, then closed his eyes and with a loud grunt lifted a flat stone off the top of the altar and set it aside. He reached down into the circle of stones that formed the altar and withdrew an object wrapped in leather. Slowly, he unwound the straps and unwrapped the package. He withdrew a small pyramid-shaped object with a ball perched on top.

"The ancient one's light," White Eagle whispered as he passed it to me.

The object was heavy. The surface of the pyramid looked like polished stone while the ball on top appeared translucent. It was amazing. I had never seen anything so beautiful.

"The ancient one and the Hatalii could make light come from here." White Eagle pointed at the ball. He walked back to the pictographs.

I could imagine the rays in the picture as light. "Can you make the light?" I asked.

"No, only the ancient one and our first Hatalii could make the light." White Eagle went to the final pictograph and pointed again. "After they died no one could make the light. We kept the gifts here in this sacred place waiting for the ancient one's return. But I am getting old, and my people are dying. Soon no one will be left to guard them. I have watched you and believe you can be trusted. I will give them to you. You must keep them safe till the ancient one returns."

White Eagle retrieved two other leather wrapped articles and gave them to me. "You must go now," White Eagle whispered. "I will close the cave forever."

I took one last look at the pictographs. The last one showed two people, one tall, one short, lying side by side. The ancient one and the shaman, I supposed. Then in a moment of enlightenment, I knew.

They are the mummies.

White Eagle guided me out of the canyon, helped me onto my horse, and pointed the way back to camp. I started out and turned to wait for White Eagle. He was gone.

I arrived back at the camp, and went directly

to my tent and hid the gifts in my pack. Then I wandered about the camp until Colonel Stevenson returned from supervising the loading. "Colonel, how is the packing going?" I asked.

"Ah Vladimir! Things are proceeding nicely. We could have used your help though. Wandering off to look at the canyons wasn't much help," the colonel said.

I was shaken. Did the colonel suspect something? "Tomorrow, I will help," I said.

The colonel laughed. "No need to get the tsar's representatives hands calloused. We've finished. Tomorrow, we will get this expedition wrapped up and have this shipment on its way to the Smithsonian."

I asked, "Colonel, now that the expedition is finished, I would like to visit some more of this beautiful country of yours. Perhaps I will visit California?"

"That's fine with me. What about your tsar?"

"Oh, I will write him. It will be fine." It was settled as easy as that. I would head west while the colonel headed east with the shipment.

Translator's notes - This was the last journal entry but on the back page of the journal there were a few badly burnt notes

*All of the antiquities, including the **(unintelligible)**, safely reached the Smithsonian. I monitored the archeological journals but as I expected **(unintelligible)**, the shipment's*

*contents were **(unintelligible)**, but nothing was published except **(unintelligible)**.*

*I told the tsar of **(unintelligible)**. The tsar said he would continue to send my annual stipend if I sent him some artifacts. I sent several including the **(unintelligible)** to Tsar Alexander for the Moscow Museum, but I kept the three from the cave with me.*

Amy flopped back in her chair. Wow, the artifacts did indeed come from the Navajo, but who was the ancient one that could make the stone light up. And why did it light up the other night?

Chapter 10 - The Cell

Winnipeg, Manitoba, Canada
Aug 4, 2002 - 6:45 pm

You'd think that a relatively small airport like this could get your bag here a lot quicker, Yusof Ekstrom thought. They must have carried each bag from the plane by hand. There weren't more than thirty people on the flight.

The luggage, from Air Canada flight AC962, from Vancouver to Winnipeg started arriving. Yusof was standing beside another man who was making similar comments about the slow service to his attractive companion. The man had a southern accent. Arrogant Americans, Yusof thought, always criticizing and impatient.

Yusof grabbed his luggage from the carousel and made his way to the car rental booths. The bag was almost empty. He would only be staying one night and could have gotten by without luggage, but since

Haleef Al-Jabar was caught smuggling a trunk full of radiological waste and explosives across the border to the U.S., everyone seemed to be on increased alert. Haleef apparently planned to explode the car in the parking lot at Quest Field as fans were leaving a Seahawks football game. What a waste of time. Soon we will have the money to deal a much deadlier blow to the Americans. But now, because of Haleef, he had to be extra cautious. A man with his complexion traveling without luggage might be suspicious, even if he had blue eyes.

Yusof inherited his blue eyes from his father, Jon, and his dark completion from his mother, Hadifa. Jon met Hadifa in Aden where he worked for the Canadian Embassy. Hadifa's father, Yusof Saleh, was one of a number of prominent men Jon met in his work and Yusof invited him to his house for one of the local festivals. It was there where Jon first saw Hadifa. He had met her before, but she had been covered head to foot in a *hijab* and veil, in the strictest Muslim tradition. But here, in the privacy of her home, she was exquisitely dressed in expensive western clothes.

She had been accepted in the political science program at Carlton University, and Hadifa's father wondered if Jon might help her get settled in Ottawa. Jon willingly agreed to help her settle in when she arrived in Ottawa. He did more than that. Before Hadifa graduated, they were married.

To the delight of Hadifa's father, they decided to name their son, Yusof, after him, and they promised to bring him up as a Muslim. Hadifa and the young

Yusof spent many months in Yemen, and Yusof became fluent in Arabic and the customs of Yemen. He attended a religious school and could recite many passages from the Koran by heart. Other than his blue eyes, he could easily pass for a Yemeni. With the proper contact lenses, he could hide those eyes whenever he needed.

The car rental agent was courteous and efficient, and Yusof was soon on his way to his motel. Amil Fawaz would arrive from Montreal and stay at a different motel. They planned to meet at the Door to Beirut, a Lebanese restaurant, owned by Fadi El Khoury.

Fadi was the leader of their cell and was their only contact with the Priest, the Egyptian benefactor, who financed their operation. Fadi operated out of Montreal for years. It was an ideal operations center; a high percentage of the population of Canada was latently, if not openly, anti-American. This was especially true in the province of Quebec and the city of Montreal. But after the September 11th attacks, he was worried that the CSIS and the RCMP were paying too much attention to the Middle Eastern communities in Montreal, so he moved to Winnipeg and opened a new restaurant, Door to Beirut. It was successful and actually made a profit. It was not simply a money-laundering operation.

Yusof checked into his motel, showered and changed his clothes. He wore a suit on the flight. Now he changed into a pair of dark gray pants, a muted golf shirt and a light weight bomber jacket. Hopefully, nobody would take much notice of him at

101

the restaurant. He arrived at 9:30. By this time, most of the evening diners had left. Fadi saw him enter and waved him toward a door in the back. This led to a small private dining room where Amil Fawaz was nibbling on Lebanese sweets and sipping strong Yemeni coffee. Amil stood and walked over to Yusof.

"*As-Salāmu `Alaykum*," Amil said, as he kissed Yusof on both cheeks.

"Careful Amil, if these Winnipeggers see you, they may get the wrong idea.

Amil let out a roar. "Let the bastards think what they may."

Amil was rotund and bearded. He always reminded Yusof of the Egyptian chap that is always there to help out the hero in those adventure movies. He even had the same demeanor, a sort of irreverent competence. He held Yusof by both shoulders at arm's length and looked him in the eyes.

"It's been too long, old blue eyes," he said, and then he began butchering one of Bing Crosby's old songs.

"Enough, enough."

Yusof broke loose of the powerful grip.

"Someone is sure to call the police," Yusof said.

Amil bellowed out another loud laugh and pointed to a chair.

"Sit, sit, have some coffee, it's Yemeni. And…and some sweets perhaps. Some *ma'amoul* stuffed with pistachios? And Fadi promised some *tabbouleh* once you arrived."

"Coffee, just coffee, right now. I'll wait for the

tabbouleh. Have you talked to Fadi about the project?"

"No, he said that we would wait for you. The only thing he said was that tens of millions could be involved."

"Tens? Not tens. Surely, you must have misunderstood," Yusof said.

"No, no, he said tens of millions. With that much money, we can do anything, perhaps even a suitcase nuke. Then we will show the American bastards," Amil roared.

"Shhh, the walls are not soundproof."

Yusuf worried about Amil's inclusion in the cell. Amil lost his wife and son in the 1982 Israeli invasion of Lebanon. He helped plan the attacks on the American and French barracks in Beirut in October 1983. He blamed the Americans for the ongoing Israeli aggression, and would have flown one of the September 11 planes if he could have.

"To hell with the Jews," Amil whispered.

"After the Americans, we will deal with them. With ten million, imagine what we could do. We could—"

He stopped expounding on the damage they could do as Fadi entered the room.

"My good friends," Fadi said, "welcome, I have wonderful news. But first some food. I will tell you what good fortune has befallen us as we eat." He turned and poked his head out the door and nodded to a waiter. He returned and sat at the table with Amil and Yusof.

Amil could not contain himself. "What is it?" he

said.

Fadi signaled for him to be quiet as the waiter entered and served the food. When the waiter left, he said, "Eat and listen."

Amil and Yusof listened intently.

"So?" Amil said when Fadi finished. "We simply obtain the scroll and sell it to a museum. Surely a museum would not buy stolen goods. What was the name of that museum again?"

"The AC Archeological Museum," Fadi said. "It was formed by the famous oilman Arthur Calvert."

"I don't understand why they would buy it," Amil said.

"The curator for antiquities, an eighty-three year old matron, has had many questionable dealings in the past. Either she buys this artifact or the museum and her reputation...ah, how do they say it? Yes, yes, or their reputation is toast."

Fadi smiled at the phrase, and Amil burst out laughing.

"So the plan is set. I will travel to Yemen to obtain the scroll," Yusof said.

"I will go with you," Amil said.

"No, you are not welcome in Yemen. You can't come with me. The Yemeni secret police are watching for you after your last actions there."

"He deserved killing," Amil said.

"That may be so, but he was a member of the government and close to the President. You are no longer welcome in the country and would risk the mission. Yusof will go alone," Fadi said.

"So be it then. I will go back to the United States

and start some more fires. I'll give the Great Satan something to do," Amil said, with a roar.

They finished their meal confirming details of the operations. In theory, it was quite straightforward. The Priest had found out that the scroll was on the market in Yemen. They simply had to find the person offering it for sale, and buy or steal it. Fadi would look after the sale to the museum.

By the time they finished their meeting, the restaurant staff had left. Amil and Yusof left, and drove back to their respective motels. Fadi stayed behind to lock up the restaurant.

"The Priest will be pleased," he muttered to himself as he locked up.

Chapter 11 - Friends and Lovers

Los Angeles, California
August 5, 2002 - 9:00 am

The three days at Disneyland were a success. Kurt had never seen Robby have so much fun. Now that they started their trip back to Joleen, things changed.

"So, Robby, how did you like Disneyland?"

"It was real good, Dad. Can we go again some time? Will Mom let me?"

"I'm sure she will. Maybe we could go to the Florida Park next time."

"Could we all go together, you, me and Mom?"

"I don't think so Robby, but you and your Mom could go."

Robby sat quietly for a long time after that, and then asked, "How long will it take to get home?"

"Two days. I promised your Mom I'd have you home tomorrow, so we are in for a couple of days of nothing but driving."

Robby nodded and slumped back in his seat.

****

It was Saturday, October 3, 1992. Kurt was preparing to visit Joleen and the Organ Pipe Cactus National Monument. He walked head down toward the café. This week they had finished the launches from their simulated cockpit and were preparing to head back to Montreal to make required design adjustments. Kurt had mixed emotions. The test's success was good, but leaving Joleen bothered him, even though he'd only seen her twice so far.

"Hey, wait up," Roy called out from behind. "What's the rush?"

"Oh, I'm going down to see Joleen."

"Again? Is something up here? I've never seen you take this much interest in a woman."

Kurt kicked at a stone and said nothing. Roy turned around and walked backwards in front of Kurt. "Come on, what's up, Kurt?"

"Nothin'."

"Don't try and bluff me, Kurt."

"Well, I guess I really like her. I don't know why. And we leave on Tuesday. I wish I had more time."

"Come on, Kurt. We'll be back in a couple of months for the air-to-air test. I hope you aren't going to do anything foolish." Roy tripped as he backed into the steps leading up to the cafe and ended up sitting on the middle of three steps. "Ah, fu...feathers, you could have warned me."

Kurt smiled down at Roy and went into the cafe.

Roy followed slapping his butt trying to get the dust off.

As they ate breakfast Roy tried to bring up Joleen again, but Kurt changed the topic to the air-to-air test they were planning.

As they were about to leave, Roy said. "Ok, you don't want to talk about Joleen. I get it. But I mean it, Kurt. Don't do anything foolish."

He reached in his pocket and threw a couple of condoms on the table. You better take these along."

"She's not like that," Kurt said. But, as he rose, he scooped them up. "I've borrowed Nick's truck. See you later."

Kurt arrived at Joleen's and found her waiting on the front porch. A couple of backpacks sat beside her.

"Grab these," she said, pointing at the packs. "You didn't wear very good shoes."

Kurt sported his best Nikes but Joleen wore hiking boots plus loose fitting khaki shorts, a khaki army shirt and a large brimmed hat.

"You have a hat?" she said.

Kurt shook his head. Joleen disappeared into the house and reappeared with an old British army safari hat.

"This will have to do." She smiled and tossed the hat to Kurt. "Let's go."

As Kurt drove south out of Ajo, Joleen filled Kurt in on the Organ Pipe Cactus. "They are a type of cactus that looks like..." Joleen smiled and looked at

Kurt.

"Organ Pipes?" Kurt said.

"Oh, you brilliant PhDs." She smiled and his heart skipped a beat. "They grow in only one place in the United States. It's a very small area at the Mexican border. It's so unique that it was made a National Monument."

She continued to explain the history of the area, its native peoples, mountains and the wildlife. Obviously, she found the area fascinating and explained that she planned to take Kurt on a hike through the park to the old Victoria Mine site so he could see some of the sights for himself.

That explained the backpacks with food, water and the clothes. She finished her detailed natural history lesson just as they drove through the town of Why.

Why indeed, Kurt thought to himself, would anyone want to live here? Just then, Joleen changed places with the two backpacks that had been sitting between them. She snuggled close to him. Ah, now he was the two headed pick-up driver that Roy always pointed out. He put his arm around Joleen just as she slid her hand up his leg. The shock caused him to swerve and almost hit the ditch on the narrow road.

"Oops...later," she said, as she looked into his eyes. "We wouldn't want to roll Nick's truck, would we?" Kurt was temporarily tongue-tied and just drove on without answering.

The walk through the National Monument was spectacular. A heavy two-day rain a few days earlier washed away a year of dust. The desert was suddenly alive. Kurt hadn't noticed from the road on the drive down, but small flowers had sprung up in almost every low spot. What, from a distance, appeared to be tall dead sticks had tiny green sprigs protruding from tiny holes, and at the top tiny red buds prepared to bloom. Joleen named them all—from the dead-stick Ocotillo, to the towering Saguaro. They walked south from park headquarters to an abandoned mine site where she allowed Kurt to rest.

The two months away from the gym had taken its toll on Kurt. The trail to the mine crossed numerous ridges and intervening valleys, and Kurt started to fall behind his guide.

"Half way." Joleen laughed, as she passed Kurt some water. "We'll have some lunch when we get there. Unless?" She paused. "Unless you're hungry now?"

"No, the water will be fine. But, what do you mean half way? Aren't we at the mine?"

"Naw, there's not much here, just a few holes and some tailings. The real mine is over that ridge. It's much better preserved and more interesting."

Kurt looked up. "That's not your average ridge, looks more like a mountain."

Joleen pointed. "See that cairn. The mine is just down the other side and across a small valley."

Kurt could just make out a small cairn made of a pile of rocks atop the hill.

"Who put that there?" he asked.

"Who do you think?"

"You…you got to be kidding, we are climbing that?"

"Yes and no." Her grey eyes twinkled.

Kurt could see she was having fun with him.

"I did build that cairn, but we will go around the ridge to the mine. There is a narrow valley just to the southeast of here. We'll go through it and loop around. It looks like the climb would wear you out, and I want to keep you reasonably fresh for a little surprise."

"Thank God," Kurt sighed.

Once they crossed up and through a small pass, the journey became easier. They turned west along the southern side of the ridge and worked their way down a gently sloped valley that ended at the mine site. Joleen was right. This site was a lot more interesting. In addition to the tailings and shafts, there were a number of ruins along with some old mining equipment. To Kurt's surprise, there was another group of tourists at the site as well.

After poking around for a while, Joleen put her finger to her lips and motioned for Kurt to follow her. They slipped quietly away from the tourists and made their way around the edge of what appeared to be a solid rock cliff rising up behind the mine site. She looked back to ensure they weren't followed, climbed a few feet up the cliff and disappeared into one of many crevasses that notched the cliff wall. She poked her head back out, and motioned for him to follow. The crevasse was narrow and sloped steeply upward. Kurt struggled to maneuver his larger body and backpack through the twists and turns, and he fell behind. When he arrived at the top and climbed out of the crevasse into a small canyon, he realized that was Joleen's plan.

A trail of clothes led past a solitary Saguaro cactus to a pool of perfectly clear water that contained a naked Joleen.

The sun was shining directly into the pool and glistened on Joleen's skin. "Surprise," she said.

Kurt stood motionless; the canyon, cactus, pool and the naked Joleen were just too much for his senses.

"Well, are you going to join me or are you going to tell me you don't like my surprise?"

"No, I mean yes, I…I mean yes, I am going to join you, and no, I'm not going to tell you I don't like your surprise."

Kurt stripped and stumbled into the pool. The water felt surprisingly cold in comparison to the heat of the desert. He didn't have any time to comment on that. Joleen started where she left off at Why and kissed him. Soon they were making love.

Joleen was wilder than anyone Kurt had been with—not that there were many. She groaned and screamed in ecstasy. Kurt was sure that if the tourists were still at the mine site or anywhere in the valley, they would have assumed the mine was haunted. Even the Saguaro agreed. It stood at the edge of the pool, fingers pointed to the sky, making a "*shushsssss*" sound, as the wind wound through its needles. They lay back, holding each other close in the cool water.

"Getting cold?" Joleen said.

Kurt nodded. The water in the desert pool had to be spring fed.

"Come on," she said. Joleen went to one of the backpacks and retrieved a blanket which she spread on the ground. Kurt joined her, and they lay there in each other's arms drying in the warm desert sun. Then she opened the other backpack, and they ate a nude lunch.

Kurt never knew anyone so uninhibited.

After lunch they made love again. He thought about the condoms in his jeans, but he hadn't used one in the pool so why start now? This time the lovemaking was more tender and quiet. The Saguaro seemed to approve and made no disciplinary sounds. The sun disappeared behind the canyon wall. Joleen sat up. "We better go. We don't want to be walking around amongst all these cactuses in the dark.

Joleen seemed to find the walk back even easier that the trip out, but it was all Kurt could do to keep up. When they arrived back at Nick's truck Joleen snuggled up to him, put her head on his shoulder, and closed her eyes.

She wasn't asleep, but thankfully she didn't have any more surprises for him. The sun was well down when they arrived at her house.

"Folks will be worried," she said as she gave him a peck on the cheek. "Call me tomorrow." And she was gone.

Kurt sat there aware of two new loves in his life, the desert and Joleen. As he drove back toward the base and his motel, he knew. This was the girl he wanted to marry.

****

"Dad, are we being punished? Is that why my hand is like this."

"What, no. What makes you say that?"

"Well, I heard Mom talking to one of the neighbors after bible study class. And Mom said that she was being punished because she had to get married. Didn't you want to marry Mom?"

"Robby, I've told you before that I really loved your Mom and I still do, but sometimes religion takes over a person's life. Sometimes they believe that God is punishing them and—"

"Did God make my hand like this? The lady at Mom's bible study said that was the reason."

"Robby, do you think God would punish you? Why would he do that?"

"Mom told the lady it was because you had to get married. Who made you get married, Dad?"

"No one, Robby, your Mom and I got married because we loved each other and wanted to."

****

Kurt wandered into the Gila Bend Motel Diner at noon. He was normally an early riser, but the previous day's activities more than exhausted him. In the booth across from the entrance, Nick and Roy sat like two Cheshire cats from the Disney, *Alice in Wonderland*, movie. They didn't say anything but just stared at him with those silly grins. Roy with perfect teeth, and Nick with a wide gap between his two front teeth. Kurt sat down. He knew from those silly grins what was coming. "I came for my truck," Nick said.

"Oh, sorry, I forgot."

More grinning. "It's okay; I hitched a ride over with Gunny. Thought I'd join Roy here for afternoon tea. That's what you Canucks drink in the late afternoon, ain't it?"

Kurt didn't think it possible, but a bigger grin spread across Nick's face.

"Okay, okay, cut it out, and I'll pay for lunch."

"Deal," Nick agreed, still grinning. In fact, he still had a lecherous grin pasted on his face as he left the diner to get his truck.

Roy sat quietly after Nick left, just staring at Kurt. Kurt knew Roy wasn't going to give up as easily as Nick. He would have to explain yesterday, but a diversion might work.

"Nick sure likes to stick it to a fellow, doesn't he?"

Roy said nothing.

"What did you do yesterday?" Kurt said.

Roy paused for a few seconds. "How'd you and Joleen get on?"

"Hope Nick wasn't too upset about having to come get his truck. What do you think?" Kurt said.

Roy crossed his arms and looked Kurt in the eye, and said, "So, what did you and Joleen do that made you sleep so late?"

Roy wasn't going to give up.

"Well…ah, well," Kurt said, and then stopped.

"What do you mean, ah, well?"

"Well, we were in this pool of water, a… ah…ah, a spring"

"In the desert?" Roy said.

"U-huh, and we…" Kurt paused. "Just leave it alone, Roy, you don't need to know the details. All you really need to know is that I picked her up; we spent the day hiking in the desert and ended up at this mine site with a secret entrance to a little pool fed by a spring. You can imagine the rest and quit grinning. You look dopey."

Roy continued to grin. "I can imagine. Hope you used my gifts."

"No, they weren't handy."

Roy's grin faded. "Ah, Kurt, if you are going to have a fling in the desert, you…you…I told you not to do anything foolish."

"It's not just a fling. I really like her; in fact, I am going to ask her to marry me."

"You're what?"

"I'm going to ask Joleen to marry me."

Roy's mouth hung open for a few seconds. "Let's go to the bar," Roy said. "You need some more serious counseling here. In addition, I could use something more than the toast and coffee you so generously sprung for. What that cost you, two bucks? How about a beer and pizza at that little bar down the road?"

"Okay, if you quit lecturing me, I'll buy."

****

"Kurt, are you sure about this marriage thing?" Roy said, as he took a bite of pizza and a swig of beer.

"What? You have to finish chewing that piece of pizza and quit talking into your beer if you expect anyone to hear you. And if you want me to pay, no lecturing, remember?"

Roy chewed for a while and said nothing.

"Well, Kurt, we haven't known each other for that long but from what I've seen you're a straight arrow type who doesn't rush off half-cocked. But here you are, you've known Joleen for what, a week, and now you plan to marry her."

"It's two weeks."

"Yah, well, one week or two, it's still not long. So I figure you're either a nerd who's never even held a girl's hand, and up and marry the first one that can bring herself to kiss you, or she's some kind of sexual minx or siren that's ensnared you."

"No, Roy, you're wrong. She's…I'm not a nerd and she's not a minx. She's, well, I don't know. We just have a great time together. I get along well with her family; I even went off to church with them last Sunday."

"Oh, and that's another thing. They belong to some sort of holy-roller sect or something, don't they? That could lead to trouble. I've never seen you demonstrate any religious leanings."

"They aren't what you call holy-rollers. They are just Baptist, a little stricter than some churches but not extreme. You know my folks are of Scandinavian heritage, and I was brought up Lutheran. I can remember when they frowned on men and women dancing."

"Ah, there we have it. You proposed to the first woman that danced with you."

Kurt frowned. "So Roy, what religion are you? I suppose you're an atheist?"

"Not sure what I am. Look around you. Was this random chance, creation or perhaps a mix of both? For me, the jury's out, but I know formal religion's not for me. Look at the Old Testament. It's mainly about who smote who, one battle after another with, ah, say the Philistines. I think that carries on to this day, doesn't it, with Israel and the Palestinians. Philistines and Palestinians, sounds almost the same to me."

"But Jesus was all about peace and forgiveness. That's the New Testament's message."

Roy nodded. "Yah, but we're not having much success, are we? Would you say our little project down here testing an air-to-air missile was about peace?"

"Well, we have to. We need to defend ourselves."

"I agree; you can rationalize anything. But the problem with the more extreme protestant religions is they set all these high standards, and you are either shown to be a hypocrite when you fail to meet the standards, or you carry all this guilt and expect to be punished."

"Protestant, why only protestant?" Kurt said.

"Well, the Catholics were smart enough to create

confession. They can create these same high standards, but they expect you to fail from time to time, and you just go to confession and try harder next time. Smart guy, the Pope, eh?"

Kurt sipped his beer and stared at Roy.

"Ah Kurt, I didn't mean to put you in a funk. It's just my little hang-up with formal religions. I'm sure you and Joleen will be fine. Here have some more pizza; I'll get us a couple more beer."

The next morning Kurt went to Ajo and proposed. Joleen accepted. Her family was delighted.

After that everything seemed to move at light speed. Kurt asked Roy to be has best man. He agreed. Kurt and Roy went back to Montreal to make the required design changes and plan the air-to-air tests. Joleen planned the wedding. Two months later they were back for the air-to-air tests and the wedding. Both went off without a hitch and three months after the day in the desert Mr. and Mrs. Sigurdson were moving to Montreal. The timing was excellent as Joleen's pregnancy wasn't showing yet.

Bellingham, Washington
Thursday, August 8, 2002

Kurt dropped Robby off with Joleen on time and without incident.

He had decided not to confront Joleen about Robby's belief that they were being punished. That could wait for another time. Kurt also didn't want to tell Joleen about Robby's incident at the mine, and since Major Wilkinson asked them not to tell anyone, he was able to persuade Robby to keep their discovery a secret.

Chapter 12 - O'Shanigan

Charles de Gaulle Airport - Paris, France
August 12, 2002 - 8:20 am

Father Terry O'Shanigan's flight from Sana'a to Paris via Frankfurt arrived on time. He collected his luggage and walked out of the terminal. Father Paul Richards waited in the usual place and jumped out of the car to open the door.

As Terry settled back into the Mercedes he rubbed his hand across the leather seats. A nice perk for a priest, but pride is one of the seven deadly sins; I should really help Paul load the luggage.

Father Richards slid into the driver's seat. "You must be tired; it was almost midnight when you left Sana'a. How is your arm?"

"I see you are in your typical, bright-eyed and questioning form this morning, Paul."

"Sorry."

"No, no, that's fine. My arm is fine." Terry

adjusted the sling supporting his arm. "It's healing slowly, but no longer hurts, and surprisingly, I'm not tired."

"Successful trip?" Paul said.

"Yes, the Cairo effort went well. It appears our competitors, the École Biblique, found out about the site you discovered. They want access, and are submitting a competing proposal. But, I am sure we will prevail. Our work is superior, even though we have a much smaller staff."

"Pride, good Father, be cautious of pride," Paul said.

Terry smiled, "Yes, I know. Still, I am sure we will continue to have exclusive access to the site."

"And Sana'a?" Paul said.

"The trip to Sana'a was not as productive." Terry hesitated. He felt that twinge of guilt as he lied to Paul. "Nothing conclusive there."

Perhaps, if I can actually acquire the scroll, Terry thought. Then I could…could what? Tell Paul…tell him what?

École Biblique - Paris, France
April 3, 1988

Father Paul Richards had been Terry's closest friend and ally since that early April morning in 1988. Terry was working on his PhD at the École Biblique, under Paul's supervision. For several months, they carefully unrolled the Copper Scroll, cut small sections off, and pressed each brittle piece between two flat glass plates so it could be examined. The previous day they had presented the status of their work to the department head. It seemed to contradict many of the conclusions previously published by the École scholars. After the meeting, Terry returned to the lab to continue his work. He lost track of time and worked through the night into the morning. There was a knock at the door and he looked up to see Paul, a sinister expression contorting his face; an expression Terry had not seen before, or since.

"Terry, you must work faster. Those who want to shut down access to outsiders are growing in power. I fear we shall soon be shut out. I am copying all my research and storing it offsite. I suggest you do the same."

"Are you sure? Why would they do that?"

"I think they want to control the message. Our work has brought their conclusions into question, and they are worried about what we will find if we complete our analysis of the Copper Scroll. Our suggestion that the Copper Scroll was made by another group, not the group that made the rest of the Dead Sea Scrolls, seems to have disturbed them," Father Richards said.

"How long do we have?"

"The next board meeting is in six weeks. I think they will decide then. We should accelerate the work on the scroll."

Howie Erickson

École Biblique - Paris, France
May 9, 1988 - 4:40 pm

The board meeting was now just one day away. Father O'Shanigan and Father Richards had unrolled the complete scroll, and were working to record and interpret its message. What they had discovered so far was a document with six columns of text, each organized into six paragraphs. They seemed to be disorganized entries. Some paragraphs described vessels used in rites carried out in the temple in Jerusalem; some described what seemed to be records of harvests; another column of six paragraphs indicated that there were treasures hidden somewhere. But other than that the text held little of real significance.

For the past two nights, Terry had been testing his translations of the ancient languages on the Copper Scroll by running various translation programs using the École Biblique's large computer system. He had been working late again, since access to the facility might soon be lost, but he was getting tired, so for his final run that night, he made slight alterations to the input data and selected the program to process it. He accidently ran a program that tested for simple encrypted messages. It was something he had developed on his own and planned to test, but the threat of losing access to the Copper Scroll had put that project on hold.

Before he realized his mistake and cancelled the program, it indicated with an incessant beep—beep--beep, that it had found a pattern. He let the program complete its job and ran the resulting output through

124

his translation program. A completely new story emerged.

There were descriptions of two other scrolls, one made of gold and one made of silver, and a partial description of three treasures belonging to someone called the Master. It mentioned the First Apostle, and the Chosen One. Terry read the text again. The First Apostle must refer to Andrew, but the Chosen One, could that refer to Jesus? Perhaps. Was this why the École wanted to restrict access to the Copper Scrolls?

Should I share this knowledge? No, I will decide what to do with this discovery later. For now, no one must know. Not even Father Richards.

Terry deleted his programs from the École Biblique's computer system and finished copying his files to diskette. He could run his program using more limited computer facilities outside of the École Biblique.

At eight in the morning, two hours before the board meeting, Terry left with the last of his records. Later that day, he was informed he would no longer have access to any material at the École Biblique. But, he had the information from the Copper Scroll; all he needed to search for the antiquities was money.

After unsuccessfully searching for a sponsor for several months, he discovered that Arthur Calvert, a rich oilman and collector, was sponsoring projects. At first Terry was reluctant to tie himself to a big private donor. He was afraid it would limit his freedom. But when he couldn't raise even a fraction of the required money from small donors, the church, or governments, Terry finally gave up and went to Arthur.

He was pleasantly surprised. Arthur sponsored a large number of charitable foundations and institutes. As long as they made effective use of his money, he interfered very little. A quarterly progress report and a formal financial audit was all that was usually required. In Terry's case, however, his successes in discovering antiquities, and Arthur's interest in acquiring and protecting them brought the two men much closer together.

For the initial grant, Terry found it necessary to inform Arthur that he had decoded a portion of the Copper Scroll and that he believed this would lead to additional treasures. He also informed Arthur that the École Biblique was no longer allowing outsiders access to the Copper Scroll, and they would have to proceed with what he had discovered. Arthur agreed to keep this fact secret, and he was true to his word.

Arthur's first grant to Terry's Institute of Biblical Archeology was a staggering ten million dollars. Terry couldn't believe it. He rented a small office in Paris and hired a secretary. Then he proceeded to convince a number of priests and brothers who were not too closely connected to the mainstream church to join him. They all had advanced degrees in archeology and were only too eager to go on a dig for Dead Sea Scrolls. When Terry told them they were going to Machaerus in Jordan, rather than Qumran on the West Bank, where the original Dead Sea Scrolls were discovered, they were disappointed. But they would be on a well-financed dig and as

Father Richard, the first one to join with Terry, said, "Who knows? There is so much history in the area; we are bound to turn up something."

Father Richard didn't have any idea how prophetic those words would be. Arthur's connections got them into the country in record time, and Terry's mysterious sense of where to look, plus the ground penetrating radar that Arthur Calvert's money bought, allowed them to quickly identify three sites. The digs began and yielded numerous scrolls and other mysterious artifacts that they were surprisingly allowed to take out of the country. Arthur's connections at work again, Terry knew.

Arthur was so pleased with their success that he donated another five million dollars and insisted they set up a formal research site. He sent one of his real estate agents to Paris and soon they were in a refurbished building on the outskirts. Its unobtrusive exterior hid a first class research facility with all the latest computer and analytical equipment. A set of suites on the top floor housed Terry and his key staff.

"Arthur is going to make this life so good no one will risk expulsion by leaking any secrets," Terry explained to Father Richards.

They quickly analyzed what they found and made two more forays into the remote area before anyone else could get organized. Terry picked the area clear, and no other expedition found anything of significance. What the others did find, the local government confiscated for their antiquities department.

Institute of Biblical Archeology - Paris, France - August 12, 2002 - 9:40 am

The drive from Charles de Gaulle Airport to the institute took over an hour. "Oh, I almost forgot," Paul said, as he pulled up at the Institute of Biblical Archeology. "This morning you received a telephone call from Father Ernesto Gonzales. He's from Our Lady of Guadalupe Abbey in Oregon. He insisted on being put through immediately. I had never heard of him, so I told him that you were on a plane, but I could pass along a message when I picked you up. He insisted I instruct you to call him immediately."

"That's fine. I know him. You can put the call through as soon as I'm in my office."

Once Terry was back in his office, Father Richards put the call through.

Terry answered, "One moment, please."

He needed to be sure this was the real Father Gonzales and that nobody could listen in. He took a small notebook out of his pocket and flipped it open. The book contained a series of lines numbered from one to a thousand. Each line contained a unique sixteen digit hexadecimal code. He selected a line number. "Zero, seven, nine," he said and waited.

If the person on the line was whom he said he was, he would have an identical list of sixteen digit hexadecimal numbers.

The voice on the other end said, "Zero, seven, nine."

"Correct," Terry said.

Terry unlocked a drawer in his desk, and set the

telephone handset in a cradle in a small black box. He keyed the sixteen digit code into the keyboard to activate the scrambler. He put on the scrambler's headset and waited for the person at the other end to enter an identical sixteen digit code.

"Hello, Terry, hello," a voice said, when the scrambler on the other end synchronized.

"Ernesto. What is so urgent that you risk a direct call?"

"Remember the boy I told you about the last time we met?"

"Refresh my memory," Terry said. "What is his name?"

"Robby, Robby Sigurdson. He is nine years old."

"Yes, I remember our discussion. I asked you to begin monitoring him. He is one of several we are monitoring around the world. What is so urgent?"

"I think he may be a Master," Ernesto whispered.

Terry leaned forward and pressed the earpieces on the headset tight to his ears. "You think he's a Master? Why?"

"I don't have all the details but he was on a trip in the Algodones Dunes with his father and…well, they found something. The boy, Robby, fell into an opening and strange lights came on. When Robby left, the opening closed by itself."

"Where are the Algodones Dunes?"

"In south eastern California."

"It must have been a well or abandoned mine or something. Why do you think it is linked to the Six and the Master?"

"It happened the evening of July 31, the same

time as the Master's Light awakened in Paris."

"Yes, there might be a connection. But it could be just a coincidence. Anything else?"

"The boy told his priest that the walls inside of the opening just seemed to glow. There didn't seem to be any real lights. And there were strange letters on the wall. That's about all we know."

"Yes, I think you are right. I need to see that parish priest and perhaps the boy. Can you give me the priest's contact information?"

Terry took down the particulars.

"Thank you, Ernesto. I think you did the right thing breaking protocol and calling me directly."

Terry hung up, and walked out of his office and handed the information to Father Richards. "Can you get me an appointment with this priest, Father James, in Bellingham, Washington, and arrange a flight to the nearest large airport. Leave the return leg open. I am not sure how long I will be."

Terry returned to his office and looked out the window at the Paris skyline. His years of work were finally yielding results. After years of searching, he had located the gold scroll. It would surely lead to the other artifacts of the First Apostle, but he couldn't convince the jeweler to part with it. At least not for what he could offer. He would need to use his other resources, and he would need to do it quickly before the jeweler put the scroll on the open market.

****

Father Richards tapped on Terry's door. "I have your reservations to the United States. The flight leaves at four thirty. We will need to hurry to get you to the airport on time. Do you want me to help you pack?"

"No, I can handle that. You bring the car around to the front of the building."

The activation of the Master's Light, the discovery of the location of the Gold Scroll and now the boy—things are getting complicated, Terry thought. Should I tell the others about the boy, even if I'm not certain? No, I will call the Brotherhood of the First Apostle together after I see the boy.

Chapter 13 - The First Apostle

Gobi Desert, China
Approximately 1 BC

A freezing wind blew from the north onto the western limits of the Gobi Desert. Blood dripped from Xiong's fingers and froze as it hit the ground forming little star-like splatters amongst the sharp rocks at his feet. He reached down and turned over three small stones so that the side with the desert varnish faced upward trying to hide the grave as the Master requested.

Many days earlier they had exited the Gansu Corridor, making their way to Turfan on the northern portion of the Silk Road. As the Silk Road turned north, and they crossed a section of the Great Wall, the Master said, "We have overstayed. You must soon find a place for my grave. It must be unmarked, and no one must find it."

Xiong found a campsite a few miles north of the

Great Wall. It was set well back from the road under an overhanging cliff. A large sand dune curved between the cliff and the road, protecting the site from casual observation. Xiong removed wood from one of their camels and started a fire. He helped the Master get settled up against the wall in the reflected warmth and then tended to the camels.

The Master said, "Bring me my bag." Xiong retrieved a large leather pouch tied to his camel's saddle, and the Master pulled out a small stone pyramid with a ball at its apex and set it in the sand. Then he retrieved a scepter-like object. The handle was about six inches long with grooves for the Master's fingers. The Master grasped the scepter with his left hand. He placed his thumb in an indentation in an egg-shaped orb at the top of the scepter. Hair-like filaments, that covered the orb, immediately stiffened and stood erect. At the same time, heat and light began to radiate from the ball atop the pyramid.

Xiong saw this many times before, but each time he fought the impulse to run. If it were not for the gentle and kind nature of the Master, he would surely have run from such a sight.

The Master seemed to gain strength as he warmed. He again reached into the bag and produced a small stone item that looked like part of a circle. Xiong had never seen it before.

"Take these three keys to enlightenment." The Master handed the item to Xiong and pointed at the pyramid and scepter. "Follow wandering star along the Silk Road to the west, then journey to Judea, to the city of a king called David. There will be others from the south with similar items. Search them out and join them."

"How will I find them?" Xiong said.

"There will be three men in fine garments searching for a baby. Ask for those seeking the baby."

Xiong nodded.

"They will have items similar to these." The Master pointed again at the three items. You must convince them to join you. You must help this child. Teach him what I have taught you. Help him become a leader of men, and he may bring peace to the many peoples of this world. If you fail, your world may be lost to us, forever."

"Lost forever?" Xiong said.

"Yes, we believe that the time is right for the world to begin its journey, away from violence to enlightenment. If we are right, this baby may be the spark to light man's way. You must guard these three items and the baby until he matures. If you are sure he is the one, you must help him enlighten the world."

"How can we be sure?" Xiong said.

"When the boy becomes a man, and reaches the age of knowledge, thirty years old, give him the first key." The Master held up the scepter.

"Let him use it. Watch him. If he uses its power for good, he is the one. If not, retrieve the key and leave him."

"But, by the time he is thirty, I will be old. I will not be able to help him for long."

"Yes, you are right; you must select others to help you. The journey to enlightenment will take many years. You must join with others of good nature. You must teach them so they can give counsel to the people after you and he are both gone. When your world is ready, we shall return."

"We? Are there others?"

"Enough talk. I am weak and time is short. You must prepare. You must reach the land of Judea before the wandering star dies."

Xiong made some tea and finished setting up the camp. Who were the others? How did the Master know these things? He would ask again after the Master rested. He'd seemed stronger as he gave the instructions. Perhaps he was not dying.

Xiong turned to see the scepter fall from the Master's hand; the light on the little pyramid went from warm yellow to brilliant white and faded to nothing. Xiong rushed to the Master and cradled him in his arms. The Master's face looked gray, his eyes black and lifeless. Tears formed in Xiong's eyes. He sat there holding the Master until the cold forced him to tend to the fire. He packed the three objects back into the Master's leather pouch and planned his next actions.

He would not be able to explain a body tied to his camel so the gravesite had to be nearby. But the sand dunes were continually shifting and could not be counted on to hide a body for long and the area not covered by dunes was littered with small rock. A major disturbance, such as a gravesite, would last for years. He selected a site as close as possible to an advancing dune. He cut a piece of canvas from his tent and laid it on the ground, and then he removed each surface stone from the planned gravesite and set it on the canvas. Next, he dug the grave and stockpiled the subsurface material on a nearby dune. The digging was arduous. He'd expected mainly sand under the rocky surface but there were many razor sharp stones. Once the body was in the grave, he placed the larger stones directly on the body and covered it with fill from his stockpile. Then he replaced the surface rocks, which he had saved on the canvas, one by one, with the desert varnish facing up.

He stood and looked at his work. It was good, but not perfect. He vowed to stay until the desert winds or his adjustments made the grave undetectable.

For several weeks, he stood guard over the grave. Blowing sand scoured the site, and the dune advanced over the grave. When he was sure the grave was undetectable, he loaded his camel and left.

Before he arrived at the city of David, the wandering star was gone.

Saskatoon, Saskatchewan
August 19, 2002 - 1:30 pm

As Kurt pulled up in front of the apartment, where he had lived since taking the job with the Canadian Security and Intelligence Services, his cell phone rang. The call display indicated it was Joleen. Oh, oh, what's wrong? Joleen didn't call unless there was a problem.

"Hi Joleen wha—"

"How could you, Kurt? You know I…we always agreed that lying was wrong. How could you tell Robby to lie to me? How could you? If it wasn't for Father James, I would never have known." Joleen started to sob.

"Father James, how'd he get involved?"

"Robby went to confession. He told Father James he lied to me, and Father James told him he should tell me the truth."

"You sent Robby to confession? Isn't he too young for that?"

"That's not important. Father James looks out for Robby because of his problem. Because…you know…anyway Robby could have been killed. He…he fell into a mine. Why didn't you call me?"

"Joleen, nothing serious happened. Robby wasn't hurt. I didn't want to upset you."

"Well, I'm upset. I'm more than upset. I don't think you can take Robby on a vacation again. Not if you don't tell me when something happens. I'm going to have to think about it. Goodbye."

"Joleen, Joleen!"

Kurt sat there staring at his cell phone. Should he call her back? No, she wouldn't answer. He'd let her cool off for a few days, and then call.

The phone rang. Joleen?

Kurt looked at the call display. No, it was Michael Walker. What does he want?

Kurt answered.

"Kurt, I have a special assignment for you. It will

take a couple of weeks out of the office," Michael said.

"What is it?"

"Not on the cell phone. Check your s-mail." Michael hung up.

Kurt parked the car in the underground garage, and went up to his apartment and signed in to his secure email.

Sana'a, Yemen
Monday, August 23, 2002 - 10:45 pm

Jack Thompson gripped the armrests as Lufthansa Flight 623 twisted and turned on its final approach. Final approach—couldn't they pick a better term? It sounded like it was the last landing you were ever going to make.

Jack didn't like flying, especially into third world airports with heaven knows what kind of air-traffic control. He pressed his nose to the window. He could see a few lights but no mountains. That's good. The Sana'a airport is at an elevation of 2350 meters with mountains around at—what the hell did the briefing book say? Yah, mountains at 3650 meters, that's over 11,000 feet. Sure hope the pilot knows where he is.

He recalled Wolfgang's words. "Here you are, Jack. Lufthansa gates are right through there. Good luck on your trip." Then he added with a big smile, "Or as we Germans say, 'fly Lufthansa die Lufthansa.'" He could have done without that comment.

"Whoa," he said under his breath. The plane landed fast and hard. Altitude and heat required more speed to maintain lift someone at UNICEF had warned him. Well, they were on the ground now, and he wouldn't have to worry about that until he took his return flight. As he left the plane and walked across the tarmac, he realized that it wasn't hot. In fact, it felt pleasantly cool and refreshing.

The terminal was another thing. It was hot and dirty. The immigration control line for foreigners was long and slow. No, that was an understatement, it hadn't moved for twenty minutes. Then a new agent showed up, and things proceeded quickly. The visa, which UNICEF obtained for him, got him a quick stamp in his passport and a wave through to customs. The customs area was chaos. Bags were everywhere. There were more long lines and extensive searches by the custom agents. There were also a lot of tough looking guys in military uniforms with rifles standing at the exits.

This could take all night, he thought. The plane landed at 11:00 pm, and it was already close to midnight. But then he saw him. A rather slight Yemeni stood near the luggage carousel with a tiny sign that said "Thompson UNICEF."

Jack walked over. "I'm Thompson."

A big smile lit up the young man's face. "*Salaam 'Alaykum.*"

Jack responded, "*Alaykum As-Salaam,*" as Wolfgang had instructed.

Ali smiled at Jack's attempt and nodded. "I am

Ali. I will be your driver while you are here. Where are your luggage tags? What color are the bags?"

"Dark green." Jack reached into his pocket and produced the tags. Ali took them and disappeared into the melee around the carousel.

The carousel wasn't turning, and luggage kept coming down the conveyor. There were several men standing at the conveyor attempting to distribute the luggage. They had built a pile of bags, and as each new piece arrived, they placed it onto the pile. From there, the bag slid down and out across the floor. The heavier the bag, the further it went. As Jack watched, two people were mowed down by a large bag that careened into crowd.

In what seemed like only seconds, Ali reappeared with his bags.

"A magician," Jack muttered.

"Follow me," Ali said, as he walked to the head of the line, and handed the agent a letter, and what appeared to be a little something extra. The agent waved them through, and Jack followed Ali to a small white van jammed in amongst other waiting cars and drivers. Ali tossed the bags in the back and gestured for Jack to get in.

"Have you come to Yemen before?" Ali asked.

"No, this is my first time."

"If you wish, I can show you some of the sights. The old city or Wadi Dahr? Will you have time?"

"Perhaps. My meeting at UNICEF will only take one day, and my return flight is not until next Monday. That will give me a couple of free days."

"Yes, yes, I can show you a lot in that time."

This could be quite fortuitous, Jack thought. He was unsure on how to go about his assignment, but Ali might be able to help.

"I must find Abdul Hasheem. He is a jeweler."

"Abdul, the Jew. Yes, I know his shop. I can arrange for you to see him. Does he know you are coming?"

"He should, but I don't yet have a time for a meeting with him. Can you arrange that?"

"Yes, but tomorrow. It is too late tonight," Ali said as he sped through empty streets.

Jack looked out the window as the shops flew by. They all had bright blue doors. The van slowed at an intersection where a group of soldiers, with a heavy machine gun, sat in a sand-bagged fortification. That ought to keep people off the street at night, he thought. They passed several other checkpoints before they turned up Dahr Himyar Street to the Sana'a Sheraton.

Ali helped him check into the hotel and agreed to pick him up at 9:00 the next morning. Jack's meeting at the UNICEF office was scheduled for 10:00. Ali assured him that was enough time to get to the UNICEF office. "It's very close. It's on Al Hasaba Amram Road next to the Water and Sewage Authority. Very close."

Chapter 14 - The Gold Scroll

Jerusalem - 43 AD

Xiong and John followed as Stephen was dragged out of the city by an anti-Christian mob. John, Stephen's brother, wanted to be one of the seven elders of the Christians in Jerusalem, but Xiong worried about the hostility shown to the Christians and spoke against it. John followed Xiong's advice and was pleased when the followers selected his elder brother as the first among the seven, and thus the leader of the Christians. Today, Xiong was proven right. He pulled John away from the crowd. "There is nothing you can do. We must leave before they turn on us. We must protect the Master's gifts. We must keep them safe until the Master returns."

John looked back as they climbed a small hill. The mob ebbed and flowed as it moved down the valley. It surged forward as instigators urged them on, and then hesitated, as the Christian believers pleaded for mercy. The crowd stopped on a large rocky area and formed a circle with Stephen at its center. The mob stood uncertain, quiet. A single large rock arced out of the crowd narrowly missing Stephen. He knelt, folded his hands, closed his eyes, and bowed his head in prayer.

Another rock, larger, found its mark and hit Stephen's shoulder. A large gash appeared, oozing blood. Calls, soft at first, then louder, came from the heart of the mob. "Death to the Christian." Then dozens of rocks arched high from throughout the mob. Many missed but enough hit their mark and Stephen tumbled forward blood reddening his hair and running down his neck. He twitched, as each additional rock hit, but he did not die. The process was long and cruel.

John turned to go back and help Stephen.

"No, one martyr is enough for today," Xiong said, as John struggled to free himself. They crested the hill and John turned to see someone move forward and slam a large rock down on Stephen's head.

The twitching stopped. It was over.

Tears streamed down John's cheeks. He took one last look back. The crowd was melting away, shame on many of the faces. A few of the Christians lingered. Once it was safe, they would collect the body and take it for burial.

John wiped his eyes and looked at Xiong. "What will we do, where will we go?"

"You must gather the others I have selected. The six of us will disappear into the desert. We will hide there, like the grains of sand hide in the great dunes.

We will become the Six, the Brothers of the Sand, moving with the winds, hiding amongst the grains, protecting the gifts. I will retrieve them. We must leave tonight."

For almost two years, they wandered the deserts, from Jerusalem to the Dead Sea, and finally east to the Oasis of Ein Gedi.

"I am in my eighty-second year. I am old and can go no further," Xiong said.

Xiong placed three small wooden boxes on the ground in front of him. He opened each. The first box contained a thin stone, shaped like a third of a pie and covered in small markings. The second box contained a small scepter.

"We will hide these. But this one," Xiong said, as he opened the third box to reveal a small pyramid with an orb at its apex. "This one, we must keep with the Six."

"Why?" John asked.

Xiong pointed to the small orb on the pyramid. "This will light the way for the Master's return. We must watch and prepare for the light. This treasure must never be left alone. It must always be watched by one of the Six."

"But we will also get old. When will the Master return?" John asked, as he had many times before.

"I know not when the world will be ready. The Master seeks peace for the world so we can gain the knowledge. If we cannot achieve peace and the knowledge, he may never come."

"What if…what if he does not come before we die? Who will watch for the light? And the treasures, they will be lost," John said.

"Yes, we must prepare. Each of you must find six others you trust and each of those six must find six more, until we are six, times six, times six, times six, times six, times six. Keep the members of your Six secret but pick one of those six to replace you and leave his name in a sealed scroll with the Master's light. When you die the remaining five will open that scroll and invite your choice into our Six. Each level must do the same. Each member of a lower Six must not know more than you, their six and the six reporting them."

"But what of the three treasures, who will guard them?" John said.

"The Master's light will stay with us and we will hide the others treasures and record the locations on three gold scrolls. You, John, as a goldsmith, will make the scrolls."

The Six watched as Xiong removed the pyramid from its box. He set it down and pushed some sand up around it.

"I will take the first watch," Xiong said. "Three brothers must always stay near the pyramid so it can be watched night and day. The other three may go about the business of the brotherhood. And so it shall be until the Master returns to make us a holy Seven. Now sleep, I will call one of you when my watch is up."

As the others wrapped themselves in blankets and lay down, Xiong pushed more sand around the little pyramid, and began quietly chanting, "May the sands protect us. May the sands hide the secrets of the

Master until peace reigns across the world. Let the light of the Master return. Let the Master return to guide us." He repeated the verses six times as the others fell asleep

Sana'a, Yemen
August 24, 2002 - 9:00 am

Jack slept surprisingly well considering the time change from New York. The two days in Frankfurt with Wolfgang probably helped. He showered, dressed, and caught a light breakfast. No ham, his breakfast favorite. That was to be expected in a Muslim country; good thing Wolfgang treated him to some good German sausages during his stay in Frankfurt.

Wolfgang had turned out to be a good guy, but most of the underground antiquity dealers Arthur sent him to meet were pretty shady. How did Arthur Calvert, the president of Calvert Oil meet all these sleaze-balls in the first place? Well, that didn't matter. This would be his last job for Arthur.

As Chairman of the Calvert Oil Children's Trust, Jack was doing a lot of good, but what Arthur had him doing was ethically questionable if not illegal. So, Jack and his wife decided that he should resign and take a job offer from California State Children's Aid Society. The pay would be significantly less, but at least it would be legal work. And besides, the work Arthur had him doing was getting riskier. For the first time he was asked to personally bring back an artifact. He carried papers from the Yemen National Museum, German Department of Antiquities, and Stanford Department of Eastern Studies that would help him get the item through the various customs. But, what if the papers weren't enough? What if they were forgeries? He could be arrested.

He already broke the law by not reporting that he carried $500,000 in bearer bonds, effectively cash. He would trade these for the scroll if Abdul actually had it. Another $250,000 had already been deposited in a numbered Swiss account, and a final $250,000 would be deposited in the same account once the scroll's authenticity was verified. This must be something unique. He had never made any payment over $150,000 before.

As he left the dining room, he saw Ali waiting by the revolving doors. They exited into bright sunlight and a pleasant breeze.

"Wait here. I will get the car," Ali said.

In a few minutes, Ali showed up with the white van. "I called Abdul, the Jew. He says he does not know you. He wishes to know why you want to see him."

Ali is efficient, Jack thought. "Tell him Wolfgang sent me, and that I would like to see him today. Ask him if he has the object he and Wolfgang discussed." Ali nodded and repeated the instructions.

"That's good. Can you make the arrangements while I am in my meeting? I hope to be through by noon," Jack said.

"I will try," Ali said, with a smile as they pulled

up at the UNICEF office. Ali was right; it wasn't far.

Ali guided Jack into the office and to the reception desk. A woman dressed in the traditional black from head to foot greeted him. She was the first woman outside of the staff at the hotel that he saw without a veil. Her dark eyes sparkled, and she smiled as she informed him in perfect English that the director was expecting him.

"I will go now," Ali said.

"Yes, please run that errand and be back by noon," Jack said.

The receptionist showed Jack to the director's office. He was a young Brit by the name of James Bondish.

"That's Bondish 006¼," he said, with a grin. "Welcome to Yemen, birthplace of the most popular beverage in the world." James held out a cup for Jack. "Coffee."

"Coffee?" Jack said.

"Yes, in the early 17th century Yemen pretty well had a monopoly in the growth and trade of coffee. You must try some of the various local brews while you are here. This one is quite mild, but they are all excellent." James stuck his head out the door and asked the receptionist to bring some milk for the coffee. "You'll see, it's great."

James then started on a dissertation of historical Yemen.

"This is the land of the Queen of Sheba, you know. Her capital was Marib. There was an impressive dam built there, several centuries BC, to collect the spring floodwaters for irrigation. It supported a city of up to 40,000. The Incense Trail ran from the Arabian Sea through Marib to the Mediterranean. There's a large city, Shibam, in the middle of the desert, made up of ancient ten story buildings. The honey from that region is famous. One of the Three Wise Men is supposedly buried in Yemen." He rattled on with fact after fact.

"The country is just brim full of history."

"Yes." Jack said, looking at his watch.

"Oh yes, the meeting. Sorry old chap, but it's postponed to this afternoon. Mohamood Salleh is unavailable this morning."

Mohamood was a local businessman who was funding three schools in Sana'a specifically for girls. Since girls in rural areas seldom received an education, UNICEF pressured Mohamood to set up some rural schools. He agreed to set up the schools if UNICEF would help with the funding.

James Bondish made a proposal to the Calvert Oil Children's Trust and was granted $500,000 over five years. Jack was here simply to sign the agreement, plus of course, to complete his extracurricular assignment.

Jack hoped the formal activities of the meeting with Mohamood would take only a couple of hours leaving time to meet Abdul. It was not to be. Mohamood insisted on showing him the local schools and would not sign any agreement until Jack and James came to his house for the evening meal. With James' encouragement, Jack accepted the dinner invitation.

James insisted that Jack ride with him, in the

UNICEF Mercedes, on their tour of the schools, and Ali reluctantly left with instructions to postpone Jack's meeting with Abdul and to meet Jack at the hotel the following morning. During the drive through the city, James briefed Jack on the local culture and what to expect at the evening meal. Mohamood was quite westernized, and they could expect to eat the meal at a table rather than seated on mats on the floor. After the meal, they would retreat to a top floor room and sprawl on mats for a Qat chew. Qat, James explained, was a local plant, the leaves of which were chewed. It had an effect similar to an amphetamine.

At a stoplight, James pointed to a large SUV beside them. The driver sat with a branch in one hand, picking leaves and putting them in his mouth. A large lump pushed out his cheek, and a little green saliva ran down his lip. Similar lumps bulged the cheeks of three others in the SUV. Their light was still red, but when the light for the cross street turned yellow the SUV lurched forward almost running down a pedestrian. Then two occupants of the SUV stepped out onto the running boards, waved Kalashnikov rifles, and cursed the hapless pedestrian.

"Well, those guys are hyped. Is that the Qat? It must be a drug? How does a Muslin culture that doesn't accept alcohol accept a drug?" Jack said.

"They are partly hyped, but a lot of it is just the macho culture. If you don't have a big car, just get out of the way," James said. "And surprisingly, they don't seem to see Qat as a drug. Perhaps, it stems

150

from the fact that about fifty percent of the internal economy is derived from the Qat trade. It results in a flow of money from the city to the countryside, and the government is probably happy to let that continue. You will get to judge for yourself tonight."

They toured the schools which were clean, well equipped and full of young girls eager to learn. Jack thought that this would be a worthwhile project for the trust, and he felt better about himself. It wouldn't be just a clandestine collector's trip.

After the tour, the Mercedes made its way back to the Sheraton so he could shower and change. Ali was waiting and wanted to drive him that evening but James would not hear of it and insisted that he and his driver pick Jack up on the way to Mohamood's.

Everything went as planned. The driver and James arrived on time. "I have a jar of prized honey from Wadi Hadramaut. You can give it, as a gift to Mohamood," James said. Mohamood's house was large by any standard. It was three stories tall and covered half of a city block. James explained that several extended family members lived in the house, so it wasn't as extravagant as it seemed. Jack presented his gift, which was graciously accepted, but not opened, as was the custom. Mohamood's wife and other women of the house served the sumptuous meal. Then, they quietly disappeared and let the men eat alone.

The men ate, talked, and then adjourned to the third floor Qat room. Jack lounged on the mat beside James and Mohamood and picked leaves off what he was assured was a prime branch. In no time, he formed a small chewed ball of leaves in his cheek, and he began to feel the effects. He was not high or anything, but he did seem more alert. After the chew, Mohamood brought out the documents, which he and Jack signed, and gave to James to witness and look after. The evening then broke up.

As they left Mohamood's house, they encountered a waiting Ali, and Jack decided to go back to the hotel with him. He shook hands with James and thanked him for all his help.

"I will forward copies of the documents to you in New York," James said.

As Jack climbed into Ali's little white van, he looked up to see two veiled women walk by. The effect of the Qat made their eyes look even more intense as they peered out through the small gap between their veil and head covering. As they drove back to the hotel, Ali tried to convince Jack to go on a tour the next day. "Perhaps to Wadi Dahr?" Ali suggested.

Jack had decided that wandering around a strange country with $500,000 in bearer bonds in a money pouch attached to his calf, was not a good idea and declined. "Just pick me up when it is time to go to Abdul's," he said. "What time will that be?"

"Abdul wants you to come for Qat so you will need to be ready by 5:00 pm."

Not more Qat, Jack thought

West of the Dead Sea - 45 AD

Xiong watched John work on the final scroll. John was an excellent goldsmith and worked almost non-stop since their arrival at the oasis of Ein Gedi. They had insufficient gold for three scrolls, so they made one of gold, one of silver, and one of copper. The gold and silver scrolls were complete, and the final copper scroll would soon be ready. Once it was ready, they would hide the two treasures and the three scrolls, and begin the watch of the Master's light.

John looked up and smiled. "I am finished."

Xiong lay back against the wall of the small cave high above the Ein Gedi oasis. He was weak. The journey to Ein Gedi had been hard, and he knew he could go no further. He forced himself to sit up again. "Call the others," he said to John.

John gathered the others around Xiong. "The time has come," Xiong said. "We have been careless. We must never have all of the treasures together again, not until it is time for the Master's return. Go and hide them as set out in the scrolls. I will remain here with the Master's light until you return. Then we must select another to take my place and we must find a safer place for the Master's light. I am too old for another journey, and will die here."

"No, you can come with me to Qumran. It is not far," John said. He looked to the others for support but found none. They knew Xiong was right.

Sana'a, Yemen
August 25, 2002 - 6:00 am

Jack Thompson checked his watch. It was almost 6:00 am The damn Qat left him wide-awake for most of the night, and now he seemed to have no appetite. No wonder the Yemenis were so thin. At least he wasn't going on the tour Ali had proposed. He'd skip breakfast and give sleep another try. He woke just before noon and forced himself to eat.

Ali picked him up as scheduled at 5:00 pm, and explained, "Abdul lives in the old city. It is walled, and we cannot drive inside. We will park at Bab-al-Yemen, the Gate to Yemen, and go the rest of the way on foot. Did you know that the United Nations has declared the city a World Heritage Site?"

"Yes, I have seen the pictures," Jack said as Ali parked the car near the gates.

But as Jack stepped out of the car, he realized the pictures didn't do the site justice. The buildings were narrow and several stories high. Dull sand-colored bricks were interlaced with whitewashed arches that outlined windows and doors. Staggered white cornerstones framed the edges of each building. The buildings stood slightly askew, each one leaning at a different angle to the others. Jack stood, looking in turn at each building until Ali said, "Do you want me to take your picture here? Do you have a camera?"

"No, that's fine. Let's go."

Ali led him through the Spice Suq. It was a narrow street lined on either side with baskets of colorful spices, great wads of compressed dates, coffee beans, and occasional piles of amethyst and other semi-precious stones. Jack ignored the sights and clutched the small pouch inside his light jacket. It was probably not the wisest thing to be on foot in these tight quarters with so much money. They rounded a corner and walked up a street that was only slightly wider. One side was lined with small jewelry stores.

"The Jews own most of these stores," Ali explained. "Many Jews lived here until 1948, that's when Israel was formed you know. After that, most of them moved to Israel. But some of the jewelers stayed. They are very good, the best in the country."

They passed a small enclosure with two standing camels arrogantly looking down their noses at Jack like some old English aristocrats. Ali pointed to the next shop. It was closed.

"This is Abdul's shop. Go in. Abdul will be waiting for you. I will wait here while you complete your business."

Jack was glad they finally arrived but still felt uncomfortable. What did Ali know? Jack opened the door to the shop and poked his head in. A small man sat on a stool against the far wall which held an array of jewelry on narrow shelves lined with dark velvet cloth, and illuminated with brilliant lights.

The man rose from the stool. Dispensing with the traditional Arabic, he greeted Jack. "Mr. Thompson, I am Abdul. Welcome. Welcome." He proceeded to shake Jack's hand furiously. "I welcome you to my shop. Please, please come in."

"Thank you, please call me Jack."

"Yes, yes, and please call me Abdul."

Abdul continued to grip Jack's hand. He pulled him around the shop pointing to various shelves, describing pieces of jewelry. "You are married? Yes?"

Jack nodded.

"Please pick a piece for your wife."

"No, that's not necessary," Jack said.

"Ah, please. I would be honored if you would accept." Jack pointed to a necklace of what looked like dark black pearls with accompanying earrings. "Ah," Abdul said, "very pretty, but it is only hematite. It is not expensive."

"That's fine. I am sure this would be my wife's choice."

Abdul took the items from the shelf and placed them in a small case with a velvet lining. "May God bless you and your wife, and may your days together be long and joyous," Abdul said, as he passed it to Jack.

Inexpensive or not it looked quite beautiful. Jack was beginning to feel less uncomfortable. Abdul seemed to be genuinely friendly. "Thank you," he said, touching his hand to his heart as he remembered what James said was an appropriate gesture.

Then Abdul then led him upstairs to the Qat room where he was introduced to Abdul's two brothers, three cousins, and some other assorted relatives. They spent a couple of hours picking leaves and chewing. The relatives kept Jack busy answering questions about New York, his impressions of Yemen, the weather, the trust, and what seemed like a million other things.

Finally, Abdul stood, looked at the others, and said, "We have business." Without another question, everyone stood, said their goodbyes and left.

Abdul walked to the corner of the room where a small velvet bag lay on an octagonal table with inlays of Frankincense wood. He motioned Jack to follow as he loosened the drawstring on the bag, and pulled out a highly polished wooden case about twelve inches long and two inches wide and two inches in height. There was a single clasp on one side. Abdul released the clasp and opened the lid to reveal a small velvet bag which he lifted clear. Underneath was the unmistakable glint of gold. Jack stepped forward for a closer look. There were two polished wooden handles on what appeared to be a gold scroll. Jack reached out.

"Do not lift it," Abdul said with reverence in his voice. "It is extremely fragile, and a few pieces have broken from it over the years. Do not worry. The pieces, they are all here." He held up the small velvet bag.

"Is it gold leaf?" Jack asked.

"No, pure gold."

Wow, Jack thought. No wonder it's worth so much.

"Can it be transported?" Jack said.

"Oh, yes. The handles are secured with clips at each end. The scroll does not move unless they are released." Abdul pointed to two small fasteners.

"Good. It will have to bounce around in my carry-on."

Jack produced five hundred thousand dollars in bearer bonds. Abdul checked them. He nodded and placed the small velvet bag in the case and gently closed it. He latched the single clasp and slipped the case into a larger velvet bag.

"It's yours," Abdul said.

Jack picked up the bag. "The rest of the funds will be deposited in your account as soon as the scroll's authenticity is verified.

Abdul nodded and guided Jack down the stairs.

"God be with you, my friend." Abdul shook his hand furiously and opened the door.

Jack stepped outside and looked both ways. Now, where was Ali? He said that he would wait here.

Jack turned and noticed a tall veiled woman walking toward him. The Qat must still be affecting me, her eyes look odd. Damn it, Ali, where are you? He felt vulnerable in the dimly lit alley. At least he wasn't alone. A lone woman would not be wandering about if it was dangerous.

She brushed by him in the narrow street. He looked away. A hand grabbed his mouth from behind, and before he could move, he felt a blade sever his throat.

He could make no sound and only gurgled as he tried to call for help.

He spun around and fell to the ground. He saw Ali around the corner sprawled at the feet of the camels, a red pool of blood leaking from his neck, coloring their hooves.

The veiled woman bent down. A bloodied hand reached out and picked up the velvet bag. Dark blue eyes peered at him from above the veil. Then everything slowly faded into darkness.

Chapter 15 - The Ship

Algodones Dunes, California
August 26, 2002 - 11:45 pm

A week had passed since Michael sent Kurt back to Edwards Air Force base to work with Major Roger Wilkinson. For some reason, the discovery was given a high-level security classification. It was well above both his and Roger's clearance levels, but here they were flying back and forth above the Algodones Dunes in a slow moving, high-wing Twin Otter. Roger suggested that since they were already involved, using them limited the number of people who knew about the discovery. That was probably right, but what about the priest at the back of the plane—why was he involved?

Kurt stared at the cabin wall of the small aircraft. It glowed a flickering blue-green, as if lit by an alien campfire. But, the dim light escaped from a more earthly origin, four green oscilloscope screens and the screen of a data-processing computer, which added a bluish tint.

Roger was sitting in front of the screens adjusting the sensitivity of an array of magnetometers being towed behind the plane. He shook his head. "Kurt, the data coming from the magnetometers is so poor that there is no value added by processing the data. Either the sensitivity is so high that it shows variations in the surface of the sand dunes, or it's so low that it shows only the almost flat surface of the bedrock below. This seemed like a good idea when it was suggested, but now it looks like I'm not going to get it to work."

The co-pilot poked his head between black curtains that separated the passenger cabin from the pilots. "That's the fourth time through the search grid, sir. Do you want to try it again?"

Kurt thought for a second. He didn't want to give up, but was there any hope? He looked at the Roger seeking some support. "What do you think, Roger, another pass?"

Roger would not have been Kurt's choice to operate the complex equipment strung out behind the plane, but security concerns prevailed. The military had searched through the officers with the required clearance and technical skills and settled on Roger. Judging from his success so far, security concerns may have trumped the need for reliable data acquisition. Damn military security processes—surely there must be a topnotch technician who could be trusted?

Roger stared at the computer outputs, and said,

161

"We've about used all our ammo on this. It has me buffaloed. I guess we could give the grid one more pass at a lower altitude to see if we can see the shi…"

He carefully rephrased. "At a lower altitude we might be able to pick up the boundary effects of the phenomena, sir."

Sir, again, Kurt noted. He'd tried a couple of times to get Roger to call him Kurt, but without success. He was not accustomed to being called sir. And, as a civilian with CISS, the Canadian Intelligence and Security Service, a Major in the U.S. Army certainly didn't need to call him sir. It seemed though, that folks in the U.S. used sir a lot more than Canadians. It appeared to be a matter of respect, as well as rank. Perhaps, it stemmed from the fact that a lot more individuals in the U.S. passed through some formal military training. Whatever the reason, Roger seemed quite sincere with the sir. Kurt's train of thought returned to the problem at hand when Roger turned toward him, signaling he was awaiting an answer.

"I think we should go for one low-level pass at the grid. How are we doing for fuel?" Kurt said, as he shifted his gaze to the co-pilot.

The co-pilot pulled his head back through the curtains into the pilot's compartment for a moment then stuck it back through the curtains like some comic in a vaudeville performance.

"We have enough to fly the grid one more time and make it back to the Yuma Base with sufficient reserve."

His eyes expressed a less than enthusiastic look, but his speech gave no hint of his feelings. But then, the co-pilot's words confirmed the look in his eyes as he offered. "With all this low flying though, we'll certainly raise the interest of any sand jockeys playing around down there."

That may have been true earlier, Kurt thought, but after midnight there probably weren't many people riding around in dune buggies. Besides, the sand jockeys, as the co-pilot called them, seldom explored this rather uninteresting area of the dunes. It was obvious the co-pilot was ready to leave.

"It's your call, Mr. Sigurdson," the co-pilot said.

Kurt noted that there was no sir from the co-pilot this time, just a stiff, Mr.

Kurt turned to the third passenger in the darkened cabin, the grim faced Father O'Shanigan. He was barely visible in the back of the cabin, where he observed the proceedings. Kurt wondered if he should be called Father, even though he wore no clerical collar, gave no indication of his religious connection, and had been introduced only as Mr. O'Shanigan. But Kurt overheard one of the pilots wondering why a priest was on board and in charge.

Kurt suspected that Father O'Shanigan was here because of Joleen's meddling. He was sure O'Shanigan was connected to Father James, Joleen's parish priest. It was puzzling though, how did O'Shanigan manage to get U.S. military security clearance for this mission? Even more puzzling was the decision-making authority the father exercised. Although he said almost nothing during the discussion of options, all final decisions were O'Shanigan's. Kurt vowed that once he got back to work with Roy, he would use all the resources at his disposal to develop a profile of this Father O'Shanigan.

"Father O'Shanigan, do you agree, we'll re-fly the grid at the lower altitude?" Kurt said.

There was no response.

O'Shanigan? Kurt assumed he had a first name, but none was volunteered. Tracing this guy might be difficult if O'Shanigan wasn't his real name. He tried again using the non-religious title. "Mr. O'Shanigan, do you agree to another grid search at low altitude?"

"No," O'Shanigan said after a long pause.

"I think it is important that we delineate this phenomenon. May I ask why you disagree?" Kurt said.

Again, an unusually long pause left Kurt dangling. This guy certainly wasn't like most people who jump to fill a silence with resulting foot-in-mouth problems. Kurt stared into the face in the dark rear portion of the cabin, trying to get some type of reading. Nothing. This guy would be good at poker, that is, if priests played poker.

Finally, O'Shanigan said, "As the pilot said, we don't want to pique the interest of the sand jockeys."

O'Shanigan seemed even more concerned about security than the military folk. But the sand jockeys weren't really a concern. The military cordoned off the area of interest and released some misinformation to cover the operation. They'd aired a story that a helicopter carrying some highly toxic chemicals and radioactive material went down. Talk about a stupid cover story. It was likely to attract hordes of environmental and nuclear protesters to the area tomorrow. Why transport these things in a helicopter, why in an aircraft, why transport them at all, why even make them? If the media noticed this, these questions and more would be asked. The misinformation campaign was likely worse than no information at all, but how do you cover up this operation?

Well, too late now, the military would have to act quickly to clean up the public relations nightmare and get their people out of the area. The phenomenon, as everyone was calling it, had gone undetected for hundreds of years, and if attention wasn't drawn to the area, it would probably remain undetected by anyone else. With these things in mind, Kurt said quietly, "Mr. O'Shanigan, since we want to keep this discovery secret, we are going to have to scale back our activities. This might be the last time we can try to delineate things from the air."

"No."

That was the reply, with no further elaboration. Was his real goal here to ensure the mission didn't succeed? Kurt wondered.

"Okay, I'll tell the pilots," Roger said.

He poked his head through the curtains into the pilots' area and gave the order. "We can head back to base as soon as I get the equipment reeled in."

Roger returned to the glowing screens. "Holy crap," he whispered.

"What is it?" Kurt said, as he and O'Shanigan

turned their gaze to Roger.

Roger just stared into the back of the cabin.

Kurt looked back at O'Shanigan and his heart skipped a beat. Those eyes were as cold as any he had ever seen.

Kurt asked again, "What is it?"

"I think I just detected a boundary effect. It was sharp as hell, and now it's gone. I think it was the edge of the ship."

The word "ship" slipped from Roger's lips. That wasn't supposed to happen, Kurt thought. Did anyone notice? O'Shanigan's eyes gave no answer. Hopefully, the pilots didn't hear. If the priest heard, he would likely raise hell with Roger's superiors. That's if priests were allowed to raise hell. Kurt smiled inwardly erasing the effect of those cold eyes.

"But we're about a half mile from the hatch. That would make the phenomenon at least half a mile long," O'Shanigan said. "Impossible, that's impossible."

"Right, it would be point four nine miles long," Roger said.

Kurt noted that O'Shanigan hadn't followed Rogers lead and called it a ship. Maybe no one else noticed.

But Kurt noticed something, a slip by O'Shanigan. The father, or whatever he was, had far more technical skill than he let on. O'Shanigan knew exactly where they were from the computer readings and was able to estimate the ship's size, as quickly as Roger. On the other hand, Kurt understood, in only a general sense, what Roger was doing. Obviously,

O'Shanigan wasn't your average parish priest.

"We should make another pass," Roger and Kurt said simultaneously.

They both knew it would be good engineering procedure to confirm what appeared to be the edge of the phenomenon.

"No," O'Shanigan said, "it's impossible…it's a mistake. Retrieve the equipment and let's go."

"But—"

"No buts," O'Shanigan said. "Let's go."

Before Roger turned back to the screens, he answered Kurt's unasked question.

"I never thought we would be looking for anything so big. On the other runs, I turned the resolution down until we were about a quarter mile from the target. I didn't want to have a bunch of residual stuff from the bedrock messing up the recordings."

"Damn. Damn!" Roger said.

There was no further conversation in the cabin. Kurt looked back at O'Shanigan. There was no emotion in his face, but his eyes were dark and threatening. Kurt continued to watch O'Shanigan as the light from the equipment faded, and the cabin dimmed.

He felt a strange foreboding as O'Shanigan's face slowly faded and retreated into a cloak of darkness. He could feel an ominous presence even when he could no longer see O'Shanigan. To Kurt, it somehow seemed fitting to associate this man with darkness.

The pilots were obviously eager to get on with

what they thought were more important things. Roger barely had time to copy the contents of the search to a CD and clear the computer of any of their recordings before they landed at the Yuma base, and the three passengers were disgorged at Hanger A.

While Kurt and Roger looked around for the jeep to take them to a barracks for the night, Father O'Shanigan, one arm in a sling, walked over and climbed into a waiting white King Air. Its only visible markings were its registration letters CLV-2. As soon as O'Shanigan was aboard, the combination door-stairs was raised, and it taxied away for takeoff.

Roger looked at Kurt and breathed out a quiet. "Well, I'll be go to hell."

"Yep, and you will probably meet O'Shanigan there," Kurt said.

Chapter 16 - The Mesa

Southern Arizona
August 27, 2002 - 1:20 am

The white King Air rose from the runway heading south then banked to the left continuing its climb. It reached cruising altitude and set a course for Montana. O'Shanigan settled back into one of four large leather seats. It was a pleasant way to travel and would save him from the punishment of several long waits in airport lounges. He'd have to thank Arthur for his thoughtfulness when he landed. He pushed a small yellow button on the armrest. Immediately, an attractive young woman dressed in western attire emerged from a door to the forward cabin.

"Can I get you something, sir?"

O'Shanigan smiled. Priest or not, this woman aroused a primal instinct in him. Arthur Calvert was somehow able to surround himself with a number of women who caused a similar reaction. How was he able to find so many young and….

"Sir," she said.

Terry returned from his reverie. He blushed. The young woman smiled; she had obviously seen this reaction before. "My name is Rosa. We have a full range of food and beverages on board. Can I get you anything?"

"How about a black coffee and Danish?"

She returned in a few minutes with a small tray which she attached to the bulkhead. It was within easy reach but did not obstruct the small working table directly in front of Terry.

"Anything else, sir?" she asked with a look that made his loins ache.

"No, just close the door, please."

When she left, Terry picked up the phone, pushed the scrambler button and dialed a number in Montana. The phone rang only once. A feminine voice answered, "*Yes?*"

"It's Terry. Can I speak to Arthur?"

"One moment, please." There was silence, no elevator music while he waited.

"Terry, how'd you make out?" A deep and somewhat raspy voice asked.

"I'm afraid that there actually is something there, and it's much, much bigger than we expected. This is going to be exceedingly difficult to contain."

"Don't worry, we'll put a lid on it," Arthur growled. The scrambler seemed to give his voice an even more powerful tone than it had in person.

"What about that Canadian, Sigurdson?" Arthur

170

said.

"He's going to be a problem. To damn smart to be put off easily."

"I'll get someone working on that. Leave him to me," Arthur said. "We have some connections in Canada. But enough of that, I have some good news; we should have another artifact in our possession in short order. I have someone retrieving it at this moment."

"Sana'a?"

"I'll fill you in when you get here. Let's not discuss it over the phone, scrambled or not. You should be here in less than four hours, I would guess. It can wait till then." There was a slight click as Arthur hung up. Then a red light on Terry's phone began to blink indicating the scrambler lost synchronization.

He sat back in the leather seat, picked up the Danish and coffee, and reflected on the day's events. The CD in his briefcase would be of little value. It showed only that the ship, if that's what it was, was much larger than anyone imagined. More would need to be done, but he needed to control those involved in any further examination. He would certainly need to monitor Sigurdson's involvement.

Laguna Military Base, Arizona
August 27, 2002 - 1:30 am

The jeep took Kurt and Roger to a nearby barracks where Kurt thanked Roger for his effort.

"Yah," Roger said. "What you mean is thanks for nothing. I screwed it all up. I only detected one boundary effect on our last pass, and that damn O'Shanigan ran off with the only data disk I made."

"That's fine. It gives us a rough size of the thing. No one would have expected it to be that large," Kurt said, trying to restore Roger's bruised faith in his own competence. "Besides, O'Shanigan would have just run off with the data anyway. I always thought this would be handled better by a ground search. Flying around at night with stuff hanging off the back of a plane will just bring the curiosity seekers. We should be able to cordon off a relatively small area now and get on with our research."

"Well, I guess you are right, but if I had a little more time to get acquainted with the equipment, I could have done a better job. It's been a while since I actually twisted any knobs."

"I know," Kurt said. "Just because you lead a team doesn't mean you can do everyone's job. Damn security protocols got in the way."

"Thanks for the vote of confidence. See you later," Roger said over his shoulder, as he wandered off to find his room.

"Okay," Kurt said, not knowing if they would ever cross paths again.

Kurt was eager to get back to C-CAF, the secret Canadian Security and Intelligence Services facility in the middle of Saskatchewan, and check out O'Shanigan, but that would take some time. He needed to catch a military flight to San Diego in the morning. From there he would travel to Vancouver, then Calgary, and finally Saskatoon. From Saskatoon, he would make the two and a half hour drive to C-CAF. Well, unless you had a King Air like O'Shanigan, travel time was just part of the equation.

As soon as he could get a secure line set up, he'd call Roy and get him working on O'Shanigan. Kurt had grown more and more confident in Roy's abilities since their work on the Firefly missile. If anyone could dig into this guy's background, it would be Roy Matacowski.

Calvert Mesa, Montana
August 27, 2002 - 5:00 am

Terry looked out the window as the King Air circled. The ranch was covered in a thick overcast, and the pilots were using the ranch's beacons to carefully position themselves for the drop through the clouds. This was important since the ranch lay in a narrow valley bounded on three sides by rugged mountains. Even in clear weather, the approach to the airstrip was "interesting" as Arthur understated on Terry's last visit. But, Terry had the utmost confidence in the pilots and equipment they were flying. As the sole owner of Calvert Oil, Arthur could afford the best of both.

There was a light knock on the forward door, and Rosa appeared. "We are preparing to land, sir. The pilots think it could be a little rough until we get through the clouds and suggest that you fasten your seatbelt." Terry held up his hands to show a fastened belt. Rosa smiled. "We should be at the hangar in about ten minutes. There will be a vehicle there to take you up to the ranch house."

Ranch house indeed, Terry thought. Arthur Calvert selected a mesa shaped mountain in which to build the residence. The mesa stood in the center of a u-shaped valley. The surrounding land sloped gently up to the foot of a circular wall of two hundred foot cliffs. Around the base, tucked right up against the cliff walls were the typical ranch buildings including a barn, machine shed, and simple open-sided buildings for hay storage. The residence itself was built into the mesa. The rooms and balconies appeared here and there, cut unobtrusively into the rocks. The construction had all been done from inside to minimize damage to the mountain. Atop the mesa were a few narrow footpaths for guests to wander about. You reached the residence via an elevator from the garage, which was built into the base of the cliff. The visible portions of the residence were constructed of natural stone and from any distance were invisible. Amazing what you could do, if money was no object.

The King Air touched down softly, and the stewardess announced, "Welcome to Calvert Mesa."

Terry climbed into the back seat of the SUV waiting for him at the end of the runway. It was a two-mile drive to the facility. The driver was polite but quiet. Terry was happy about that. He wasn't looking for conversation; he needed quiet to try and figure out how he could suppress this latest discovery. Years of painstaking work could be lost if this got out of control. That woman, Joleen, was going to be a problem. He'd have to work closely with her parish priest to monitor her. She seemed more than just religious, she seemed unstable.

And her husband, how did some university professor from Canada get to be flying around in U.S. military aircraft? Granted, he was in on the discovery, but that doesn't normally get you invited along on a secret government mission, let alone designated as second in the decision-making hierarchy. Perhaps one of Arthur's many sources could find out. If not, he would use the Brotherhood's network.

The driver pulled the SUV up in front of two oversized garage doors built into the face of the cliff. The door on the right opened, and they drove into a tunnel large enough for two-way traffic. It led back into the mountain for about a hundred yards and then opened into a large underground garage with room for fifty or more vehicles. The vehicles currently parked there ranged from a couple of Hummers to snow-removal equipment. The driver pulled up in front of a set of elevators, jumped out, and opened the door. As he stepped back, Terry could see the butt of a gun poking out from a shoulder holster. Driver and security, Terry thought.

"Take the elevator on the left to level six, sir. Mr. Calvert is waiting for you. I will ensure that your luggage gets to your room."

Terry followed the driver's instructions. Although he had visited Calvert Mesa several times, he had only been to levels five and six. Level six was the level that allowed access to the top of the mesa. The rooms there were mainly for Arthur Calvert's private use. They included the library, dining rooms, meeting rooms, and Arthur's personal suite with its panoramic view of the surrounding valley. Level five included guest rooms, a staffed bar which offered light snacks twenty-four hours a day, more meeting rooms, and computer systems for guest use. Terry assumed that levels two to four included staff quarters and service facilities such as power generation, water, and sewage. It was amazing what could be done with enough resources; if Arthur thought he would need it, he would have it.

The elevator door opened. Arthur was there with his hand extended.

"Welcome, Terry, welcome."

Arthur was a small man, with head and hands that seemed oversized for his body. Small piercing grey eyes seemed to look into one's soul, which on first impression was unsettling. But Arthur's personality overcame these negatives. He was warm and seemed genuinely interested in everyone he met. Terry was sure that trait allowed him to build his father's small oil company into the largest independent oil company in the world. And as the only shareholder, he could spend the company's money on anything he wanted, subject of course, to the ever present Internal Revenue rules.

Arthur pumped Terry's hand. "How was the flight? I hope Rosa looked after you. She's one of the more striking attendants, don't you think?"

"Yes, Arthur, Rosa is beautiful as well as efficient. Once again, flying your personal airline made me reconsider my priestly vow of celibacy."

Terry had been told Arthur knew the names of each of his staff right down to the janitors of his various offices, and if he didn't know them, he would stop and spend a few minutes talking to them, even with a U.S. Senator in tow. He had a photographic memory for people and their stories as well as a genuine interest. He could tell you a personal story about every staff member he met, and knew the life history of his close personal staff. That probably explained the fierce loyalty his staff had to his company, and, more importantly, to him personally.

"So, you want to give up the priesthood?" Arthur slapped Terry on the back and let out a powerful roar of laughter. A laugh more suited for someone of much larger stature, but so natural, that you laughed with him. "Well, you are in luck; a few of our regular staff at the mesa are on vacation, so you will see her again. She will be helping out in the dining room until CLV-2 flies you out of here."

CLV-2 was the King Air Terry had arrived in. Arthur referred to his aircraft by simply using their call letters. Somehow through his connections, Arthur got the FAA to reserve CLV for his company, Calvert Oil, and each of his planes had a similar designation. CLV-2 was the civil aviation designation for Calvert Two, the King Air, and CLV-1 was the designation for Calvert One, a long range Airbus.

177

"I understand that you plan to stay overnight and leave early tomorrow."

"Yes, I need to get back to Paris," Terry said.

"I'm sure we can get you to stay an extra night. We have lots to discuss. We could use a full day."Arthur never seemed rushed, like a lot of executives, and always had time for thoughtful and thorough discussions of key projects.

"I'll bring in Calvert One, and we will get you back to Europe faster than using the CLV-2 and commercial airlines. I could arrange for Rosa to travel on the flight." Arthur winked and let out another roar of laughter.

Terry nodded. "Okay."

He knew it wasn't any use to argue with Arthur. Arthur would always beat you with the simple addition of money. Calvert One, the Airbus, for example, could fly non-stop from the mesa to anywhere in Europe.

"Good, very good. This will give you time to rest today. We can have lunch in the dining room and get right to work this afternoon. You know the way to your room; it's the same one as usual, the one with the southeast exposure for an early riser."

Arthur always seemed to know more about him than Terry expected. Was that just Arthur's own abilities, or did he have some help? Terry suspected the latter. Arthur probably knew more about most of the people he dealt with than they knew about themselves, but that was not the case with Terry. His secret was buried too deep.

"Lunch will be at one. I will have Rosa call you at

eleven just in case you over sleep."

"A little rest would be good. We were prowling around over the desert half the night," Terry said as he looked for the stairs that would be the easiest way to his room. Arthur pointed to a door marked "SE rooms 1-6," and walked off in the other direction.

Terry took the stairs and found his room. It was a large room with a king-sized bed, an easy chair and loveseat, a desk complete with computer and printer, a bathroom with a Jacuzzi tub, a combination walk-in multi-headed shower and steam room, and finally a sauna. There was a large balcony facing the southeast.

Terry's suitcase had been opened, and his clothes were hung neatly in the closet, or placed in the chest of drawers. His briefcase was unopened by the desk. He walked over to decide what to wear. Everything that needed pressing was pressed. In fact, his jacket still felt warm. Arthur kept him busy just long enough on the sixth floor. Amazing.

Terry showered using the large rain-like overhead nozzle, then crawled into the bed and fell asleep.

Chapter 17 - Crisis

Laguna Military Base, Arizona
   August 27, 2002 - 4:00 am

Kurt rose at 4:00am, a habit he learned from his days on the farm. He showered, shaved, dressed in a golf shirt and slacks, and went looking for a phone. He found the duty officer who showed him to a vacant office with an outside line. The officer assured him that he would not be interrupted since the regular inhabitant was on leave.

Kurt dialed a 1-800 number that connected him to the University of Saskatchewan. A typically annoying recording came on. Push 1 for this, push 2 for that, blah, blah, blah. If he selected one of those options, he would have been connected to the appropriate office, or more likely, given more options. Instead, he pushed the # key, followed by a three digit personal identifier and an eight-digit security code. He obtained a dial tone and dialed

Roy's extension. It was a relatively easy way to get to C-CAF, and yet, eliminate stray or unwanted calls.

After the tenth ring, he was about to push the * key which would have allowed him to leave a message, when Roy picked up. "Why's the turkey farmer calling in the middle of the night?"The three digit ID identified Kurt as the caller on Roy's screen and allowed Roy to make his cocky greeting.

"What do you mean? It's ten after six in Saskatchewan, almost quitting time."

"Yah, for a farmer maybe. What's up?"

"Ah, Roy, I'm not sure how secure this line is. Activate your scrambler."

"Oh-oh, this sounds serious, I'll turn it on. Are you ready?"

"In a bit, just stand by until I get my end active." Kurt pulled two small black bags connected to a tiny black box and headset from his briefcase. Kurt placed one bag over the mouthpiece and the other over the earpiece of the phone. Then he put on the headset and punched a code into the black box. "Are you there, Roy?"

"Yep, say, why are we using the scrambler?"

"For some reason, there is no cell service allowed here, some kind of interference worry or something."

"Where the hell are you, anyway? Roy asked once the secure communications link was set up."

"I'm near Yuma, at the Laguna Army testing base in Arizona," Kurt said.

"What are you doing down there?"

"Roy, I'll fill you in when I get back. But for now, could you just not ask any questions?"

181

"Sure, why'd you call then?"

"I want you to do some in-depth research on someone. His name is O'Shanigan, or more likely, Father O'Shanigan."

"A friggin priest, you got to be kidding?"

"It appears so, but that's about all I have on him. He wasn't much of a communicator, but he has high level security clearance. That should give you something to get going on. I should be back late tonight if I don't miss any connections in Vancouver or Calgary."

"Okay. But you're not stopping by to see Joleen and Robby?" Roy said. "The weekend's coming up you know, and her place is only a few miles south of Vancouver."

"No, Roy, some things happened on my vacation with Robby and...well, I think I will let her cool down a bit before I visit again. It's a long and complicated story. For now, just check out O'Shanigan, will you?"

"Sure, see you when you get here, bye," Roy said.

Kurt thought about what Roy said. If he had some time in Vancouver, he would call Joleen.

****

Kurt was pleasantly surprised when he checked on the military flight that was to take him to San Diego, where he would continue via commercial airlines to Canada. The duty officer informed him that there was a military flight headed for Alaska that was stopping for fuel in Vancouver. If Kurt could be ready in twenty minutes, he could hitch a ride.

Kurt held up his bag. "I'm ready. Which way to the plane?"

As the plane flew north, he looked down at the Washington coastline. He tried to figure out where the aircraft should be and what the coast looked like at Ferndale where Robby and Joleen lived. Robby had shown him around town before their trip. They had driven by Robby's school, past the bank where Joleen worked, and along the coast to pick up the dune buggy. Yet, he couldn't figure out which city was Ferndale. Things looked a lot different from the air, beautiful, but different.

He remembered the day he and Joleen flew into Montreal. It was evening, and looking down from the air, the city lights were beautiful. Joleen could not contain herself and squealed with delight. Montreal was very different from Ajo.

How could something, that started so wonderfully, have soured so badly? All over simple cosmetic surgery for Robby. Then there was Joleen's flight from the Baptists to an obscure religious fundamentalist group, and finally to the Catholics. Five years of confusion, and then the separation and divorce.

But there were good times, too.

The snow on the mountaintops reminded him of their first winter in Montreal. Joleen was seven months pregnant and used to tease him about how nervous he was. He drove from their apartment to the hospital several times to pick the best route. He used to go out at least once an evening to ensure the electric block heater was working so their old car would start. Joleen hadn't ever heard of a block heater growing up in Ajo, and used to say, "Kurt, you're just like a cowboy. You tie your car to a hitchin' post every night, and you go out and check up on her every few hours."

Her eyes flashed with amusement, and she giggled every time he looked at his watch. She knew he was wondering about the car. Well, it was lucky he did. Joleen went into labor early, and the doctor said that if she had arrived at the hospital a few minutes later, Robby might have arrived in the car. After they brought Robby home, she was eager to buy a newer more reliable car in case Robby became sick. They bought a new car, and Kurt had a remote-start kit installed as part of the deal. He justified it by saying she needed it so she could get into a warm car at work where she parked outside. By the time they made their last trip down to Ajo to see grandma and grandpa, Robby had mastered the procedure, and delighted in showing grandpa how he could start the car from inside the house. Joleen took the car as part of the divorce settlement.

"She won't need that down there," he said under his breath, as he looked down at the lush coastline.

His mind bounced, like the ball in an arcade game, from memories of the car kit, to nights in the discothèques, to ski trips to the Laurentians.

A bored southern drawl interrupted. "Ah, could the passenger please fasten his belt for our descent into Vancouver International Airport."

He arrived at the Customs and Immigration station at 7:40 am. He waited while the agent interrogated a man with a swarthy complexion.

****

Yusof Ekstrom handed his passport to the immigration officer. The officer looked at the passport picture and then at Yusof. Yusof's complexion was dark, perhaps middle-eastern, and Yusof knew what the immigration officer was doing. He was profiling Yusof as a potential terrorist. They do not even follow their own rules, he thought.

Yusof stood silently as the officer paged through the passport. "Ah, Mr. Ekstrom, you arrived from Frankfurt on AC 693?"

"Yes," Yusof said. He was confident. This was a genuine Canadian passport that he'd used many times. It listed his name as Yusof Richard Ekstrom.

"Did you visit any countries other than Germany on your trip?"

"No." He found that it was best not to offer any information, and just let the immigration officer pursue his line of questioning.

"What was the purpose of your trip?"

"I visited my father; he is working on a contract in Germany." This was true and could be verified if required. "It was his birthday." Yusof looked directly at the officers. Today, his blue eyes were an asset.

The officer paused.

Yusof smiled. The blue eyes always worked.

Terrorist didn't have blue eyes.

"Do you have anything to declare?" the agent said.

Yusof smiled his most pleasant smile. Typical stupid bureaucrat. Can't you see where I have checked off the box indicating a gift of a hundred and thirty-five dollars in value? Then Yusof said, "Yes, I am bringing back a gift for my girlfriend. It's a jewelry box."

Yusof had removed the scroll from the wooden box and placed it in a tube with a number of blueprints. He sent it to his office in downtown Vancouver, via FedEx, along with several other tubes of blueprints.

The agent persisted. "Do you have any other goods that are not accompanying you?"

"No," Yusof said. This was not a lie. The blueprints should already be at his office

The agent marked something on Yusof's landing card and handed it and his passport back to him. Yusof glanced at the card and back at the agent. Suspicious fool. He knew from the notes on the landing card that his luggage would be subject to further scrutiny. Who are they going to catch with all of these questions and futile searches, a few tourists trying to smuggle in a gold necklace or an undeclared dress, or perhaps a teen trying to bring in a few joints, while the ports and couriers moved thousands of unchecked items in and out of the country each day.

****

The other lines were almost empty when the agent finally waved the man through and motioned Kurt forward. As the man walked away, he turned and looked back at the agent.

Kurt could see the anger flash in the man's blue eyes.

There must have been a shift change scheduled because the agent quickly processed Kurt and closed his station. Kurt proceeded through customs and threw his bag on the conveyer belt for his connecting flight to Calgary.

He had enough time; he could call Joleen before she drove Robby to school. Should he? It might be dicey. Joleen had not spoken to him since she'd found out that Robby had fallen into some mysterious hole in the desert. Whenever he called, she'd just let the phone ring. Call display had its disadvantages if you were the caller. Maybe this time she'd answer and let him talk to Robby.

****

Yusof waited at the carrousel for his luggage. When it showed up, he pulled out the retractable handle and headed for the exit. Sure enough, he was stopped and directed to a customs agent. She seemed to delight in looking in every nook and cranny of his bag including the laundry bag. She opened the hand crafted scroll case. She looked at him. "It's empty," she said.

"It's a jewel box. I declared it."

"Is this the hundred and thirty-five dollars you declared?" she asked.

"Yes."

"Do you have a receipt?"

Yusof pulled his wallet out of his back pocket and produced a crumpled receipt from a shop in Frankfurt. He passed it to her. "It's in Euros. It converts to about hundred and thirty-five dollars Canadian."

"Okay, that's fine." She handed the receipt back to him and laid the scroll case on his open suitcase. "Have a good day, sir."

Yusof rearranged and zipped up his suitcase. He smiled to himself as he put the scroll case back in a velvet bag, placed it in his small carry-on bag, and stuffed the receipt for hundred and thirty-five dollars back in his wallet. If she knew that by tomorrow afternoon this small case would once again hold a gold scroll worth many millions—a gold scroll which would provide the means to bring this sinful country and the Great Satin to the south to their knees, would she wish him a "good day?" He picked up his bag, and made his way to the bus which would take him to long-term parking and his car.

Ferndale, Washington
August 27, 2002 - 7:55 am

Joleen awoke with a start, looked at the clock and

realized she hadn't set the alarm. They would have to hurry. She poked her head into Robby's room. "Robby. Robby, we're late. Hurry, get up."

They had attended a parent-teacher meeting the night before, and it hadn't gone that well. His teacher reported that Robby wasn't paying attention in class. Since that damn trip with his dad, Robby had been more than a handful. He constantly pestered her to let him call his dad. They argued all the way home from school and well past Robby's normal bedtime. What is happening to us, she'd thought. We'll go and see Father James tomorrow. He'll be able to help.

In about fifteen minutes, Robby walked into the kitchen. He had her blond hair and blue eyes, but even at nine, she could see hints of Kurt's stocky frame and muscular body. Robby was dressed in an old pair of jeans and an oversized Montreal Canadians jersey that Kurt had given him.

"How about corn flakes and milk?" Joleen said. "It's fast, and we are running late."

Robby nodded.

"You can't wear that jersey to school, you know the school rules."

"I got a regular shirt underneath. I'll take it off before I go in."

"I thought we would go and see Father James after school. What do you think?"

Robby shrugged. "If you want."

Robby finished his cereal first. "I'll start the car."

"No, go and get your school stuff organized."

I wish Kurt never had installed that remote-start kit. Ever since he gave us the car, Robby always wants to start it. I guess that's because it's a link to his dad. But we don't need it, it's not cold here, and it just wastes—.

"Mom, it won't take a second."

"Robby picked up the controller.

The phone rang.

"No," Joleen said. "I mean it, Robby."

She grabbed the phone.

"Don't hang up," Kurt said.

"I told you not to call. What do you want?"

"Is it Dad?" Robby jumped up smiling. "Let me talk to him."

"No. You can't talk to him."

"Is that Robby?" Kurt said. "Can I talk to him, please?"

"No. You can't…and…and you, and that damn remote car starter thing…and, I don't know. You and that trip…you…you've ruined our son."

"Mom, can I start the car? Did Dad say I could?"

"Ah, I don't care, Robby. Go ahead," Joleen said.

"Joleen, slow down, stay calm. What is this all about, surely not the car starter?"

"He's having trouble at school, and he's always arguing with me."

Robby looked out the window at the car on the street, turned toward his mother, head down, as he fiddled with the remote controller.

Joleen sat down as Robby pushed the start button. "And I am calm, I mean…"

Whaoump, a shock wave hit the house. The front window blew out. Shards of glass flew across the room striking Robby in the back. Robby fell

190

forward.

"Ieeeee, Mom, Mom, my back."

Joleen rushed to Robby. There was glass everywhere. Blood started to ooze through the back of the jersey.

"Robby, don't move. I'll call an ambulance."

"Joleen, what happened?" Kurt said.

Joleen hung up and dialed 911.

Chapter 18 - Suspicion

Airport - Vancouver, B.C., Canada
August 27, 2002-8:10 am

"Joleen," Kurt shouted into his cell phone. Heads turned to look at him as he ran out of the departure lounge, back through the terminal and out of the secure area, past startled security staff. They tried to stop him, but he brushed past them, made his way to the Hertz counter, threw down his priority card and asked for any car that was ready. He tried to call Joleen. A busy signal.

"All we have ready is a Suzuki jeep," the agent said after she checked her computer.

"Nothing bigger?" Kurt said.

"We will have a full-size ready in about half an hour."

"No, I'll take the jeep."

He dialed again. Still busy.

On the forty-five minute drive to the border, Kurt

tried Joleen's number several more times. It no longer rang busy. It just rang and rang.

Finally, someone answered. "Hello."

"Who's this?" Kurt asked.

"This is Officer Hanson, who's calling, please?"

"It's Kurt Sigurdson. What happened to Joleen and Robby?"

"What is your relationship to the subjects, sir?"

"Husband, father. What the hell happened? Are they all right?" Kurt shouted.

"Control yourself, sir. Where are you?"

"I'm at the Peace Arch border crossing." Kurt said, as he pulled into the line at U.S. Customs and Immigrations. "Ah damn," Kurt said as he realized he'd left his briefcase in the departure lounge.

"What?" Officer Hanson said.

"Nothing, nothing." Kurt checked his shirt pocket to make sure he had his passport. It was there. "Sir, are you okay?"

"Yes, yes, how are my wife and son?"

"She's your wife, sir?"

"My ex-wife."

"Ex-wife?" Officer Hanson said, and then paused.

He was obviously considering Kurt's possible involvement.

"Listen, she's my ex-wife, but we are on friendly terms, and Robby is my son. And, you better goddamn well tell me how they are. If you can't, you better put someone on the phone that can!"

"Okay, sir. Your son was taken to St. Joseph Hospital in Bellingham. He has serious but not critical injuries. As far as I know the woman is unhurt. Are you coming here, sir?"

"No, I'm going to the hospital."

"Okay, I'll have someone meet you there."

"Fine," Kurt said, and hung up.

He made one more call to Roy. He got the answering machine. "It's Kurt. I've run into some trouble. I'll call you later."

Calvert Mesa – Montana
August 27, 2002 - 11:00 am

When Terry awoke, the phone was ringing.

A female voice said, "Mr. O'Shanigan, it's eleven o'clock, shall we expect you at one?"

Terry nodded, still amazed at the organization. Then, realizing that the female voice couldn't see him, he stammered, "Yes, ah yes, I will be there at one."

No matter how many times he was here, he couldn't quite get used to the clockwork-like operation. He showered—this time with cool water, gently streaming from three sides, intermingled with a gentle steam mist. He sat on a little stool that folded out from the wall and meditated. He finally got his mind off the previous night and visions of Rosa. What was it about her?

He dressed, left his suite, and climbed one flight of stairs to the main dining room.

As he approached the door at the top of the stairs, it opened to reveal Rosa in an elegant, low-cut, dress. She held a glass of Terry's favorite single malt scotch.

"A Glenmorangie with a wee nip of water to wake her up." She passed him the glass and took his arm. "Mr. Calvert is in the small anteroom. Please come with me."

God forgive me, but could this be heaven, he thought.

The lunch was a delight of good food, whiskey, and wine. Arthur kept the discussions away from their projects. When he tried to open the discussion, Arthur put him off. "Plenty of time for that later, now that Calvert One is on her way. Just enjoy the view." Arthur moved his arm to indicate the canyon wall and mountains in the distance, but his glance, and the twinkle in his eye let Terry know that he knew that wasn't the only view Terry was taking in. Terry relaxed and enjoyed the moment. He had not let himself take a break for some time.

A male steward came in and whispered in Arthur's ear.

"Terry, there is something rather serious I need to attend to. Let's meet again for dinner at 6:00 pm."

Bellingham, Washington
August 27 - 11:00 am.

Kurt parked at the St Joseph Medical Centre, and jogged to the Emergency Admitting desk, and asked about Robby and Joleen. Robby was in surgery on the fourth floor. The nurse directed him to the appropriate waiting room where he found Joleen sitting in a corner sobbing quietly. He walked toward her. When she saw him approaching she jumped up, ran to him, threw her arms around him and began to sob convulsively. He held her tightly and waited for her to stop sobbing. When she did, he said, "How's Robby?"

She sobbed again, more loudly. He waited. He could feel his heart rate rising. How bad was it?

"Joleen, please, is Robby okay?"

"It's terrible; his back is full of glass. The pieces went right threw his shirt." She sobbed again. "It's like…like his shirt is nailed to his back with glass."

More sobbing.

Kurt whispered, "Joleen?"

"I think he lost a lot of blood. The doctors said it would take several hours to get all the little pieces out and stitch him up, but…" She took a deep breath. "He was in horrible pain but talked to me after they gave him something. We have been here for about two hours." She started crying again.

Kurt led her to a chair and sat her down. He pulled up another chair facing her, grabbed both her hands and sat quietly. Questions strained at his lips, but he held back. He waited several minutes until she finally quit crying. "Have they given you anything to calm you?"

She looked up. "You know what I think of tranquilizers."

"Sorry," Kurt said. He knew Joleen thought tranquilizers were used by the government to gain control over you.

He started again. "What happened?"

"The car exploded. Robby pushed the remote start, and it exploded. It blew out the front window and sent glass across the room. It...it..."

She started sobbing again. Kurt waited. "Your damn remote starter. It could have killed him or blinded him. Only a few seconds before, he looked out the window at the car, if...if he had pushed the button..."

"Damn your remote starter," she whispered.

"I don't see how the remote starter could have caused—"

"Well, it did. It did."

Kurt couldn't deny that it seemed that the remote starter caused the explosion. But that didn't make sense. The remote starter acted just like turning the key to start the car. It did nothing else. He couldn't see how that could cause the explosion. Maybe another car hit his and caused the explosion, or a propane bottle exploded, and the timing was just a coincidence.

"Was there another car or something?" Kurt asked.

"No, the car was ripped open like a sardine can. It was your damn starter."

Kurt was sure that wasn't right, but he had no better explanation. He just sat there dumbfounded waiting for Robby to get out of the operating room.

In about an hour, a doctor walked into the waiting room. Joleen jumped up. Panic showed on her face.

The doctor flashed a broad reassuring smile. "I'm Doctor Ross," he said. "I have been looking after Robby."

"How's Robby?" Joleen said.

"Well, he was extremely lucky. He had a tough nylon hockey jersey on and another shirt underneath. The jersey acted sort of…well, like a bullet-proof vest. When we removed it, almost all the glass shards came with it. In fact, his injuries were minor. Lots of blood, but only a few deep cuts. He needed only ten stitches for his wounds."

"Thank God," Joleen whispered.

"When can we see him?" Kurt said.

"He's in the recovery room. You can go in now. He will be groggy for a while yet, but he should recognize you and be able to talk in about fifteen minutes. Follow me."

As they prepared to follow Dr. Ross out of the waiting room, the largest policeman Kurt had ever seen stepped in to block their path. "Mr. and Mrs. Sigurdson?" he said.

"Yah, sort of," Kurt said. "We're divorced."

"Yes, well we would like to talk to you, both." A body-less voice drifted from behind the monolithic policeman.

A head popped out. "I'm Lieutenant Sm…" Kurt couldn't quite grasp what he said from behind the monolith. "And this is Patrolman Rodriguez. We would like to talk to you about the explosion."

"Can't you guys wait?" Joleen said. "My son is hurt, and we are just on our way to see him."

"We could come with you," the Lieutenant said.

"No, you won't." Joleen pushed passed Rodriguez.

"Ma'am."

"Don't you, ma'am, me," she said, looking over her shoulder.

"You go on ahead to Robby. I'll handle this. I'll catch up," Kurt said to her back. Not that she needed anyone's permission; she was going to Robby, even if she had to deck Rodriguez to do it.

"Okay, do we really need to do this now?" Kurt looked at the lieutenant. "Lieutenant, I didn't catch your name, but can't we find out what was wrong with the car later?"

"I'm Lieutenant Smith from Homicide. And no, I think it is important we get on with this right away."

"Homicide? Was someone killed?"

"No." Smith paused, apparently looking for the right words.

"Then, why are you here? It was just an accident caused by the remote-start system. Wasn't it?"

"Well," Smith said. "It appears an attempt was made on someone's life. Perhaps your wife's or son's. Do either of them have any connections to the drug world?"

"Wha…, what do you mean, drug world? My son's only nine, and, and my wife will barely touch Aspirin, let alone illicit drugs. You guys are crazy. You must be wrong about the car."

"No, we're not. Our bomb squad has already identified the explosives. Something rather exotic, they tell me. What do you do for a living, sir?"

They suspect me, Kurt thought. What the hell is going on? Joleen said Robby was having trouble at school. Maybe it was drugs. No, I was just with Robby for three weeks. He was fine then. You don't get involved in the drug culture that fast. And Joleen, who could possibly want to kill her? Did she have a new beau? One of those loonies from one of the fringe religions she experimented with. They were known to do weird things. No, that wasn't likely either. Robby would have told him if a new man was sniffing around. What then? They must be wrong, must be.

"Mr. Sigurdson, what do you do for a living?" Smith said.

Better use my cover identity, a lecturer at the University of Saskatchewan. If I tell them I am with the Canadian Intelligence and Security Service, they might think I have access to explosives.

"I'm…." Then he had second thoughts. They would want to know where he was for the past few days. What would a lecturer be doing at a U.S. military base? Better stick with the truth.

"Sir?" The Lieutenant appeared to be trying to muster some authority in his voice.

Kurt explained that he was a Canadian Intelligence and Security Service employee, and he couldn't tell them what he had been doing for the past few days. The officer was obviously suspicious. Kurt could not show him his airline tickets or boarding passes since these were all in his forgotten briefcase somewhere in the Vancouver airport. He explained this, but Smith wanted more. All he could do was give Smith the Yuma Base Commander's phone number, and promise to provide more proof of his recent activities once he caught up with his briefcase.

Smith seemed unimpressed, but finally let Kurt go to see Robby.

Kurt checked with the nurse for directions to the recovery room and headed for the elevator. Smith followed him and joined him in the elevator. He was obviously making sure Kurt wasn't using the visit to Robby as a means of escape. He continued along without speaking and took up his station outside the recovery room. This guy is no slouch, Kurt thought, as he entered the room.

Robby was already sitting up, smiling and talking to Joleen. That was a good sign. When he saw Kurt his smile faded. "Dad, I'm sorry. I didn't mean to blow up the car. I just pushed the button, same like I always did."

"I know, Robby. It wasn't your fault. It was…ah, it was something else." An explanation eluded Kurt. He didn't want to upset Robby by calling it a bomb. And Joleen, she'd go ballistic. No need to subject Robby to that.

"How are you feeling?" Kurt asked, changing the subject.

"I'm okay. I want to go home."

That was a good sign.

"We'll take you," Joleen said.

"Not so fast. We need to talk to the doctor," Kurt said. "Robby might not feel so good after the pain killers wear off."

Joleen said nothing. Robby just frowned. They sat quietly for a while, and Robby closed his eyes and drifted off to sleep.

Joleen grabbed Kurt's hand and put her head on

his shoulder and fell asleep, adrenaline exhaustion catching up with her. Kurt sat as still as possible, trying not to disturb her. He ran over the day's events in his mind repeatedly. Was the explosion actually a bomb? Was Lieutenant Smith right? Could the bomb have been intended for Joleen or Robby? It didn't make any sense. Who would want to harm them and why? He went over and over the facts. Could it be connected to the discovery that he and Robby made? Nothing seemed to connect.

Joleen stirred. "We need to talk," Kurt whispered, and gestured toward the doorway. Joleen shrugged, stood up, rubbed her eyes and walked out the door. Kurt followed.

Smith was still there, hunched over in a chair. A real Colombo type, Kurt thought. He intervened before Kurt could say anything else to Joleen. "I have a few questions, ma'am, if you don't mind, please."

"No," Kurt said. "Let me explain it to her."

Smith nodded.

Kurt proceeded to explain that Smith believed that the explosion was not an accident, but a bomb. Joleen reacted with unexpected calm. Her eyes simply widened with fear. Kurt explained Smith's theories about Robby and drugs. Joleen shook her head.

"No way, no way," she said.

"Are you sure, ma'am?" Smith said.

"Yes, no way, there's no way."

"Is there anyone who might want to hurt you? Perhaps, a jealous boyfriend? "Smith eyed Kurt, monitoring his reaction to the question.

"No, I'm not…I haven't seen anyone since Kurt and I…" She looked at Kurt. "Since we divorced."

"Okay, you two think about this. Do you have any enemies? Would someone want to exact revenge for something? Or, even Robby, for that matter? There are some crazy kids out there these days, and they can get lots of bomb building instructions on the net."

"I thought you said this was an exotic explosive?" Kurt said.

"Yah, that's what the lab boys tell me. But, that was just preliminary results. If it's verified, it would rule out kids and make this a professional hit."

"Professional hit?" Joleen's eyes widened, and she looked at Kurt. "Is this connected to your job?"

Smith widened his eyes and tipped his head toward Kurt, obviously pleased that he wasn't the only one with this thought.

"I can't see how," Kurt said.

"Okay, as I said, you folks think about this, and I'll get back to you. Let Patrolman Rodriguez know how to get in touch with you when you leave the hospital. I'll send him up here."

Joleen and Kurt walked back into the recovery room. A nurse was there, checking on Robby. She walked over to them. "He's fine," she said, smiling.

"When can we take him h…?" Joleen looked at Kurt. "We can't take him home, can we? It might not be safe, and the house is a disaster, glass everywhere. What if someone tries again?" Tears started running down her cheeks. "Where will we be safe?"

The nurse looked puzzled. Kurt looked at her, and said, "When will Robby be ready to leave the hospital?"

"I'm not sure. A day or two, you will have to ask the doctor."

Joleen started to cry in earnest. "What am I going to do? I'm afraid."

"Look. Robby will need to spend some time out of school to recover. Why don't you let me take you both to Eric and Susan's farm? Robby liked it there, and you will certainly be safe. You can stay there until we get this thing sorted out. That shouldn't take too long."

"Okay," she said, and sat down by Robby. "You get it organized."

Kurt thought for a minute. He'd need to get his luggage and briefcase from Vancouver. Could do that on the way? No, that little jeep wasn't going to handle the three of them and their luggage. Robby would probably want to lie down. A van would be best.

He formulated a plan. "You have your cell?"Joleen checked her purse and nodded. "Okay, check for messages every so often. I'll call Eric to let him know we are coming, and I'll get a bigger car. I'll keep you posted," Kurt said.

He gave Rodriguez his cell number and left.

Calvert Mesa – Montana
August 27, 2002 - 6:00 pm

Terry arrived in the dining room and to his disappointment was met by a male steward. He was once again escorted to the small anteroom where Arthur sat sipping a black coffee. Arthur motioned for him to take the chair across from him, facing away from the window. No distractions this evening, Terry thought. Arthur is ready to work.

The steward brought Terry coffee and took his meal order. Arthur stared down uncharacteristically into his cup. When he looked up there was no twinkle in his blue eyes, only sadness.

"Bad news…very grim news. Jack Thompson is dead," Arthur whispered, as he looked back down at his coffee. Terry was surprised. He met Jack a few times. He was the youngest of Arthur's inner circle of assistants, and seemed quite healthy. If Arthur had announced one of the others had died, he wouldn't have been surprised.

Arthur remained silent, so Terry said, "What happened? An accident…heart?"

"No! He was murdered on assignment in Yemen. He was there to pick up the gold scroll."

Terry's eyes widened. "Murdered?"

"Right," Arthur said. "I should have insisted on a bodyguard. Jack always refused to take one, but I should have insisted this time. The country is extremely dangerous, and the artifact was too valuable. Damn…damn."

Terry could see tears well up in those tough grey eyes, and he watched as several trickled down

Arthur's cheek. He had never seen this tender side of Arthur before, and it shocked him a little. In the past, Arthur always seemed in control of his world. But as a priest, Terry knew death could come to anyone at any time. It was the one inevitable thing man could not control.

Arthur reached down, retrieved his napkin and wiped his eyes. He recovered and was ready for business. "As you suspected, the scroll was in the possession of the jeweler. It had been with his family for generations, but he was willing to sell it to us for a million U.S. dollars."

"A million dollars?" Terry said.

Arthur nodded. "We're not sure if the transaction took place, but when they found Jack's body, he had neither the bonds nor the scroll on him. And as one might expect, we can't find the jeweler. They did find Jack's driver, but he was also murdered. His last contact outside of the hotel staff at the Sheraton was a UNICEF officer."

"UNICEF?" Terry said.

"Jack was there to give a grant from the Calvert Oil Children's Trust to some of the local schools. It was a good cause and a good cover for his trip. But not good enough as it turns out. Damn."

The steward returned with more coffee.

The steward left, and Arthur continued, "If the jeweler is alive, we'll find him and find out if he'd given Jack the scroll. Hopefully, it's in his possession, and he will still sell it to us. That may be tough though. I assume, if he's still alive, he'll be a bit jumpy. The bearer bonds, on the other hand, are pretty well untraceable, and we will just have to write them off."

"If the scroll was stolen," Terry said, "perhaps, the thieves don't…"

A light rap at the door interrupted him, and Tran Ng stepped into the room. Terry wasn't sure of his age, but he'd been around for a while. He was a covert agent for the CIA in the Vietnam War, a DEA agent, a security consultant, and was now head of security for Calvert Oil.

"Tran, you know Terry, don't you?"

"Yes, of course." Tran came over to shake Terry's hand, and then he turned to Arthur. "A little more information came in on Jack."

He paused and looked from Arthur to Terry, and back.

"Go ahead, Tran, Terry's plugged in on this," Arthur said.

"Well, even though Jack never wanted a bodyguard, I often assigned a covert tail to cover his ass. Because of the risks in Yemen, I had a three-man team keeping an eye on him twenty-four seven. They were good men. I'd used them a number of times for various jobs in the Middle East."

"Do they know anything?" Arthur said.

"I'm afraid there is bad news there, too. One was found under some hay in a stable near where Jack was found. He was the guy watching Jack that night. His throat was slit just like Jack's. One of the off-duty guys was found in his hotel room, same scenario. Throat slit from behind. The third guy was in a local restaurant eating and took a bullet in the shoulder. He's okay. I guess, whoever we are dealing with, is better with knives than guns."

Arthur frowned. "Can he tell us anything?"

"Not yet, he's still recovering from surgery, but he's safe. My contacts in Yemen's security service have him under guard in the same facility that treats their pPresident. It's the best we can do there. Once he's out of the recovery room, I will arrange to talk to him. I don't think we will find out much. This wasn't a random robbery; it was a professional hit. I don't think we will find many tracks—the ballistics maybe, but I doubt it."

"Thanks, Tran. I feel a little better knowing Jack wasn't out there on his own, but he's still dead, and I want to know who did it."

"I am trying to get the Yemeni authorities to release the body. I have arranged a plane to fly it back," Tran said.

Arthur nodded. "Have you notified his wife?"

"We haven't located her. She is visiting a niece, and they've gone on a road trip. As soon as they use a credit card, we will be able to trace them."

"Keep me posted," Arthur said.

Tran left, and the steward brought their meals.

"Another collector, do you think another collector is behind this?" Terry said.

"Perhaps, but who could it be, and who would be so ruthless? There are only four or five private collectors who have the money to buy something like this, and I know them all. Any of them might bend the rules, to various degrees, but not murder. No, not multiple murders."

Arthur's face seemed to become more austere. The eyes lost the look of sorrow, and he said, "We'll get the bastards who did this, Terry. We'll do it for Jack."

They ate silently for a while, then Arthur said, "I need to do a few things. Let's break and meet in the library tomorrow morning. You can use the time to make phone calls or send emails."

"Okay," Terry said, but he knew he wouldn't do that. He only made routine communications from the mesa. You never knew if Tran monitored the phone lines and computers. Using a secure phone from the mesa might look suspicious, and apparently the latest eavesdropping systems could remotely record keystrokes before things were encrypted, even if he used his own computer. He'd wait.

Chapter 19 - The Dossier

Terry entered the library. Tran was sitting at a large oval conference table with a small wireless keyboard and mouse in front of him. Arthur was sitting at the head of the table. He looked up and motioned for Terry to sit down in the chair across from Tran. On the wall at the end of the table a large computer screen displayed various items. One was a large picture of Kurt Sigurdson, another a somewhat blurred picture of Joleen and Robby

"Tran was just about to bring me up to date on what he's found out about Sigurdson so far."

"Okay," Tran said. "This guy was easy to trace until about five years ago. He was born in Saskatchewan in 1962, went to high school in Davidson, Saskatchewan, and was a bit of a star with the Davidson High School team."

210

Tran worked at the keyboard for a few seconds. A close-up of Kurt Sigurdson's face framed in a football helmet appeared on the screen. "This is from the yearbook."

"After high school he went to the University of Saskatchewan and ended up with a PhD in Control Systems Engineering. He went to work for Orva Aerospace Ltd. out of Montreal. They were working on some kind of missile project for the U.S. Air Force. He worked on the project at the Goldwater Air Base in southern Arizona. Now, we aren't sure yet, but that's probably where he met his wife. She's from a small town called Ajo just south of the base. One of my guys is trying to find out more about her. Anyway, they ended up in Montreal in 1990."

****

Kurt and Joleen moved to a small apartment in Montreal. Joleen embraced the French Canadian culture and especially enjoyed visiting the city center, with its many women's clothing shops She was always amazed how fashionably the French-Canadian women dressed. She was disappointed that her increasing girth restricted her attempts to imitate their fashion sense, but vowed to get her figure back and get into the shops as soon as she gave birth.

Kurt was happy at work. He continued working with Roy on the Firefly missile project in Montreal. The technical results were exceptional. Better than anything deployed or in development by anyone.

They were convinced that would put Canada in the lead in air-to-air missile technology. Michael Walker worked non-stop to get the required government backings to complete the project. Once in production, the Firefly would bring several hundred skilled jobs to Montreal, perhaps even more in the long term.

Joleen went into labor two weeks early. Kurt woke in the middle of the night to find her sitting in a chair by the bed. "I think it's time we go," she whispered.

The contractions were coming fast and furious by the time they reached the hospital. Kurt was happy he had scouted the route. He got to the hospital in record time. A nurse checked her and wheeled her straight to the delivery room. Kurt hung around feeling kind of useless until an orderly brought him some scrubs so he could go into the delivery room. He hurriedly dressed in the green smock, green cap, and green shoe coverings.

As he was led to the delivery room, he caught his reflection in a glass door. "Look a bit like Kermit, the frog," he muttered.

The orderly smiled.

By the time he got into the delivery room, the main event was over. "What took you so long?" Joleen said.

"They couldn't find me the Kermit costume," he said, doing a little hop.

Joleen laughed.

"It's okay, even my doctor didn't get here. It's a boy," she said, pointing at the intern who was doing all those little things they do with newborns.

Kurt noticed that he looked a little nervous. Just a beginner, probably his first delivery on his own, he thought.

Joleen motioned him closer and gave him a loving hug, a kiss and whispered in his ear, "We can start working on number two, soon."

"I thought it was supposed to be the guys who are super horny after all this pregnancy stuff," he whispered, hoping the medical staff hadn't heard.

Joleen winked and held him closer.

Dr. LaPorte walked in. He came over to Joleen and apologized for not getting there on time. Then he went over to the intern who was finishing up his work. There was some animated discussion with a lot of gestures. French-Canadians, Kurt smiled.

Dr. LaPorte wrapped the baby in a blanket and brought him over to Joleen. "Do you have a name selected?"

"Yes, Robert Arnold, after my grandfather and my dad."

"Very nice," the doctor said, and then looked at Kurt and continued, "I'll be back in a few minutes." Once outside the room, where Joleen couldn't see him the doctor motioned for Kurt to follow.

Kurt went to the door. "I'll be right back, Joleen. I want to ask the doctor a few things."

The doctor was waiting outside with a serious look on his face.

"Kurt, don't worry now, but Robert has a small non-serious birth defect. He has an extra finger on his left hand. I didn't want to upset Joleen. We won't have to tell her until tomorrow. We'll be taking the baby soon, and she won't see him again until morning."

Kurt thought for a while. "No, let's tell her now. She needs to know, and she'd be furious if we wait till tomorrow."

"Do you want me with you when you tell her?" the doctor said.

"No, I'll do it alone. You come back in a few minutes to explain our medical options."

Joleen looked up as Kurt walked in. Tears streamed down her face.

"He…he…he has six fingers. Look."She held his tiny left hand with five fingers curling over her index finger, the thumb wrapped underneath. "What did we do? Oh, oh, we sinned. God is punishing us." She began to sob uncontrollably.

The doctor returned and explained that an extra finger was not uncommon and could easily be corrected. Joleen would not listen and kept crying. She was convinced this was God's punishment for their pre-marital sex and Robby's conception. This was pretty well the start of the end of their marriage.

Other than the extra finger, Robby was a healthy child. Various doctors and Kurt tried to convince Joleen to have the extra finger removed, but Joleen refused. She insisted that it was God's will, and the finger would remain as a reminder of their sin. Kurt finally gave up. He would let Robert decide when he came of age.

Joleen rebuffed Kurt's sexual advance after that, and they grew further and further apart in the first year of Robby's life.

Just after Robby turned one, Joleen's father, Arn, called to inform her that her mother had cancer. Joleen immediately packed up herself and Robby, and they left to be at her mother's side.

****

"We don't have a lot of information on them in Montreal, but about a year after Robby's birth, Joleen went back to Ajo," Tran said.

Arthur looked at Terry. "Do you have any information on Sigurdson's wife?"

"I don't know that much," Terry said. "What I know is second hand information from her parish priest. He thinks she is emotionally unstable. She was raised a Baptist, but after her son was born slightly deformed, she tried out a couple of other religious groups, and then switched to the Catholic Church. Apparently, she felt God was punishing her, or at least that the Baptist God was."

"What kind of deformity?" Arthur said.

"Oh, nothing significant. He was born with an extra finger on his left hand. It could have been easily corrected surgically, but she would not allow it. She confessed to her parish priest that she was pregnant when she was married. She felt that she and Kurt were being punished for having sex before they were married, and her son's extra finger was to be their constant reminder."

"Kind of punishing the child for the sins of his

father," Arthur said.

"Apparently, that's what led to their marriage break up," Terry said. "Can't be sure but that's what the parish priest tells me. As far as the boy is concerned, I have never met him, but I understand he is a typical youngster."

Vancouver, B.C., Canada
August 28 - 10:00 am

The Lone Ranger and Tonto were charging through his dream dodging exploding cars. That didn't seem right. Then slowly he awoke to his telephone ringing with the William Tell Overture ring tone. He grabbed the phone. It was Joleen.

"Where are you?" she said. Kurt looked at his watch and realized he had slept for twelve hours. "I'm at a motel near the Vancouver Airport. I went to Vancouver to get my luggage and pick up a bigger rental car. I needed some sleep. I left you messages."

"Well, we need you. The doctor says Robby can get out this afternoon."

"I'll be there in a couple of hours."

Now, as he showered and got dressed, he reviewed the previous day's events. Kurt had driven back to Vancouver in the Suzuki jeep to pick up a van. Soon after leaving the hospital, he received a call from Michael Walker. Walker told him his briefcase was picked up by airport security as unattended luggage, x-rayed, and searched. It had been linked to his baggage which was pulled from

216

the plane and searched as well. Airport security alerted the RCMP, and they tried to find out about Kurt at his cover number at the University of Saskatchewan. That led them to Walker who told the RCMP to call off the Airport Security investigation, and secure the luggage and briefcase.

Kurt explained that there was an explosion at Joleen's house, and that his son was injured. He omitted the fact that it might have been a bomb.

After getting the van, he picked up his luggage and briefcase, and called his brother Eric to tell them they were coming. Eric asked a lot of questions since he hadn't seen Kurt and Joleen together for some time. Kurt put off the explanation, just saying that they needed to go to the farm. Then he left Joleen a message that said he was going to head to a motel for a few hours sleep before he drove back to Bellingham. He realized it was close to thirty hours since he'd slept.

Now, he hopped out of the shower and looked at his watch. Better get a move on, I don't want to give Joleen time to change her mind about taking Robby to the farm. He'd be safe there.

But he still didn't understand why someone would want to hurt Robby. Was it connected to Robby's discovery, was the priest involved, the government, the CIA perhaps? No, they wouldn't assassinate a child on U.S. soil—or would they?

Calvert Mesa, Montana
August 28, 2002 - 11:00 am

"Okay," Arthur said. "I think we could use more information about Joleen and the boy. Tran, you get some of your guys on it, and Terry could you see if the parish priest has, or can get, more information?"

Terry and Tran nodded in agreement.

"Tran, what else do you know about Sigurdson?" Terry said.

"Well, that's a bit of a mystery. Sigurdson worked on the missile project in Montreal until it was cancelled. That's where his trail goes black."

****

Kurt had been alone for about six months. Joleen had stayed with her mother and drove her back and forth to Phoenix for cancer treatment. Then one day, the rest of his life went into freefall. He arrived at his office just east of Dorval Airport at 7:30 am. Normally he was the first one in the office, but today he was late and arrived to see a stone-faced Michael Walker sitting in his office with Roy.

Roy looked up. "We're another Arrow!"

"What?" Kurt said, tossing his coat onto a chair.

"The government has cancelled the Firefly just like old Dief cancelled the Avro Arrow! Bastards. Government turkey butts, damn..." Roy stood up and cursed his way to the window.

Kurt couldn't hear the rest of the expletives. He

218

looked at Michael. "Is it true?"

"I'm afraid so. I just received the call from the Deputy Minister of National Defense; we are going to buy American made missiles for our fighters," Michael said.

"Just like the Arrow." Roy turned from the window. "You know, the story is Prime Minister Diefenbaker went for a canoe ride with President Eisenhower, and he talked Dief into canceling the Arrow and installing some crummy Bomark surface-to-air missiles instead. Those turkeys were obsolete in a couple of years, and we were stuck buying U.S. fighters that were nowhere near as good as the Arrow. That set Canada's aerospace effort back for a decade at least. Most of the engineers went off to NASA or other industries. Now we are almost back in a leadership position, and they do it to us again. What are those goddamn bastards in Ottawa thinking?" He turned back to the window, muttering.

"This could be tough on our staffing," Michael said. "Don't discuss this with anyone else. There won't be an official announcement for a couple of days. I'll have a better idea of the fallout by then, okay?"

Roy turned and shrugged.

"Right," Kurt whispered.

He left work early and arrived home to a ringing telephone. He picked it up. "Hello."

"Where have you been?" Joleen said, she was crying. "I called your office, they said you'd gone home, you didn't answer…I, I called your cell, our house, where were you?"

"Joleen?" Kurt said. "What's wrong? I'm sorry my cell was off…sorry…stop crying, I can barely understand you. Is it your mother?"

"No, it's Arn. He…he had a heart attack. He died. The assistant manager just called. I have to go back to the hospital to see Mom. How can I tell her? She's been so happy lately with her cancer in remission. This may undue all that progress. I can't lose them both…oh, Kurt. We're being punished. It's just like Robby. It's our fault because…look what we've done."

"Joleen, just stay with your mom in Phoenix, I'll catch the next flight down and drive back with you." There was no answer, only soft crying. "Joleen, do you understand."

"Yes, we'll wait for you."

"Okay, I'll get my flight organized."

He arrived in Phoenix just after midnight, rented a car and arrived at Joleen's motel around 2:00 am. She had reserved a room for him and left a message to meet for breakfast.

To Kurt's disappointment, Robby hardly recognized him. Obviously, Joleen had not talked to Robby about his father. That didn't surprise Kurt. The breakfast was a cool affair. Joleen kept insisting that Robby's extra finger, her mother's cancer, and her father's heart attack were all punishment for their sins. When he told her about the cancellation of the Firefly project, she added that to the list.

Nothing would change her mind and, although she let Kurt help with her father's funeral, she shared little else with him. After the funeral, she insisted that he leave. That was it. Their marriage was over. If not for Joleen's mother, Alice, he probably would never have seen Robby again. But Alice's cancer remained in remission, and she insisted Robby see his father twice a year, at Christmas, and during the school summer vacation.

After Arn's funeral, Kurt arrived back in Montreal to more chaos.

"It's a turkey shoot," Roy said. "We're being reorganized, and there're bound to be layoffs. So, you know, everyone is positioning themselves for a job. Most people are so confused they're running around stabbing each other in the chest. Damn fools. How'd you make out with Joleen?"

Kurt explained the situation.

"So, do you think she'll ever come back?"

"No, it doesn't look like it, and to top it off, I might not have a job."

"Ah, don't worry, Walker and I looked out for you."

"How's that?" Kurt said.

"Well, it seems that old Diefenbaker weaseled some concessions out of Eisenhower. In a trade-off for the Arrow, he received a guarantee that we, Canada, that is, would be plugged into the secret computer stuff going on in the U.S. intelligence arena. Well, as it turns out…" Roy paused and looked around to ensure nobody was in earshot. "As it turns out, we got us a bang up, super duper, first class, science fiction type, secret computer and communications counter-espionage center hidden away. All on account of old Dief-the-Chief. How about that?" Roy paused.

"And?" Kurt said.

"Okay, here's the kicker. Because the Firefly was canceled and we're going to purchase American stuff, Canada and the U.S. have updated Dief's agreement. The secret site is going to be upgraded with the latest super-computers and communication equipment to do anti-terrorist and counterespionage work. You and I buddy—we'll be in charge."

"You and me?"

"Well, Walker will be in charge, but you know how he is—he'll be out selling and getting funding for projects, while we'll be doing all the fun work."

"Where is the facility? Here in Montreal or Ottawa."

"No," Roy whispered. "It's part of the Diefenbaker Dam complex in Saskatchewan. It's called the Canadian Counterespionage and Antiterrorist Facility or C-CAF for short."

****

"Tran, what do you mean his trail goes black?" Terry said.

"I mean he seems to disappear. He sells his house in Montreal, puts his furniture in storage and, for almost a year, there is no trace of him. No address, no job, nothing. And then…" Tran said, and pointed to the screen showing a University of Saskatchewan course brochure. "Then he shows up as a professor of engineering at the University of Saskatchewan.

But here's where it gets downright strange. No one has ever taken a class from him, and when you try to sign up for one of his classes, they always show up as full. Now that implausible, isn't it?"

"No more implausible than a priest being in command of the mission in the Algodones Dunes," Arthur said.

"Right, but we know how Terry got there, don't we?" Tran said, with a smile.

"Anything else on Mr. Sigurdson?" Arthur said.

"Well, we've kind of dead-ended there, sir. We'll have to keep working on his dossier."

There was a tap at the door, and one of Tran's assistants poked his head in.

"Tran, sorry to interrupt; it's urgent. Yesterday, there was an explosion at Sigurdson's ex-wife's house."

He moved to Tran's keyboard and tapped a few keys. Several pictures of a mangled car appeared.

"That doesn't look like an accident," Tran said.

"No, my agent couldn't get too close because of the police but look at the way the car is split open right behind the windshield. The explosion wasn't the gas tank or engine where you might expect an accidental explosion. No, it was most likely a bomb under the front seat."

Arthur jumped up. "A bomb? Someone's after Sigurdson's family. Why? Is something else going on here, Tran?"

Tran shook his head. "I don't know. Could be. Why do you think that?"

"Well, Sigurdson and his kid—did they just

accidentally stumble on that site or are they somehow connected to our other project?" Arthur said.

"I'll follow that up, but I don't see the connection," Tran said.

"Can you put some protection on the family just in case?" Arthur said.

"Yah, good idea. I'll get surveillance set up on the family. I'll update you as soon as we get anything new."

Arthur looked at Terry. "I don't see why someone would target Sigurdson's family? Surely, it can't be related to the artifacts and Jack's murder. There must be some other reason."

"I'm sure Tran and his crew will find out," Terry said.

"I hope you are right. He is very good, but sometimes things just don't work out as we wish. Well, we certainly can't do any more right now. We need to break for lunch anyway. You will have the afternoon to catch up or relax. Calvert One will be ready to take you to Paris this evening."

Chapter 20 - Dead Sea Scrolls

Over Saskatchewan, Canada
August 29, 2002 - 11:00 pm

Terry sipped on a coffee and looked out the window of Calvert Air, CLV-1 as it climbed to cruising altitude. He wondered if they would fly over Regina, the city where he grew up and attended Miller Composite, a local Catholic high school. His thoughts drifted back to his high school days. He had above average athletic ability, and one of his friends convinced him to try out for the football team. Miller had an excellent team. It was well coached and always had a surplus of hulks for positions on the line and to his surprise, sure hands and exceptional speed landed him a position as a wide receiver. He was on his way to setting a school record for most yards gained by a receiver when his football career was dealt a devastating blow. A tough linebacker broke his right arm and shoulder with a clean but explosive tackle. After that, it was off to the hospital for a few incisions and a couple of pins.

As Terry left, his doctor announced, "You're as good as new."

But he wasn't. That injury ended his football career and dogged him to this day. He rubbed his arm. Hopefully, the recent surgery would be the last.

He closed out his athletic career on the track team where others were just a little faster. Coming second, third, or fourth, no matter how fast you ran, never garnered much glory, so Terry concentrated on academic activities and ignored all social activities. This didn't win him many real friends, but that mattered little as he finished with the highest average anyone had ever attained at Miller, and he would probably never see any of these classmates again. His parish priest helped him get a scholarship to the prodigious Jesuit run George Washington University. A little pressure from his priest, and some of the Jesuits, convinced Terry to pursue a degree in divinity.

Terry took the last sip of his coffee, stood up, and moved toward the rear of the plane.

Rosa appeared magically. "Anything you need before retiring?" Terry's heart rate jumped at the sound of her voice

"No, nothing," he said, fighting off a number of impure thoughts. "Just call me about an hour before we land in Paris. That's about six hours, right?"

"Six hours and twelve minutes," she said.

The plane could probably hold two hundred and fifty people if set up as a commercial airline, but

Arthur Calvert had designed this layout himself. At the front, just behind the pilots' compartment, was a meeting area with seating for twelve. It boasted all the latest communications and audio-visual equipment one would expect in a large ground-based office. Behind that was a section of first class airline seating for eighteen, followed by a couple of elegantly laid out washrooms.

Further to the rear, there were two private sleeping quarters for Arthur and another privileged guest. In this case, Terry was that guest. Finally, at the back of the plane were the galley and crew area, which included not only first class seats, but also small rooms for crew members who needed rest. On this flight, there was a second flight crew of two pilots. That flight crew would ensure CLV-1 would not be on the ground long once Terry disembarked in Paris. In a few hours, the plane would be back at Arthur's disposal.

Southeast of Davidson, Saskatchewan, Canada
August 29, 2002 - 11:30 pm

Kurt, Robby and Joleen flew from Vancouver to Saskatoon. They picked up Kurt's car at his condo and headed for the Sigurdson farm. It was 11:30 pm when they arrived, and Joleen and Robby headed for bed. Kurt swore Eric to secrecy and then told him the story, at least the parts he could, including the police suspicions that it was a bomb. He finished the story and headed for C-CAF.

"I'll look after them," Eric said as he saw Kurt off.

Eric secured the gate to the farm with a chain and a padlock as Kurt drove off. He never had to do that in the past, but now the kids who came out for a wiener roast seemed to not care about other people's property. Most of the damage was usually minor, a few loops with a pickup through the fields, a few broken beer bottles, and some miscellaneous garbage strewn about. But last summer, someone decided to build their bonfire next to one of his wooden granaries and it caught fire. He couldn't save the granary, but he stopped the fire from spreading to his crops. If he hadn't acted quickly, the fire could have spread all the way up to the farmhouse. So, now the partiers could use the road allowance a mile and a quarter to the south to go down to the lake.

He went into the house and found Susan sitting at the kitchen table sipping on a cup of tea. In her typically efficient manner, she had cleaned up the kitchen while he was seeing Kurt off. You'd never know that only moments before they had prepared and eaten a snack with Kurt.

"Want me to nuke you a cup?" she said, holding up her favorite oversized red mug with the big "We Love You, Mom" emblazoned in crooked green letters. Eric had taken their twins, Charli-Ann and James, to a pottery class when they were just five, and they had made it for her. The twins were ten now, just one year older than Robby.

"Sure, that sounds good. How about mint? Do we have that?"

228

Susan nodded and went to the cupboard for the tea bag. "The kids will be excited to have Robby here. It's been a long time since they've seen him. Too bad they're spending the night at Jim and Mary's, and weren't here to greet him."

"It's probably a good thing. Robby and Joleen need to get some sleep. Jim will have the kids back here bright and early. They'll have lots of time with Robby. Kurt thinks he'll leave Robby here while they go back to fix up the house."

"What about his school work?" Susan said.

"We'll work something out."

They sat sipping their tea.

"You know, Kurt's holding back. Something just doesn't seem right." Susan looked down into the little pool of tea left in her large cup.

"Reading tea leaves, are you?" Eric said.

"You know Kurt's job, kind of top secret. The explosion at Joleen's…I don't know. It all just doesn't seem right."

"No, it's nothing to do with his job."

She looked into the cup again. "And it's not tea leaves. Tea bags don't leave tea leaves. I just think there's more to this than what he told us."

"Well, we didn't have a lot of time to talk. Maybe Joleen can fill in some more of the details in the morning."

"Maybe," she whispered. "But, you know Joleen; she sees the hand of God in everything she can't explain."

Eric nodded but said nothing.

Susan stood up. "I'm off to bed, you coming?"

"No, I'm not sleepy. It's a clear night. I think I'll go up and look at the stars."

They left the kitchen and climbed the stairs to the second floor bedrooms. It was a large house with five spacious bedrooms. They had recently remodeled the old farmhouse and added three on-suite bathrooms. Susan was pleased and thought that the old farmhouse was now just as nice as any city house. As they reached the master bedroom, Susan turned to give Eric a kiss.

"Sure you don't want to come up, there's no moon tonight, and the sky should be great?" he said.

"No, I'm really too tired, you go."

Eric proceeded to the end of the hall where there was a steep staircase leading up to a small door. He climbed the steps, and stepped up into a mini observatory. Eric loved astronomy and had built a number of telescopes. When they renovated the farmhouse, Susan had suggested that they build a small observatory where he could set the telescopes up more permanently. She hadn't expected it to be part of the house, but after the contractor showed her the design drawings, she agreed. It actually improved the look of the roofline. The contractor built a kind of balcony into the peak of the roof with a unique retractable canvas roof that could be opened to provide a view of most of the night sky.

It was a perfect spot for an observatory. Davidson, the closest town, provided very little light pollution. It was a relatively small center and was about twenty miles to the northwest. Yard lights from surrounding farms were not visible, and Eric installed on-off controls for his own yard lights right in the observatory. However, he rarely used the yard lights. He truly liked the night.

He looked over the edge of the low wall surrounding the observatory and saw the final glow of artificial light in the farmyard flick out as Susan turned off the bedroom light. Darkness wrapped the farmhouse in its protective arms. The spruce trees and valley walls provided a black wall around three sides of the farmyard. On the fourth side, the land sloped away to the dark silvery grey of the lake.

He stared into the night, letting his eyes adjust to the darkness. In a few minutes, he would begin to see the individual spruce trees. He looked up to find the constellation, Orion. Whenever it was in the night sky, he would begin his observations by looking at the Orion Nebula. It was the first nebula he had ever seen. He had been using a simple four inch telescope then, and the nebula's beauty had amazed him, as it still did today.

Now, with the twenty-four inch reflector that he finished making a couple of months ago, it seemed like he could reach out and touch Orion. He had made at least two adjustments to keep the nebula centered in the mirror as it moved slowly across the sky when he heard a loud metallic snap. Raleigh, the big Shepherd-cross, let out a couple of loud barks. It was quiet for a few seconds then there was a long low squeak.

The gate, Eric thought. He grabbed his binoculars, popped his head over the balcony wall and focused on the gate. The light-gathering ability of the binoculars and the time in the darkness allowed him to see quite well. There were two men crouching by the gate and a third in an SUV. One of the men by the gate carried what appeared to be a large bolt cutter and was slowly pushing the gate open. Each time the gate let out a squeak he stopped and began moving it more slowly. The other dark shape held a—what was it, another bolt cutter. "Damn, they have Uzis," Eric said to himself.

He dashed down the narrow stairs and into the master bedroom. "Susan." He shook her awake.

"What?"

"Shhh," he said. "Don't turn on the lights. There are guys with guns at the gate. They must be after Robby and Joleen. Follow me." He led her to the gun rack in a small closet in the hall. He pulled two twelve-gauge shotguns from the rack and handed them to Susan. He grabbed a couple of boxes of shells and led her to the head of the stairs. "Lay down here and blast anyone who tries to come up the stairs. Load up both guns so you don't run out of ammunition."

Susan's hobby was skeet shooting. She was number one at the Davidson Gun Club, so Eric knew she would have no problem loading the guns and protecting the stairs.

"Shoot?" she whispered.

"Yes, as soon as anyone starts up the stairs, let them have it. And keep your head down, it looks like they have machine guns." He turned and dashed back to the gun cabinet and grabbed a semi-automatic 222 and a bolt action 303. He couldn't find the ammunition by feel, so he closed the closet door and turned on the light. "Uhh," he said, realizing that the light, even though it was only a 40-watt, was going to kill his night vision for several minutes. But, he needed the right ammo. He loaded both rifles, threw the extra ammunition in a canvas bag, and flipped off the light. He blindly felt for the stairs and climbed into the observatory.

C-CAF – Saskatchewan, Canada
August 30, 2002 - 3:45 am

Roy sat in front of his computer screen gathering information about Father O'Shanigan. He muttered one unique curse after another as his computer presented each new fact and added it to a dossier titled "The Dark Priest." He entered another command. A female voice responded, "I'll be right back." The female figure on his screen exited through a doorway labeled "Data Retrieval." Roy, a science fiction buff, added his own 2001 HAL-type presence to the system, and whenever he was alone, he would activate his assistant. He also added a sexy female voice and appropriate figure to his assistant, but was having trouble animating the face, so a yellow happy-face adorned the trim body. He called her LISA—which stood for "Logical Interrelation Swan Analysis." The program used statistical techniques and fuzzy logic to identify relationships between seemingly random events. Occasionally, it would find a black swan.

The door opened, and Kurt walked into Roy's lab just as LISA reported, "Roy, probability of relationship between O'Shanigan and the CIA increased from 80.6 to 87.5 percent."

"Where the hell have you been? You're two days late," Roy said.

"Left you a message."

"Sure. 'Some trouble, I'll be late.' Great message, and by the way, you look like the walking dead."

"Thanks for the compliment. What did LISA say about O'Shanigan and the CIA?"

"A lot. If I didn't know LISA's capabilities, I wouldn't believe it. But it's 3:45 am, and as I said, you look like a zombie or something. Go have a shower, and I will heat up a couple of frozen pizzas. We can trade info over pizza and coke."

Kurt paused like he was about to protest, then nodded and wandered off to the showers. C-CAF was fully equipped with living quarters and a well-stocked kitchen. You could spend several weeks there without the need to leave the facility. Kurt arrived in the kitchen just as Roy was pulling the pizzas out of the oven. Kurt grabbed a couple of cokes from a fridge and sat down at one of several empty tables. There was nobody else around since the place basically ran itself.

Roy brought the pizzas over. "Pepperoni or pepperoni, sir?"

"I think I'll have a pepperoni if it wouldn't be too much trouble."

"I'll see what I can do," Roy said, as he plopped the pizzas on the table.

"I think I will complain to the management. Your serving style leaves something to be desired, and you need a shave."

"Won't do you any good, government owns the place," Roy said.

Roy picked up a piece of pizza, and said, "So, where the hell were you?"

Kurt told his story, the call to Joleen, the explosion, and the hurried trip to Ferndale. He finished with the police's assertions that the explosion was a car bomb, not an accident.

Roy listened to each point without question, but when he heard about the car bomb, he couldn't hold back. "And you think this Father O'Shanigan might have something to do with it?"

"I don't know, Roy, it seems highly improbable. But, it could be one of your black swan events, I guess."

"Anything else before I start? Roy asked.

"Well...I brought Joleen and Robby back with me."

"They're here?" Roy said.

"No, I left them at my brother's farm. They have no place to stay. We can't start to repair the house until the police finish their investigation. Even then, it will take a couple of weeks to fix things up. At Eric's, they're only a couple of hours away. Once the police are through, Joleen and I can go back and organize the repairs while Robby stays on the farm."

"You think they're safe there?"

"Why not? How would anyone know where they are? Why...don't you think they'll be safe there?"

"I'm not sure. LISA is starting to turn up a lot of strange stuff. The probability of some of it being linked to your Father O'Shanigan is increasing as the analysis progresses. Nothing solid yet, but perhaps, they'd be safer here."

"Here? At C-CAF?"

Roy recognized the concern showing in Kurt's eyes. "Yah, why not, we have lots of room."

"No, I don't think that's necessary. Besides, that could get our asses booted out of here, and we need LISA's help on this. It's bad enough that we are using her on this without authorization. Now, tell me what you have on O'Shanigan so far."

"Okay, over in the lounge area—in the soft chairs, this could take a while."

Sigurdson Farm - Saskatchewan, Canada
August 30, 2002 - 4:15 am

Eric grabbed the binoculars and focused on the gate. It was fully open, but only one man was standing there. He was facing the farmhouse. Where were the other guys?

Then Eric saw a red flash, it was brake lights. Their SUV was coasting downhill toward the farmhouse without lights and they needed to brake. Not too professional, they could have used the emergency brake. Probably overconfident, don't think anyone is watching. He scanned the farmyard looking for the third man. Back in the SUV, he hoped, but Eric could only make out the driver through the tinted windows.

Raleigh barked and then charged out of the barn toward the gate, growling. The man by the gate turned and lifted his weapon. Phtt, phtt, phtt—phtt, phtt, phtt. There was a yelp from Raleigh, then nothing.

"Silencers, bastards—Raleigh—you bastards will pay for that," he whispered.

The dark SUV stopped in front of the house.

No brake lights—must be using the emergency brake this time, Eric thought. Bastards are looking more professional all the time. Silencers, and who knows what else.

He was beginning to worry about Susan and the third intruder. The guy who shot Raleigh was still at the gate. Where was the other guy?

Eric heard Susan shout from the hall below. "Stop where you are."

Then, phtt, phtt, phtt—phtt, phtt, phtt from the silenced guns, and BLAM, from the shotgun.

A distinctive "Uuuug" of a male voice.

Another BLAM, from the shotgun.

"Get me out of here, I'm hit."

Good for you, Susan, Eric thought, as he poked the 222 rifle over the balcony. He flipped on the yards light and took three quick shots at the man at the gate. Eric was accurate and his target fell to the ground, got to his knees and crawled to the ditch. Eric fired two more shots at the SUV as it spun around to face away from the house. The enemy was clearly surprised by the lights and worried that Eric controlled the high ground. But, it didn't take them long to recover.

The window of the SUV opened a couple of inches, a barrel poked out. Phtt, phtt, phtt—phtt, phtt, phtt. Wood splinters flew up around Eric. He dove for the floor. Phtt, phtt, phtt—phtt, phtt, phtt. The yard light went out.

"Damn," he shouted, as he poked his head up.

He could just see the SUV as it backed up and stopped in front of the porch. A man jumped out the far side and crouched behind the SUV. Eric squeezed off a couple of shots. "Stop him," the crouched figure shouted.

Phtt, phtt, phtt—phtt, phtt, phtt. More splinters.

Eric ducked, waited a second, and poked his head up. He could make out a man being dragged around the back of the SUV. "Hurry," one of the assailants said.

Eric took aim. Click. "Damn, empty." He reached for the 303. He shoved it over the edge of the balcony just as the lights on the SUV went on, and it started to spin out back toward the gate. Phtt, phtt, phtt—phtt, phtt, phtt— phtt, phtt, phtt. He ducked. They were trying to keep him down while they escaped. He popped up. They were at the gate and the wounded assailant in the ditch crawled into the SUV. Eric got off one shot before they were out of sight behind the trees. He had no idea if he hit the SUV or not. "Susan," he shouted down the stairway. "Are you all right?"

"I'm okay, I'm going to check and see if everyone else is okay."

Screams were coming from the bedrooms below.

He took another look over the edge of the balcony to see if the SUV was gone. It flew over the lip of the valley and disappeared. Eric smiled triumphantly, then just as quickly, the smile faded. He realized it was just luck that he was up looking at the stars and heard the lock being cut.

By the time he got down the stair, Susan was with Robby and Joleen. No one was hurt, at least physically. Joleen, on the other hand, was weeping uncontrollably, an emotional wreck.

"Susan, you call the RCMP. I'll call Kurt."

C-CAF – Saskatchewan, Canada
August 30, 2002 - 4:30 am

As they walked over to the soft chairs, Roy realized Kurt had not eaten any of his pizza. "I think it's time for me to do the talking. I'm sure you're hungry," Roy said. "How about some rum with that coke?"

"Yah, I could use that, but what about O'Shanigan?"

"What do you know about the Dead Sea scrolls?" Roy said.

"Not very much. Why?"

Roy pulled a bottle of Captain Morgan dark rum from a shelf behind a small bar. "Dark, I presume." He held the bottle up.

Kurt nodded.

"Well, your Father O'Shanigan is a bit of an expert in the area. He graduated from Georgetown with a doctorate in Divinity. Apparently, his field of specialization was ancient Hebrew and Aramaic. He has a number of papers on record at the university, some of them on the interpretation of the Dead Sea scrolls. His work was well-received, and quite a number of other people reference those papers as authoritative works, at least according to LISA. But here's the anomaly, he finished his doctoral work and went off to work with the École Biblique in Paris, but then, he never published anything else."

"Maybe he lost interest," Kurt said.

"No, LISA found some fairly recent news clipping stating that the Jordanian government gave a team headed by O'Shanigan permission to use some specialized type of ground-penetrating radar to search archeological sites for more scrolls. Your good Father O'Shanigan is an expert in the operation of the equipment. He apparently spent a year on site at the University of Pennsylvania working with a group of graduate students on the device. The Jesuits have a patent on it."

"Jesuits?" Kurt said.

"Yep."

"Well, that explains how O'Shanigan could interpret the readings Major Wilkinson was taking over the dunes," Kurt said.

"Who's Major Wilkinson? Roy said.

"I'll explain later, but O'Shanigan, he's involved with the Dead Sea Scrolls?" Kurt said.

"Yep, up to his eyeballs, and the whole thing has been rather clandestine. Lots of activity, but most of it behind closed doors. Not much of substance published since the scrolls were discovered in 1946-47."

"They were discovered in 1946," Kurt said. "Wow, and nothing much has been published?"

"Yah, it looks like some sort of cover-up if you ask me. But there's much more." Roy stopped to finish his last piece of pizza and take a swig of his rum and coke.

Kurt still hadn't started his pizza.

"Thought you were hungry?" Roy said.

Kurt looked down, shrugged, picked up a piece and stuffed it in his mouth. "More," he said, his mouth stuffed with pizza.

"One piece at a time. One piece at a time." Roy grinned.

"No, you turkey, I mean more about O'Shanigan."

Roy just sat there with a grin. "Eat your pizza."

Kurt complied. They sat quietly for about fifteen minutes while Kurt finished his pizza.

"Good," Roy said, and held up the rum bottle. "A top-up?"

Kurt nodded, and Roy plodded off to the fridge for a couple more cokes. He returned, threw Kurt a can of coke, and began.

"Before I get to O'Shanigan, let me finish up what LISA has so far on the scrolls.

"The original scrolls were discovered near Qumran at the north end of the Dead Sea. Legend has it they were discovered in a cave by a Bedouin shepherd-boy looking for a lost lamb. I doubt that. Most of the caves were high up on a cliff wall, and it seems unlikely a lamb could find its way up a cliff. He was probably goofing off and made up the lamb story to cover his ass."

Roy saw Kurt's impatient look and realized he better stick with the facts.

"Anyway, over a period of time, it appears that maybe a thousand scrolls were discovered. Nobody knows for sure since a black market quickly developed, and private collectors squirreled away many of them, or at least their fragments. LISA even found advertisements in the Wall Street Journal in the mid-fifties for what appeared to be portions of the scrolls."

"Didn't the government get involved and protect them?" Kurt said. "They must have known this was a great archeological discovery."

"I'm not sure. I asked LISA to detail the political set-up at the time. In 1947, the area was part of the British Mandate of Palestine. Of course, the British bureaucracies looked after things like this wherever they ruled. At that time, any discovery was turned over to the Antiquities Department and stored in the Rockefeller Museum."

"Rockefeller?" Kurt said.

"Yep, I guess they put their oil monopoly money to some good, and some of the scrolls actually ended up there. But there are probably all kinds of vested interests that don't want them published. Take the religious communities. The Christians, for example, what could the scrolls reveal about Jesus and his life? Could it upset long-standing dogma? The Jews—could it upset Rabbinic teaching? And countries—what would the scrolls say about ancient Palestine? What potential impact would that have on the present-day boundaries of Israel and Jordan, let alone the formation of a new Palestinian state? That could certainly pique the CIA's interest."

"Wow," Kurt said, as he exhaled. He had apparently been holding his breath as Roy rattled off the list of potential villains. "So, O'Shanigan fits in with the religious interests, right?"

Roy shrugged. "That's the most likely conclusion."

Chapter 21 - The Signal

C-CAF - Saskatchewan, Canada
August 30, 2002 - 4:40 am

Kurt's cell phone burst to life with the William Tell Overture.

"The Lone Ranger rides again," Roy said, with a chuckle.

Kurt dashed across the room to answer his phone before the message system answered. "Kurt Sigurdson, here," he mumbled, through his mouthful of pizza. "Oh, hi Eric—what? Anyone hurt? Susan shot him?"

Roy was on his feet, eyes wide, looking to Kurt for an explanation. "Someone attacked the farm. Susan shot one of the attackers, but he got away." Kurt held his hand up, signaling Roy to wait while he got more information.

"Eric, none of you were hurt, right—yah, I imagine Joleen has gone off the deep end, but none of you were physically hurt…? Good. How in the hell did you see them coming…? That was lucky as hell. What about the police…? Good, I'll leave right away. I should be there in a couple of hours…okay, keep an eye out in case they come back. Bye."

"What in the hell was that?" Roy said. "Did I hear right? The farm, Robby, and Joleen were attacked?"

"You heard right, and I'm sure it's got something to do with goddamn O'Shanigan."

Kurt proceeded to fill Roy in on what he knew from talking to Eric.

"I'm going back to the farm," Kurt said.

"Not without me. You're like a zombie. You'd be in the ditch before you made it half way there."

Kurt nodded.

"Have you any idea what you are going to do when we get there?"

Kurt thought for a while. "No, not really. I just need to get there to calm Joleen down, and look after her and Robby. I need to get them somewhere safe."

"What about here? That's two attempts that someone has made on Joleen and Robby's lives. There could be more. This place is off the grid, and if we lock her down, you'd need an A-bomb to get in. Wait here," Roy said, and then he turned and left the room without waiting for an answer.

Kurt didn't move. "What in the world have I gotten us involved in?" Kurt asked the empty room.

Roy returned with two M16 military issue rifles, two 45-magnum pistols and a duffle bag full of ammunition. "We aren't going anywhere without a little fire power. I raided the firearms locker. Let's

245

grab some chocolate bars and a few cokes, and get going."

Kurt nodded, and silently followed Roy.

When they were a few miles down the road, Roy looked at Kurt slumped in the passenger seat, starring down the road.

"You look terrible. You need to get some sleep."

"Can't. Not yet. I have to figure out what's going on."

"I'd like to help, but ever since you came back from holidays, you've been holding something back. You know, I can't help if I don't know what you're up to."

Kurt stared forward for a few minutes.

"Okay, but you're sworn to secrecy. You probably guessed, it started while I was on vacation with Robby."

Paris, France
August 30, 2002 - 11:00 am

Rosa woke Terry just as CLV-1 was beginning its approach to Paris. They landed and went directly to a private gate.

It must have cost a bundle to get a landing slot in this airport, Terry thought, as he left the plane.

It took only moments to clear immigration and customs. Father Richards met him at his gate and escorted him to where Jennie was to pick them up. "The limo is in the shop and Jennie is driving the van; she will meet us here," Father Richards said.

She never showed up, and now, Terry waited with his luggage while Father Richards was on a mission to find Jennie. Terry watched the activity around him. It seemed like the culture in Europe had changed over the years. No one seemed willing to serve, even if they were paid well. They all seemed to believe it was beneath them. This, he thought, was in sharp contrast to the hospitality industry in the U.S.A., especially the south. Whether they meant it or not, they always smiled and gave you a "You all come back now." when you left.

Father Richards returned with Jennie.

"She was waiting at the wrong place," Father Richards said. "She doesn't have a cell phone so when she couldn't find us, she parked the van and came looking for us. It's too far to carry the luggage so we'll go get the van."

Terry nodded.

Terry positioned himself against a pole with the luggage piled in front of him and retrieved a disposable cell phone from his briefcase. He had a few private calls to make.

Gravel Road – Saskatchewan
August 30, 2002 - 6:00 am

Roy sped down the gravel back-road that was the shortest route between C-CALF and the farm. Kurt sipped on a coke.

"How about finishing that explanation," Roy said.

"Oh, yah. Well, we were out on the Algodones

dunes. It was our last night. We were going to explore the Old Plank Road the next day, and then head to Disneyland. Robby was exploring the dunes behind our camp. It wasn't dark yet, so I just let him explore. You know how Joleen is? He hardly gets to do anything on his own."

Roy nodded.

"Anyway, he wasn't gone for very long when I heard a cry for help. I followed his trail up a dune and fell down the other side. He was down a hole. I thought it was a mine or a well—"

"Whoa," Roy said, as he slammed on the breaks and swerved. "Hold the story. Someone rolled their truck."

He stopped and backed up so that the headlights illuminated the wreck, flipped on his four-way flashers, and jumped out. Kurt followed. There was nobody in or around the vehicle. The air bags had gone off, but the big red and black Yukon SUV wasn't badly damaged.

"Looks like it just rolled on its side. From the skid marks it looks like they caught that ridge of gravel on the right, started into the ditch, tried to pull back at full speed and rolled—common mistake. But, why in the hell would they just leave it here, sticking out onto the road? Someone could easily smack into it. We almost did."

Kurt walked to the back of the SUV. "It's a Budget rental from the Saskatoon airport. Damn, I've seen this truck before. I remember the odd red and black two-tone color. I thought it was rather ugly when I first saw it behind me in the rental exit at the airport. I saw it again when I stopped at my apartment, and then at Davidson on the way to the farm."

"Do you think it was following you?"

"It fits. What's the likelihood of someone being in all those places and ending up on this back road? Isn't this another one of your black swan events?"

"Yep," Roy said. "Did you see them following you on this road after you dropped off Robby and Joleen?"

"I saw headlights behind me in the distance for a while, and then they disappeared. I didn't think anything about it at the time. It could have easily been a farmer turning off to his yard. But, where are the occupants now?"

"I don't know, but we can't leave this truck like this. Someone is sure to hit it. We will have to stay here until we can get a tow truck or something. Check your cell. Do you have coverage?"

"Yah, I have a strong signal."

"Okay, call the RCMP and see if this is already reported, and how long it will take them to get here."

"No way. We aren't staying here. We're going to get Robby and Joleen."

"Kurt, we can't leave this thing sticking out onto the road. Somebody might hit it"

"Then we'll push it into the ditch and tell the RCMP where to find it."

Back on the road, Kurt called the RCMP and explained what they had done and where to find the SUV. After he assured them that there were no injuries and the SUV was of no danger to anyone else, they took his number, and he hung up.

"They hadn't heard anything about the accident. I think that confirms our suspicions about whoever was in the vehicle. They didn't want to answer any questions, so they abandoned the car. You want to bet that a farmer near here is missing a vehicle, and we won't be able to trace whoever rented this ugly black and red unit?"

About twenty kilometers down the road, Roy looked over at Kurt. "You awake?" he whispered.

"Yah."

"Feel like finishing the story?"

"Huh? Oh, yah, right."

Kurt described the strange things that happened after he found Robby in the hole at the base of the dune. The strange lighting, the odd-looking markings on the walls, the way the sand seemed to float up when Robby touched one of the figures on the wall, the ladder that appeared, and the door that slid shut when Robby climbed out.

Then Kurt slumped back in his seat and closed his eyes. "So Roy, what do you think it is?"

"Doesn't sound like any mine or well I've ever seen. If I were a UFO nut, I'd say it was a spaceship, but I expect it is actually some U.S. military installation."

Kurt smiled. "Well, get out your UFO t-shirt and tinfoil hat."

"You got to be kiddin'; you think it's some kind of space craft. Could it be some kind of U.S. experimental craft?"

"No, from the way everyone has reacted this

certainly isn't U.S. military, and the reaction of the sand…well, it certainly doesn't appear to be earthly technology."

Roy thought about what Kurt told him. He said nothing for several minutes while he tried to make sense out of what he'd been told. They were just turning onto the pavement of Highway 11, which leads from Saskatoon in the north through Davidson, to Regina in the south, when Roy said, "When did you and Robby turn that spaceship on?"

"It was July 31, about eight pm. Why?"

"Six-E-Q-U-J five", Roy said.

"What's that?"

"The WOW, that's what," Roy shouted.

Montreal, Quebec, Canada
August 30, 2002 - 8:30 am

The phone rang. Rahim, the Greek, rolled over and struggled to find the receiver. "Hello…hello," he said.

"Report," a voice on the phone said.

"Who is this?" Rahim said

"Report," the voice said again.

Rahim recognized the voice; it was the priest. He sat up.

"I'm sorry, I must have fallen asleep."

There was no response.

"We missed the boy at his house in Ferndale," Rahim said.

"I am aware of that. Where is he now?"

"At a farm in Saskatchewan. We have mounted an operation." Rahim checked his watch. "It should be underway now. I will call you as soon as it is done."

"No, I must dispose of this cell phone. I have had it too long. Once I get a new one, I will call and give you a new number. No mistakes this time."

"No, no, we will complete the mission this time."

The line went dead. Rahim checked his watch.

"Soon," he muttered.

Near the Sigurdson farm – Saskatchewan
August 30, 2002 - 6:30 am

"So, what's a WOW?" Kurt said.

"You know about SETI, right," Roy said.

"Sure, the Search for Extraterrestrial Intelligence, I have my home computer tied into the Planetary Societies network; it provides idle computer time to process signals. So, how does that relate?" Kurt said.

"Well, back in 1977 at Ohio State, Jerry Ehman wrote WOW on a print-out of a signal that appeared to be from an extraterrestrial source. They have searched that area of the sky ever since and never detected a repeat. But guess what?" Roy said.

Kurt shrugged and looked at Roy. "Are you just going to sit there with that silly grin or are you going to share?"

"Okay, on July 31, at 7:47 pm Pacific time, SETI picked up an exact repeat of that WOW. Washington's working on convincing the SETI scientists that the signal originated from a military satellite, but I think we might know better."

Kurt shook his head. "Roy, are you sure of this?"

"You bet. I'm sure there was a WOW. I didn't pay a lot of attention at the time. You know, most of these things turn out to be explainable signals of earth origin. I'll follow up on this once I get back to C-CAF. In the meantime, just think about what it could mean. That thing you and Robby found might be connected to that communication."

"Okay, Roy, let's say your wild hypothesis is correct. What about O'Shanigan?"

"Right, so how did this Father O'Shanigan get involved?" Roy said.

"Okay, here's how things unfolded. Robby and I stayed in the camp overnight. The next morning I took my hand-held GPS, and we walked back to the opening Robby discovered. From what you and I know now, maybe we should call it a hatch. Sand almost covered it, but you could still see its smooth surface. If you didn't know better, you'd say it was just smooth rock under the sand. I made a note of the exact location from the GPS, went back to the camp, packed up and left.

"I contacted Walker and told him the story. He called me back and told me to call a Major Roger Wilkinson at Edwards Air Force Base. I did. He was very cordial, but I expected that was the last I'd ever hear about it."

"Yah, but what about O'Shanigan?" Roy said.

"Patience, I'll get to him," Kurt said. "Remember the t-shirt!"

Roy looked at him and chuckled. His favorite t-shirt pictured two vultures sitting on a branch. One saying, to the other "Patience, my ass, I'm going to kill something."

"Anyway, I decided that it would be best if we didn't tell Joleen about our little discovery, and on our way home from Disneyland I convinced Robby that we should keep it a secret. That was a mistake. Before I got back home, Joleen was on the phone. She'd taken Robby to her parish priest, a Father James, and Robby told him about falling in the hole. Father James told Robby he shouldn't keep secrets from his mother so Robby told her. She was almost hysterical and I couldn't reason with her. She said she might not let me see Robby any more.

"Then just after I returned to my apartment in Saskatoon I got a call from Walker. He sent me down to Edwards to help Major Wilkinson analyze the discovery. I was told not to tell anyone, not even you. We were set to go back to the Algodones Dunes when Washington told us to hold off."

"Washington? How'd they get involved?" Roy said. "Did someone report the discovery to Washington based on the word of a Canadian intelligence officer? I doubt it—they would need to check it out themselves, first."

"Right, Roger and I were about to do that when Washington called us off. We had to wait for O'Shanigan," Kurt said.

"Man, this O'Shanigan is connected pretty high up. I'm going to have to be careful researching him."

"Right. Well, to finish up the story, Roger,

O'Shanigan and I conducted an aerial survey with some kind of magnetometer instrument."

"You mean one of those units you tow behind a plane."

"Yah, it was something like that."

"Well, that wouldn't find anything. It wouldn't be sensitive enough," Roy said.

"That's what I thought, but Roger assured me this was some new stuff the military developed to detect underground caverns. You know, terrorist hiding spots, secret labs and weapons storage, stuff like that. Anyway, we couldn't seem to find anything, and we were reeling in the unit when we got a hit. It showed the ship was about half a mile wide or long."

Roy let out a low whistle.

"Roger and I wanted to make more runs to confirm this, but O'Shanigan would have none of it."

"O'Shanigan was in command?" Roy said.

"U-huh, I forgot to mention that. The plot thickens, eh? Anyway, that's pretty well it. You know the rest. I was on my way back when the explosion went off at Joleen's, and now here we are heading to my brother's, where he's just come through a firefight. What the hell is going on?"

"Watch out, Roy, the turn to the farm is coming up."

Chapter 22 - Safe Haven

Sigurdson Farm - Saskatchewan
August 30, 2002 - 7:15 am

As they approached the farm, an RCMP officer stopped them. The RCMP had the area sealed off. After they explained who they were, the officer allowed them to follow a narrow roped-off path to the farmhouse. Susan had convinced Joleen to take a sedative, so she was relatively calm when Roy and Kurt arrived. Robby had gone back to bed. Eric and Susan were going over the happenings one more time with a senior officer. Roy and Kurt sat down and listened. It was an astonishing story, several assailants with machine guns held off by his brother and sister-in-law. Kurt could see the bloody trail left by the guy Susan hit; the stairway was riddled with bullet holes. It was a miracle no one in his family was hurt.

Eric looked at Kurt. "The bastards killed

Raleigh." A tear ran down his face, and he walked over and hugged Kurt. "What have you gotten us into?"

The RCMP crime scene team finished their work in the house and let Susan reclaim the kitchen. Soon, the smell of coffee and bacon brought everyone to the kitchen table.

At the table, Roy took over. He was sure Robby was the key, and whoever the assailants were, they would make another attempt on Robby's life. "We need to get him to a safe place, and quickly, before those guys regroup and launch another attack. Eric and Susan, you should come, too."

No, we have farm animals to look after. We can't just leave. Anyway, we can protect ourselves," Eric said.

Roy looked around. "Yah, we can see that, but how long will the farmhouse last? Any more bullet holes and it'll fall over."

"We're staying," Susan said.

"Okay, we have some pull," Roy said. "We can get an RCMP officer or two set up here for a while. If those guys don't come back soon, they won't likely come back."

Roy, Kurt, Joleen and Robby left for C-CAF about 6:00 pm. They followed the same route back, but this time, as Roy drove, Kurt kept a constant watch out the rear window to see if they were being followed. Roy pulled over in a hidden driveway occasionally, and waited to see if anyone was following at a distance. He even made a couple of detours and circled back. When they were sure they weren't being followed, Roy headed for C-CAF at high speed.

"We might as well die at the hand of the gunmen as in a car wreck," Joleen said.

Roy ignored her, and they made it to C-CAF by nightfall.

C-CAF - the following morning
August 31 2002 - 6:00 am

"Dad. Dad, look," Robby shouted as Kurt wandered into the kitchen area bleary eyed. It was 6:00 am and Robby sat in front of a large computer screen with what appeared to be spaceships and laser beams flitting across the screen.

Roy sat at a small table eating some cold pizza. He looked up, glanced at Robby, and then winked at Kurt. "I developed an interface to a little multi-player game so LISA can provide the opposition. It's a lot better than the weak opposition the game provides in single player mode. I've set LISA up to take it easy on him. He's pretty good though."

Kurt stared at Robby for a moment, and then said, "Great use of government resources."

"Ah, LISA could handle a couple of thousand of those games and not even break into a sweat," Roy said.

"Yah, I know. I'm beginning to think she's taken over as your love interest. If you ever get her a female face instead of that yellow happy-face, I'm sure you'll marry her." He opened the fridge. "Any

258

more of that pizza?"

"No, Robby and I cleaned it up, but you could whip up a new one in no time."

"Nah, I better have some real breakfast. When did you and Robby get up?"

"Never been to bed. Just caught a few winks here," Roy said, as if he'd slept for a week.

"Ah shi…ah, don't tell Joleen, or you'll be in deep you know what."

"Robby, why don't you head off to bed," Kurt said. "If your Mom finds out you haven't been to bed…well, you know what will happen."

"Just hit ShiftAlt, and the game will pause until you come back," Roy said.

Robby wandered off to bed, and Kurt prepared some oatmeal. "What the hell were you thinking? You know Joleen. When I left Robby with you last night, I thought you were going to send him to bed."

"I did, but he came out after about 30 minutes saying he couldn't sleep. He sat beside me at the terminal for a while, pumping me with questions about LISA, so I thought I'd let him challenge her until he got tired. And ah, well, you know how it is. Time just zipped."

The microwave dinged.

"Better tend to your gruel," Roy said.

"And you, I'm sure you didn't stay up all night just to watch Robby and LISA battle it out. What were you and LISA up to?"

"Following up on the WOW."

Kurt looked up from his bowl of oatmeal, a confused look on his face. "What?"

"Shit, Kurt, all this activity must have addled your brain. You're memory is usually better than this. Just fill you're trap with some of that gray gruel you like to eat, keep quiet, and I will reboot that brain of yours."

Kurt nodded and began to eat. Roy was right. The last few days had knocked him off the rails. Not much of a spy when it came to action involving people you really care about. They told him that in his training, but until now, it was just words. His brother and wife reacted like agents in the movies during the action at the farm. And it was his fault they needed to do that. He never considered that he'd be followed. It was only luck that some of his pursuers rolled their SUV or they would know about this place, too.

"Okay," Roy said. "As I explained last night, SETI, the Search for Extraterrestrial Intelligence, detected a signal from space that they thought might be from a distant civilization, the original WOW. The folks at the Planetary Society and others have analyzed that signal to death. They revisited that area of the sky numerous times but never received another signal. Well, it turns out that at 7:56 pm on July 31, the approximate time you and Robby were poking around your little spacecraft, the SETI folks detected another signal from that region of space. It was longer, contained some of the same code, but a whole bunch more. A whole group of SETI scientists just about peed their collective pants."

"Wow," Kurt muttered through his oatmeal.

"WOW, is right; and ever since, the government

and military have been telling the SETI community that the signal was from a military satellite. Not a lot of takers though, since it's hard to believe that there were satellites in the same spot in 2002, and in 1977, and that a portion of their transmissions would be identical. The only fly in the ointment is that the signal was extremely powerful. That means the signal originated from near earth, so the SETI folks are losing interest.

"So they are giving up?" Kurt said.

"Maybe, but in addition to playing games with Robby, I put LISA on the case. She's come up with some interesting coincidences. At the same time as the signal was generated, there was a localized shutdown of power and internet communications at the UCLA campus. Then the next day, there is a post on a blog asking if anyone had any strange happenings with Navajo artifacts at about 8:00 pm on the 31st. The blogger mentions a pyramid with a little ball on top. There was a picture on the blog. I printed it out. Take a look."

"What is it? Is there a connection?"

"I don't know. That's all LISA has so far. The connection to our little mess may be just a coincidence. But, you know, LISA and I don't believe in coincidences. Anyway, she's churning away on the possibilities. I'll let her work while I take a shower."

About 7:30 am, Joleen wandered into the lounge, blinking and rubbing her eyes. "Where's Robby?"

Kurt looked up from the computer screen. "He's sleeping."

"Good, when did he get to bed?"

"Oh...shortly after you I think. You want something to eat? There's lots of stuff in the pantry. I can whip up some waffles for you."

"No, I'll just have coffee for now. I'll eat when Robby gets up."

That could be a while, Kurt thought.

She got her coffee and plopped herself down in a recliner. She looked quite haggard. Her hair was tousled, what was left of her makeup was smeared, her clothes were dirty. She hadn't looked this depressed since her dad died.

"Joleen, I'll make you some breakfast. You need to eat. No telling when Robby gets up."

Joleen didn't reply.

Kurt went to the kitchen and whipped up some waffles. "Come on. We have real maple syrup." He held up the can, and then poured some on the waffles. "I've fixed a couple for you."

"Mmmmm. That's good." She ate quietly for a while. "Kurt, how long do we have to stay here? You know Robby is missing school. You and your spy stuff." She started to cry.

Kurt waited until the crying stopped. "What do you know about Father O'Shanigan?"

"Why? How do you know about him?" Joleen

said.

"Well, he was with me last week, following up on the thing Robby and I found."

"He was with you?"

"I know it sounds crazy, but yes, he was not only with me, but he was in charge of a U.S. military operation. I'm trying find out more about him. Maybe he's connected with the explosion at your house or the attack at the farm."

"You think a priest is involved in those attacks? That's crazy."

"Well, I think he's not your average priest. What can you tell me about him?"

"Not much, Father James called and asked if I would speak to a Father O'Shanigan. I said I would and then a couple of days later Father O'Shanigan called"

"What did he want?" Kurt said.

She paused for a while. "He asked a lot of questions about Robby. He wanted to know about his hand. He asked what happened in the desert, how Robby was involved."

"What did you tell him about what we found in the desert?"

"I told him that Robby fell into this hole and lights came on. I told him Robby said that there were all kinds of lights and strange writing on the walls. That interested him. He said he wanted to come and meet with Robby sometime, and that he would arrange it through Father James. That's all I told him. Why would he want to hurt us?"

"I don't know. I'm not sure he does; that's why

I'm checking up on him."

Joleen finished her waffle in silence. She looked down at her clothes. "I'm filthy. Do you have a washing machine in this hideaway?"

"Yah, right at the end of the hall, past the bathrooms. There's a washer and dryer, even an iron and ironing board."

*****

Roy returned a little after 8:30 am and selected his favorite recliner. "I feel a lot better now. Has LISA come up with anything?"

"A lot of stuff is up on the screen, but I'm was making waffles for Joleen so—"

"Burrrrring, buring—burrrrring, buring." The phone beside Kurt interrupted with a distinctive ring letting them know the call was routed through the cover site in Ottawa, and was for Roy. Roy held his finger to his lips signaling Kurt to remain silent, and said, "Push the speaker button."

"Hello, Roy Matacowski here."

"Hello there, my Mister Big Bang." Kurt looked at Roy and raised his eyebrows.

Roy waved and mouthed. "Later."

"Lisa, I'm glad you called back. I need…"

"I don't give a damn about your needs, you horny old man. You don't call me for three weeks, and then you call asking me about one of my hot, young, grad students."

"She's your student?" Roy said.

"You're trying to tell me, you didn't know?" Lisa laughed. "Then, why did you call me?"

Roy squirmed in his chair. Kurt smiled. Let's see him get out of this.

"I had LI…ah, I had my…" Roy walked over and picked up the phone and cut off the speaker. "I had my computer here doing some research, and it picked up her blog. She didn't leave an email address, and I didn't want to contact her publicly on the blog—"

"No, her picture wasn't on the blog, just her name, Amy Philips-Moore."

Roy looked at Kurt and shrugged. "Lisa, I promise I will call more often, but I really need to talk to her."

Kurt could see Roy was struggling.

"Well, my computer dug up her name but couldn't come up with a phone number or address. Her blog came out of UCLA, so I thought you might know her. It was just a coincidence that she was a student in your department. Can you get her to call me…no, I think this is important enough that I meet with her. I'll come down. I'll let you know as soon as I get a flight. We can have dinner, and you can chaperone me while I talk with her…."

"Great, I'll get back to you. You see if you can find Amy and get a meeting organized. Bye."

"Trouble with Lisa, eh? I think I know where your computer's name came from. You've been holding out on me. Who is this Lisa, and how long have you known her?"

Roy didn't answer. He walked over to a keyboard

265

and typed in instructions for LISA to get his reservations.

"Can I fill you in later? I need to get packed. LISA will pick the fastest route, either through Calgary or Saskatoon. She'll work in the driving time. You know, this is a terrific place except if you're suddenly a field agent, getting in and out is hell. You can keep an eye on the analysis of the WOW stuff."

"Okay, and I'll do some more follow up on O'Shanigan and his connections."

Roy returned a few minutes later with a carry-on bag.

"Anything interesting?" Roy said.

"Not sure. LISA keeps spouting about correlations, but they make no sense to me. I'm trying to find out more about O'Shanigan. Are you off?"

"Yep, L.A. via Saskatoon. See you in a couple of days." Roy looked over his shoulder as he walked to the exit. "Let me know if LISA gives us any leads."

"The exact words I was going to say to you."

Chapter 23 - Brothers of the First Apostle

Institute of Biblical Archeology – Paris
August 31, 2002 - 4:00 pm

Terry completed the last of his secret calls—calls to the members of the Brotherhood of the Sand. They would meet September 4, once the last member arrived in Paris. He turned off his disposable cell phone and locked it in his desk.

*****

Terry joined the Brotherhood shortly after he received that mysterious telephone call on May 15, 1989. He had just returned from a field trip to one of his Dead Sea excavations when he received the call.

"Father O'Shanigan, I am Brother Ross from the

Trappist Monastery in Lucerne. I am a Dead Sea Scroll scholar like you. I would like to meet with you."

Terry didn't know Brother Ross, and he knew all of the scholars of any significance. "Well, Brother Ross, I am not prepared to discuss my research at this time. I suggest you talk to the scholars at the École Biblique." Terry was about to classify Brother Ross as just another researcher or reporter trying to pry some information out of him. "I am sure the École Biblique will—"

"I know of the gold scroll," Brother Ross said.

"What?"

"I know about the gold scroll."

How could that be? The published work on the copper scroll only mentioned the possibility of another scroll. No one knew of Terry's discovery of the silver scroll, and its description of a gold scroll.

Terry agreed to meet with him.

Brother Ross said that he would arrange for a car to pick Terry up. Terry was surprised. A monk with money? It didn't seem right. He was more surprised when the car turned out to be a limo with completely opaque rear windows. You could see neither in nor out. They drove to an underground garage where he was transferred to a windowless Beauvais Laundries van. After another half hour of driving around, the van stopped, and someone got in. He was separated from Terry by a large rack containing towels and other linens, so only his shoes were visible to Terry.

He began. "I am sorry I can not reveal my true identity to you unless you agree to our proposal."

Our proposal, Terry thought, this brother is not acting alone.

He continued. "I am a follower of the First Apostle. Do you know of us?"

"The…the Brotherhood of the Sand?"

"Ah, so you did recover the silver scroll in your diggings at Ein Gedi. We suspected something when you appeared there suddenly, and began digging at such an unusual location. Was it the Copper Scroll that led you to the site?"

Terry hesitated. He shouldn't have mentioned the Brotherhood. No, he would say no more, he would let his host do the talking.

After a long pause, the brother continued. "We followed your work on the Copper Scroll for a number of years and suspected that you had decoded a portion of the scroll. When the École Biblique forced you out we monitored your work but you published nothing. The École Biblique continued restricting access to the scrolls until they were pressured into making a partial release in Chicago. But you didn't need that. You had already succeeded in finding the secrets contained in the Copper Scroll, correct?"

The brother waited for a reply, but Terry resisted. "We have an offer for you. We, the Brothers of the Sand are but six, one less than the seven in the original Christians' council. One seat on our council always remains open in honor of Stephen, the Martyr. That place shall be filled when the Master returns. While we wait, we protect the great secret and guide the world toward peace. When peace is achieved, the Master will return."

"Six, there are only six? How can you have any effect on the world? What secret do you protect?"

"One question, I will answer. The others will only be answered if you accept our proposal. The brothers are six, but the Brotherhood is six times six, six times over."

Terry tried to do the math in his head. Six to the power six. He was still working on it, when the brother said, "That's forty-six thousand six hundred and fifty-six. But each brother knows only thirteen others in the brotherhood, and would die before revealing their names. If you accept our proposal, you must be willing to do the same. You will have six days to decide. If you accept, you will become party to the secret."

"Six days…what is your proposal?"

"I am a brother of the sixth level, the highest in the order. One of us has died, and we have the responsibility of selecting a replacement. Normally, we select from the fifth level, but you present an extraordinary case. Your research and contacts could help us if you were to join us, and, on the other hand, you could do enormous damage if left to your own devices. So, we have decided to offer you the position of one of the six."

"I will need more information," Terry said.

"No more, unless you accept. And let me assure you, if you don't accept, your research will be thwarted at every turn, and if you decline and tell anyone of this meeting, you will soon be discredited. I will call you in six days."

Terry heard the van door open. "Wait," he said. The door closed and the van began moving. The brother was gone, and Terry was on his way back the way he came, the van to the basement garage, and the limo back to his office. He noted the license number as it drove off, but he suspected it was a fake.

When he checked, he found it listed as a fifteen-year-old Volkswagen, and there was no record of a Beauvais Laundries or Brother Ross at the Trappist Monastery.

C-CAF- Saskatchewan
August 31, 2002 - 10:00 am

After Roy left, Kurt sat staring at the wall. Things didn't make sense. Why were people after Robby and Joleen? How was Lisa's grad student connected to them? And O'Shanigan, how did he fit in?

LISA beeped and broke his concentration. He moved to the nearest computer screen and typed in his password.

Search 0168 - Alert 1
Unexplained power outage August 1, 2002 - 3:57 am GMT
Tower of London.
Correlation probability 52%.
Continuing search.

Search 0168 - Alert 2

271

Unexplained communications outage July 31, 2002 - 3:57 pm GMT (7:57 Pacific Time)
UCLA campus.
Correlation probability 78%.
Continuing search.

Search 0168 - Alert 3
Unexplained power outage Paris, France August 1, 2002 - 3:57 am GMT
Correlation probability 35%.
Continuing search.

What was Roy up to? An explanation would have to wait until his return from LA. In the meantime, Kurt continued his research on O'Shanigan. He hit Ctrl S. A small box appeared on the screen requesting a search number. Kurt typed in 0165. LISA responded.

Search 0165 - Summary - Terry O'Shanigan
*Born Regina, Saskatchewan //**More***
Graduated High School - Miller Composite //
More
*Undergraduate degree Bachelor of Arts // **More***
*Doctor of Divinity // **More***
Post Doctoral Studies. - The Dead Sea Scrolls //
More
*Formed the Institute of Biblical Archeology in 1989 // **More***
*Accepted $10 million in funding from Calvert Oil // **More***
Discovered new cache of ancient scrolls in 1989

// ***More***

Appointed Special Advisor to the Vatican 1992 // ***More***

Appointed to U.S. President's Special Committee // ***More***

Presented Paper entitled The Copper Scrolls at a Conference // ***More***

Appointed Special Advisor - Biblical Antiquities - London Museum // ***More***

The list continued with a number of papers and talks given on behalf of the Institute of Biblical Archeology.

Kurt clicked the ***More*** that followed each line. LISA responded with detailed information. This guy is sure well connected, Kurt thought. The line for date of birth yielded information about his family. Kurt followed the link until ***Incomplete - continuing search*** appeared. The line for high school produced a yearbook picture. How did LISA do that?

He continued looking at each line until he came to the line on the President's Special Committee. When he hit ***More,*** Lisa displayed a flashing ***Restricted - Security Clearance Alpha C Prime required - Enter ID and Security Code.***

Alpha C Prime? What the hell. There's no such security level—at least as far as I know.

He clicked on the line, and an entry box appeared. He entered his ID, and then, his security code.

LISA responded ***Access Denied***.

Damn it. This link probably showed O'Shanigan's connection to the military or CIA. He sent LISA on a plain old internet search for him, then a search of government departments. Nothing. Guess this will have to wait for Roy. He proceeded to examine the various papers that O'Shanigan had written or presented.

Paris, France
May 20, 1989 - 7:00 pm

Terry agreed to the brotherhood's request and was instructed to go to a small bookstore called La Chambre Biblique. When he arrived, the store was empty except for one man behind a desk. The man locked the door and hung a closed sign in the window. "I am Brother Oswald. Follow me, please."

Terry followed Brother Oswald down a long flight of stairs that ended at an arch covered in gold leaf. A simple beige curtain blocked the view of the room beyond. There were three hooks on each side of the arch. Four were empty. On the other two, hung beige monks' habits with sky-blue hoods. Brother Oswald silently put on a robe and motioned for Terry to do the same. Then he led Terry through the arch into the sanctuary. Four others were waiting in similar attire.

The sanctuary chamber was a hexagon with beige walls and a sky-blue dome. The only entrance was the arch through which they entered. The four brothers were standing on the points of a six-pointed star almost hidden by fine sand. What little light there was emanated from small torches behind each of the brothers. Each torch was on a short stand and was covered with a metallic hood. The light that escaped shone directly on the back of each brother's blue hood. There were two unlit torches. Brother Oswald lit the torches, and motioned for Terry to stand on one of the two unoccupied points of the star. Terry stood to the right of Brother Oswald and turned to face the center of the room.

They stood silently for several minutes, and then Brother Oswald began a chant. "May the sands of the Master protect us." As he repeated the chant, "May the sands of the Master protect us," the brother on his left joined in. Each time the chant was repeated another added his voice to the chorus. "May the sands of the Master protect us. May the sands of the Master protect us. May the sands of the Master protect us. May the sands of the Master protect us."

Terry was last and once the six completed the chant, the brothers knelt facing the center of the room. The light from the torches behind them, which were no longer blocked by their hooded figures, illuminated a large silver sphere hanging from a chain in the center of the dome. It looked like the sun shining out of a clear-blue sky. Except, this sun was different. A fine stream of white sand fell from a small hole in the bottom of the sun, and much like the sand in an hourglass, the sand formed a cone where it landed on the floor.

Brother Oswald began again. "May the sands hide the secrets of the Master until peace reigns across his world." Again the chant was repeated as each brother joined in. "May the sands hide the secrets of the

275

Master until peace reigns across his world. May the sands hide the secrets of the Master until peace reigns across his world. May the sands hide the secrets of the Master until peace reigns across his world. May the sands hide the secrets of the Master until peace reigns across his world."

Brother Oswald leaned forward and placed his hands into the sand. He chanted, "With peace let the knowledge of the Master return." Then he pulled the sand gently toward himself. The others followed and pulled some of the sand toward themselves. "With peace let the knowledge of the Master return. With peace let the knowledge of the Master return. With peace let the knowledge of the Master return. With peace let the knowledge of the Master return. With peace let the knowledge of the Master return." They sat back revealing a small pyramid, with a ball on top, sitting in the remaining sand.

Brother Oswald began to chant again. "Let the light of the Master return to guide us." He picked up the small pyramid, stood, and extinguished his torch and left the room. Each remaining brother, in turn, recited the chant, stood, extinguished his torch, and followed Brother Oswald. "Let the light of the Master return to guide us. Let the light of the Master return to guide us. Let the light of the Master return to guide us. Let the light of the Master return to guide us. Let the light of the Master return to guide us." Terry was the last to exit the sanctuary. After the brothers left the chamber they removed their robes and took the small pyramid to a windowless room on the second floor. They placed the pyramid in the center of a hexagon shaped table and took up seats facing the pyramid.

Brother Oswald sat across from Terry. "Brother Terry, the ritual you just participated in has signaled the assembly of the six since the First Apostle formed the Brotherhood. We protect the treasures of the Master and await his return. We watch the Master's light atop the pyramid for the signal that he has returned.

"The Master's light rested in a sanctuary in Nuits St Georges and remained dark for many centuries. Then in the middle of the sixteenth century, it came to life only to fall dark once again. In May 1915, it sprang to life for several days, and then once again in 1977 it came to life for a few minutes. We moved the sanctuary from Nuits St Georges, here to Paris, after the Master's Light came alive in 1977, but since then, it has remained dark.

"Now you join us, a Brother of the First Apostle, a Watcher in the Brotherhood of the Sand."

Chapter 24 - Escape from LA

Los Angeles Airport
August 31, 2002 - 4:30 pm

Lisa Cathy May Donald did not possess the kind of beauty currently gracing magazine covers, but she would certainly not go unnoticed entering a room. Her fiery red hair was cropped in a style that said she was a businesswoman but hinted at something else. Medium green eyes with a darker green border in the outer fringes of the iris highlighted an angular face with a prominent nose and mouth. Her body was trim but not extraordinary in any of the often-noted features. She had a bearing that exuded confidence, and sometimes impatience.

That impatience showed as she paced back and forth waiting for the Air Canada flight to land at LAX. The flights from Saskatoon all ended up coming into the international arrivals area, and it could take forever if a few jumbos from who knows where landed at the same time. That reminded her, she was going to have to get Roy to explain to her one more time, why an obviously high-powered computer analyst, working for the Canadian Government in Ottawa, always ended up flying to L.A. out of Calgary or Saskatoon. The last time she asked him, he gave her some kind of blather about university computing systems.

He's probably seeing some floozies in those cities. She smiled. Now, there's some jealousy showing. She had no right to expect Roy to be seeing only her. In fact, one of the things that attracted her to Roy was the lack of demands he placed on her. He did not want to possess her. The control the others tried to exercise was the reason she never married. She thought for a moment, no, there was another reason. She could never seem to find someone who could discuss things with her, as an intellectual equal. Roy was her equal, and the irreverence and wit he displayed while discrediting conventional wisdoms, delighted her. She knew he was the first man she loved, and she was not going to drive him away by trying to possess him. She would give of herself and enjoy what he freely gave to her. No less, no more.

They had met at a computer conference eighteen months ago. Roy was interested in a new processor IBM was developing, and she was there to hear a paper on using computers to decrypt ancient writings. They ended up sitting next to each other. At the end of the seminar, Lisa asked him if he understood what the computer types were trying to say. He volunteered to explain it but only over dinner. That was the first time they ended up at Toni's restaurant. They spent the evening explaining their specialties to each other, and ended the night at Lisa's. Since then they met whenever their schedules permitted

She looked up at the monitor. Flight AC1169 began blinking "LANDED."

Roy appeared. He's a little bleary eyed, she thought, as she threw her arms around him.

"How's my Mister Big Bang?" she said. They both smiled, and a matronly lady next to Roy gave Lisa the evil eye. "Come on let's get out of here." She grabbed his arm and led him through the terminal to the garage and her car. He silently obeyed. Once inside she pulled him close and gave him a long inviting kiss. "Well?" she said. "You still haven't answered my question. How's my Mister Big Bang?"

"You know, I had pretty well convinced that old lady that I was a nice guy. She sat beside me on the way down, and I was on my most gentlemanly behavior. I told her I was on my way to meet a lovely lady with a PhD in Archeology who was a professor at UCLA. Her granddaughter was planning to study Archeology at some university. She couldn't remember which one, but now that she's seen how raunchy the professors are, I'm sure she'll have her sent to a convent."

Lisa elbowed him in the stomach as she started the car.

"So, did you get a meeting set up with Amy?"

Roy said.

"Yes, I did. But, she has an evening class and won't be available until 9:30. That gives us some time for a little R&R at my place, followed by dinner at Toni's. You game?"

Roy reached over and slid his hand up her skirt.

"Enough, a simple 'yes' would suffice. Remember I have to navigate these L.A. freeways. That's hard enough without added distractions."

Roy smiled, leaned back and closed his eyes. "I could use some rest. That lovely old lady talked the whole way. She spent most of the flight describing her hometown of Rosebud, Alberta. It has a population of less than a hundred and boasts an active theater attended by people from all over the world. She's on her way to some sort of a workshop in L.A. Then, she told me all about her granddaughter, and then asked what was I doing, who was I going to see? The only thing she missed was politics and religion."

Lisa touched Roy's hand as he drifted off into a deep sleep. She let him sleep for the hour it took her to get to her house. Once inside the garage, she sat and watched him for a while. Roy wasn't obviously handsome. In fact, he was a little on the short side and carried a few too many beer and pizzas around his middle. But, she knew from the way other women reacted to him, she wasn't the only one attracted to him. She gave him a little jab in the ribs powered by this thought.

"Ouch," he said, rubbing his eyes. "What was that for?"

"For those other women."

"Huh. I haven't even looked at another woman since we met."

She giggled. "Okay, let's get you cleaned up then. I can smell that little old lady's perfume on you."

They spent an hour together in her large shower getting him 'cleaned up', and ended up entwined on the shower floor with the warm water gently caressing their skin.

"Hmmm, remind me to sit by an old lady the next time I come down," Roy whispered.

"Enough with the other women. We better get going, or we won't have time for dinner before we meet Amy."

When they were seated at the restaurant, Toni, the owner, came over to see them. "Ah, Miss Donald, so lovely to see you again. And, I see you have brought a new gentleman with you tonight."

Toni had overheard them teasing each other one evening and now he always joined in.

"Ah-ha. The truth at last. Toni, you are a gentleman. I've been hearing about other women all afternoon."

Toni gave one of his brawny laughs. "A nice bottle of Chianti, tonight?"

They agreed, and Toni wandered off chuckling. He returned in a few moments with the wine. After the ritual tasting and approval, Toni signaled for a waiter. "I recommend the Veal Scaloppini, tonight, with a delicate lemon sauce"

They both opted for Toni's recommendation.

They sipped the wine and sat enjoying each

other's company for a while, then Roy said, "Tell me about this grad student, Amy Philips-Moore."

"Well, she's a brilliant young woman. She's doing her doctorate on the early Navajo civilization. She's been quite successful in uncovering new material. On her latest field trip, she uncovered a number of new cave paintings and is working on interpreting them. But, that's not what's of interest to you. Several weeks ago, someone left me an old box labeled old Navajo stuff. There was an old diary in it. It was in Russian."

"Russian?"

"Yes, odd as it may seem, there was a representative of the tsar on an 1882 expedition to Canyon de Chelly. A lot of people were interested in archeology in those days, mainly for treasure I expect, so they financed a lot of the early expeditions. The Canyon de Chelly Expedition was extensive, but nothing was ever published."

"Where is this Canyon de Chelly?" Roy said.

"It's in eastern Arizona, a little north of Interstate 40."

"So, how did the artifacts end up in that box, any idea?"

"Well, the tsar's representative never went back to Russia. He stayed in America studying the Navajo culture and eventually started a museum."

"Where is that?" Roy said, as he cut a piece of the veal.

"It was in San Francisco. Only problem is, the museum was destroyed in the 1906 San Francisco earthquake and fire. The box of artifacts must have been saved somehow."

"Were there items in the box, other than those shown on her blog?"

"You can ask her. We should hurry; we are to meet her in forty-five minutes."

Los Angeles, California
August 31, 2002 - 9:20 pm

Lisa parked her VW Jetta in front of Amy's apartment. "Perfect timing," she said. "That's Amy getting out of that car."

They scrambled out of the Jetta and walked over to where Amy was now struggling with the security door. "Amy," Lisa called out.

Amy turned to greet them. "Oh, hi. I just got home."

Lisa made the introductions, and then Amy said, "Let's go up to my apartment. That's if we can get in." She entered her code. The door buzzed, and she gave it a tug. "Damn thing's stuck again. The building's pretty old."

That's a bit of an understatement, Roy thought. The building was a three-story walk-up. There were numerous bricks missing from its façade, and all the exposed wood could have used a coat of paint. One of the panes in the security door was covered with plywood. But, it was in no worse shape than the surrounding apartments. The whole neighborhood looked a bit seedy.

"I would like to move, but it's tough on a grad

student's income." She looked at Lisa. "And it's the only place that I could find that allows pets."

"Give it another try," Roy said. Amy keyed her code again, and the door buzzed. Roy gave it a massive tug and it opened. He looked at the lock, pulled out a small piece of metal and held it up. "Looks like someone was trying to jam it open and failed."

"Yah, people are always doing that." Amy shrugged. "Let's go up. I'm on the third floor."

Amy directed them to the stairway. "Watch your step. The nosing is loose on a couple of steps." She unlocked the door to her apartment and pushed it open. "Noodles," she called out, as she flipped on the light.

She screamed.

Noodles, a large German Shepherd, lay just inside the door in a pool of blood with three small holes in his chest, and one in the head.

Roy pushed by Amy, who was frozen in the doorway. There was more. The body of a woman lay on a worn blood soaked futon. Roy rushed over and felt for a pulse, but as soon as he got close he knew it would be useless. Blood oozed from her chest and a bullet that had entered the back of the skull had blown part of her face away.

"Mrs. Gonzales, Noodles, no, no." Amy's legs began to buckle, and Lisa grabbed her.

"Get her back into the hall," Roy said.

Lisa pulled Amy out and laid her down. Roy checked the suite to ensure the assailant or assailants were not still there. Lot of good I could do if they were. Might be time to start carrying a firearm. He dialed 911 on his cell as he walked into the hall. Amy was sobbing, and Lisa was trying to calm her. "Amy, what's the address here?" Roy said.

Nothing. "Amy, the address?"

The 911 operator answered, and Roy reported the situation. He knelt by Amy and grabbed her hand. "Amy, the address?"

She whispered it to Roy, and he relayed it to the operator. He hung up and looked back in the room. The place was a mess. It had been tossed, but the TV, stereo and an iPod were all still sitting there. This wasn't a random robbery.

"We better stay out here in the hall until the police show up. Don't want to mess up the crime scene," Roy said, but he was sure the police wouldn't find anything. This was a professional job gone wrong. Mrs. Gonzales and Noodles were not expected.

Roy was surprised at how quickly the police arrived. He hurried downstairs to let them in and led them to the suite. Amy was still on the floor, sobbing, head cradled in Lisa's arms. The police took a quick look inside and confirmed that Mrs. Gonzales was dead. They came out and said everyone needed to remain outside until the homicide detectives arrived.

Roy walked over to Lisa and whispered, "Don't mention the artifacts, just say I was interested in her work."

Lisa looked up, a question in her eyes, and was about to say something, when the officers separated them to take their statements.

Roy went with one of the officers to the far end of the hall. He answered the questions without mentioning anything about his real reason for being there. He stated that Amy was one of Lisa's students, and they were meeting her after dinner. He hoped Lisa's story would agree. It was obvious Amy wouldn't be of much help to the officers tonight.

Once the officer was satisfied, Roy walked back and sat down beside Lisa. Amy quit sobbing and was lying quietly with her head on Lisa's knee.

"Okay, Roy," Lisa whispered. "What the hell is going on? Why didn't you want me to tell them why we were actually here?"

"What did you tell them?"

"Just that I was here to talk to Amy about her research. She is my student, and that's essentially true. But why not mention the artifacts?"

"Well, I think the artifacts are connected to the killings."

"So, why not tell them?"

"I don't think it would help their investigation. If we tell them my suspicions, they will probably take them in evidence, even if they don't know why, and I need access to them."

"Amy, were the pyramid and other artifacts in your apartment?" Roy said. She didn't respond. "Amy?"

She looked up. "Why would someone hurt Noodles and Mrs. Gonzales? Noodles wouldn't hurt anyone."

Roy took her by the shoulders and looked directly

into her eyes. "Listen to me. The artifacts, were they in the apartment?" She stared back at him blankly. He shook her gently. "Amy, answer me. Were the artifacts in your apartment?"

"No, no...at the university, in...in my research locker."

Roy looked at Lisa. "We have to get those artifacts before whoever was here figures out where they are. We need to get going."

Roy went back to the officer and asked if they could go. At first he refused, but just then Amy broke into a convenient bout of hysterical sobbing. "We need to get her to the hospital." Roy pointed at Amy. "If we don't, she could have a complete breakdown."

The officer used his radio to see when the detectives would show up. Apparently, they were tied up at some other murder, so they were allowed to go.

As they left Amy's apartment, Roy noticed a small white Civic parked down the street. There appeared to be two men slouched down in the front seat. It was not the typical big black SUV that was always the bad guy's choice in the spy movies, but Roy was suspicious. "Was that car here when we went in?" he asked Lisa.

"I don't know. I wasn't paying attention; do you think someone's watching us?"

"I don't know, but we'll find out. Here's your car. Let's get going." He helped Amy into the passenger seat while Lisa got in the driver's side. "I'll get in the back and keep an eye on our suspicious friends.

Go to the corner and make a u-turn, and drive back the way we came. Don't drive too fast."

Lisa started the car and made the u-turn. She drove back down the street toward the Civic. "Don't look at the car. Amy, you look at Lisa." Amy followed Roy's instructions. She seemed to be in a state of shock and didn't understand what was going on. Roy leaned forward between the two and tried to appear uninterested in the car, but he covertly looked at the occupants of the Civic. They leaned toward each other and began kissing.

"Ah, it's just a couple of love birds," Lisa said.

"You weren't supposed to look, and just because they locked lips when we drove by doesn't mean anything. A mixed gender team would be good tactics for many reasons. The woman could follow you into a woman's washroom, for example. Or, as they have done here, they could pose as a couple. Just keep driving." Roy turned and peered out the rear window. The Civic didn't move. "I think we are okay," he said, as the Civic was just about out of sight. He turned back to the front just as they passed a parked SUV. It was black with tinted windows so he couldn't see who was in it. It flicked on its lights as they passed and pulled out behind them. "Shit."

"What?" Lisa said.

"I think the SUV that just pulled out may be a problem."

"Sure you aren't being paranoid? First, the Civic, and now, the SUV. What kind is it? How many people in it?"

"It's a black Yukon, and I don't know how many

289

people are in it. Its windows are all tinted, even the windshield. Isn't that illegal down here? I know it is in Canada."

Lisa's voice shook a little, as she said, "Yah, it's illegal here, too."

"Just keep driving like we are going to your house, not the University, but nice and slow. If those are just your average folks, they should pass us as soon as we get to a four lane street."

Lisa drove on for a few blocks, and the Yukon continued to follow at a respectful distance. She turned right onto a major four-lane street that would ultimately take them to the freeway. The Yukon sat at the corner for a while and then pulled in to follow them. "That's not too suspicious," Lisa said. "They could be heading to the freeway."

"We'll see. Pull in at that corner store." Lisa stopped in front of the door. Roy stepped out and wandered into the store. He asked the attendant for a pack of cigarettes while he watched for the SUV. It passed. He fumbled in his pockets. "I left my money in the car," he said, and left the store. Back in the car he looked at Lisa. "Did it stop?"

"No, it kept on going. I lost sight of it as it rounded the curve. Guess we're just a little jumpy after what we saw at Amy's. You know she lives in a pretty rough neighborhood. It was probably just a break-and-enter gone wrong. Where to now, the university?"

"Is it the same direction as your apartment?"

"No, we would have to take the freeway north rather than south."

"Well, then head south for a while. I'm still not convinced we are in the clear."

Lisa rejoined the traffic on the street. It wasn't very busy, so Roy easily saw the white Civic pull into the traffic from the next side street. It took up position behind them. In about four blocks, the black Yukon joined the parade behind them.

"They're back," Roy said.

C-CAF - Saskatchewan
September 1, 2002 - 1:50 am

Kurt spent most of the time since Roy left reviewing LISA's output on O'Shanigan. Joleen and Robby came by a couple of times for some food, but Joleen insisted Robby needed more sleep, and they went off to their rooms. The latest paper LISA provided was something that O'Shanigan presented on the use of ground penetrating radar in archeology. It discussed his success using an airborne radar unit to delineate underground structures and caverns. Well, that might explain why he was on that flight with us.

"You bastards." Joleen burst into the room. "Robby just told me you and Roy let him stay up most of last night playing computer games. That's why he slept for most of the day. How…how could you? You lied to me." She started to cry. "He needs his sleep. He's just a kid. Why? How could you? You and Roy, how could you let him play those games all night?"

"Joleen, calm down. Robby has been through quite a bit these last few days—the explosion, the glass in his back, the hospital, and that stuff at the farm. He needed something to get his mind off all of that. Roy's spaceship game was just the thing he needed."

"But his school work, he needs his sleep so he can do his school work." She sat down and put her head in her hands.

Kurt walked over and put his arm around her. "Is he awake now?"

"No, he went back to sleep."

"Well, you said he slept a lot yesterday, and he's asleep again. He's going to be just fine. I will help him with his schoolwork. You can call his teacher in the morning and find out what he needs to study. Everything will be okay."

Joleen looked up; her eyes were red and swollen. "Do you really think so?"

"Sure, this will all be cleared up in a couple of days. But, you need your sleep, too. Why don't you go back and get some more rest. Did you take one of the sedatives the doctor at the hospital gave you?"

Joleen shook her head.

"Well, maybe you should."

Joleen nodded, and wandered back to her room.

"Remember, the sedative," Kurt called after her. He was about to follow her to ensure she took it when the phone rang with three short rings indicating it was for him. The three short rings pulsed through the room once again before he grabbed the phone.

292

"Sigurdson," he said.

"It's me," Roy said.

"Oh, Roy, glad to hear from you. LISA is spitting out all sorts of mysterious messages about correlations and—"

"Never mind LISA. There's been a murder, and we are being tailed by a couple of cars. I'm going to need some help here, and I am going to need it in a hurry, hopefully, without blowing my cover. We must have some assets down here. I need their help to get these guys off our tail. Then I have to pick up a couple of things, and I will need passage for three back to C-CAF. Preferably via a private aircraft."

Kurt was wide-awake now. "You on your secure cell?"

"Yep," Roy said.

"Good. Let me think." Kurt was silent for about a minute. Roy waited quietly on the other end. "Okay," Kurt said. "I don't have authority for all this, especially the private plane, but Walker could do it, and he trusts us. How long can you give me?"

"Maybe twenty-five minutes. We can continue to drive around for that long, but if we take too much longer those dudes following us may do something drastic."

"Okay, I'll call you right back." Kurt dashed to his office and called Walker.

Los Angeles, California
August 31, 2002 - 11:55 pm

"Okay, what the hell is going on," Lisa said, when Roy hung up. "What's this 'never mind Lisa' and 'blow my cover'?"

Roy shook his head and nodded in Amy's direction. Lisa said, "You're a goddamn spy."

"Amy," Roy said.

"She's asleep. Emotional exhaustion, I assume. This was pretty hard on her, you know, with her dog and neighbor dead."

Roy nodded. "Yah, poor kid."

"But you. Damn it, what haven't you told me? Assets, private planes, blow your cover? My Mr. Big Bang isn't who he claims to be. I think I deserve an explanation."

Roy nodded and began to fill her in. It took about fifteen minutes for Roy to tell her about C-CAF, the Canadian Counterespionage and Antiterrorist Facility; and about the explosion at Joleen's, the firefight at the farm, Kurt and Robby's discovery, the mysterious Father O'Shanigan, the link to the WOW, and the potential link to the artifacts in Amy's locker.

Lisa drove, wide-eyed, and said nothing as Roy told the story.

"We need to get those artifacts," he said as he finished the story.

"Roy, we are almost at the exit to my apartment. Should I take it?"

"No, stay on the freeway. We don't want to get in a situation where those guys can corner us."

294

"I don't have much gas left."

"Shit. Come on Kurt. Not much time left." The cell rang. "Thank you," Roy shouted.

Amy bolted upright, slumped back and began to cry softly.

"Yah," Roy answered.

"Roy Matacowski?" the voice on the other end asked. It wasn't Kurt.

"I'm Roy."

"Okay, call me Sam. Where are you?"

Roy asked Lisa and relayed the information.

"Do you have a cell besides your secure cell?" Sam said.

"Lisa, do you have your cell with you?" She nodded and handed it to Roy.

"Yes, we have one," Roy said.

"Okay, dial this number and when it's answered just leave it on. We are going to use it to trace you."

Roy dialed the number. The same voice answered, "Sam here."

Roy set the phone down on the seat and waited. He kept his secure cell to his ear. 'Okay," Sam said, "we have you located. Now here's the drill. Keep on the freeway at no more than fifty miles per hour. Once we are set up, we will tell you which exit to use. When you're off the freeway, a light will turn red just as you get to it. Run it. If the folks following you run it, we will have some cops in place to ticket them. If they stop, it's going to turn into one of the longest red lights they have ever seen." Sam chuckled. "They are sure to get impatient and run it. If they do, the cops are going to be the slowest ticket writers you have ever seen."

"Listen, Sam," Roy said. "These guys may be connected with a murder at…" He paused for a second, and then gave Amy's address to Sam.

"Okay, we'll cook something up to hold them for a while if we can, but we don't have anything to link them to the murder without blowing your cover."

"Well," Roy said, "now here's an anonymous tip. A suspicious Civic and a Yukon with the license numbers…ah…you fill in the details, were reported parked near the murder site, etc., etc."

"Good idea. We should be able to take them into the station and find out who they really are. Doesn't sound like they will be carrying real licenses, but…just a minute…okay, we're ready. Take the third exit. Go through three sets of lights and turn right. It's a narrow street. Slow down so the two cars following you get close. It's a long block with no exits, so once they are in there, they're trapped."

"Hold on Sam. I'm not driving so I need to relay the plan to the driver."

He looked at Lisa. "Just follow my instructions."

Lisa nodded.

"Okay, Sam. We are ready."

"Exit coming up," Sam said. Roy relayed Sam's instructions to Lisa. It worked just as planned. The Yukon ran the red light and was stopped by the police. The Civic stopped but eventually became impatient, backed up and made a u-turn. They were stopped for making an illegal u-turn.

Sam, in a "Tommy's Carpet Cleaners' van, waited for Roy and his troop several blocks further on. Lisa and Roy piled into the back of the van with a confused Amy in tow. Sam arranged to have Lisa's car driven to her apartment and parked in her regular parking spot. If anyone checked, it would look like she had driven home.

The van took the trio to the university where they picked up the artifacts, and then proceeded to a private airport where a Lear jet waited. Amy didn't want to go with them, but Lisa and Roy convinced her that her life was in danger if she didn't.

Once they were in the air, Roy called Kurt to let him know they were all safe, and they would be landing at Saskatoon so that they could use Roy's car to get back to C-CAF. Then Roy opened the small bar, passed around sandwiches and a strong drink for each of them.

Chapter 25 - The Big Bang

When the private plane arrived at Saskatoon's airport with Roy, Lisa, Amy, and the artifacts, they picked up Roy's car and drove to C-CAF.

Now, Amy, Lisa and Joleen sat around a large table in the lounge with the three artifacts in the middle of the table. Robby was piloting one of Roy's exotic starcrafts through some far off galaxy with LISA providing realistic company. Joleen seemed to be in better spirits as she discussed the situation with Lisa and Amy. She even let Robby take a sandwich back into space with him, and for once, she wasn't upset about him playing a computer game.

"Having Lisa and Amy here seems to be helping Joleen cope," Roy whispered to Kurt, as they walked over to the table where the artifacts were displayed.

"I hope so," Kurt whispered. "Robby needs some

stability.

"Now, what about these artifacts? Anybody have any ideas?" Roy said.

"Do you think the people following you were after them?" Joleen said. "Are they the ones after Robby?"

"It sure looks like it," Roy said. "I think that Robby somehow activated the artifacts when he was in the mine."

"How?" Joleen said.

Roy shrugged and began examining the artifacts. He tested each piece with a small magnet and passed them around. "The material is hard and scratch resistant. It's not magnetic. It could be some exotic metal, but the artifacts definitely don't appear to contain any ferrous metals."

Kurt turned the pyramid with the orb over to look at the bottom. "It looks like stone. Amy, you said light came from the orb. It doesn't seem possible. I can't see any visible seams. Maybe we should check it under a microscope?"

"That's a good idea," Roy said. "Let's take the artifacts back to the lab, and you see if you can figure out what material they are made of. I want to set up another little experiment, but I need to set the computer up first. That'll take me a couple of hours. Let's get back together at five. Is that okay with you gals?" Roy said.

"We'll make something for dinner," Lisa said.

"Right, something better than pizza," Joleen said, with a grin.

Cairo, Egypt
September 1, 2002 - Sunset

The priest's sanctuary was situated in a small house built in the third or fourth century. Like so many others from that time, it backed onto an old fortification, in this case, a Roman fortress. The city grew up and around the house over time, and now what used to be windows were now brick walls. An exit led down a two foot wide passage that ran under other structures and emerged into a wider alley that led to a major street fifty feet away. He seldom used this entrance; instead, he accessed his sanctuary through a secret entrance in the Hanging Church.

The Hanging Church, or Saint Virgin Mary's Coptic Church as it is now called, was built on top of the old Roman fortress. The secret passage, forgotten in the dust of time, was built by the followers of the First Apostle. It was accessed from the church, and sat unused until he uncovered an old papyrus scroll detailing its existence. As a Coptic priest he could slip in and out of his sanctuary unnoticed. But, he would have special visitors arrive through the other entrance, the long alley. Today, he sat at his small desk waiting for the visitor. He had removed his clerical garb and now wore a short-sleeved golf shirt and denim pants. Cool air, well, cool relative to that outside in the Cairo streets, wafted down on him from a small ceiling fan. He leaned back in his chair, looked at his watch, and listened. A faint wail struggled through the stone. The call to prayers. He turned to the southeast, knelt, bent forward, head on the floor, and prayed. A soft knock interrupted his

300

prayers, and he returned to his desk to admit his visitor.

The Greek had been here before and knew his way—first the alley, then the dingy passageway to the electronically controlled door into the sanctuary.

"Why did you come? It is not wise to meet in person," the priest said. "You could have been followed."

"I was careful and used my British passport. The authorities are quite suspicious about Canadian passports these days. They're too easy to get."

"Yes, yes, but why did you come?" the priest said.

"Ah, I was in Sana'a with Blue Eyes. I have good news; he has the gold scroll."

"So he succeeded again? When can I have it? You do not get paid until I have the scroll."

"He is back in Canada and should soon have the scroll. We sent it to his office in Vancouver via courier to avoid customs. When he gets it, he will send it to me immediately. You still wish to pick it up in Montreal as planned?"

The priest nodded.

Good, everything is set. But…," the Greek said.

"But? Is there a problem?"

"Well, it's Amil; the U.S. authorities have requested that the Canadians pick him up. They will probably link him to Blue Eyes and Winnipeg, and well…"

"Perhaps you should straighten things out with Amil and Yusof when you get back."

"Yes, once the scroll is on the way to Montreal, I

will hold a special meeting with Amil and Yusof."

"And the boy? You have failed twice. Do you know where he is.?"

"No, but when we do, we will eliminate him."

"Like the farmhouse?"

"Well, that was unexpected, somehow they saw us coming. They held the high ground, and they were well armed. We will be more careful this time."

"I hope you are right. But, now you must go; we risk much by you coming here. And I must finish my prayers. Do you no longer pray?"

"When necessary." The Greek rose and left the way he came.

The priest returned to his prayers.

C-CAF – Saskatchewan
September 1, 2002 - 5:00 pm

Roy entered the lab, grinning and waving a piece of paper. "You know, the longer I run that random correlation program that I wrote, the smarter I look. I think I'm due for a whopping raise…and probably, a big promotion."

Kurt looked up from analysing the physical properties of the artifacts. "I'm not having much success. I need a break, but you gotta quit patting yourself on the back. You'll break your damn arm. And what's a random correlation program? Sounds like some kind of an oxymoron to me, perhaps, written by a real moron."

"Hah, hah, stop with the show-off words. What I

did was write a program that LISA runs continuously in the background. She—and here's the random part—she picks a news story, at random, off the wire service, say an increase in the number of murders in Montreal. She scans for similar stories at a different time or place. Then she picks some other random thing—say the temperature at that time, or perhaps, a list of people who rented cars around that time, all without direction from me."

"Sounds like a lot of dead ends."

"Sure, but LISA's patient and never sleeps. Anyway, she has a good solid lead for us." He paused, smiled and waved the piece of paper again, waiting for Kurt to bite. Kurt turned back to his work. "What, you're not interested?"

Kurt turned back and spread his hands out in front of himself, palms up in an "okay out with it" gesture.

Roy walked closer. "Well, about half an hour ago, I received a secure email from the LAPD guys working on the murder of that lady in Amy's apartment block. It appears that there was a computer science student living in the building who became so pissed off at all the break-ins that he rigged up a spy camera in the corridor. Good thing it was in the States, the damn Privacy Commissioner up here would probably declare it illegal, and we would have to destroy the tape. You know that office has to go, it's—"

Kurt put his hands up to stop Roy in what was an all too familiar tirade.

Roy shrugged. "Okay, well, the forensics guys, they uncovered this camera. It was wireless by the way; the guy built it himself. Quite a neat piece of technology I understand. Maybe we should hire him, when he graduates."

"For god's sake, Roy. Get on with it."

"Oh, yah, a bit short of sleep, I guess. Anyway, they find this guy and get his recordings. It covers the time of the murder, and they pulled off pictures of two or three unidentified guys entering the building around that time. They couldn't match them to anyone on file but guess what?" Kurt motioned for Roy to continue. "Well, a few months ago LISA's random correlation program linked several series of forest fires in the U.S. with an Amil Fawaz. His border crossings into the U.S. and his motel stay correlated quite nicely. We'd never have come up with that without the program LISA was running. It was a terrorist idea we hadn't thought about. Imagine the damage, economic as well as environmental, that a relatively small group of terrorist could do, if they set a large number of concurrent fires throughout the U.S. and Canada. We'd be overwhelmed.

"Walker thought it was important enough to put a field agent from the RCMP on it. She hasn't uncovered much yet, some notes on movements, a few photos of him and unidentified associates. But, she uploaded all the photos. When the photos of the guys from LA came in, I asked LISA to see if she could find a match. Well, this guy Amil Fawaz, a suspected terrorist, was in L.A. in Lisa's apartment building when that lady was killed."

"But why? Couldn't it have been just a coincidence?" Kurt stood up.

"Sure, and a bunch of guys just coincidentally wandered in and shot up your brother's farm, too."

"What's on that paper you've been waving about?"

"Oh, Amil's picture, plus those of his associates to date." He held it out for Kurt.

There were eight photos on the page. "A bit small, don't you think. Is that the best we can do?" Kurt said.

"No, of course not, come on." Roy walked over to a computer screen, logged on to LISA, and called up full screen images. He paged through them a couple of times. "Recognize anyone?"

"One more time, slowly."

Roy paged through again, pausing at each photo. "Whoa," Kurt said, "something about that one." It was an excellent, almost portrait quality colour photo of a handsome man with a swarthy complexion and unexpected blue eyes. "He looks familiar, for some reason. I have no idea why. Who is he?"

"We don't know, yet. There's only one agent on this case and only part time at that. LISA's random correlation program has only been running for a few months. This was LISA's first real hit. Walker didn't want to spend too much of his discretionary budget on an unproven technology, so we just have one junior agent working on it part-time."

"The quality of that photo is unbelievable for a surveillance shot. Where was it taken?" Kurt said.

Roy clacked a few keys. "Winnipeg, at a Lebanese restaurant called Door to Beirut. Ever go to Winnipeg?"

"Twice, once as a kid, and once when we landed there to wait out a snow storm in Toronto." Kurt shook his head. "No, I didn't see him in Winnipeg." He moved closer to the screen and looked at the image. "It's the eyes. You don't expect those eyes. Where? Where did I see them?"

Roy didn't say anything. A couple of minutes passed.

"Vancouver, this guy was standing next to me at the luggage carousel when I was on my way back from Yuma. Just before I called Joleen," Kurt said.

"We can find him then." Roy pushed Kurt back from the terminal and began typing.

"How? You can't find him just from that, can you?"

"Just watch the magic." Roy chuckled. "First, I'll have LISA check your flight from Yuma, she has that on file. Just need to access the airline files." A few moments passed. "Look at that, they still have the carousel that your luggage came out on. Let's see what other flights came out there?" More typing, a few more seconds.

"Ah, only one, AC 632, Toronto to Vancouver, with a stop in Winnipeg. Now, let's hope the Human Rights commissioner isn't listening, we'll search the passenger list for Middle Eastern names." LISA responded with a list.

"Eight possibles," Roy said, as he scanned the list.

Kurt peered over Roy's shoulder. "There, Mr. Yusof Ekstrom. That sounds like a blue-eyed sheik to me."

"Good pick. That's likely him. I'll call Walker in the morning and see if we can ask the RCMP to follow up. In the mean time, I'll task LISA to find out all she can about Mr. Ekstrom."

He hit a few keys. "She's on it; let's go see what the gals have whipped up for dinner—maybe it's a deluxe pizza."

"Not likely," Kurt said with a grin. "I'll meet you in the dining area."

*****

Kurt walked into the combination dining area, lounge and kitchen with several large sheets of paper. He spread them on one of the large tables and looked around for Roy.

"Kurt, come here." Lisa, standing between Amy and Joleen, motioned to him. "We need you."

"Ah, always gratifying to be needed by the fairer sex. What can I do for you?"

"Well, we found these nice steaks in the freezer. Do you have a barbeque in this facility of yours, or do we have to make them in the fry pan?"

"We have a gas grill in the back room. It has an exhaust hood, the works; you won't even need to go outside."

"Not me, the BBQ is male territory." Lisa laughed.

"But, I have some interesting stuff on the artifacts to show Roy."

"Mister Big Bang isn't here, and it can wait till

after dinner," Joleen said. "You need to burn the beef."

"Joleen, not you, too. What's this Mr. Big Bang stuff? What do you know that I don't?"

The three girls laughed. "Roy can tell you at dinner," Lisa said.

The steaks were delicious, and everyone ate quietly. They all were in need of a good meal. Robby finished and asked to be excused.

"No more computer games today," Joleen said.

"Okay, Mom. I'll go and look at that list of homework you got for me today."

Kurt looked at Joleen. "I called Robby's teacher this afternoon," she said.

Lisa started clearing the plates. "I saw some Rocky Road ice cream in the freezer. Everyone game?"

There was a chorus of agreement.

Kurt looked at Roy. "Well, Robby's not here so this might be a good time to explain why everyone here but me calls you, Mr. Big Bang."

"Elementary, my dear Kurt," Roy said. "Tis because of my great unifying theory. You know, the stuff all the great scientists, since Einstein, have been chasing. Haven't I ever told you?"

Kurt shrugged and shook his head.

"Okay, then, it's all about scale. From the very, very small to the very, very large. Everything repeats. For example, if you move far enough away from our universe, way out there until you are actually outside it looking down, it would look solid. In fact, my theory suggests it would look like a person. And if you were to move farther away, you would soon see other people. All of them really just another universe."

"Fine. But how does that lead to Mr. Big Bang?" Kurt said.

"Patience." Roy chuckled.

"Patience, my ass, I'm—"

Roy held up his hand. He knew the rest of the saying. "Well, you see. Every once in a while a couple of those people, ah universes, get together and copulate. And what do you get?" Roy paused.

"Ah, that's it?" Kurt laughed.

"Right. You get a new little universe created by…"

"A Big Bang." Kurt completed the story. "Cute, really cute. I bet you tell that to all the girls."

"Nope, only Lisa." Roy grinned up at Lisa who was returning with bowls and the ice cream.

"Liar," she said. Then she looked at Kurt. "So, now you are party to Roy's Unifying Theory of the Universe."

Everyone sat down and offered an opinion on Roy's theory as they devoured the ice cream.

"Okay, enough fun," Kurt said, as he put his dish in the dishwasher. "I want you all to come and look at this." He went to the table in the lounge area and spread out several large sheets of paper.

"What is it?" Amy asked, as she bent over to get a closer look.

"It's the surface of your pie-shaped artifact magnified twelve hundred times."

"It looks like writing," she said.

"It is. Here, look at it with this magnifying glass."

Lisa took the magnifying glass and bent over the sheet. "Yes, it is some kind of writing. However, it's certainly not English. Why didn't you make it larger?"

"Twelve hundred power is all we have on site. But, now look at this." Kurt put another sheet in front of her.

"It looks like pictures—stick people and animals." Lisa handed the magnifying glass to Amy. "Here, take a look."

They all took their turn. Roy was still looking at the various sheets, when Joleen asked, "What does it mean?"

"I don't know," Kurt said. "That's why I wanted all of you to look at it. Any ideas?"

"The stick figures look a little like Navajo wall art," Amy said.

Roy looked up from scanning the sheets. "You know, I think these are good enough that we could use the high resolution scanner, and LISA could clean up the images."

"Do you think that would work?" Kurt said.

"Can't hurt to give it a try. I'll run a couple of these through to see what it can do. "Amy, why don't you come along?"

"Joleen, I think I'll go along with them. You want to come?"Kurt said.

"No, I'm going to help Robby with his homework. Remember, you said you would help him, too."

"Yah, I can catch up with Roy later, after Robby's

asleep. Let's go help Robby."

Chapter 26 - Betrayal

Vancouver, B.C., Canada
September 4, 2002 - 1:00 pm

Yusof took the elevator to the top floor of a small building just off Robson Street and proceeded to room 505 where a small sign identified "Jenifer's Office Services. A receptionist looked up. "Mr. Franks. Good morning. I haven't heard from you for a while. Were you away?"

"Good morning, Jenifer. Yes, a little business trip to Chicago. Did a courier package arrive for me?"

"Well, nothing from Chicago, but a box of blueprints arrived from Germany. I'll get it. It's in the storage area." She hurried away and returned in a few moments with a box.

"I would like to look at these. Is one of the offices available?" Four rooms were equipped with a desk, a phone, and a computer for Jenifer's clients. A nice set up, especially for Yusof's purpose. Jenifer was competent and could be relied upon to send and receive packages and messages without asking questions. Most importantly, nothing could be traced to him. She had no way of getting in touch with him. He always called from a pay phone or disposable cell, and paid her invoices in cash.

"You can use any office, nobody else is here. Why don't you use number three? It has the best view." She laughed. It was the only office with a window. It looked directly at the back of another building.

"I'll use number two. It's closer." He didn't want anyone looking in the window at what he was doing, remote as that possibility might be. "Do you have one of those medium-sized courier boxes that I could use?" His plan was to courier the scroll to the Greek in Montreal.

"Sure." She retrieved a collapsed box and handed it to him. "You'll have to put the box together. It's not hard, it just folds up. Do you want me to pack it for you?"

"No, I can handle it."

"Okay, have fun." She smiled. "You had a couple of calls, Mr. Franks. Mr. John Jacks called wanting to know how your trip went. He left this number." She handed him a phone message slip.

Ah, Mr. Jacks is wondering about the scroll, he thought. John Jacks was an alias the Greek used.

"And an Amil called. He sounded upset and wanted you to call as soon as possible. I told him you only picked up your messages every few days, but he seemed sure you would check in soon. He didn't leave a last name, said you would know who he was. He left this number. It's in Vancouver." She handed him a second slip. "Those are the only messages. Would you like me to phone them for you?" It was another service she provided. It made it seem like her clients had their own private secretary placing calls.

"No, I'll handle it myself." Yusof entered office number two and closed the door.

Something's not right, Amil shouldn't be in Vancouver, and he shouldn't have used his real name. Yusof dialed the number Amil left.

"Royal Hotel."

The Royal was a scruffy hotel down near the waterfront. It was primarily the haunt of hookers and those down on their luck.

What is Amil doing there? Yusof thought.

"Yah, what do you want? I ain't got all day."

"Ah, could you connect me with Mr. Amil Fawaz's room, please?"

"Ain't here."

"Has he checked out?"

"Naw, just gone out."

"Do you know when he will be back?"

"What the hell do you think I am, man? Some kind of a nursemaid? He'll be back when he's back." There was a click, and the line went dead.

Guess I couldn't leave a message, even if I wanted to, Yusof thought. He sat for a while trying to figure out what was going on. It doesn't make sense. I'll finish here and then call him again.

The courier package from Germany contained

several tubes of blueprints protected by bubble wrap. The gold scroll wrapped in purple velvet and secured in a tube, was hidden in the center of the bundle. Yusof did not remove the cloth but carefully placed everything in the wooden scroll case, wrapped the case in the bubble wrap and placed it in the courier box.

It was ready to send, but he wasn't comfortable. When the Greek insisted they send the scroll via courier from Germany to Vancouver, Yusof couldn't believe it—an item worth millions in a courier package. The Greek insisted it was safe and less likely to be found than if Yusof tried to carry it back. That proved to be correct. The scroll surely would have been found when his bag was searched at customs. But now, in Canada, why risk sending it via courier? He could easily fly to Montreal with it. He made a decision. No, he wouldn't send it. He'd call first.

The Greek picked it up after two rings. "John Jacks."

"Mr. Al Franks, here." Yusof said.

"Ah, Al. Has the present arrived?"

"Yes, the present arrived safely, but I was wondering if I should bring it over personally?"

"No, no, carry on as planned. I need you to do something else. Our good friend Alex called." The Greek used Amil's alias. "He is upset, very, very upset. His trip didn't go well, and he was unable get the gift for his wife."

Amil had called the Greek, too. That's worrying, Yusof thought.

"Alex is in town and called me, too. I tried to call him, but he was out," Yusof said.

"Yes, it is not good," the Greek continued. "I am afraid Alex will do something silly. I need you to pick him up and take him to your place and settle him down."

"My place, is that a good idea?"

"Yes, your place is best. He needs to talk to someone and calm down. It will only be overnight; I have friends there. I will call you tonight; I'll have some place where you can take him tomorrow. In the mean time settle him down."

"Okay," Yusof said.

"And the gift. Send it before you pick up Alex."

"It's ready to go. I'll send it right away."

"Good, I'll call tonight. If you aren't there yet, I'll leave a message. Goodbye."

Yusof stood motionless for a few minutes. What happened to Amil? Why is he so upset? He grabbed the courier package and walked out to Jenifer.

"Could you send this off for me?"

"Sure. I need a walk. Nothing's going on here." She grabbed her coat and headed for the door. "It'll take me about twenty minutes. There's a FedEx place about three blocks away. It's Friday so I probably won't come back. Make sure the door is locked when you leave."

Yusof went back to the office and called Amil again. This time he got through. He convinced Amil to stay in his room until he picked him up. Then he left, locking the door as Jenifer requested.

A few minutes later, Jenifer returned with the

package. There was a gas main leak, and the street where the FedEx outlet was located was blocked off. She'd have to check her computer and find another FedEx location.

C-CAF Lounge
September 4, 2002 - 2:00 pm

We're becoming quite a team Kurt thought as he walked into the lounge. Each time they gathered there for a meal, it turned into a mini team meeting where they shared information.

Amy was busy trying to trace Vladimir Villdeff, the Russian archeologist. She had not been very successful. There was only one entry in a catalogue at the Kremlin Museum in Moscow. It listed a letter sent from Vladimir Villdeff to Tzar Alexandra III in 1882. There was no additional description in the catalogue, so she convinced Lisa to request more information using her position at UCLA.

Roy enhanced Kurt's enlargements of the pizza artifact using LISA. So now, they were busy enlarging and organizing overlapping sections of the artifact. Joleen took over the operation of the microscope, and Lisa was doing the scanning and merging of images on her namesake, LISA. They were about one quarter complete.

With all the help, Roy and Kurt were free to investigate other avenues of research. Roy explained his suspicions about the artifact that resembled the child's rattle or small scepter. Kurt was skeptical and worried. Roy's plan to test his hypothesis involved Robby. "I don't think Joleen will go for this," he said, when Roy laid out his plan.

"Then, you'll have to convince her," Roy said.

They agreed on a plan. They would present it at today's team meeting. Hopefully, the others could help convince Joleen to go along.

Kurt kicked off the discussion once everyone else had given a status report. "That's great. We're making progress." He looked over at Joleen and tried to assess her mood. She was sitting with Robby, smiling and seemed to enjoy being part of the team. As good a time as any, he thought. "Roy has a theory about the artifact that looks like a little rattle. He thinks it is designed for someone like Robby."

He hesitated and looked at Joleen. "Someone with six fingers." He walked over to another table where Roy had placed the artifact and picked it up. "You see the five places around the handle that seem to be designed to accept fingers, and this small indent in the ball on top. That would accept the thumb."

He handed the artifact to Lisa. She wrapped her fingers around the handle and placed her thumb in the indentation.

"You're right. It fits perfectly. Well…it fits, except that there is a place for an extra finger." She passed the artifact on to Joleen.

Everyone waited as Joleen turned the artifact over and over in her hand, and then she grasped it as Lisa had. "Perhaps, perhaps it's a sign from God."

She set the artifact on the table beside her and looked at Roy. "Roy, do you think that's why these people are trying to hurt Robby?"

"I'm not sure if that is the case, but it might—"

Robby picked up the little scepter wrapped his fingers around the handle and was about to place his thumb in the indentation.

Roy stood up. "No. Robby, no."

He was too late. Robby pushed his thumb down. Small hairs on the ball at top of the artifact suddenly stood perpendicular, the lights in the lounge went out, and LISA crashed. Robby dropped the scepter. After a few moments, the lights came on, and LISA started an automatic reboot.

"Shit," Kurt said as Joleen grabbed Robby. "Is he okay?"

"I'm sorry, Dad." Robby looked startled but unhurt. "I'm okay, I'm sorry."

Roy picked up the scepter. "It's okay. It was our fault. We should have been more careful." He put his hand on Robby's head. "But, you're fine, so that alleviates one of our concerns and confirms another. We can't have you playing with this near any critical electrical equipment."

Kurt moved over and sat down beside Roy. "Let's leave this for a while, Roy," he whispered.

"Yah, that's okay by me. I need to ensure that LISA's okay."

Lisa looked up. "I'm okay."

"The computer LISA, I mean," Roy said.

"Oh." Lisa smiled, as Roy left to tend to the computer.

Tower of London
September 4, 2002 - 8:00 pm

Peter Robbins followed Smithers' progress through the museum on the computer screen. Each time Smithers logged in at a control station, the time and his RF card number would appear on the screen in front of Robbins. Why am I always stuck on shift with that old bastard?

There was little camaraderie between Peter and the rest of the guards before that little event with Smithers a few weeks back, but now everyone hated Peter. The Sergeant at Arms put them both on report after he investigated that cockamamie story Smithers cooked up to cover his ass.

There was no fire. The old bastard just panicked when the power went off and then tried to lay the blame on me. I was almost back. If he'd waited a few minutes before heading out on rounds that day we could have easily completed them in an acceptable window. But no, just to screw me, he headed off at the earliest start time. Then that story about the fire, the doors not opening and all that other crap. What a bloody crock. And of course, all the other guards believed him and blamed me. Wonder what he's up to now.

Peter looked at the computer screen. It showed that Smithers had just logged in at the last control station. Peter turned and watched as Smithers returned to the control room via the museum access door. Smithers glared at Peter but said nothing as he walked across the room toward a small fridge and a table. The guards stocked the fridge with a supply of sodas and kept their lunches there. Smithers took his lunch pail out of the fridge and flung it down. It slid across the table and banged the wall near the row of switches for the control room lights. The lights went out.

"What the bloody hell are you doing?" Peter shouted. He stood up and was just about to walk across the room to turn the lights back on when the computer screens behind him dimmed, and the room went pitch black.

La Chambre Biblique, Paris
September 4, 2002 - 8:00 pm

The brothers took their designated places in the windowless meeting room, six stories above the sanctuary. Brother Oswald placed the pyramid in the small indentation in the center of the hexagon shaped oak table. It would sit in a place of honor at the center of the group until the meeting adjourned. Then it would be returned to the sanctuary, and a brother would remain with it as a Watcher.

Since the First Apostle formed the Brotherhood, the pyramid was never left unattended. For hundreds of years, the Brothers recorded its periods of awakening and sleep. Now there was new hope. Brother Terry was going to tell them why.

"Brothers of the First Apostle, Brothers of the Sand," Terry said. "I have news of the strange discovery in a desert in America. There appears to be an extremely large…ah, what should I call it? I'm not sure, but it is either an underground habitat or perhaps a vessel. But, I am sure it is linked to the Master."

"The Master?" Brother Antonio said. "Could it be…in America?"

"Yes, I know it seems—" Terry pointed at the pyramid. " Look."

The orb on the pyramid was glowing. It grew brighter, and the lights in the room failed.

"It's a miracle," Brother Joseph whispered. "A miracle."

The brothers watched silently for a few minutes, and then, the pyramid dimmed and went out.

"Is the Master back?" Brother Joseph looked at Terry, tears welling up in his eyes.

"I don't think so, but I do think it is connected to the desert in America and a young boy." He paused and looked around the room. "There is so much to tell. Let me start with the boy."

Vancouver, B.C., Canada
September 4, 2002 - 4:00 pm

Yusof drove around the block again. It had taken him over an hour to drive through town from his office to the Royal Hotel which was even more run down than he had expected, and there wasn't any parking. I guess they don't expect any of their clients to drive, he thought.

He spied a car pulling out about half a block ahead, parked there, and walked back to the hotel.

Even at 4:00 pm, there were a number of hookers trying to get his attention. He wove his way around several street people or drunks sleeping against a wall next to the entrance to the Royal. Yusof dodged a drunk. Canada and the United States pretend to be so much better than we are, but look at how they treat their poor. They deserve everything we will deliver to them.

The hotel lobby was even worse than the outside. It was dirty and poorly lit. Obviously, the owner had not put any money into maintenance for some time. The city designated the area for an urban renewal project some years back. Nothing came of it, and the whole area became even more run down as a result. Speculators simply bought the properties and became slum landlords while they waited for government money for the renewal projects. Capitalist and politicians preying on the poor, Yusof thought, as he walked up to the front desk.

The attendant looked up. "Yah," he said. Yusof had heard the same voice over the phone earlier.

"Do you have a house phone?" Yusof asked.

"Yah, sure, it's at the concierge desk. Who the hell do you want?"

"Mr. Amil Fawaz." Yusof raised his voice. This guy was beginning to get to him.

"Keep your shirt on, asshole." The attendant looked him straight in the eye with a threatening stare. He dialed a number and handed the telephone to Yusof. "Here's your goddamn house phone."

Yusof took it, put it to his ear and turned away.

"Amil, it's Yusof, I'm down in the…ah." He

323

looked around. "I'm down in the lobby. Meet me down here, and we can get going." Yusof handed the phone back to the attendant. "He's checking out. What does he owe?"

"Nothin." The attendant smiled. A gold tooth gleamed at Yusof. "Cash in advance."

Place like this, I should have known there'd be no credit. Yusof wandered over to the elevator to wait for Amil. The door opened, and Amil stumbled out. His left arm was hanging at his side, and his face was pale. Yusof took the small carry-on bag Amil was struggling to carry. "Let's get out of here. My car's just down the block."

Yusof threw the bag in the trunk and helped Amil into the front seat. "What happened to you?" What's wrong with your arm?"

"Dog attacked me," Amil said.

"What? Where? Have you been to a doctor?"

"I was afraid to."

"Why?" Yusof looked at Amil. Amil was shaking. "You need to see a doctor."

"I can't."

"Why?" Yusof asked again.

"I traced down the girl who has the artifact and found out where she lives in L.A. I saw her go out and was breaking into her apartment but an old lady opened the door. I covered her mouth and pushed her back into the suite. She was no problem, but then this big dog came out of nowhere and grabbed my arm. It was all I could do to get my gun out and shoot him. It took three shots to stop him. And, and, the old lady, she started screaming, so I shot her, too."

"Did you find the artifact?"

"No, I took a quick look around and then got out of there. The gun was silenced, but I was worried someone heard the old lady screaming. I was afraid to go to a doctor in case someone reported it and made the connection. I bandaged my arm as best I could and flew here. I knew you would help me. I couldn't go home, my family, they...they would ask questions."

"Right," Yusof said, but thought, why didn't Amil just go home? Even if I get him fixed up, his family will have questions. And now, we will be seen together. Ah well, it's too late now.

"Do you have your medical card with you?" Yusof asked.

"Yes."

"Okay, I'll take you to the General Hospital to have your arm looked after. Then we can go to my place for the night. The Greek is going to call with another place where you can stay until you go back home."

Amil nodded.

It took about four hours to get Amil patched up at the emergency ward. The arm was infected and required seventy-five stitches, but nobody seemed too concerned about how it happened. Amil and Yusof agreed to the story that it was a farm dog and that it had already been put down. Everyone seemed to accept that.

They arrived at Yusof's apartment at 11:00 pm

"How about something to eat? I have some

canned soup," Yusof said.

Amil flopped down on the couch and sighed.

Yusof noticed the answering machine on the end table next to the couch was blinking. "It looks like the Greek called." He pushed the play button on the machine.

The room lit up in a blinding flash. Yusof was flung across the room and out the large floor to ceiling window of his apartment. As he fell eighteen stories to his death, he had a brief moment to wonder what happened. Amil died instantly from the blast. He ended up in the galley kitchen covered in pieces of the couch.

Chapter 27 - The Test

It took Roy most of the night to get LISA sorted out. The power failure caused by Robby's episode with the scepter not only stopped LISA but caused several disk errors and program malfunctions.

Now, the team was meeting for breakfast. Roy arrived last. "Guess what?" he said. "Kurt, remember those correlations LISA was giving you about power failures?"

"Yah, I remember asking you about them, but you never explained what they meant."

"Sorry, here's the explanation. I sent LISA looking for anything that happened at the same time you and Robby activated the ship and created the WOW."

"What's a WOW?" Joleen asked.

Roy explained.

"So you think that somehow Robby and Kurt's actions at that ship created a repeat of that mysterious signal from space?" Lisa said.

"Exactly. In fact, that's how we discovered Amy and these artifacts. LISA detected a power outage that happened around UCLA at the same time Robby caused the WOW from out in the desert. Then LISA found Amy's post about the strange events she witnessed, and I tasked LISA to look for other power failure events that occurred at the same time. The correlations LISA was listing for Kurt showed other potentially linked events." Roy stopped and looked at everyone.

"And?" Amy said.

"First." A big smile lit up Roy's face. "First, there was another WOW detected last night at precisely the time Robby fired up the scepter. It was extremely short, but the SETI folks are going wild again. This is the third signal they have received from that region of space, and it is a repeat of the others. But, that's not all. One of the potential correlations that Kurt asked about also repeated."

"What was it?" Lisa asked.

"A power failure at the Tower of London. Now figure that out, ladies and gentlemen."

Nobody said a word for several minutes. Then, Amy said, "They must have an artifact. But why at the Tower of London."

"Aha, my dear Watsonette," Roy said. "That is still to be determined. I suggest we give LISA more time to look for answers while we give the SETI people another WOW. We'll send Robby and Kurt

328

ten or twenty miles from here, and Robby will fire up the scepter. That should be far enough away that it won't affect us." He looked at Joleen. "You okay with this?"

She nodded. "As long as I get to go along with Robby."

"Okay, let's do it then. Kurt, there's a park about twenty miles south of here without a house or major utility installation for at least three miles. That should ensure we don't cause a blackout when Robby fires up the scepter again. You need to take the pyramid with you, as well, because it also seems to affect the nearby utilities."

"Joleen, can you get Robby ready?" Kurt said.

Joleen nodded and left the lounge to get Robby.

"Now remember," Roy said, "once Robby fires up the scepter, we will be out of contact. You will need to time how long he keeps it active. Do you have a mechanical watch?

"No, it's quartz or something," Kurt said.

Roy removed an old beat up watch. "Here, use this. It was my dad's; it's one of those old self-winding mechanical jobs. You can lend me yours. Shouldn't need it though; LISA's clock will be just fine as long as she stays up and running." Roy walked over, and quietly asked, "Is Joleen going to be all right with this? She didn't say much."

"She's okay. We talked it over last night, and as long as she's with Robby when he handles the scepter again, she's okay with any tests we do."

"Okay, take this portable radio. The test might knock out cell service and who knows how long it will take to come back up. The portables are stand-alone and should come back up quickly. I'll be in the computer room, radio me when you're ready. Use channel 16 and be careful what you say. These radios aren't secure."

"Okay, I'll get Robby and Joleen, and we'll get going," Kurt said.

Vancouver Airport, B.C.
RCMP Office - September 5, 2002 - 10:00 am

Officer Connie Wilkinson was waiting for Michael Walker in the RCMP office at the Vancouver airport. She was a petite brunette, dressed in brown pants, white blouse and a loose fitting brown jacket. She could have easily passed for an office worker. She was at a small desk reviewing some documents when Walker entered. She sprang to her feet and walked over to Michael. "Agent Walker, I assume?" she said, her dark brown eyes sparkling with enthusiasm.

"Ah…just Mr. Walker or Michael, please, I'm not and…well, just don't call me agent."

Connie nodded. "Sorry about that. What is your interest in this surveillance project on that suspected terrorist cell in Winnipeg? My boss tells me one of the suspects, Amil Fawaz, might have been involved in a murder, in addition to setting fires. You identified this other fellow in my photos as Yusof Ekstrom. How are they connected?"

"We're not sure, that's why we asked you to add

Yusof to your surveillance."

"Well, we didn't get much before the two of them were killed in that explosion at Yusof's apartment last night."

"Did you find out anything?" Michael said.

"We got one lead. That's why we asked you to come here. We traced Amil's phone calls and located an office that Yusof used here in Vancouver. He operated out of it, using an alias but the secretary there identified him. And with help from you folks at CSIS, we did manage to get a search warrant for the office this morning."

Connie walked back to the desk and picked up the warrant she'd been reviewing when Michael arrived. "Ready?"

Michael nodded. "Okay, let's see if he left any clues at his office."

Diefenbaker Lake Park, Saskatchewan
September 5, 2002 - 11:00 am

Kurt pulled into the small provincial park a few miles from C-CAF. It consisted of a parking area, a few fire pits, three picnic tables, a trail leading down to Diefenbaker Lake, and an outhouse.

"Pretty basic," Kurt said, "but it serves our purpose. There is nobody around." He grabbed the radio and scepter. "Let's set up on that picnic table." He pointed to the better of the three tables.

Joleen set the pyramid in the center of the picnic table and stepped over the seat and sat down. She patted the place beside her. "Robby, sit by me."

Kurt sat across from them with the scepter in his hand. "Ready?" He looked at Joleen and Robby. They both nodded. "Okay." He keyed the radio. "We're ready."

The little radio crackled with Roy's response. "Okay, at zero then." He began the countdown. "Ten, nine, eight…" Kurt gave the scepter to Robby. At zero, Robby put his thumb in the indentation in the orb at the top of the scepter. The radio immediately went dead, and the small ball on top of the pyramid began to glow. It gave off a soft yellow light and radiated a pleasant heat.

Kurt looked at his watch. "Okay, ten minutes."

Joleen held Robby's right hand tightly but said nothing.

"Are you okay, Robby?" Kurt asked.

"Yah, Dad, no problem. This is weird, huh? That little golf ball thing on the pyramid is warm, like a campfire."

Kurt moved his hand closer to the pyramid. The amount of heat generated by the ball decreased. "It seems to have a built in safety device so it doesn't burn anyone," he said. Then he sat back and monitored the time.

"Okay, Robby, times almost up. Get ready to give the scepter to me. Ten seconds…five…okay, give it to me." Robby handed it over, and the light on the pyramid died.

"Anyone there? Anyone there?" Roy voice crackled from the radio as it came back to life.

Kurt keyed the radio. "We're here, and we're all

332

fine. Be back in about fifteen minutes. How'd it go at your end?"

"Fine," Roy said.

C-CAF - Saskatchewan
September 6, 2002 - 9:00 am

Everybody was seated around the breakfast table waiting for Roy and his analysis of the effects of the previous day's scepter test. "Where's Roy?" Joleen said.

"With LISA, I guess," Kurt said.

Lisa, who appeared lost in thought looked up, a question in her eyes. Kurt held his hand up. "Not you, the other LISA." Lisa frowned and looked down.

Kurt thought everyone seemed a little glum. Lisa and Amy were complaining that the cut and paste method for enlarging the printout of the pie-shaped artifact was taking too long, and they were beginning to question its value. Roy was too busy to write a program to do the work, and things progressed very slowly. Joleen was worried about Robby missing formal classes, and the need to get his stitches out. Only Robby seemed happy. His lessons were taking a lot less time than those in a formal classroom, and the help with his homework meant he had lots of time to play games on a super computer.

Roy burst in waving a few sheets of printout. "Good news." He looked at everyone in turn. "Shit, you folks look like you've been eating rotten sauerkraut for breakfast."

"Language," Joleen said, and nodded in Robby's direction. Robby grinned and looked away.

"Sorry." Roy shrugged. "We've had considerable progress overnight. LISA found the unique id of O'Shanigan's cell phone so she started a trace on his movements. It took a while, but LISA finally worked up a detailed record of his calls going back two months. The information gives details down to the cell tower that he was connected to at any point in time, and that gives us a pretty good idea of his movements. He showed up in the U.S. just before Kurt went on that survey of the ship out of Yuma. He made some calls to Washington. I can't seem to get any information on them. They must be classified."

"So, that's it, that's the good news?" Kurt said.

"No, shit you folks are impatient," Roy said.

Joleen raised her eyebrows and tipped her head towards Robby.

Roy ignored her. "Anyway, Father O was in Paris for awhile, most of the time near that institute he runs. Then he showed up at the Paris airport, and we lost track of him for a while. He showed up next in Frankfurt, a couple of hours later. It's too far to drive in that time so he must have flown. But, and this is important, he doesn't show up on any passenger list, so he must have flown under a false identity."

"Are you sure?" Kurt said.

"Positive. He must be trying to keep his movements secret. We double-checked; he did not fly as O'Shanigan on any commercial or private flights. Oh, that reminds me, we did find out that he arrived in Paris on a private aircraft owned by Calvert Oil. It originated out of Montana."

"Just a minute," Kurt said. "O'Shanigan left Yuma on a private plane." He pulled out a notebook and flipped through a few pages. "Yah, here it is. It was a private King Air with CLV-2 as an id."

"I'll have LISA check that out," Roy said. "But first, back to Father O's travels. The next time his cell shows up, he's in Cairo. His cell comes on just outside the airport, and then he heads into town. He's stationary for a while, and then he heads back to the airport. We lost track of him again while he was flying. Then he shows up in Yemen."

"Yemen, where did he go there?" Kurt said.

"Don't know. He only used his cell once from the airport to call his institute in Paris. The next time he showed up, he's back in Paris, first at the institute, then at a different location. LISA indicated that he's connected via that cell tower a number of times in the past, so I'm calling it Unknown-1." Roy stopped talking and smiled at his audience.

"And?" Lisa said.

"And two things. Firstly, you know I had LISA checking to see if there were any other power failures at the time Robby did that little ten-minute experiment with the scepter artifact. Well, in addition to one more at the Tower of London, she has come up with one in Paris that matched exactly with our experiment. And guess where that power failure was?" Roy waited.

"At Unknown-1," Robby shouted.

Joleen frowned.

"Right on, my little detective," Roy said. "The Unknown-1 cell site that O'Shanigan was linked to, reported a blackout at the time of our experiment, with no identifiable cause. And you know what that would mean."

"Another artifact?" Amy said.

"I don't know, but it certainly is suspicious, and we need to follow up," Roy said.

"Can you figure out exactly what building he was in using cell tower triangulation?" Kurt said.

"Right, Roy," Lisa said. "You should have my namesake figure that out. If we knew where he called from—and, what about the first time, when Robby grabbed the scepter? Was there a power failure there then, too? Did LISA find—?"

Roy put up his hands. "Whoa, give me and LISA a little time, will you? LISA's good, but even the fastest computer needs a little processing time. Besides, I'm not that fast, and I need to give her some direction. You folks finish your breakfast, and take a break or work on the enlargements. I'll get back to you as soon as I find out what other events Robby's little ten minute experiment with the scepter produced. Maybe, we'll know where Unknown-1 is by then."

****

Kurt followed Roy to the computer room. "Roy, I got some news from Walker this morning. The

RCMP located those individuals you identified. Amil Fawaz, the one linked to the fires in the U.S., and Yusof Ekstrom. They are both linked to Fadi El Khoury, a restaurant owner in Winnipeg. One of the RCMP agents who was following Amil located Yusof in Vancouver. Yusof picked up Amil in a rather run-down hotel. They went to the Vancouver General Hospital emergency room where Amil's arm was treated for a dog bite."

"Amy's dog?" Roy said.

Kurt nodded. "Probably. After Amil was treated, they went back to Yusof's apartment. The RCMP had it staked out, and an officer was sitting outside in a car when the whole front of the apartment blew out. Parts of the damn couch landed on the roof of the officer's car. There were body parts everywhere. The apartment itself was totally burnt out. They weren't able to get anything useful from the wreckage."

"What about the restaurant owner? Did you pick him up?" Roy said.

"No, while the RCMP was waiting for a warrant to pick up El Khoury, his place went up in an explosion. But in this case, the coroner said that El Khoury died from a single gunshot to the head, not the explosion. Walker said he sent us pictures of everyone entering and leaving the restaurant that night. Let's pull them up on LISA."

Roy selected a set of pictures that showed the last individual to leave the restaurant. It was a priest with his hat pulled well down, and the collar of his coat is turned up. He walked with his head down, so the pictures showed only the top of a hat, a chin, and a priest's collar.

"Can't do much with this," Kurt said.

Roy pointed at the screen. "Look, his left arm is in a sling. You said O'Shanigan's arm was in a sling. I knew it. That story you told me about your search for the ship that night. It didn't sound right. It's him, isn't it, Kurt?"

Kurt studied the picture. "Could be. I can't tell for sure."

"Yah, it's him. It all fits. His connection with Unknown-1—the way he flies around under an alias. I'm going to get LISA to concentrate on him."

"And one more thing. Walker wants us to take Robby back to the ship. He said it was your suggestion."

"Oh, right. The military folks have been unsuccessful at opening the hatch again. I suggested that Robby could do it."

"Roy, I wish you'd have discussed that with me first. I need to discuss that with Joleen. She won't be happy."

"Sorry, the idea just popped into my head."

"Anything else just pop into your head?"

"Ah, well…," Roy said. "How about I explain after we visit the ship again? I should check and see how LISA is doing on her analysis, and I could use something to eat."

Kurt studied Roy for a few moments. "Okay, later then."

"Great. I'll meet you back in the lounge."

*****

Amy, Lisa, and Joleen were kneeling on the floor taping together printouts of the enlargements of the pie-shaped artifact.

"How's it going?" Kurt said.

"I think we're finished," Lisa said. "We each took part of the little pie-shaped artifact and completed the microscopic enlargements. It took eighty-seven pages of printout to cover each section. Of course, we needed to be sure they all overlapped so we may have a few more than absolutely necessary."

"Let me tell you, we could have used a bigger printer," Joleen said. "It took us forever to cut and paste it all together." She stood up and pointed at their work. "It takes up about ten square feet, and probably could be enlarged more, but to do that you'd have to use the whole lounge."

Lisa walked over and stood beside Joleen and Amy. "We'd need Roy to develop a program for that, but we know he's been busy. Anyway, this is probably as good as we can do manually."

"It does give you a feel for what's on the artifacts," Amy said. "You can see the little characters are arranged in concentric circles on the disc, similar to how data is stored on a CD. But, we have no idea what the characters mean. They appear to be a bunch of little drawings that don't appear to make any sense."

Roy walked into the lounge. "How about some pizza?"

Lisa shook her head. "Is pizza the only thing you

eat around here?"

"Nope, I have coke along with the pizza, or if I'm on my own time, I have a beer. But food can wait. I just checked, and LISA's compiled some more information. First, there was a ten-minute WOW signal that matched Robby's most recent test with the scepter. The SETI folks are going wild. Of course, they think the signal is coming from some distant galaxy, but we know better. The elapsed time, from Robby starting up the scepter to the receipt of the WOW signal, wouldn't have even allowed a signal to get out of the solar system. LISA has done some rough calculations from the time delays she logged, and it looks like whatever is sending that signal is out near the asteroid belt."

"But you said that all of the WOWs originated from the same location in space. That would be damn difficult. And why, why would anyone do that?" Kurt said.

"Why someone would do any of this, is still anyone's guess. But, I agree that arranging for the signal to appear to come from a point in space would certainly be difficult," Roy said.

"Can you explain why that would be difficult?" Amy said. "Couldn't someone just put up a satellite near the asteroid belt?"

Roy paused for a minute. "I guess, but that satellite would have to be in orbit around the sun. It would be just like a planet. Planets wander across the sky, and depending on where the earth is in its orbit around the sun, they appear to move forward and backward. They sometimes even trace out loops. A distant star, on the other hand, is so far away that no matter where the earth is in its orbit, the star appears fixed in space relative to other stars. So, if the signal came from the asteroid belt area, the satellite or whatever, it is would have to constantly adjust its orbit to have the signal appear to come from the same point in space each time." He paused. "Did I explain that well enough?"

Amy nodded. "Okay, but then, why couldn't the signal come from some star then?"

"I guess it could, but then the little scepter would be capable of faster than light communications. And that, ladies and gentlemen, would be mind-blowing. And since that actually could be what happened, I think I need a pizza."

"And a beer," Kurt said, as he followed Roy to the fridge.

Chapter 28 - Return to Yuma

Laguna Military Base, Arizona
September 9, 2002 - 9:50 pm

The lights in the cabin of the helicopter dimmed and went out as it took off from the Laguna Military Base. Robby grabbed Kurt's hand. "Dad, the helicopter feels weird."

"I know. Don't worry though, these pilots are the best."

Robby strained to see out the window. "I can't see anything. It's too dark."

The helicopter flew low across the desert and landed beside a large Quonset hut surrounded by military equipment and armed personnel. The building was almost buried in the sand amongst the dunes. Kurt and Robby were ushered inside by a marine guard. Sand had been removed from the around the hatch, and the floor glistened under a number of spotlights.

Roy called out, "Robby, Kurt, over here." Roy was sitting on the floor holding a kerosene lantern and a small cloth.

"So Robby, does this look like the door that you found when you and your dad were camping here?"

"I don't know. It looks different. There was just a little shiny spot at the bottom of the dune. Now it's all shiny, the whole floor is shiny." Roy pointed to an area of the floor and wiped it with the cloth. "How about here? There's a small square that is just a little darker than the surrounding area. Does that look like the door?"

"Maybe. I'm not sure."

"That's okay, Robby," Kurt said. "We'll give it a try. Push on the square."

Robby reached out with his right hand and pushed on the square. Nothing happened.

"Try your other hand," Roy said.

Robby pushed the spot, and an oval section of the floor dropped away and moved to the side. Kurt grabbed Robby to keep him from slipping into the opening. All of the spotlights went out, and the three were illuminated by Roy's kerosene lamp.

"See, Dad. That's what happened. It opened just like that, and I fell in."

"Okay, then what happened?" Roy said.

"It was really dark until I stood up and…yah, I stood up and touched the wall, and lights came on."

"Okay, lean into the hole and touch the wall. Your dad will hold you, so you don't fall."

When Robby touched the wall soft reddish light began to illuminate the inside of the opening, and a ladder about eight feet long emerged from the wall. Fine particles of sand that lay on the shiny surface in the Quonset began to float up.

"Great job, Robby," Roy said. "We're going in."

"I don't want to go in unless you go in, Dad. Are you going in?"

"No," Roy said. "You and your dad are going to stay here so you can open the door if it closes. No one else can do that. I'll go in with some soldiers."

Major Roger Wilkinson from Edwards Air Force Base walked towards them from the other side of the Quonset. Roger was carrying a rifle, a sidearm and a large kerosene lantern.

"Thanks for the heads up on the lanterns, Roy," Roger said.

Soldiers began lighting more lanterns and soon a ring of soft yellow light flickered around the steady red glow emanating from the oval opening.

Roger climbed down the ladder first, looked around and signaled for the others to follow. Roy and several soldiers followed with lanterns and a spool of thin line.

Roy looked up at Kurt. "We have lanterns, and we'll lay out the line so we can find our way back if the lights go out. But, you and Robby keep the lights on and the door open, okay?"

Kurt nodded. "Good luck."

Robby and Kurt sat by the opening waiting. "How long will they be gone?" Robby said.

"They've been gone thirty minutes. It could be a couple of hours. It depends on what they find."

A marine signalman, Semaphore flags tucked

under his arm, called up from below. "Sir, they've reached the end of the coil of line, that's about five hundred feet. They're coming back."

"Dad, I have to go to the bathroom. I have to go really bad."

Kurt looked around. There was a portable washroom set up against the wall of the hut. "Robby, you have to wait," Kurt said. "You have to stay right by the door or it will close, remember?"

"Signal them that they need to hurry," Kurt said to the marine.

The marine sent the signal. "Message sent, sir."

In about five minutes, Roy stood at the base of the ladder, looking up at them.

"That was fast," Kurt said.

"Yah, we were almost back when we got the signal to hurry. What's up," Roy said, as he followed Roger up the ladder.

"Ah, Robby has to go to the bathroom."

Roy nodded and turned to the marine standing by Robby. "Everybody out?"

"We just need to get the body bags up, sir. About five minutes."

"Aliens?" Kurt said.

"Nope," Roy said. "We found three bodies. They looked like prospectors or something. The bodies were pretty well desiccated, but there didn't seem to be any bacterial action or decay, so I took some skin samples for DNA analysis, and I took a few pictures. Digital camera wouldn't work, as I expected, so I used an old mechanical film-based camera. We will need to get the film developed."

"I can look after that," Roger said. "There's a film lab back at the base."

Once everyone was out of the ship, Robby stood up and ran to the portable washroom. The lights in the opening faded, the door slid closed, and the floating sand particles slowly drifted back down.

"The exploration of the ship is going to be a bigger job that I thought," Roy said. "You wouldn't believe it. This thing's immense. It's like a maze with all sorts of side passages and doors that we couldn't open. I think we will need to take Robby down next time, that's if you can convince Joleen."

A marine walked up to Kurt. "Sir, the helicopter is ready to take you back to the base. Your plane is waiting to take you back to Canada."

****

When the Department of National Defense jet reached cruising altitude on course to Saskatoon, the co-pilot came back and looked at Robby. "Okay, Robby, you still want to come up front?"

"Dad, can I?"

"Sure, but don't touch anything and do what the pilots tell you," Kurt said.

Roy smiled. "He's a lucky kid; helicopter rides, up front with the pilots on a private jet, beats my childhood."

"Yah, but he's been away from school and his friends for a long time. Kids need more than just adults; they need others their own age to play with.

And we need to get his stitches checked."

"Ah, don't worry, Kurt, there will be lots of time for that. He's a great kid, and he's having the time of his life, especially with both you and Joleen around."

They sat for several minutes, the hum of the engines the only sound. Kurt looked at Roy. "Okay, I got Joleen to agree to this expedition, and you promised to explain your theory to me once the test was over. It's over, time for the explanation."

"How about a couple of government issue sandwiches? I'm not quite ready; we can have a bite while I check with LISA."

"Lisa, why? What's she got to…oh, you mean electronic LISA. Roy, you really need to change the computer's name."

Roy nodded and retrieved a couple of sandwiches from a small fridge at the front of the cabin. "Ham and cheese or ham and cheese? There's no pizza, too bad."

Kurt took the sandwich and watched as Roy set up a link from his laptop to LISA. "Damn, this link is slow. It will take a while." Roy took a bite of his sandwich. "Not as good as pizza but—"

"Quit stalling, Roy."

Roy leaned closer to Kurt and lowered his voice. "Okay, here's what I think. We all pretty well agree that Robby is an integral part in this mystery. But how do all the parts connect? The artifacts from Canyon De Chelly, the ship down there, the WOW, the simultaneous power failures throughout the world, and Robby?" Roy's laptop chirped, and he turned away.

Kurt watched as Roy entered a few commands.

"Okay, LISA has confirmed my theory. The WOW is triggered by a transmission from the ship. When the door is opened by Robby, or he activates the scepter, the ship sends out a signal and the point in space responds. I shut LISA down because of the artifacts at C-CAF, but I set up a number of other computers to collect data for her. There were power failures at C-CAF, in London, and Paris. They all matched the time we had the door to the ship open. So that confirms: one, that the artifacts and the ship are connected; two, there are likely two more artifacts; and three, Robby can activate them all."

"Okay, that's not really earth shattering, we already came to that conclusion," Kurt said. "But why Robby, and only Robby?"

"You know I believe it's Robby's polydactylism. It's the sixth digit on his left hand that somehow gives him the power."

"Roy, the CIA guys already tested a couple of polydactyl individuals at the ship. Nothing happened. you're probably wrong."

"No, Kurt, even though they tested a number of others with the condition, I still think it's the key. Robby is different. In most cases of polydactylism, the digit is just a portion split off from one of the other fingers. It isn't really a sixth digit. In Robby's case though, he has six fully functional fingers. But that's not all.

"The book of Genesis talks of fallen angels, or Nephilim. They are said to have mated with human females. The Nephilim's offspring were said to have six fingers. Or, in the Book of Enoch, it describes the watchers. They were supposedly angels sent to earth to watch over the people. They eventually mated with the human women and had children with six fingers on one hand."

"So Roy, are you honestly trying to tell me Robby is some sort of descendant of God. You, an avowed agnostic, have you gone religious? Think about what this idea would do to Joleen? I mean—is that what you're telling me?"

"No, no, not exactly. There are ancient statues and drawings all over the world depicting six-fingered gods. I think that all these ancient stories have an element of truth. Over the years, they were handed down from generation to generation orally, and slowly changed, or perhaps, they were changed intentionally by priests or priestesses to control their citizens. Anyway, the stories of six-fingered humans who descended from the gods are remarkably similar all over the world.

"Now, we just left a ship that is obviously not of this world. We still don't know when it came here, where it came from, or anything about the crew. Could the crew have had six fingers and could they have mated with humans? Would their offspring have six fingers?"

"Maybe," Kurt said. "But, Robby can't be—"

"Can't be what? Can't be genetically linked to some ancient visitor from another world? Think about it, a boy with six fingers on his left hand can make that ship come alive. Is there any other conclusion?"

"That would mean Joleen or me, or maybe both of us, are genetically linked to…to these ancients, these aliens."

"Right," Roy said. "That's why I had Robby's DNA tested."

"What, when?"

"I sent out a sample when I first came up with the theory. I just got the results back. Robby has some very special DNA."

"When were you going to tell me?" Kurt said.

"I wanted the results first. I mean it really is a wild theory and—"

"Shit Roy. When Joleen finds out, she's going to be upset."

Robby returned from the cockpit. "What's mom going to be upset about—about me going up with the pilots?"

"No, no, she'll be fine with it. What did you see?"

"It's really neat, Dad. The plane flies itself. They enter where they want to go in the computer, and then they just watch."

"So, we don't need pilots?" Roy said.

"No, they told me they were needed to take off and land, to set up the computer, and to watch for other planes. They said they would let me come up again when it was time to land. Can I do it, Dad?"

"Sure," Kurt said. "Roy and I can finish our discussion when you are up front. Come here by me and look out the window." Kurt put his arm around Robby's shoulders and closed his eyes.

Chapter 29 - Emergency Room

Ding, the microwave spoke.

Roy jumped to its command, and announced, "Pizza's ready."

Joleen looked up from an animated conversation with Lisa. "Roy, it's not healthy. You have to eat more than pizza, you know."

"Well, everyone was so focused, I didn't want to interrupt. Somebody had to make dinner."

"It shouldn't have been you," Lisa said. "We've had enough pizza. It's just about the only thing we've eaten since we arrived here. I'll roast some potatoes and make a salad. You and Kurt can burn some steak. You did a good job last time."

"I'll help," Joleen said. "Robby needs something more nutritious than pizza."

Roy took the pizza out of the microwave. "Whoa

351

now, pizza is one of the four components of Health Canada's Food Guide. The others are beer, bacon, and ice cream."

"Four? I thought there were seven. What happened to popcorn, nachos, and French fries?" Kurt said.

"Gone, it's just pizza, beer, bacon, and ice cream, that's all you're supposed to eat now." Roy laughed.

"Okay, you two, enough already. Remember, you're role models for Robby. What if he were in the room now, what would he think? Huh? What would he think?" Joleen said.

"Joleen, I thought we agreed—Robby's a smart kid. He'd know we were joking, and with the computer power here, he'd be up on the net looking up the real guide to show us," Roy said. "He'd—"

Whummph, the floor and walls shook, and the lights flickered.

"Was that an earthquake?" Amy said.

Roy rushed to the nearest terminal and pushed a couple of keys. "Shit, they've found us."

"Who? What's happened?" Joleen said.

"They've blown the outside door and are coming down the tunnel," Roy said, as he punched in a couple of queries on his keyboard. "They must have disabled the intruder alarm to get to the doors without us being alerted. Must be pros."

"Who?" Joleen and Lisa said in unison.

"Don't know, but they don't look friendly. They have balaclavas, laser sighted rifles, and night vision goggle and...ah shit, it looks like they have more than enough explosives to blow the inner door."

They all gathered around Roy just in time to see one of the figures raise his rifle and fire at the monitor. The screen went blank.

"That's not good," Kurt said. "We've lost track of them now."

"Who are they?" Joleen asked again. "Robby, where's Robby? They're after Robby, aren't they?"

"I'll get him, Joleen, you stay here." Kurt dashed out of the room and returned in a few seconds with Robby.

Joleen grabbed Robby's hand and pulled him close. "Robby, what have your father and I done to you?"

"Kurt, they're checking out the second door. We better get ready. I think we're going to use some of the combat training HQ insisted that we take," Roy said. "We'll need the guns from the arms locker, especially the rifles; we'll need those to match their firepower. Anyone know how to handle a rifle?"

"No, never even held a gun," Lisa said.

"Me, either, "Amy said. " I'm afraid of guns."

"I can," Joleen said, as she pulled Robby even closer. "I used to shoot tin cans with my dad."

"Okay, only Roy and I will need side arms," Kurt said. "I'll get two pistols and rifles for those who know how to use them. Lisa can help Roy, and Amy can look after Robby."

"Roy, see if you can find out what those guys in the tunnel are up to," Kurt said. "Amy, look after Robby. Joleen, come with me to get the rifles and ammo, and Lisa, you get the three artifacts. I have an idea."

In a couple of minutes, everyone returned—Lisa with the artifacts, and Kurt and Joleen with the pistols, three M-16s, and a tote bag with twenty fully loaded magazines.

"Joleen, give Roy one of the M-16s and some ammo."

Lisa and Kurt joined Roy at the monitor. Kurt could see five figures, two at a door working on the keypad, and three standing back, rifles ready. "Thought they shot out the camera?" Kurt said.

"They did, but there is a second one facing the door. It's hidden in a light fixture, so they don't know it's there. Someone had foresight, or maybe it was just a little blind-ass luck."

"Okay, I have an idea. Can we turn off the lights?" Kurt asked.

"Sure, we can control that from this console, but they have night vision goggles." Roy pointed at the screen. "It would give them the advantage."

"Ah, but we have something that will take that advantage away. Something they will never expect." Kurt held up the scepter.

"Huh, oh, never thought of that. It'll work. How do you want to set it up?"

Kurt looked around. "You ready, Joleen?"

She nodded. "I think I can handle a reload. I'm as ready as I'm going to get."

"Roy, show Lisa how to turn the lights off and on, and how to open and close the main door. And Roy, you fire up the hall from your position as soon as the door opens."

"Okay, Robby, take the scepter, hold it in your

right hand," Kurt said. "Amy, take Robby over to the corner and get behind that steel cabinet. Put the little pyramid and the other artifact in a drawer. We don't want the pyramid's light showing them where we are. Joleen come here. Lay on the floor here with your rifle around the corner pointed up the hallway. I will stand above you with my rifle. Robby, when I shout now, grab the scepter like before with your left hand. When I shout stop, take it back in your right hand. Understand?"

Robby nodded.

"Better hurry. They are setting out some explosives," Roy said.

"Okay, Lisa kill the lights," Kurt said.

The room went dark. Lisa sat at the console basked in a dim glow from the computer terminal.

"Lisa, I want you to open the hallway door when I say open, and close it as soon as you can after Robby shuts the scepter down and the computer comes back up," Kurt said. "Joleen, Roy, stay back until I say shoot, then move out and start firing as fast as you can up the hallway. Keep firing until I say stop."

"I'm ready," Lisa said.

"Okay, here goes. Everyone get ready. Lisa, open the door."

Red beams from the laser sighted rifles knifed down the dark hall.

"Robby, now," Kurt shouted.

The red beams disappeared. Angry shouts came from the hall. A voice shouted, "What the hell. My goggles have conked."

Another voice said, "Mine, too."

"Okay, shoot," Kurt said.

Kurt, Roy, and Joleen leaned into the hall and began firing. The unsilenced weapons were deafening in the closed space.

The intruders, surprised by the failure of their equipment and the counterattack, failed to return fire for several seconds.

"Ahhh, my leg, I'm hit," one of the intruders called out.

"My neck, my neck," a different voice called out. "Shi…, uugh."

From the tunnel entrance, a voice rose above the gunfire. "Lay down some covering fire, ga'damn it."

Suddenly the tunnel lit up with flashes from the silenced rifles of the intruders. Bullets whipped over the defenders heads and ricocheted off the concrete walls, but Kurt, Joleen and Roy kept firing.

One of the intruders called out, "How many hit? Count off."

"One."

"Three. But I can't walk. It's my leg."

"Four"

"Two, are you down?" the voice shouted.

There was no response.

"Fall back, regroup."

The flashes from the silenced weapons moved back up the tunnel.

"Okay, Joleen keep firing as fast as you can," Kurt said, and then shouted, "Robby, stop."

Kurt could see the laser sights from the rifles become active again. "Okay, Lisa, shut the door."

"She's waiting on the system," Roy shouted.

"Okay, it's back up."

Kurt couldn't see if the door closed. "We need the lights, Lisa."

"Is everyone okay," Kurt said, as the room lights came on.

"Wait, don't leave me," a figure on the floor wearing a black balaclava shouted as the door slid shut.

Kurt rushed forward, kicked two laser sighted rifles away and pointed his own rifle at the prone man. "Don't move." He turned to examine the other downed assailant. He was dead. Shot in the neck and head. Out of the corner of his eye, Kurt saw a movement. He turned to see a handgun being pulled out from under a bulletproof vest.

"Kurt, look out," Joleen shouted.

Kurt pulled the trigger on his rifle. Click.

A smile formed on the lips protruding through the balaclava as the wounded figure pointed the pistol at Kurt's head.

Bang, a shot rang out; a bullet struck the hooded figure between the eyes. Kurt turned to see Joleen staring down the sights of her rifle at the dead man.

"Thank God for tin cans," Lisa muttered.

Montreal, Quebec
- September 11, 2002 - 9:15 pm

The Greek sat waiting, a disposable cell phone in his hand. Twenty-five minutes had passed since he placed the call from a pay phone and left a coded message with the cell number. The priest should call soon. It had never taken him longer than twenty minutes to return a call in the past.

The phone rang. "Hello," the Greek said.

"Status?" a voice answered.

He recognized the voice as the priest's. "The operation is underway as we speak. It should be over soon."

"And the boy will be dead."

"If he is there, he will die."

"He is. My intelligence is solid. Do not fail me again."

The Greek knew what happened to Yusof and Amil. He would not fail the priest again.

"We will not fail. Do not worry."

"How long?"

"Maybe ten more minutes. I gave the go ahead for the operation about thirty minutes ago. It should be over soon."

"Notify me when it's over. I will instruct you on what to do with the scroll. Then destroy your cell phone." The priest hung up.

That was it. He held the phone in his shaking hands, waiting for a call from the team confirming the kill. He could not fail again.

C-CAF – Saskatchewan
September 11, 2002 - 6:40 pm

Joleen started to cry. "Oh, Lisa, I've…I've killed. It's a sin."

Lisa grabbed Joleen by the shoulder and shook her. "Joleen, he would have killed Kurt, and maybe Robby. You had to protect your son and…and Kurt. Thank God, you shot those tin cans with your dad."

Joleen nodded. "Yes, thank God. He will forgive me. I was protecting Robby."

"Kurt," Roy said. "It's not over. Get over here. They are getting ready to blow the door, and that trick with the lights and night vision goggles won't work again. It looks like they are coming in low tech this time. They have flares instead of night vision goggles."

"We need to get out of this open area. We need a more defensible position," Kurt said. "But where?"

"The fire emergency room. It's at the far end of the complex. It has a fire door, and enough emergency air to last several days. But…"

"But what?" Kurt said.

"Well, I tried to get an emergency message out. They must have cut the land lines and blocked the cell system. I can't reach anyone. We are on our own, and I don't know if those fire doors can take C4 explosives."

Kurt looked at the screen. "Well, it will have to do. They look like they are about to blast the tunnel door. Come on everyone, grab the rifles and ammo, and follow Roy. Amy, Robby, bring the scepter and other two artifacts from the drawer. Once we are hidden we will turn off the lights again. No need making it easy for them."

"Dad, help," Robby said.

Kurt turned. Amy was standing beside Robby

clutching her shoulder. Blood was running down her arm. The color drained from her face, and she leaned up against a file cabinet and sank to the floor.

"Dad!"

"Joleen," Roy said. "You help Amy. Kurt and I will handle the weapons. Robby, you bring the three artifacts."

Robby nodded.

"There's a first aid kit in the emergency room. We can look after Amy there. We need to go right now," Roy said.

Roy led them to the fire emergency room and secured the doors. "Okay, let's get behind these steel cabinets and set up to defend ourselves when, ah… if they get through the doors."

"Won't be long before they figure out where we are," Kurt said. "Joleen, get Robby and Amy down behind those cabinets in the back and put the pyramid and other artifact in a drawer again. How bad is Amy's wound?"

"It's her arm. I don't think the bone is hit, but there's a lot of blood. I need to keep pressure on the wound."

"I need you here, get some gauze from the first aid kit and show Robby how to apply pressure, then come over here. We'll take up our positions here. Roy and Lisa, you set up on the other side of the room. Joleen, once Robby has pressure on the wound, make sure he can use the scepter to turn off the lights."

"Robby, keep pushing this gauze on Amy's arm. I have to help your dad," Joleen said.

Joleen joined Kurt. "Get ready with the rifles," Kurt said. "Robby, you might as well turn off the lights."

They sat silently in the dark for a few minutes. Whuump. The floor shook.

"That's the tunnel door. They're in the facility," Roy said.

They could hear angry shouts. They were getting louder. The handle to the fire door rattled, and a voice shouted, "They're in here. Bring the plastique."

"Shit," Roy said.

Chapter 30 - JTF-2

Emergency Room - C-CAF
September 11, 2002 - 7:10 pm

They waited for the explosion.

The other side of the door erupted in gunfire, and then there was silence.

"What happened?" Lisa said.

"I don't know, but those weren't silenced rifles. Our friends with the explosives carried silenced weapons," Roy said.

There was a light tap at the door. "Roy, Kurt, you in there? It's Michael, Michael Walker. Are you all right?"

"Yah," Roy shouted. "I'll open the door."

Roy pulled the door open. A blinding light from a flare penetrated the room.

"It's okay. It's me Michael Walker. You can lower your weapons," a voice shouted from the behind the light.

"Kurt?" Joleen aimed her rifle towards the voice.

Michael Walker stepped into the light. "Joleen, it's okay. We're the good guys. We are all on the same side." Four figures in jet-black uniforms with masks over their faces followed Walker into the room. "You can put down the rifle; you're safe now. These guys are Canadian Special Forces, JTF-2."

Joleen set her rifle down and went back to where Robby and Amy were hiding.

"Is anyone hurt?" Michael asked.

"Yah, back there with Joleen," Roy said. "You have a medic with you?"

A voice out of the darkness responded. "Yes, the Special Forces have medical personnel with them. Get a medic in here."

Kurt looked past Michael. A small well-dressed man with piercing blue eyes was standing just outside the doorway. "And get Rosa, she's a fully qualified trauma nurse." When their eyes met, the man strode forward hand extended, a smile warming his face.

"Rosa? Who's Rosa, and who the hell are you?" Kurt said.

Michael held up his hand, palm outward. "Kurt, you have been out of the loop on a few things. This is Arthur Calvert. Once we get everybody on the planes, I'll explain."

"Planes? You have planes. How many?" Kurt said.

"We came in on helicopters from the Canadian Forces Base, Moose Jaw. We have the Hercules that the JTF-2 guys and I came in on, and Arthur's plane is waiting for us in Moose Jaw. It is lucky we were already on our way when your communications went out or…"

Michael stopped and peered out the door. "Give the JTF2 guys a few minutes to clean up. It's kind of bloody out there. No need for Robby to see…well, you know." He looked around. "Where is he?"

Kurt pointed. "He's behind the file cabinets. He's applying pressure to Amy's wounds.

"Okay, we'll see if we can get the lights back on and get you folks packed up," Michael said.

"I think we can fix that. Robby, the lights. Turn the lights on," Kurt said.

Robby took his thumb out of the small indentation on the scepter, and the lights came on.

"Robby and the scepter?" Michael said.

Kurt nodded.

Arthur Calvert moved to where a medic was treating Amy. "Medic, can the injured person travel?"

"Yes, sir. There's blood everywhere, but she doesn't seem to be injured."

Amy walked out from behind the file cabinet. "I'm…I'm fine." She pulled the sleeve of her blouse up. "There's a small mark on my shoulder. But I was shot. I don't understand."

The medic came out from behind the cabinet. "That's it, sir, a small scratch is the only injury, but I don't see how it produced so much blood."

"That can't be," Joleen said. "I saw the wound."

Arthur motioned toward the door. "Okay, that can wait. Let's get everyone loaded on the planes and get out of here. The guys that attacked you may have friends nearby, and who knows what they could be up to."

Michael peered out the door. "Okay, they have most of the carnage covered up. They'll finish cleaning up once we leave, and the sooner, the better. The helicopters, gunfire, and a bunch of special forces are going to require quite a cover story."

"Terrorist attack on the power station should work," Roy said.

Michael nodded. "Okay, get your stuff together and meet me at the exit tunnel."

"LISA, what about LISA? We need her," Kurt said.

Michael turned. "It's okay. Everyone is coming with us."

"No, Kurt means the computer. I nicknamed her LISA. All our work's there. We need access to the computer," Roy said.

"Oh, no problem. All your data is backed up in Ottawa, and you will have access to that data and all the computing power you need at the Mesa," Walker said.

"Where?" Kurt said.

Michael held up his hand. "On the plane—keep all that till we're on the plane. Anything else you need, Kurt?"

"Just the artifacts and our handmade diagrams. Roy, you gather the artifacts and head up to the surface. I'll go to the lounge and get the diagrams. I'll meet you there."

The group left the safe room and made their way around pools of blood and sheet-draped bodies as they headed up the tunnel to the surface.

On the way, Arthur Calvert joined Roy and Lisa. "Roy Matacowski, the computer genius, I assume?" He extended his hand to Roy. "I can assure you we have more than ample computer power and communications at the Mesa for you."

He looked at Lisa and extended his hand. "And, you must be Lisa, the anthropology professor. I must say your pictures don't do you justice."

"Pictures?" Lisa said, as she shook Arthur Calvert's hand.

Canadian Forces Base, Moose Jaw, Saskatchewan
September 11, 2002 - 10:15 pm

Calvert One climbed toward cruising altitude after takeoff from Canadian Forces Base, Moose Jaw, and the seatbelt sign went off. Rosa got up from the rear-facing seat at the front of the cabin and walked to where Amy, Lisa and Joleen sat. She looked at Amy. "Would you like to get out of those bloody clothes? We have extra uniforms in the rear. I'm sure we could find something to fit you."

Amy nodded. "That would be perfect. I look horrible."

"Okay, follow me."

Joleen touched Rosa's arm. "Is Robby all right up there with the pilots?"

"Oh sure. There's a jump seat they use when

366

there's a trainee pilot aboard. It has all the seatbelts and safety features, but it's right up there where you can see everything. I sat there a few times myself. It's interesting on takeoff and landing but a bit boring at cruising altitude. I'll check on him in as soon as I show Amy where the clothes are."

Rosa returned in a few minutes. "Maybe Robby's hungry? I have a young nephew, and we can't seem to feed him often enough. We have an extensive menu; Robby should find something he likes." Rosa smiled.

"That's a good idea. Robby probably could use something," Joleen said.

"What about you two? Can I get you anything from the bar or kitchen?" She pulled a menu from the pocket in the back of Lisa's seat. "Take a look at this. I'll be right back." She walked up the aisle to where Arthur Calvert was struggling with his seat. She said a few words to him, and he stood back. She pulled a few levers on the seat and spun it around to face the rear. She did the same with Michael Walker's seat, and, then pulled a small table from its storage position against the bulkhead. Michael and Arthur sat down facing Roy and Kurt, separated by the small table.

Lisa, who had been leaning into the aisle watching, turned to Joleen. "I'm glad she's not sitting in that jump seat."

"Huh, why?"

"Geeze, Joleen, look at her. She looks more like a model than a flight attendant. How would the pilots keep their minds on their job? She's also a trauma nurse and did you see her handle those seats?"

"What…no, I…"

"Joleen, where are you?"

"Robby saw me kill that man, Lisa. How's that going to affect him? I mean, his mom killed someone. What kind of example is that?"

"Joleen, you saved Kurt's life and probably Robby's, too. I told you that. Maybe you saved all of us. That's not a terrible example." Lisa leaned over and hugged Joleen. "Let's go up and check on the guys. Come on."

Lisa led Joleen to the table where Roy and the others were sitting. "What are you guys up to? Boys only?"

Roy stood up. "No, sit here. Where's Amy?"

"She's changing clothes. I'll go and check on her," Rosa said.

"Just a minute," Arthur said. "Rosa, let's move to the conference room. We can all sit around the table in there. We can have something to eat; I know I'm getting hungry."

"Pizza and beer?" Roy said.

Lisa rolled her eyes. "Here?"

"That's no problem," Rosa said, "pizza and beer for everyone. I'll prepare the snack and bring Robby along when it's ready."

"I guess I'll start," Michael said, as they sat down around the conference table. "But where?"

"How about there." Roy nodded toward Arthur. "So far, all we know about him is his name, and that he has a really nice plane."

Arthur smiled but remained silent.

"Good a place as any," Michael said. "Arthur Calvert is the owner of Calvert Oil. It is the largest privately held oil company in the world. As you can see from this plane, he has a lot of resources at his disposal. Anyway, after your tests with Robby and the scepter, I was directed to contact Arthur and brief him on the artifacts' strange effects. It turns out that Arthur works with a top secret group, the ACD within the United States National Security Agency."

"ACD, never heard of it," Roy said.

"And you won't. It's not listed in any directory, and none of the individuals in the group work directly for the NSA," Arthur said.

"So what is the ACD?" Kurt said.

"The Alien Contact Directorate. Our mission is to collect all the intelligence we can on past or present alien contacts and prepare for future contacts. My particular specialty is historical artifacts. Calvert Oil's private museum allows me to collect these artifacts without arousing suspicion. Well, nothing suspicious that links back to the ACD or the NSA. There's always suspicion that I am illegally plundering archeological sites. But enough about the museum; Michael, why don't you continue."

"No, no, wait," Joleen said. "Alien contact, what does this have to do with Robby?"

"You haven't told her?" Michael said, looking at Kurt, and then Roy.

"Told me what? Kurt, what haven't you told me?"

"Roy arranged to test Robby's—" A tap at the door stopped Kurt.

The door opened. Robby marched in with a huge

plate of fries and a burger followed by Rosa with two large pizzas. "Sorry to interrupt but everything is hot," Rosa said.

"No, that's just fine. Our discussion can wait. Robby, sit here by me," Kurt said.

"Okay, beer and coke coming up," Rosa said.

*****

As they ate, Arthur explained where they were going. He outlined the mesa's amenities and security features. There were few questions. Everyone seemed a bit dazed by the evening's events.

Rosa cleared what was left of the pizza as Arthur finished his explanation.

"The captain has asked that you all go back into the main cabin and buckle up in forward facing seats, in preparation for landing. Robby, you can go back up with the pilots. If that's okay?" She looked at Joleen.

Joleen nodded. "Sure." Then she looked at Kurt. "Come on, we need to talk." She led him to a pair of seats near the rear of the plane. "Okay, what haven't you told me?"

Kurt fidgeted for a while. "We had Robby's DNA mapped."

"DNA, why…why would you do that? And why didn't you ask me? It's not right. I'm his mother…no, you don't think you're his father? Kurt, oh, Kurt." Joleen covered her face with her hands.

"Joleen, it's not that. I know I'm his father." He

pulled her close. "It's not that."

Joleen looked into his eyes. "Tell me then, what is it?"

"It's Robby's polydactylism. Roy believes it's more than just the fact that Robby has six fingers on his left hand that allows him to make these artifacts work. He believes Robby has some sort of supernatural powers; otherwise, we could just put an extra finger on the scepter and trick it," Kurt said.

"Supernatural power." Joleen shook her head. "What do you mean by supernatural?"

Roy believes Robby has some unique DNA that the scepter detects. He says polydactylism is caused by a problem with one or more genes."

"We knew that," Joleen said.

"It's more than that. Robby is unique. Almost none of those with the gene have a perfectly formed sixth finger. Roy's search on LISA has turned up almost no modern cases of a perfect sixth finger. In addition, the DNA mapping showed Robby doesn't have that gene, but he has a whole section of DNA that is different from the rest of humanity. He's special."

"Well, didn't he get his DNA from us? Don't we have that same DNA?" Joleen said.

"I don't know. We will need to get tested. Somehow we passed on something to Robby. Roy thinks it's been passed down from some ancient contact with aliens. There are lots of clues from the past that point to this. There are hundreds of ancient statues with six fingers. There are myths like the Nephilim and the Watchers."

"Nephilim, the fallen angels? Roy thinks Robby—he thinks we are linked to angels or aliens?" Joleen said.

"More than just Roy. It looks like Arthur Calvert and his Alien Contact Directorate seem to think that as well."

Joleen leaned back and stared at the bulkhead for a while. "Are there no other people like Robby?"

"Probably, but nobody has located them. We would need to test their DNA or get them to try and activate an artifact."

Joleen nodded. "But—"

The plane touched down hard, and Joleen grabbed the armrests.

The pilot came on. "Sorry, folks. Bit of a crosswind. Please remain in your seats. We will be ready for you to disembark in a couple of minutes."

Lufthansa Shuttle - Frankfurt to Rome
September 12, 2002 - 8:00 am

"May I help you put that in the overhead bin, Father?" the stewardess said. "It must be difficult with your arm in a sling."

"Yes, please," he said.

"Father Francis, isn't it? You have flown with us frequently, haven't you?"

"Yes," he said, thankful that he was using the fake Canadian passport. The stewardess might have started asking questions if she recognized him, and he had been traveling under his real name.

"You were lucky. We delayed our departure since there were a number of individuals connecting from the Cairo flight. A few more minutes and we would have left you behind. You better take your seat. We will be taking off shortly."

Father Francis turned on his cell phone and checked his text messages before the plane took off. There was one message. It said "Boy escaped – on way to Calvert Mesa - unhurt!!!"

He read the message again.

How could they have failed? A boy, three women, and a couple of amateur agents against five experienced mercenaries. Is everyone incompetent?

Calvert Mesa, Montana
September 12, 2002 - 1:45 am

Arthur Calvert's staff handled the arrival of the large batch of guests with efficiency and within fifteen minutes of landing, they were all in their rooms.

Kurt, Joleen, and Robby were given a three bedroom suite. Each bedroom included an en suite bathroom and a large window that looked out over the mesa. The windows were made of special glass that was opaque until the lights in the room were dimmed. From the exterior, no one could distinguish the windows from the multitude of small indentations in the cliff face. The living area included a similar window that looked out over a small balcony.

Joleen found a note on a white terry bathrobe hanging in the bathroom. It said "Mrs. Sigurdson, in the bedroom closet you will find a selection of clothes. They should be your size. Please pick out what you like. If there is anything missing, or anything that you would like that is not there please call 366. If we have it, we will bring it right up."

Wow, Joleen thought, this Arthur Calvert runs quite an operation. She showered and selected loose-fitting powder blue terry pants and a matching top. Kurt was waiting for her in the living area. He wore brown cord slacks and a matching polo shirt.

"Clothes for you, too?" Joleen said.

"Yah, and for Robby, he's waiting for us. Wants us to help him select."

They went into Robby's bedroom and came out in a few minutes with Robby in jeans and a Mickey Mouse t-shirt.

"Mr. Calvert seems to have pretty good intelligence on us," Kurt said.

"How did he get our sizes?"

"Credit card history, probably."

"They have all that information on us. That can't be right."

"Well, Roy said he could dig that out with LISA, and I expect this Mr. Calvert has guys as good as Roy."

Joleen shook her head. "What's the world coming to?"

"You don't want to know," Kurt said. "But, come here, I want to show you something."

Kurt walked over to the opaque window and

pushed a button. The room dimmed. A number of small red LEDs bordering the room at floor level turned on. "Red lights, our night vision is most sensitive to red light, and it doesn't inhibit your ability to see in low light. Look." He pointed at the window.

Slowly the window became transparent yielding a panoramic view of the moonlit canyon below the mesa. The three of them stood there in silence looking out on the scene.

Finally, Robby said, "It sure is pretty, isn't it, Mom?"

Joleen reached out and put her arm around Robby and pulled him close. "Yes, it's pretty." Then she reached out and put her other arm around Kurt and pulled him close. Kurt put his arm around Joleen, grabbed Robby's hand, and pulled them both closer. Then they just stood there, looking out at the canyon.

"I'm hungry," Robby said. "Can I have some pizza?"

"No, Robby," Joleen said. "Roy has fed us enough pizza to last a lifetime. How about a tuna salad sandwich and some carrot sticks? You like tuna salad. And carrots, they help you see in the dark. Your dad and I will have a sandwich, too."

Robby shrugged. "I like pizza better, and I can see real good already."

"Kurt, can you see if we can order something? Rosa said twenty-four hours a day."

Kurt went to the phone and called food services. "They said ten minutes. We better get ready." He pressed a button—the window went opaque, and the lights came up.

A steward delivered the food in less than ten minutes. He introduced himself and set the food out on the small dining table. "Arthur would like you all to join him in the main dining room for breakfast tomorrow at nine. We will have a nice buffet," he said as he left.

"I wonder how many people Mr. Calvert has working here?" Kurt said as they ate.

When they finished, Joleen said, "Robby, I think it is time for bed. Go brush your teeth and get those Donald Duck jammies on. I will come and tuck you in."

"Dad, will those men come back again? Can I sleep with you? Mom, can I sleep with dad? I don't want to sleep alone."

"Sure, if your dad says it's okay."

Kurt nodded. "Okay, go brush your teeth and get those pajamas on like your mom said, and go and hop into my bed. I will be there in a little while."

Robby went to Kurt's bedroom and turned on the TV.

Kurt grasped Joleen's hand as they sat down on the couch. "Are you okay, Joleen? You look a bit ashen."

"Kurt, I killed a man today. How's Robby going to react to that? What will he think?"

"Well, first off, he doesn't know you killed someone. He didn't see any of that. He was way in the back. And you don't have to tell him until he is older, when he will understand. In fact, you never have to tell him, if you don't want to."

"I couldn't lie to him."

"You wouldn't have to lie. You just wouldn't bring it up."

"No, I'll have to tell him. He will have to know and judge me."

"Okay," Kurt said, "but when he's older and better able to understand."

Joleen nodded.

"Okay," Kurt said, "we should get to bed, too. Nine o'clock for breakfast will seem awful early. It's already two-fifteen. That gives us only about five hours of sleep."

Kurt started towards his bedroom. Joleen fell in step beside him and put her arm around him. "I don't want to sleep alone tonight either."

Kurt squeezed her close. "It's a king-sized bed. Room enough for three."

Chapter 31 - Confessions

Calvert Mesa, Montana
September 12, 2002 - 8:50 am

Joleen, Robby and Kurt stepped onto the elevator on their way to the dining room. "Six floors in the complex, that's pretty amazing," Kurt said, as the elevator doors started to close.

"Hold the elevator, hold the elevator." Roy stuck his hand between the closing doors and pushed them open. Lisa and Roy stood there—Roy with a broad grin lighting up his face and Lisa with a small smirk on her's. She winked at Kurt.

"Interesting sleeping arrangements last night," Lisa said.

"Yah, we all slept in one bed," Robby said. "It was real big."

Joleen looked down and started to blush.

Lisa cocked her head and looked at Joleen. "Well, I'll be. I wasn't talking about you folks. I was talking about me. I slept alone."

"Why, what happened?" Kurt said.

"Ah, Roy was up all night with the other LISA and a bunch of her friends. He—"

Roy was bouncing up and down in the corner of the elevator and could no longer contain himself. "Kurt, you wouldn't believe it. I have access to LISA, Ottawa headquarters and three supercomputers. Me, only me, with control of three super computers. It's unheard of—they are all working on all our analysis. They're kicking out results faster than I can look at them. Apparently, there's a large eighty-two inch plotter on-site. I have it printing out huge enlargements of the pie-shaped artifact. I've—"

The elevator doors opened, and a smiling Arthur Calvert greeted them. "Good morning, everyone, I trust that you all slept well and found everything you needed. I hope you have recovered from yesterday's ordeal. Come this way, please."

Arthur extended his arm toward the dining area with its panoramic view of the canyon below. "Michael Walker and Amy are already here. Sit anywhere. John will bring us coffee, tea, or juice—or anything you like. And to keep it simple this morning, we are going to have a buffet. It should be ready in a couple of minutes. Robby, anything particular you would like?"

"Oh, no, Mr. Calvert, Robby can have what's on the buffet," Joleen said.

"Arthur, just Arthur please, we are quite informal here on the mesa. If the buffet's okay that's fine, but if Robby wants something special, please don't hold back."

As John served the group beverages, Arthur said, "Roy, I hope the computer and communication facilities here are to your liking?"

Roy nodded. "I've never had so much computing power at my disposal."

"That's good because we have a special problem for you to work on. Michael, why don't you explain."

Michael took a package out of his briefcase. "We had followed Yusof to an office in Vancouver. Just one of those shared office fronts with a company phone number, and a shared secretary. The secretary was to have sent this off via courier, but the street around the FedEx office was shut off due to a gas leak so she came back. We caught up with her just as she was going out to try again. She was nice enough to hold the package until we served a warrant. Lucky break."

Walker set a polished wooden box on the table in front of Roy and Kurt. "This is what was in the package." He opened the box and removed a small velvet bag revealing a gold scroll.

"Wow," Roy said, "that must be worth a chunk of change. Was this all about money?"

Arthur, who sat quietly through Walker's story, said, "The text on the scroll appears to be written in ancient script We hope that you, Mr. Matacowski, with your computer skills, will be able to decipher our gold scroll."

"Gold Scroll. You have the Gold Scroll?" Terry

O'Shanigan shouted as he entered the room from the stairwell access.

Roy jumped up and turned to face Terry. "You, what are you doing here, and where's the sling? What do you know about the scroll? Michael, what the hell is he doing here?"

"Well, Terry, you seemed to have caused quite a commotion. I see some of you know Terry. For those of you who don't, this is Father Terry O'Shanigan. He has been one of the key members of the ACD for some time."

"Sorry to get so excited, Arthur," Terry said. "But the Gold Scroll, you didn't tell me it would be here,"

"I didn't know either. Things happened so fast, I think we are all lacking complete information. First thing after breakfast, we will have a roundtable discussion in the conference room where everyone can be brought up to date."

"But the scroll, I must see the scroll," Terry said.

"Terry, it's not going anywhere. The buffet is ready. Please everyone, help yourselves."

*****

After breakfast, everyone except Joleen and Robby gathered in the conference room. Joleen had arrange for Rosa to take out Robby's stitches. "Kurt can fill me in tonight. I don't think I have anything new to add to the discussion," Joleen said, as she left with Robby.

"Okay," Arthur said, "Roy, why don't you

381

explain your theories."

"What about him?" Roy nodded toward O'Shanigan. "Why doesn't he go first?"

Arthur looked from Michael Walker to Roy, and back to Michael, "What's the problem here, Mr. Walker? Mr. Matacowski, you seem to have a problem with Terry?"

"I'll tell you my problem," Roy said. "We don't really know who this guy is. According to Kurt, he showed up without explanation and seemed to be running things when they were trying to delineate the ship. Then he disappears and doesn't offer any help. And then there is the fact that his arm was in a sling. We have a picture of a priest with his arm in a sling at Fadi El Khoury's restaurant. He was the last to leave the night of the murder. So I'd say Father Terry is probably the killer. How's that for a problem?"

"I can assure you, Father O'Shanigan is not the killer. Firstly, the night of the murders Terry was here at the mesa with us; and secondly, Terry and I have worked at the ACD together for a number of years," Arthur said. "But to ease tensions a bit, Terry, please give us a run-down on your work."

Terry looked at the individuals seated around the table. "I am not sure where to start. Perhaps, it would be best to go back to before I met Arthur. After I graduated, I specialized in Biblical Archeology. I worked for a while on the Dead Sea Scrolls. But suddenly, the group that controlled them withdrew my access to them. A few days earlier, I discovered a key to unlock the secrets hidden in the Copper Scroll from the Dead Sea collection. I discovered that there was another scroll, a Silver Scroll.

"Arthur responded to my search for research funds, and I was able to set up the Institute for Biblical Archeology in Paris. With Arthur's resources, I recovered and decoded the Silver Scroll which described another scroll, the Gold Scroll. Recently, we were close to recovering the Gold Scroll, but—"

Arthur held up his hand. "Let me explain that," he said. "I sent one of my most trusted employees, Jack Thompson, to Sana'a, Yemen to collect the Gold Scroll. He was murdered, apparently just after he obtained the scroll. We had no lead on who committed the murder, or where the scroll was. The authorities in Yemen were of little help, but it did seem like someone knew we were going after the scroll and followed Jack until he obtained it. They killed him to get it. We now believe that was your Mr. Yusof Ekstrom."

Roy nodded and glanced at O'Shanigan. "So, what about the sling?"

"An operation a few months ago, an old football injury that never healed properly, and the sling came off just two days ago. Why is that so important?"

"Well, statistically what are the odds of two priests with slings on their left arms being involved in this? Pretty low, wouldn't you say?" Roy said.

An odd look came over Terry's face. "Could I see the picture of the priest you suspect of committing the murder?"

"Sure," Walker said. He rummaged in his

briefcase for a moment and then passed a picture across the table to Terry.

Terry stood up and reached out for the photo. He took one look and fell back into his chair. "No, no, it couldn't be, it…"

"Do you know him?" Walker said.

Terry nodded and whispered, "Father Antonio. It's Father Antonio. All these years, and…how, why?" He leaned back in his chair and stared at the ceiling.

"Is he one of your six buddies?" Roy said.

Terry jumped to his feet. "The Six, how do you know about the Six?" He looked at Arthur, then sat down and stared into the palms of his hands.

"Terry," Arthur said softly. "It appears that you have been keeping some secrets of your own."

Terry kept staring into the palms of his hands.

"Well then, Roy, can you explain what you are talking about?" Arthur said.

"Sure. When Kurt first contacted me after he and Robby discovered the ship, he asked me to check up on O'Shanigan. I did a few online searches—found a number of his papers on the Dead Sea Scrolls and a reference to his institute in Paris. My computers did a little digging and found his cell phone's unique identification number. I traced his movements using that information. He gets around but never showed up here.

"The correlation analysis I ran on his movements found that he went to a location in Paris served by a particular cell tower once a month, and here's the kicker. It turns out there were five other cell phones registered all over the world that turned up at the same time. So, it appeared that six of them were in that general location once a month. I don't believe in plain old coincidence, so I assumed they were meeting. That's how I came up with six.

"And some of you will probably be wondering if any of those cells were at the murder site. I don't know. I am still trying to trace the location of the six cell phones on the night of the murder. Only two, one in London, and one in Mexico have shown up so far. If O'Shanigan was here, we still need to locate three."

"Well, Roy, your ability to trace people's movements using cell phone data is rather unsettling. I will have to get my security team to look at some countermeasures," Arthur said. He turned to look at Terry who was still staring at his hands. "Terry, do you have anything to say?"

Terry looked up at Arthur. "Could we meet alone, Arthur?"

"Okay, if the rest of you don't mind, let's take a break and meet in the dining room at noon. We can continue with this after lunch."

Hallway - Calvert Mesa, Montana
September 12, 2002 - 11:00 am

"Roy," Tran said. "Could you show me how your cell tracing program works?"

Roy looked at him. "Countermeasures?"

Tran nodded.

"Not much the average person can do except use disposables. And that approach is not particularly good if there are a lot of people who need to contact you. Relays are another way, but they take time to set up and manage. Simplest solution is cash, and a lot of disposable cells. But with enough computer power, access to telephone company records, and a little time, I can probably trace your movements."

"So, not much the average person can do," Tran said.

Roy smiled. "Come on down to the computer center. I'll show you."

They proceeded down to a windowless room on the second floor of the mesa.

"Okay," Roy said, "where should I start?"

"How about your trace on Terry's five associates. How did you do that?"

"Well, when you don't know who's in a group, it is harder but still possible. Each cell tower has a relatively small number of cells attached at one time so if you have one person's unique cell identification number, you can follow them. If they frequent one place, you can record which other cells are there at the same time. I found Terry's cell identifier, and had LISA follow him and go back into the telephone company records. She identified a high probability that six specific cell phones were associated."

"Father Antonio," Tran said, "what do you know about him?"

"Well, LISA came up with the six phone identifiers just before the attack. Once I got set up here I tasked her with identifying and following each of them. Let's see what she's found out about Father Antonio."

Roy typed a command on the keyboard.

Hello Roy, LISA responded.

Tran raised an eyebrow and looked at Roy.

"Something I added, still working on voice commands but for now it's keyboard input," Roy said, as he typed a few more commands. "

Father Antonio. Probability eighty-nine percent - associated with two disposable cells. One disposable cell recently active. Frankfurt Airport. Currently no cells active.

"The Frankfurt Airport. Can you find his flight? If he's flying out we can arrange to have him picked up when he lands," Tran said.

"If he's flying under his own name, yes. But, if he's using an alias and his cells are off, it's just a waiting game."

"Can you keep me posted," Tran said. "I'll go see what my guys can come up with."

Roy nodded. "Will do."

Dining Room - Calvert Mesa, Montana
September 12, 2002 - 1:45 pm

Everyone finished a rather uncomfortable lunch. Arthur engaged in small talk in an apparent effort to reduce the tensions that grew after the revelations about Terry's associates. It didn't seem to be working, so Arthur stood, and said, "At our meeting, Terry apprised me of a number of extraordinary pieces of information. In fact, he pointed out that this information could dislodge the underpinnings of one or more of the world's principal religions, and perhaps lead to chaos throughout the world. After a lot of discussion, we decided that the people in this room are intimately involved, and as such, you should also hear these facts. But you must swear to absolute secrecy, and you may expect your life to never be the same again. If anyone does not want to make such a commitment, they should not attend our next meeting in the conference room."

No one spoke.

"Fine," Arthur said. "Joleen, perhaps Robby should continue his lessons with Rosa. I assume you want to attend this meeting."

Joleen nodded. "Robby, you go with Rosa. I'll come down later."

Once they were all in the conference room, Arthur began. "The six people that Roy discovered are actually in a secret group that goes back 2000 years. They protected the secret of the artifacts and their origins since the days of the First Apostle—not Paul, as described in the Bible, but Xiong, the rumored fourth Wise Man. As you might expect, this by itself could shake the foundations of Christianity. But even more unsettling is the fact that these artifacts are linked back to the ancients, known as the Watchers. I knew of the artifacts and believed that they were linked to aliens. That was the reason the ACD is involved, but I never knew about the six members of the secret society. Terry will explain more about them."

Terry stood. "I am sorry for the deception, but we have hidden this secret for so many years. We are followers of the First Apostle. Our order is called the Brotherhood of the Sand because of our ancient origins in the desert. The original six believed that the Master or Watcher as Arthur called him would return some day to make us seven. But the Brothers of the First Apostle are not simply six, but six to the power of six. We are organized in cells. My cell has six members, and we await the Master to make us seven, like the seven in the original Christian council. Each of the cells has the leader from the higher level, plus six members. So no one knows more than a maximum of thirteen members."

"That would make your secret society number roughly forty-six thousand, "Roy said. "That's an awfully large group to keep secret."

"Yes, I agree. Even though, no member knows more than thirteen others, our organization was infiltrated numerous times, and many of our members were killed but the large number of us spread over the globe allowed us to monitor worldwide activities in an age of extremely slow communication. Today, it is not necessary, but ancient traditions linger, and now our highest level is compromised.

"We also have in our possession a pyramid with the Master's light. Others, we don't know who, have been trying to gain control of the artifact for years, and now, the light may be in danger. We were hoping that the Gold Scroll would lead us to the other artifacts of the First Apostle. We had no idea there was another complete set of artifacts here in the United States, and did not dream of the existence of an alien ship."

"Actually Terry, we think there are three sets of artifacts, yours, the ones we have here, and a set in the Tower of London," Roy said.

"The Tower of London, how did you arrive at that conclusion?" Terry said.

"Well, every time Robby activates the scepter or the ship, there is a local power failure near our pyramid. There is also always one in Paris, near the cell tower where I traced you to your meetings with five other people. And there is a power failure at the Tower of London. Now, I believe that polydactylism has something to do with the activation of the artifacts. There are numerous references to Ann Boleyn having a sixth digit," Roy said.

"I was unaware of that," Arthur said.

"Well, it's not proven, but she was never seen in public without gloves. Even at her execution, she was recorded as wearing gloves. Perhaps she wore them to hide her sixth finger. She was executed for being a witch and, if she could make light come from a small round stone on the top of a stone pyramid that would make sense. How would that look to someone in the sixteenth century? In fact, how does it look to us today?" Roy paused for a few seconds and looked around.

"Magic," Terry said.

"Right, and her jewels are stored in the Tower of London. Their computer records are a mess, and I haven't found a reference to the artifacts in a catalogue yet, but—"

"I should be able to use my connections to solve that problem," Arthur said. "If the artifacts are there, I will get them here."

"That would be great," Roy said. "I have a few ideas I could check out once I see them."

"Terry, why don't you continue," Arthur said.

"Yes, the writings of the First Apostle mention the six fingers on the left hand of the Master and…" Terry paused and looked around the room at each individual. "And the writings of the First Apostle state that Jesus had six fingers on his left hand."

Joleen gasped. "Jesus. No, that couldn't be. That's not anywhere in the Bible."

The others around the table remained silent.

"I'm sure you can see why we kept these facts secret. How would the Christian world react? Or the Muslim world, where Jesus is considered a prophet?" Terry said.

Amy leaned forward. "Something else makes sense to me now. Joleen and I wondered about my wound. We're positive a bullet went right through my shoulder, but the medics and no one else believed us. They thought we made a mistake due to the stress of the battle, but what if the scepter gave Robby the power to heal, like Jesus? Could that be how Jesus performed his miracles?"

Joleen grasped Kurt's hand, "Robby…Robby and Jesus. Kurt, what will happen to Robby if people find out?"

"I agree Mrs. Sigurdson, you see why we need secrecy," Terry said.

Arthur nodded and leaned back in his chair. "Terry, is there anything else you want to reveal?"

"Yes. I never told anyone, but when we decoded the Silver Scroll it not only gave directions to the Gold Scroll, but also a scepter. When I searched the location, the scepter wasn't there. Maybe it had already been taken by looters."

Roy jumped up. "Maybe Terry's decoding algorithm will work in the Gold Scroll, as well? The other scrolls gave you directions. Maybe it will too. Who knows what it will reveal, maybe another pie-shaped artifact—maybe the scepter was hidden some place else. Let's give it a try."

Arthur smiled. "Okay, you and Terry get to work on that. Anything else?"

Michael Walker said, "I'd like Roy to prioritize finding this Father Antonio. I can assign a couple of analysts to help."

"Sure," Roy said. "Tran and I have already started on that. LISA's sorting through cell records but I haven't been going through official channels to access the phone company records. A little help there would speed up the process."

"Done," Michael said. "Anything else?"

"There are two analysts in Ottawa that are good at this sort of thing. I could use their help."

"I'll see to it. Arthur has a plane waiting to take me back to Ottawa. I'll get it set up on route," Michael said.

Computer Room - Calvert Mesa, Montana
September 13, 2002 - 2:30 am

Terry worked on the Gold Scroll for several hours, carefully pressing it between sheets of glass. He passed the finished product to Roy. "Ready for you to photograph and decode. But, I need a break. How about you?"

"I'm fine. Could use something to eat though; how about pizza and a coke?"

Terry shook his head. "How about a sandwich and a glass of milk? I've had enough caffeine for a month."

"Nah, I'll have a coke, a pepperoni pizza and coke. Milk will just put you to sleep."

Terry nodded. "I'll order pizza and coke for you, and a sandwich and milk for me."

****

Terry sat slumped in a large leather armchair, head back, mouth open, sleeping. An empty glass and a half eaten sandwich sat on the table beside him.

While Terry slept Roy photographed the gold scroll and scanned the images into LISA. He extracted the text from the photographs and was ready to run Terry's decoding algorithm. He looked back at Terry and smiled as he initiated the program. Then he sat back and picked up the first slice of his cold pizza.

Several minutes passed, and he was about to start on the last slice when LISA announced "*Decoding complete, Roy.*" Roy let the slice fall back on the plate and scanned the decoded text.

"It's done," he shouted.

Terry stirred but didn't wake up.

Roy went over and shook Terry. "Hey, that's enough sleep for a week."

Terry stumbled to his feet. "What?"

"Look here, about a third of the way through the text. I think these are directions."

"What's that?" Terry said.

"It's from the scroll. LISA decoded it."

"Already?" Terry said, rubbing his eyes.

Roy pointed at the clock. "You were out for quite a while. I warned you about the milk."

Terry scanned the text. "This doesn't make sense," Terry said, pointing to a section of text.

"Okay, let's check the input. LISA had some trouble converting photos of the scroll to text. I'll put the original photos of this section up beside the text I fed LISA."

"Here," Terry said. "You have these characters wrong." He wrote several characters down and handed then to Roy. "Use these here." He pointed at the screen.

Terry waited while Roy gave LISA the new input data and ran the decoding program.

"There," Roy said. "Does that make any more sense?"

"Here." Terry pointed at several lines." It tells where the third pie-shaped artifact is hidden. I have a team in that area on a dig. If the artifact is still there, we should be able to find it and get it out of the country without detection."

"What about the third scepter?" Roy asked. "Does it say anything about a scepter?"

Terry frowned.

"What's the matter?" Roy said.

"It gives the location for the scepter but…"

"But?"

"It's the site described in the Silver Scroll. We excavated that site years ago. I spent several months there with Father Antonio, and we thoroughly searched the area but we didn't find a scepter. In fact, we found nothing of interest." Terry paused for several seconds. "It must have been looted in the past."

"Father Antonio, he was there? Are you sure it was looted or did he take it without your knowledge?" Roy said.

Terry nodded and stared at the floor for several seconds. "You are probably right…all this time. How could I be so blind?"

"Don't beat yourself up. You never know about people."

"But I'm a priest, I'm…"

"He's a priest, too," Roy said.

"How many other people has he fooled? What else has he done?"

"Don't worry, LISA will find him, and we'll bring him in and find out. In the meantime, let's get your folks over there going on recovering that pie-shaped artifact. That's if Father Antonio hasn't taken it as well."

"No, he's never been at that site as far as I know."

"Good then let's get your team working on it."

Terry looked at the clock. "It's almost three in the morning."

"Not in the middle east. If they find it we'll get one of Arthur's private planes to pick it up, and it'll be here before you know it."

Chapter 32 - Not Till The Fat Lady Sings

Computer Room - Calvert Mesa
September 16, 2002 - 6:00 am

Roy was sitting at a small table, head down on folded arms, when Arthur and Terry entered. A partially empty beer sat against his left elbow. Strands of his hair were dangling in a partially eaten piece of pizza.

"So, he does sleep," Terry said.

Roy jumped, his elbow knocked the beer over and tomato sauce clung to his forehead as he sat up. "Ah, crap." He wiped his forehead. "Do you have them?"

Arthur held up a small box. "The artifacts from the Tower of London have arrived, but I think you should get the pizza out of your hair before we let you touch them."

Roy nodded. "What about the other pie-shaped artifact, Terry?"

"Father Richards, my most trusted aide and friend has found it. It was where the Gold Scroll said it would be. It was inside an archeological site Father Richards was already excavating. He would probably have found it without our help, but it might have taken several years. With our information, he was able to go directly to it. It's on a plane and should be here by noon."

"Great," Roy said. "I have LISA set up to scan and analyze the pie-shaped artifacts once we have them all."

"Now, only the third scepter still eludes us," Terry said.

"I've some good and bad news there," Roy said. "LISA has retrieved the text of a message to Father Antonio's cell phone in Frankfurt. It said 'Boy escaped – on way to Calvert Mesa - unhurt!!!'"

"What," Arthur said. "That means there's—"

"There's a leak somewhere," Roy said. "As soon as LISA finds the source of those messages, we should be able to close that."

"The sooner, the better," Arthur said. "So, what's the good news?"

"The next message Father Antonio received was in Rome. There was only one flight, Frankfurt to Rome, which Father Antonio could have taken. LISA is pulling up the passenger list. We should soon be able to find out what alias he is using."

"What about the message. What did it say?" Arthur said.

"LISA's working on that. I'll let you know as soon as I find out." Roy looked at the pizza sauce on his hand. "I need to get cleaned up."

"I'll get someone to come in and clean up the beer," Arthur said. "Let's get back together after lunch, after the other artifact is here."

Airport - Cairo, Egypt
September 16, 2002 - 2:00 pm

After an hour and a half wait in line, Father Antonio was motioned forward by the immigrations agent at the Cairo airport. He passed his forged Canadian passport in the name of Father Francis to the agent. He used it when he didn't want to be traced via his valid Italian passport. As far as anyone knew, he was in Rome.

The agent asked him a few questions, stamped the passport and motioned for Father Francis to proceed. His only luggage was a carry-on, and he quickly cleared customs and went out to search for a reliable cab, not an easy job.

As he stepped outside, a voice called out, "Father, Father Antonio, you need a taxi, yes?" Mohamed Ismail came forward out of the crowd waving a large red handkerchief.

"Ah, Mohamed, it is good to see you." He lied. He planned to slip into town without anyone he knew seeing him.

"I can take you. I can take you, come. The car is parked nearby. You do not have more luggages?" Mohamed said.

"No, just this. Where is the car?"

Mohamed wiped his face with the handkerchief, stuck it in his back pocket and pointed toward a mass of cars double and triple parked along the side of the road. Mohamed's taxi was against the curb; its access to the street blocked by several cars. Mohamed complained to the other drivers and leaned into the taxi several times to honk the horn. After several minutes of shouting and arm waving, Mohamed maneuvered his taxi to freedom and left the fray honking.

"Father, the traffic is very bad. Where shall I take you, the church...the residence? It will be slow today."

"The residence first, I need to shower. You can wait. I don't feel like walking in the heat. Then to the church."

Father Francis looked out the window. The traffic didn't seem any worse than usual. A chaotic ballet of cars choreographed to the incessant honking of horns. It seemed as if the cars were actually communicating—some voices loud, long, and harsh, but most were quick soft toots seeking recognition. Spaces would appear and one of the dancers would fill the space.

He took out a cell phone. Were there any more startling revelations? On his arrival in Rome the message waiting for him had said "Mesa group has gold scroll - you are found out - Mesa group knows about you."

They knew about him so he could not stay in Rome. He decided to return to Cairo to retrieve the scepter and disappear. He withdrew funds from three bank accounts in the name of Father Francis. He did not access the account in Father Antonio's name in case they were waiting for him.

Now, in Cairo, he re-read the message "Mesa group has gold scroll - you are found out - Mesa group knows about you." The scroll was intercepted. That was why it hadn't arrived as scheduled.

He checked the most recent message and gasped as he read it "Mesa group trying to locate you - are tracking all your cell phones - I will proceed with final task - this is my last communication - HIDE." He read the message again, and then turned off his cell phone.

How? How was he discovered? No matter, the Brotherhood of the Sand was no longer of any value to him. He would retrieve the scepter and disappear like a grain of sand in the desert.

"Father, we are almost at the residence. Would you like to stop at the front or rear entrance?"

"I've changed my mind, drive on. Take me to the Restaurant Al Yemeni."

"But it is not open, yet. Why not stop at the residence first. I will wait and take you when the restaurant opens."

Father Francis looked at the back of Mohamed's head as they pulled up at the residence. Was it just a coincidence that Mohamed was at the airport? Are they waiting at the residence for me? "No, drive on. I want you to take me to Restaurant Al Yemeni."

When they arrived, the restaurant was closed as Mohamed foretold. "I shall wait. You can sit in the car until the restaurant opens, and I will wait while you eat."

Father Francis handed Mohamed some money. "No, I will walk."

"But it is hot, and there is no place to sit. I will wait," Mohamed said.

"No, go. I will be fine."

Mohamed drove away, looking back over his shoulder a couple of times.

Is he just trying to make some easy money or is he working for the group at Calvert Mesa? I need to be more cautious.

He continued to watch until Mohamed was out of sight, and then he slipped down a dusty side street. He walked for a couple of blocks then stepped into a narrow entrance, hurried up a flight of stairs and unlocked a steel grate leading to a small two-room apartment. This apartment was his base when he didn't want anyone at the church to know he was in Cairo. Never before had he come here in his clerical garb, and hoped that no one saw him this time. But, as long as it provided a safe haven for a few days, that didn't matter. It would be the last time he used this place as well.

Tran Ng's Office - Calvert Mesa
September 16, 2002 - 11:45 am

Roy tapped on Tran's door as he stuck his head in. "We have a problem."

Tran spun around in his chair and waved for Roy to come in. "What's that?"

"The leak is from someone on the Mesa," Roy said.

"Are you sure? Everyone went through extensive security checks?"

"Yah, I'm sure. That cell phone text Father Antonio received in Frankfurt, the one that said "Boy escaped – on way to Calvert Mesa - unhurt!!!", it came from a number in Lisbon. LISA traced the calls made to that number. They were made from an internet phone account accessed from a computer in Warsaw. LISA broke into that. Its function is to take emails, convert them to text messages, and send them from the Lisbon number. Then we—"

Tran tapped his finger on the desk. "The short version, Roy, please."

"Sorry, anyway LISA traced the emails back to a terminal here at the Mesa. A terminal in room 3-26. Father Antonio cell has just come on in Cairo. LISA's checking to see if there are any more messages."

Tran turned to his computer and retrieved the Mesa room assignments.

"Abdul Ibrahim," Tran said. "He's the contractor we have here upgrading our Ethernet cabling. He certainly could have sent the message, but how the hell would he know that we are tracking Father Antonio's cell phones?"

Roy pulled a case out of his pocket and unfolded it to reveal a small set of screwdrivers. "I have an idea," he said, as he squeezed behind Tran's desk and removed the wall plate for the Ethernet connection. He pointed at two small wires attached to the back of the wall plate. "That's not standard equipment. There must be some kind of bug in the base plate. And look. It feeds into the cabling."

"How did he get through our personnel screening?" Tran muttered, and turned to his computer screen.

"Well, shit happens," Roy said, "more often than we'd like? Do we know where he is, right now?"

"That's what I'm checking. He needs to use his access card to enter any room, so we have a record of where he's been and where he is right now," Tran said, as he opened his desk drawer and brought out a revolver. "He's in the kitchen."

"You got to be kidding. You think he's bugging the kitchen?"

"No," Tran said, as he brushed by Roy, gun in hand.

Dining Room - Calvert Mesa
September16, 2002 - 12:00 noon

Joleen and Robby were sitting at one end of the large cherry wood table when Kurt entered. Arthur motioned for Kurt to join him and O'Shanigan at the head of the table. They appeared to be discussing a few documents spread out in front of them. Kurt nodded in acknowledgement and went over to talk to Robby and Joleen. "Sorry, Arthur wants to see me. I'll try not to be too long."

"Are you going to eat with us, Dad?" Robby said.

Kurt scanned the room. The only other people in

the room were Lisa and Amy. They were standing by the window looking out at what was normally an expansive view. But today, there was a heavy overcast. The clouds seemed to hang from the mesa, dipping away from the cliffs, obscuring everything but a few hundred yards of the valley floor below.

"We shouldn't be too long. I'll be back before they serve the food. Have you decided what you are going to eat?" Kurt said.

"I want a pizza, but Mom says I should have soup and a tuna sandwich. What are you having, Dad?"

"Let's both you and I have soup and a tuna sandwich. Okay?"

Robby nodded.

"Have you ordered, yet?" Kurt asked.

"No," Joleen said. "They seem kind of slow today. We don't even have water, yet. That's kind of funny they—."

"Kurt," Arthur said. "It will take just a minute. Then you can join your family. It's good news."

"Robby, I'll be right back." Kurt turned and walked over to Arthur.

"What are you having, Mom?"

"Well, if you and your dad are having soup and a sandwich, I think I will, too. Tuna's one of my favorites."

In a few minutes, Kurt came back. "It's over. Roy is monitoring Father Antonio's cell phone, and when he uses it again he'll be arrested. Tran and the CIA have men stationed at all the locations where he's likely to show up. He doesn't know we are on to him so it shouldn't be too long now."

The door to the kitchen opened and a waiter came out with a tray of water glasses. The glasses wobbled on the tray and one crashed to the floor bouncing on the thick carpet. Water sprayed out across the floor and the glass rolled harmlessly toward Robby. Arthur jumped up. "What are you doing here?" he said.

Tran burst through the doorway from the kitchen and raised his gun. "Abdul, stop right there."

Abdul spun towards Tran. The tray tipped towards Tran as Abdul pulled a gun from under it.

Tran fired. The shot ricocheted off the falling tray.

Abdul fired. It hit Tran in the shoulder. Tran spun to his right. His gun flew out of his hand and across the room as he fell.

Amy screamed as Lisa pulled her to the floor.

Joleen grabbed Robby and pushed him under the table.

Abdul came closer and stepped to his left so he could see Robby sprawled under the table. He pointed the gun at Robby. "Stop," Joleen screamed.

Kurt leapt out of his chair and was half way to Abdul when the shot rang out.

Abdul lurched forward. His back arched and his head snapped back. His arm flew up and he fired his gun into the ceiling.

Two more shots. Then Abdul fell, face forward, on the floor. Blood pulsed from three holes in his back.

Roy stood at the kitchen door, a gun raised, his hand shaking. "Body shot. Just like training." He leaned against the wall and sunk to the floor.

Kurt picked up Abdul's gun and rushed to Roy. "Are you alright?"

"Not as easy as training. Not as easy. I'm okay. Tran. Help Tran."

Arthur rushed to Tran. Tran rolled over, holding his arm. "Kitchen staff, in the walk-in freezer," he said.

Arthur and O'Shanigan hurried into the kitchen.

Joleen pulled Robby to her and hugged him.

Excited voices echoed out of the kitchen. Rosa rushed out with a first aid kit and began tending to Tran. "I will try to stop the bleeding but there is quite a bit of damage. Roy, help me with this tourniquet. We need to get him to a hospital."

Tran looked at Roy. "How'd you...ouch. Rosa, take it easy. How—?"

"There was another gun in your drawer."

Tran nodded, winced, and passed out as Rosa tightened the tourniquet.

"It's not good. I think an artery's cut. I'm not going to be able to stop the bleeding."

Arthur looked out the window. "With this fog we can't get a plane out. You have to stop the bleeding."

"Robby and the scepter, He could help Tran like he helped me," Amy said.

"Roy," Lisa said. "We need the scepter for Robby."

"What? Robby?" Joleen hugged Robby closer.

"Right, remember what we think he did for Amy. He might be able to do that again."

"I'll get the scepter," Roy said. "Warn everyone

there will be a power failure. Kurt, Joleen, can you get Robby ready?"

Kurt went over and hugged Robby and Joleen. "Robby, I want you to sit down by Tran and put your hand on his shoulder. We'll give you the scepter and you put your thumb in the indentation just like you did before. Can you do that?"

Robby nodded.

Joleen looked at Kurt. "I thought you said it was over."

Chapter 33 - Hello

Conference Room - Calvert Mesa
September 16, 2002 - 8:00 pm

Arthur, Kurt, and Terry sat at the conference room table while Roy readied an overhead projector.

"So, it's just a matter of time now until we reel him in," Arthur said.

"Reel who in?" Tran said.

Arthur whirled around in the swivel chair. "Oh, I didn't hear you come in. How's the arm?"

"Okay, I'm as good as new. Maybe better. The arthritis in my knees seems to be gone."

"I think you know how sensitive that information is," Arthur said.

"Yes, I've talked to Rosa about that. She's the only person in the room who didn't know about the scepter's power. But who do we need to reel in?"

"Father Antonio or Francis, whatever he calls himself. I've alerted your team leader in Cairo."

"Good, I won't relax until we catch him. Don't want any other attempted assassinations."

"Roy's just about to tell us about his analysis of the three pie-shaped artifacts," Arthur said.

There," Roy said.

Everyone looked at the overhead projection.

"Here is an enlargement of a portion of the pie-shaped artifact that Terry's man, Father Richards, found in Egypt. The characters are logographic," Roy said.

"Looks like Chinese characters to me," Terry said.

"Right, I think it is. Chinese characters have a logographic origin. When I saw the characters in the ship, I was pretty sure the language in the ship was logographic. The characters on the first pie from Amy were native petroglyphs, of similar, but not identical, logographic origins. Here are the symbols on the artifact from the Tower of London. They aren't logographic but are a form of ancient Armenian alphabet.

"The symbols on the pies are mirrored, and I was able to match the symbols one to one. Amy is familiar with the ancient Armenian scripts and the Navajo glyphs, and with her help, I was able to work out the language.

"I saw what looked like a communications panel in the ship. I think we should attempt to send a message. I have enough understanding of the language to do that."

"How long would it take you to develop a message?" Arthur said.

Roy shrugged. "Depends on LISA, few hours max. But, we'll have to go back to the ship, and I'll need Robby. Do you think Joleen would go for that, Kurt?"

"I don't know. I'll see what she says."

Kurt and Joleen's suite - Calvert Mesa
September 16, 2002 - 9:00 pm

Kurt and Joleen stood by the large window and looked out at the canyon surrounding the mesa. It was illuminated by a full moon and dark shadows emphasized the rugged cliffs guarding the mesa.

Joleen grabbed Kurt's hand and squeezed. "We're not even safe here, Kurt, surrounded by cliffs and Arthur's guards. Will it ever be safe for us to leave? Will it ever end?"

Kurt put his arm around Joleen. "Arthur, CSIS, the CIA, everybody is working on it. Once we catch Father Antonio, we should be all right."

"But so many people know about Robby and what he can do. If it ever becomes common knowledge that he can heal people when he holds the scepter…if that happens…"

Kurt pulled her closer. "We'll protect him, somehow."

"Are you sure we can? What would I have done to get him to see my mother when she had cancer? I probably would have stopped at nothing. Word will get out, and everyone will be hunting him, the good and the bad. He can't cure everyone in the world.

411

How would we decide?"

"I don't know, Joleen, but it hasn't come to that, yet. We need to learn more about the ship, and the other artifacts. There has to be a reason the artifacts were left here."

"But this has been going on for thousands of years. Nobody understands why. Whose ship is it? Where did they go? What did they do to us, to Robby?"

"We'll find out," Kurt said.

They stared silently out the window holding each other close as the moon climbed higher in the sky.

"The canyons look so pretty under the full moon. It's so peaceful," Joleen said. "I wish we could just take Robby and disappear so no one could find us. They can keep their damn artifacts. I'd be happy if we could just live out our lives in peace. Robby, can he ever have a normal life now? We have to do something."

"Roy has an idea, but it means taking Robby back to the ship again."

"Why? Hasn't he been there enough? What good would it do?"

"Well, now that we have the three pieces of the pie-shaped artifact, Roy thinks he understands their language enough that we can send a message. But it requires another trip to the ship."

" Can't he do it from here? Arthur would get him all the communications gear he needs. He could do it from here."

"No, Roy thinks he saw a communications panel in the ship, and he wants to try to send a message.

He needs Robby to do that. It means another trip to the ship."

Joleen turned and put her head on Kurt chest. "Okay, we need to do something, but I want to come."

Alien Ship - Algodones Dunes, California
September 17, 2002 - 3:30 am

The inside of the Quonset had been completely cleared of sand. A number of armed military personnel ringed the area holding kerosene lanterns. The outer surface of the ship glistened in the dim light.

"It looks like highly polished onyx," Joleen said.

"We don't know what it is, but it's not anything we have," Roy said.

"Kurt, are they using the lanterns because the ship shuts down all the electrical stuff?'

Kurt nodded.

"It's kind of eerie," Joleen said, as she squeezed his hand.

"Right, but once Robby opens the ship he can turn on the lights inside it. But, we will take a couple of lanterns, just in case."

"Here Mom," Robby said, as he pointed at a small square on the surface of the ship. The square was almost indiscernible in the flickering light. "This is where I open the door."

"Okay, Robby, go ahead, I'll hold you so you don't slip in," Roy said.

Robby placed his hand on the small square and the door slid open.

"Okay, turn on the lights, Robby," Roy said.

"Ohh…" Joleen gasped as Robby reached into the opening. "Kurt?"

"It's okay, Joleen. He's done this before."

"He… he seems so grown up."

"Watch," Kurt said.

A soft red light suddenly illuminated the inside of the ship, and a ladder extended out of the wall.

Follow me," Kurt said, and climbed down the ladder with Robby right behind him.

Joleen and Roy followed.

"Mom, isn't it neat? It's just like Star Trek. Look at all the funny letters on the wall. When I put my hand there, on the funny symbols, all the lights come on and the ladder comes out of the wall."

"Okay, we need to move on," Roy said. "Robby, you can walk with your mom."

Kurt fell in beside Roy as they moved through the ship. Roy consulted the rough map he drew on their last trip. "I hope I'm right on this. That console I saw on the last trip should be for communications. Either that or I really haven't figured out the language."

"Here we are," Roy said, as they walked through an arch into a circular room. A different looking console in each of its four quadrants. "I think this is the center of the ship, but it will take a lot more exploration to be sure. Anyway, I think that one's the communications console. Either that, or it controls the engines and we fly off to the moon."

Kurt looked over his shoulder at Joleen, then

414

whispered to Roy, "Quit joking around. Joleen's handling all this really well so far."

"Not sure I'm joking," Roy muttered. "Robby, come over to this console. Put your hand here."

Robby placed his hand in a small square on the console's smooth surface. The blank wall behind the console lit up, and a small picture of the solar system appeared. A line appeared linking earth and a small circle in the asteroid belt.

"Bingo," Roy said, "good job, Robby. Now let's see if I can do my part." He touched one of the symbols on the console. Nothing happened. "Nope, guess Robby is going to have to do it all. Robby, touch each of the symbols, ah…each of the funny letters when I point to it."

When Robby touched a letter, it flashed and came up on the screen on the wall.

"You're doing great, Robby," Roy said, as they worked through the symbols on his list. "Okay, now this one. I think it's the send button."

"Wait," Joleen said. "Kurt, what do you think? I think we have to."

"I think so, too. It's the best option for Robby's future."

Roy looked at them. They both nodded.

"Okay, Robby, make it so," Roy said.

Robby nodded and touched the symbol.

The line between earth and the circle in the asteroid belt started blinking, and the circle grew larger.

"What's happening?" Joleen said.

"Powering up? Maybe that's what it means when

that thing in the asteroid belt gets bigger. I don't really know," Roy said. The circle stopped growing. "I think something's going to—"

The circle seemed to explode, and what looked like a projectile, burst out of its side and headed away from earth. As the projectile hurtled away from earth, the field of vision expanded. Soon the whole galaxy was visible. Then, it too, receded and other galaxies became visible. Another spiral galaxy appeared, and the projectile dove into it.

"Andromeda," Roy said, "it's Andromeda, the closest spiral galaxy." The projectile arrived at a solar system in the outer regions of Andromeda and approached a double-star system with three moonless planets. There was a small circle near the second planet, and the projectile dove into it. The circle began to flash, and a line between the circle and the planet appeared. Then the screen dimmed.

"What just happened?" Joleen said.

"I think we just said hello to a planet in the Andromeda galaxy," Roy said.

"That can't be," Kurt said. "To get there, it would take a radio signal, ah—"

"About two point five million years," Roy said.

"I don't understand," Joleen said.

"Mom, radio waves travel at the speed of light and Andromeda is two point five million light years away, so it would take two point five million years for them to get there. Right, Dad?" Robby said.

"Right," Kurt said. "So what probably happened is, we started the message on its way, and the screen showed us where it's going. I'm pretty sure it wasn't registering delivery."

"Yah, you're probably right," Roy said. "I hope someone's awake up there when the message arrives at Andromeda. By the time it gets there, their civilization could be long gone. We should get back to the mesa. There's no use sitting around here. Nothing's going to—."

"Look," Robby said.

The wall screen brightened and again showed the double-star system with the three planets. A line between the second planet and the circle above it appeared.

"A response," Roy said, as the projectile retraced its track, through space, back to earth.

A series of symbols on the console lit up, stopped and repeated. Roy copied them onto a small notepad.

"What's it say?" Joleen asked.

Roy shook his head. "I don't know. I need to run it through LISA. Let's get back to the mesa."

Chapter 34 - For Good or Evil

Cairo, Egypt
September 17, 2002 - 5:30 pm

It was almost dark and the Muezzin began the evening call to prayer. Father Antonio walked, hunched forward, in a dusty burlap robe. He checked the street behind him before turning into the narrow alley leading to his sanctuary under Saint Virgin Mary's Coptic Church.

"*Baksheesh, baksheesh.*"

Father Antonio jumped back. A boy, who looked to be about twelve, sat in the middle of the alley.

The boy held out his hand. "*Baksheesh, baksheesh.*"

Father Antonio pulled his hood further down over his face and turned to see if anyone was following him. The alley was about a fifty feet long, and dead-ended about fifteen feet past his secret entrance. He was always concerned about being trapped, but other than the retched boy, no one else was around. He pushed past the boy.

The boy jumped up and followed him. "*Baksheesh, baksheesh.*"

"Go, go, can't you see, I am poor," Father Antonio said, as he unlocked the door leading to his sanctuary.

"*Baksheesh, baksheesh.*"

Father Antonio retrieved a few coins from under his robe and threw them on the ground. "Go, you will get nothing else."

The boy grabbed the coins and ran down the alley. He stopped, counted the coins, and watched. As soon as Father Antonio disappeared through the small doorway, the boy ran to the adjoining larger street. He stopped about a hundred yards down the street and pounded on a door. A blond-haired man in jeans, a golf shirt, and light brown sports jacket opened the door.

"Someone has gone in. Someone has gone in, *baksheesh* now."

"What did he look like?" the man asked.

The boy shrugged. "Tall, thin like you, but hair, it's not black but not like you."

"Egyptian?"

"No, not Egyptian, *baksheesh*, now?"

The man reached in his pocket and pulled out an American five-dollar bill. "Get back there. Come and tell me if he leaves or anyone else goes in."

The boy pocketed the bill and ran back to the alley.

The man lifted his arm and spoke into his palm.

"John, Rex here, the kid says someone has gone in. Bring the car up and block the alley. I will meet you there. If he comes out our way we will easily be able to take him without anyone noticing."

Rex waited for the acknowledgement.

"Okay, I'm on my way."

"Paulo, did you copy that? Do you have the entrance to the church covered?" Rex said.

"I've got it covered," Paulo responded.

"Good."

When Rex arrived at the alley, the boy was at his station watching the door. "Did anyone come or go?"

"No, no one."

Rex pulled out a twenty-dollar bill and held it up. "You never saw us. Understand?"

The boy reached for the bill, and Rex pulled it back."

"Do you understand? You never saw us. Or…" Rex made a slicing gesture across his throat. "Or you are in big trouble. Understand?"

The boy, his arm stretched out towards the bill, nodded. "I see no one. I never here."

"Good." Rex handed the bill to the boy who turned and ran off.

As the boy disappeared, John pulled up in an old Toyota Land Cruiser. Its body looked like it was about to drop off the frame but the motor hummed quietly. The rear section was separated from the driver's area with what looked like boxes but was really a metal divider. The rear windows were obscured with advertising for various shops. They'd capture the priest, put him in the back of the Land

Cruiser, and head for the CIA safe house. Getting the priest out of the country would be the CIA's problem.

John stepped out and walked over to Rex. John was short, sported a ragged black beard and mustache. He wore torn khaki pants, an old Hard Rock Café t-shirt, and a stained canvass jacket. He would not arouse suspicion driving the old Toyota, but Rex in his snappy jacket stuck out like the proverbial sore thumb. The two of them standing there looking up the alley would have seemed a little odd if anyone happened by. It was one of the reasons John never liked working directly with CIA agents. They just didn't seem to care as much about fitting in. He would have rather had Tran's men handle the operation, but they needed the CIA's ability to fly the priest out of Egypt without detection. So, he was stuck with the sore thumb. No, two sore thumbs actually. His partner Alejandro was teamed up with Paulo, a CIA agent on his first field assignment. Neither Paulo, a Brazilian, nor Rex, a Texan, could speak Arabic.

John listened as Rex talked to his sleeve. "You two call us if Father Antonio tries to leave the church your way. Let him see you when he shows himself. He doesn't know we know about his secret exit, so he will most likely decide to come this way when he sees you. It will be easier to grab him here. If he comes your way, let us know, and we will get the car up to the church. You two follow him, and when he gets close to the car grab him."

Rex turned his attention to John. "The longer he

waits the better. It's dark, and they'll soon lock up the church for the night. He's bound to come out this way. I'm going to check on the door."

"You shouldn't go alone. Procedure requires—"

"Fuck procedure. What can an old priest do to me? You stay with the car," Rex said.

"What can you expect from a sore thumb?" John muttered.

"What?"

"Ah, I have a sore thumb. Hope he doesn't put up too much of a struggle."

"Don't worry, I'll look after him." Rex started up the alley. He arrived at the wooden door and tried it. It opened. "Unlocked. Confident asshole," he muttered. He took a few steps down the short hall and pulled out his gun and flashlight. They had scouted the hallway the previous day and found an inner metal door with a wood façade. He positioned himself about two feet away from the door and whispered into the mike in his coat sleeve, "I'm just outside the metal door. I will wait for him here. Radio silence from here on until he shows himself."

Calvert Mesa, Montana
September 17, 2002 - 10:00 am

When the van pulled into the mesa garage Arthur was waiting for them. Roy looked at Kurt who was sitting in the back with Joleen and Robby. "Oh-oh, something's up. I've never seen Arthur waiting down here for anyone."

"Well, you folks have caused quite a stir," Arthur said. "The whole world is wondering what happened. We just got our systems fully up and running."

"We knew the artifacts we have on site would cause a shutdown," Roy said.

"It was a lot more than that," Arthur said. "Our communications just came back up a few minutes ago, and we are getting a full reading on the effects of your experiment. Let's head up to the conference room where Tran will give us a report. Does anyone need anything? Robby, how about you, are you hungry?"

"No, he's fine," Joleen said. "We all ate box lunches on the plane. Robby needs some sleep; he was awake all night. I'll tuck him, and then I'll join you."

Kurt and Roy found Arthur in the conference room

"So, what happened here?" Roy said.

"Okay, a quick overview while we wait for the others. Everyone was prepared for the power failure. Terry, Tran and I were in here with the three pyramids on the table. When the lights went out, everyone else had lanterns. The pyramids stayed lit for about an hour and fifty minutes," Arthur said.

"That's about right," Kurt said. "It was one hour and fifty-three minutes from the time Robby opened the door on the ship till we were back out, and the door closed. So that was about what we expected."

Arthur nodded. "Right, but when our local communications gear was back up and running, we still couldn't communicate. Our satellite link was down. It was restored just before you landed."

"Maybe, because, we had the three pyramids in one location at the Mesa," Roy said.

"Well, apparently the Pacific region, Japan and the east coast of China were all affected. Almost all communications, ground and satellite were lost, so I doubt it was these three little devices," Arthur said. "Terry and Tran have been monitoring the news in the anteroom while I brought you up to speed. I'll have them come in and brief us."

Joleen, Lisa and Amy came in just as Tran and Terry joined the group.

"Ah good, everyone's here now. Tran, why don't you fill us in on the media reports," Arthur said.

"Well, it's still unclear, but—"

The three pyramids at the end of the table began to glow again, and the lights went out.

"What the hell," Roy said. "Joleen, does Robby have the scepter?"

"No," Arthur said. "The two we have, are here on the table."

"I don't understand why this is happening," Roy said. "If Robby didn't—"

"The third scepter," Joleen said.

Saint Virgin Mary's Coptic Church
September 17, 2002 - 6:00 pm

Father Antonio removed the scepter from its protective glass case and placed it on a velvet cloth. It was such a simple looking artifact. How could it hold so much power? Could he…, could he also wield its power? He picked it up in his right hand, wrapped his four fingers around the handle and placed his thumb in the small indentation in the head of the scepter as he had done many times before. Nothing happened as he expected. The spot for a fifth finger was obvious. Why didn't he notice that before? Why did it take the discovery of the Sigurdson boy? Enough self-recrimination. It was time he tried.

He set the scepter down on the velvet cloth and pulled his withered left arm from his sling. He pried open the five fingers of his left hand and wrapped them around the scepter. He held his thumb poised over the head of the scepter. He hesitated. If he succeeded, they would know he had a scepter. Perhaps he should wait. No, it didn't matter what they knew now. He moved his thumb closer to the waiting indentation—an alarm buzzer sounded—he stopped.

Someone was in the secret entrance. The retched boy? He placed the scepter back on the velvet cloth and punched a couple of keys on his computer. An image from an infrared camera appeared on his screen. No, it was not the boy. Calvert's people were waiting for him. The boy was a lookout. He would have to use the main church exit. If he hurried, he could leave with some of the other clergy. He could slip out in the group.

He quickly changed into his clerical garb and pocketed a flash drive with all his computer data. He inserted another flash drive and started a program from it. The program would overwrite each bit of his hard disk, making nothing traceable.

He was almost ready. With his right hand, he placed the scepter back in his left and wrapped his fingers around the handle. He positioned his thumb over the small indentation in the head of the scepter and pulled the sling forward to hide his hand and the scepter. He would appear to be leaving empty-handed. He left his sanctuary and climbed the stairs to his small office in the back of the church.

He could hear voices in the church. The other clergy were leaving. He stepped out of his office, "Slipping out early. God will not be pleased."

One of the priests turned, "Oh Father Antonio, we didn't know you were in Cairo. It is lucky you came out of your office now, or we would have locked you in the church. Moreover, you shouldn't judge so quickly, we are still about God's work. We are going to the Sisters of Mercy Orphanage to sing with the children. Will you join us?"

"Yes," he said, as he worked his way to the center of the small group walking toward the exit. He could see two men standing just outside the church's entrance, one to the left and one to the right. Calvert's men? Could he slip by? No, the one on the right stepped forward.

"Father Antonio," he said. "You need to come with us."

The man on the left drew a gun and pointed it at him.

"What is this? This is sacred ground. Put away your gun, you can't arrest someone here," one of the

426

clergy said.

The man on the right continued moving forward.

"Paulo, stay where you are," the man with the gun said.

Paulo moved towards Father Antonio and took out a pair of handcuffs. "It's okay. I'll get him."

As Paulo grabbed Father Antonio's right hand to place a cuff on it, Father Antonio moved forward and pushed the palm of his right hand onto Paulo's chest. Paulo was now between Father Francis and the agent with the gun, effectively blocking a clear shot.

"Paulo, get out of the line of fire for Christ sake."

"Don't worry Alejandro, I got him. He's only an old priest."

Father Francis struggled to force his thumb into the indentation on the scepter.

Success. The lights went out. Paulo groaned and the handcuffs clattered to the floor followed by the dull thud of Paulo's body.

Father Antonio slipped to the right and used the wall to guide himself down the stairs.

"Paulo, where are you. Do you have the priest?" Alejandro shouted.

As Father Antonio slipped out onto the street, he heard a thud. "Oh, my hip."

One of the clergy must have fallen.

The last thing he heard as he walked down the dark street was the agent with the gun. "Paulo's down. Paulo's down. The priest is getting away. Get the car up here. Acknowledge. John, acknowledge. Ah…damn, the radios are down."

Conference Room - Calvert Mesa
September 17, 2002 - 10:45 am

Fifteen minutes had passed since the pyramids activated. Then they dimmed and the lights came back on.

"At last," Arthur said. "We'll try and figure out what just happened later. In the mean time, let's have Tran complete his report."

Tran stood. "Well, as I said earlier. It is still unclear, but most of the communications satellites and a large portion of the Pacific Rim's ground-based microwave communications systems were down for about twenty minutes. After that, it was just a matter of trying to get everything up and synchronized again. That took about an hour. Some of systems are still off-line. CNN is reporting that China has mobilized troops along the Russian border. They are accusing them of some sort of cyber attack. Russia blames the U.S. and says we detonated some sort of device out in space near the asteroid belt. The U.S. is claiming it was some sort of solar flare."

"Just a minute," Terry said. "Why was it that only the communications over the Pacific area were affected?"

"I think it was because whatever we were communicating with in the asteroid belt was directly over the Pacific. If we'd communicated at a different time of day, it would have affected communications somewhere else," Roy said. "Tran, what time did the communications go down?"

"At about 3:51 am Mountain Time, according to

428

CNN," Tran said.

Roy looked at Kurt. "Kurt?"

Kurt flipped a page in a small notebook he was carrying. "I was the official time-keeper. Good old mechanical Timex."

"Keeps on ticking while the world takes a beating," Roy said.

Arthur frowned. "I assume we caused this, but how? We initiated communications before and this didn't happen. Roy, isn't that how you obtained enough data to work up a message? Was it really us?"

"In the past, all Robby did was turn the ship on or activate a scepter, and the ship sent a communication to that thing in the asteroid belt. This time we tried to send a message, and that thing in the asteroid belt woke up and sent what must have been a super powerful message to Andromeda," Roy said. "Kurt, how about the time?"

"The device in the asteroid belt sent its signal at 3:51 am," Kurt said. "I'm afraid it was us."

"If we do this again, we need to be a lot more careful," Terry said. "CNN says we even knocked out air traffic control."

"Oh no," Joleen said, "was anyone hurt?"

"No, apparently they went to visual flight rules and their radios came back on quickly. There are still all sorts of people circling up there, waiting to land, but no one's been hurt."

"Okay, that's the news," Arthur said. "Roy, why don't you fill us in on what happened at the ship."

Roy nodded. "Well, everything went as planned. I

correctly identified—"

Tran's cell rang. "Sorry, urgent call from Cairo. I'll take it outside, please go on, Roy."

Roy nodded and proceeded to describe the how they had sent and received a message."

"We have a return message?" Arthur said.

"Right." Roy held up a piece of paper.

"You might have told us that earlier. What does it say?"

"That's the problem. I need access to LISA to decode it, and she's down because of the power failures."

"Okay, why don't you get working on that now that the power's back on? We can get back together as soon as you have it. How long will it take?"

"A couple of hours, if all goes well," Roy said. "But, we might be disappointed. It could just be a message from the device up there in the asteroid belt telling us it forwarded the message, and we should expect a response in a few thousand light-years. Remember, an actual response would mean faster than light communications."

Tran returned. "Bad news, Father Antonio has escaped."

"I thought we had him trapped?" Arthur said.

"We did. A CIA agent was about to cuff him when the lights went out. When the lights came back on the agent was down, dead."

"Father Antonio, an old man with one arm in a sling, overpowered an agent and killed him. He must have had help," Terry said.

"No, the agent appears to have died of cardiac

arrest, but we will need an autopsy to be sure," Tran said.

"Doesn't sound plausible to me; how old was the agent?" Arthur said.

"Twenty-seven," Tran said. "I know, a fit twenty-seven year old agent dies of cardiac arrest while arresting an old one-armed priest. That seems unlikely to me as well."

"Not if Father Antonio has the third scepter and can activate it for evil. Just the opposite of what Robby did for Lisa and you Tran," Joleen said.

"Yes," Lisa said, "what if that withered arm has a six-fingered hand and the scepter?"

Arthur nodded. "Okay, Roy, you work on decoding the message. Let us know as soon as you have it decoded. In the meantime, we can try and find out for sure how the agent died."

Chapter 35 - Advent

Kurt and Joleen's suite - Calvert Mesa
September 17, 2002 - 9:00 pm

Robby was stretched out on the couch, sleeping, head on Joleen's lap, feet resting on Kurt. The television on mute was tuned to late night news. Joleen whispered, "Is anything going to show up on the news? How can this be kept from the public?"

"You know my feelings," Kurt said. "We shouldn't be hiding it; I really believe we have to tell the world. I'm sure that will happen, but the question is, when. Terry O'Shanigan is concerned that it could stir up all sorts of religious turmoil. Who really knows what will happen when people find out that Jesus' miracles were the result of an alien scepter. You've kicked out the underpinnings of the Christian, and perhaps Jewish and Muslim religions. We've already seen a number of attempts on Robby's life."

"But those were just fanatics," Joleen said.

"Were they? What about the Father Antonio or whatever his real name is? He is still out there, and we don't know who he's tied in with. Father Antonio could be a Christian, Muslin, or Jewish fundamentalist. Tran thinks he was a Mullah in Iran, but he could just as easily be operating on his own, or with who knows what group. He must have some high level connections or else he wouldn't have found us. And remember, he wanted Robby dead. If you are right, and he has a scepter and can activate it—"

"What?" Joleen said. "What are you thinking?"

"Well, that would explain why he was trying to kill Robby. With Robby gone he might be the only one with the power, in his case, the power for evil. He will likely never stop looking for Robby until we catch him."

"What are we going to do, Kurt? How can we protect Robby? How?" Joleen started to cry.

"We'll be all right, Joleen. Walker's going to put us in a deep-cover program. Sort of like witness protection."

"But Kurt, couldn't Father Antonio's contacts tell him where we are hiding?" Joleen reached out to hold Kurt's hand.

"Only a couple of people will know where we are, so it is unlikely, but Robby will never be truly safe until what we've discovered is out in the open. Even then—"

The door to the lounge area flew open, and Roy charged in. "I've decoded the message," he shouted.

Robby turned his head and opened his eyes.

"Shhhh," Joleen said, finger to her lips.

"What does it say?" Kurt said.

"'We are coming,' it just says, 'We are coming.'"

Robby lifted his head and looked at Kurt. "Who's coming, Dad?"

31010882R00248

Made in the USA
Charleston, SC
03 July 2014